I0779148

WEREMAGE

A BOOK OF UNDERREALM

GARRETT ROBINSON

WEREMAGE
Garrett Robinson

The author greatly appreciates you taking the time to read his work. Please leave a review wherever you bought the book or on Goodreads.com.

Interior Design: Legacy Books, Inc.
Publisher: Legacy Books, Inc.
Editors: Karen Conlin, Cassie Dean
Cover Artist: Sarayu Ruangvesh

1. Fantasy - Epic 2. Fantasy - Dark 3. Fantasy - New Adult

First Edition

Published by Legacy Books

To my wife
Who gave me this idea

To my children
Who just make life better

To Johnny, Sean and Dave
Who told me to write

And to my Rebels
Don't forget why you left the woods

GET MORE

Legacy Books is home to the very best that fantasy has to offer.

Join our email alerts list, and we'll send word whenever we release a new book. You'll receive exclusive updates and see behind the scenes as we create them.

(You'll also learn the secrets that make great fantasy books, *great.*)

Interested? Visit this link:

Underrealm.net/Join

For maps of the locations in this book, visit:

Underrealm.net/maps

A WARNING

This book contains a scene of explicit sexual violence.

I have tried to depict it both realistically and respectfully to actual victims of such violence. A further explanation can be found in my note at the end of the book.

If this is something you'd rather not read, I completely understand, and I wanted you to know in advance.

WEREMAGE

A BOOK OF UNDERREALM

GARRETT ROBINSON

ONE

The door to their chambers opened easily under Loren's hand, and in the creaking of the hinges there were no echoes of the battle cries and bloodshed that still haunted her thoughts.

Cool air brushed her face as the room was revealed to her, and she sighed. The scents of the High King's Seat came rushing through the door, the heady salt of the Great Bay and the acrid smoke of the city's ten thousand hearths. She closed her eyes and drank them in.

"Loren?"

Chet's touch on her arm brought her back to herself. She glanced over her shoulder at him. "I am sorry. It . . . it feels a lifetime since last we were here. A span of months, not days."

"I feel the same," he said quietly. "But now that we *are* here, might we not go inside, rather than standing in the hall without purpose?"

She chuckled and took his hand to draw him in after her. Inside, they removed their cloaks and hung them on hooks beside the door. To the left were Xain's and Gem's rooms. To the right were two more rooms where Chet and Loren had once slept apart—though that had changed in the days since first they came here.

Much of the furniture in the common room was new, its wood fresh-hewn and the cushions too bright to have seen much use. The tables and chairs that had once been here must have been destroyed in the fighting. That thought further dampened what was already a solemn day—for while many in the city rejoiced at the return of the High King Enalyn, the wise knew it was no proud thing that she had been chased from her capital in the first place.

Seven days it was since the Seat had been attacked and Loren had helped Enalyn escape the fighting. Her forces had fled to the kingdom of Selvan, thinking to muster a counter-attack—but then, as swiftly as they had come, the attacking armies had fled. The fleet of Dulmun sailed east across the Great Bay, vanishing into their mighty coastal fortresses. The Shades had rowed the short distance between the Seat and Dorsea's eastern coast, and had disappeared into the Birchwood. All the scouts the High King could muster had failed to find them since, and many who were sent to do so had never been heard from again.

Since then, Enalyn had granted Loren a new position: Nightblade of the High King, her personal agent. It was a recognition of the valiant way Loren had saved the lives of Enalyn and her son, the Lord Prince Eamin. But other than a pretty name and a great honor, Loren was not quite sure what it meant. The title of Nightblade had been a childhood fancy, something she had thought up when she was a girl of the forest. The world she found herself in now was all too real, all too perilous. What good was a daydream in the face of the dangers that Loren had seen?

"Sky above. Come look at this."

Chet's voice came from their balcony. The words made her tense for a moment—but his voice held only awe, and no trace of fear. She entered their room, briefly noting the new bedclothes, before she passed through it to the balcony.

He stood leaning out into the open air, wiry arms spread as they gripped the railing. They were mayhap thirty paces high, and had an excellent view northwest across the Seat. The sun was still rising in the east, for the day was young, and the youthful warmth of its shine turned the winter air bracing rather than chilling. The city's smell struck her again, stronger than before, and she smiled without thinking.

"What?" said Loren. "What is it?"

"All of it," said Chet. "Look at it. Look at them."

He pointed. There, far below, she saw figures scurrying through the streets. A multitude of colors could be found: the red cloaks of Mystics, the russet armor of constables, the white and gold of the High King's guard, and all the liveries of soldiers and servants from across the nine kingdoms. But most wore simple clothes, and carried tools or pulled them in carts. Saws and hammers, lumber and ladders, all the accoutrements of craftsmen and artisans. They looked like a colony of ants from this high up, running frantically about in the chaos of a careless step that had crushed their hill. But their scurrying had a purpose: their home had been destroyed, and they meant to rebuild it.

"It seemed so simple when Enalyn called for them," said Loren quietly. "I know that it was not, but it seemed so. And just look how many of them have come to obey her."

"My father always said he would never take the High King's power, not for anything in the world," said Chet. "How frightening it must be, to hold such influence that your slightest whim can move an entire kingdom to action."

Loren nodded as if in agreement. But in her mind, she felt her thoughts turning in another direction.

Yes, the great and mighty could do much with a simple command—the High King Enalyn, and the Lord Prince Eamin, and even Anwar, the king of Selvan. Yet who now walked in the halls of those mighty figures? Loren of the family Nelda. The High King's Nightblade. The thought should have been terrifying—and she supposed it was, to a degree—but she could not deny that it excited her. That, too, had been part of the dream of the Nightblade.

Her hand brushed her dagger, which she now wore inside the waist of her trousers, covering the hilt with her green vest. The feel of it on her skin cast a shadow over the bright and beautiful day.

The dagger was an ever-present source of danger. She could never stop thinking about it, and was always wary of letting it be seen by anyone but her friends. If it were ever revealed, the effects could be disastrous—not only to Loren, but to the Order of Mystics who might be the best defense against the rise of the Necromancer.

Yet she could not bring herself to get rid of it. It had been her first theft. And by now she had learned two of the dagger's magical qualities—the ability to find wizards, and the sight it could grant her even in pitch darkness. These had proven beyond useful, and had even saved her life on occasion. The Nightblade could not afford to throw away her most powerful tool.

"Where has your mind gone?" said Chet, looking at her with his brow furrowed. "You have been drifting away more and more often of late. Do not think I have not noticed."

"Nowhere," said Loren, shaking her head. She ran her fingertips along his arm, sending gooseflesh rippling. "I am here with you."

He smiled and put a hand on her cheek, his question forgotten. Her smile widened—but her thoughts turned sadly to how easy it was to guide his mind, just as on the day she fled their village in the Birchwood.

They heard a gentle knock behind them and turned to see Gem. The urchin boy stood in the doorway back to their bedroom, his knuckles still held close to the doorframe as though he might knock again. He was dressed in finer clothes than Loren was used to seeing him in, though somehow he had already found a way to get them dirty.

"I have been sent to summon you," said Gem, looking at Loren.

Her stomach did a somersault. Without thinking, she reached for Chet's hand. Only once he had squeezed her fingers did she glance at him, earning a smile that should have encouraged her. But she could see a lingering sorrow behind it.

"I must go," she said.

"I know. Do not be afraid. You will do well."

"You are more confident than I am, I fear."

"I have followed you for enough leagues to know it." He stepped before her and kissed her lightly. "And what is more, I call anyone who doubts you a fool."

Gem cleared his throat a bit more loudly than he needed to. "Yes, well and good," said the boy. "Yet the council requires her presence."

Loren gave Chet's hand one last squeeze before brushing past him and into their chambers. She rushed through the common room, but Chet's voice stopped her again halfway through the door.

"Stop."

She turned, steeling herself for him to ask her not to go. He did not want her to, and she knew it. But he only came forwards and reached past her to the hook on the wall. He brought down her fine black cloak from where she had hung it, and with gentle fingers clasped it at her throat.

"The Nightblade must be the Nightblade, after all," he murmured.

"Thank you," she said, kissing him again—and this time it was not gentle.

"Sky above. *The council.*"

"Oh, still your tongue, Gem," said Loren, rushing past the boy and into the hall.

Gem scowled. "Why should I, when the two of you never do the same?"

TWO

ONLY ONCE BEFORE HAD LOREN BEEN TO THE HIGH King's council room, but she remembered the way. Therefore she did not let Gem guide her like some page, but quickened her pace so that he had to trot to keep up, though he maintained an air of long-suffering dignity.

"Who else will be there?" said Loren.

"I do not know," said Gem. "They did not summon me into the room, but sent someone out to tell me to fetch you. It is like when messengers ride day and night, relaying a letter from one to the next, except a bit more ridiculous, since it all takes place in one small palace."

Loren shook her head. Only Gem had a high enough opinion of himself that he could think of the High King's palace as small. "Did you see Xain at all?"

"No," said Gem. "In fact, I have not seen him since we came off the ship."

They paused outside the council room. One of the High King's guards stood there, resplendent in her armor. She looked down at Gem with vague disdain. The boy stuck out his tongue at her. Loren put a hand on his shoulder.

"Thank you, Gem. Now be off."

His eyes widened, like a dog whose master was displeased with it. "Might I not wait here, ready in case you should need me?"

"I do not think I shall," said Loren. "And you will likely grow bored to death, for this may take some time."

Gem's shoulders slumped. "Very well, then. You may find me in my chamber if you need me."

She watched him go until he turned the corner. Then, carefully avoiding the eyes of the guard, she entered the room as quietly as she could.

The High King Enalyn's council chamber was much like the woman herself: restrained, imposing, but not without warmth. There were some chairs around the walls—for retainers, Loren supposed, though she had yet to see anyone sit in them. The main focus of the room, of course, was the table in its center, but that table was nowhere near so large as might have been expected. Rather than feeling ornamental, it gave the place an air of wartime preparation—and that air was particularly appropriate now, with all of Underrealm embroiled in conflict.

At the head of the table sat Enalyn herself, with one elbow propped up on the arm of her chair, her chin resting on her fist. To her right sat the Lord Prince Eamin, scratching at his short, well-trimmed beard, and beside Eamin was Xain, much to Loren's relief. The wizard was often bitter and always sarcastic, but he was still the closest friend she had in this room.

But to Enalyn's left sat a woman Loren did not recognize—short, fat, and clearly old, for her hair was silver and her face bore many wrinkles. Something about her seemed similar to the High King, the sharp eyes and the severe twist to her mouth, though hers held something more of a smirk than Enalyn's did. On her shoulders was draped the red cloak of a Mystic.

The four of them looked up the moment Loren stepped through the door, and Xain hesitantly put his hands on the arms of his chair to stand. But Enalyn lifted a hand to stop him.

"Greetings, Loren," she said. "I have ten thousands of councils to hold in the time it would take me to hold ten proper ones, and so we must do away with decorum. You will pretend that these others have stood to greet you, and I will pretend that you have knelt to me. Please sit there." She pointed at the chair beside the grey-haired woman.

"Yes, Your Majesty," said Loren, hastening to obey. The woman scooted her chair over slightly to make it easier for Loren to sit.

"You two should know each other. Lord Chancellor, this is Loren of the family Nelda, Nightblade of the High King. Loren, this is Hollen of the family Konnel, the new lord chancellor of the Order of Mystics."

"Well met," said Loren, nodding. *This is the lord chancellor? I thought the Mystics were all warriors.*

Hollen flashed her a wide smile, as though she guessed at Loren's thoughts. "Well met indeed. Do not fret over my looks, dear. I am not such a bumbling old woman as I appear—but only half so much, thank the sky."

Loren's eyes widened, and her cheeks flooded with red. "I . . . I do not think . . ."

Hollen laughed, and Enalyn's lips pressed tight. "Forgive the lord chancellor. She has a habit of making people uncomfortable—which is often a useful skill— as well as a sense of self-deprecation that she finds most amusing. At another time, I might agree with her, but there are urgent matters to discuss."

"Of course, Your Majesty. My apologies," said Hollen.

Across the table, Xain caught Loren's eye and winked. She gave him a quick smile in return.

"Loren, we three have spoken about you already,

and I have come to a decision," said Enalyn. Loren did not much like the sound of that. "I know that the politics of the nine kingdoms are not familiar to you, but I cannot take the time to explain them in detail. Suffice it to say that while we balance on the brink of open war, we have not yet fallen into it, and now we must put forth every effort to keep that from happening."

That made Loren balk. "Forgive me, Your Majesty, but how can that be? A battle has already been fought."

"One, yes," said Enalyn. "But it is my understanding that you were at Wellmont. Did that battle mean that Selvan and Dorsea were at war?"

Loren pursed her lips. "I suppose not. But Selvan would have been well justified in declaring such a war."

Enalyn frowned, but across the table, Eamin's jaw clenched. Loren wondered if he dared disagree with his mother.

The lord chancellor interjected. "War brings only destruction, girl. No one should wish for that, no matter how justified they feel their cause to be. A ruler's noblest purpose is the preservation of life whenever possible. All here agree that open war with Dulmun may be inevitable. But we must do all we can to avoid it, while any chance of doing so exists."

"Forgive me, Your Majesty, for I would never think to advise you on matters of which I know little," said Loren slowly. "But is there nothing to be said for justice? Has the kingdom of Dulmun not wronged the rest of Underrealm, and should they not pay a price for it?"

The High King leaned back in her chair, steepling her fingers beneath her chin. The room went suddenly very quiet, and Loren's throat became as dry as sand.

"I have spoken out of turn," she said quietly, ducking Enalyn's gaze. "Forgive me."

"No, this should be addressed," said Enalyn. "After all, you are now an agent of a king, and therefore you ought to know the way a king's mind works. Tell me, Loren: how many people have you killed?"

"None, Your Majesty," said Loren at once. And then she felt a pang of shame as she remembered her father. "Or, one, but it was not my intent to do so. I only tried to defend my life and the life of . . . of another." She risked a glance at Xain, who met her gaze solemnly.

"That is what I have been told," said Enalyn. "You have decided that lives are not yours to take, and that if someone must die for their crimes, then that is up to the King's law. Do I have the right of it?"

"Yes, Your Majesty."

"Yet a moment ago you seemed to wish that Selvan had gone to war with Dorsea, and now you think that we should go to war with Dulmun. Tell me, Nightblade: what happens in war?"

Loren looked up with a frown. "Your Majesty?"

"You have seen battle. What do soldiers do to each other in battle?"

"They . . . they kill each other."

Enalyn nodded. "I could say that it was the fault of my soldiers for doing so. It would be easy to blame them for cutting down my enemies upon the field. But the truth is that if I declare war, every life lost is my responsibility. I say my responsibility, and not my fault, for they are not the same. I will bear that burden if I must, but I am not eager for it. You say you will not kill, and that might be called a noble vow. But if you only wish for others to swing the sword in your place, then you do not hate death—you only want to be able to tell one and all that your hands are still clean. And that is not so noble a purpose."

Loren wished that she could vanish from sight. None of the others at the table would look at her, like children sitting awkwardly while their mother chastised a sibling, only wishing for the moment to pass. But then she steeled herself and raised her head, meeting the High King's gaze.

"Again I apologize, Your Majesty." She kept her tone measured but earnest. "I am unaccustomed to sitting at so high a table, where matters such as these are discussed. I vow to you that I will learn, and I beg for your patience as I do."

Enalyn smiled, and the room's tension evaporated at once. "That is well said, and shows a humble heart. It is a wise soul who seeks to learn instead of clinging to the belief that they are right. Now, back to the matter at hand: ending the war with Dulmun before it begins."

"The key to such a strategy is making war appear not only undesirable, but hopeless," said Eamin. "That could divide Dulmun and turn the nobility against their king."

Loren cocked her head, confused, and Xain spoke up. "It is our hope that some in Dulmun may be convinced they cannot win. If the noble families think that war is hopeless, it may prompt them to overthrow Bodil, Dulmun's king, and appoint a new ruler who will make peace."

"I understand," said Loren, though that was only half true. "How may I help?"

"In all honesty, I am not certain," said Enalyn. "Yet something tells me that you have a role to play. You have displayed two talents in great abundance, Loren: an ability to gather information, and a strong sense of duty. These are valuable skills, and I regard them highly, but they are yet untempered. Therefore I mean to place you in the service of Kal of the family Endil, who sent you to me in the first place. I have raised him to the position of grand chancellor of Feldemar—the lord chancellor's former position—and he is also my Master of Spies. Under his guidance, I have no doubt you will prove yourself most useful to the preservation of the nine kingdoms."

Loren's heart skipped a beat. Almost she blurted, *You are sending me away?* She looked to Xain.

"Kal was Jordel's master also, you will remember." He spoke quietly, and she saw pity in his eyes.

She swallowed hard. *Do not be a foolish girl,* she told herself. *You entered the High King's service. What sort of servant would you be if you disobeyed her command?*

So she stilled her hands on the table and turned to Enalyn. "Very well, Your Majesty," she said. "I serve at your pleasure."

From the corner of her eye she saw Hollen give an approving smile, while the Lord Prince nodded.

"Excellent," said Enalyn. "I ask only that you obey Kal's instructions, and learn from him what you can. Never forget, Loren: our task is of the utmost importance. We do not fight for peace only to keep me on the throne. That would be a limp and insipid reason to ask so much from so many. We fight instead for the preservation of Underrealm itself, and that is a greater purpose than any one person's simple ambition. Without the order of the nine kingdoms, all would be chaos. Can I count on your aid to preserve them?"

The Lord Prince looked solemn, and his brows drew together. Loren gazed at him for a moment, wondering what must be going on inside his mind—he, the presumptive successor to the throne, and not all that much older than she was.

"You can, Your Majesty," said Loren. "And you, Your Highness, and Lord Chancellor. I have already seen the fires of war licking at the trees of the Birchwood that I call home. I will do anything I must to douse the flames, and give my life if need be."

Eamin met her gaze then, his eyes bright and his

head held high. He nodded, and though he spoke no word, she could almost hear him thank her.

"Well-spoken," said Enalyn. "Though I pray it does not come to that, and I hope you will not throw your life away needlessly. Serve Kal as best you know how, and I will consider your duty fulfilled. Arrangements will soon be made for you to go to him in the stronghold of Ammon, where he resides."

"Ammon?" said Loren quickly.

"Yes," said Enalyn. "Jordel's home."

Loren's breath caught in her throat. Jordel had meant to bring her to Ammon, her and Gem and Annis all, before he had fallen in the Greatrocks. But moreover, Annis was there, and Loren's heart leaped at the thought of seeing her friend again.

"Now we must discuss something more somber," said Enalyn. She looked to Xain. The wizard cleared his throat and sat up, folding his hands on the table before him. Loren had felt a sense of warning before, and that had faded, but it redoubled now. Whatever "decision" Enalyn had come to, this was the heart of it.

"I cannot travel with you any longer," said Xain.

The room fell to silence—except that at the edge of hearing, Loren thought she heard a high whine, like a gnat buzzing in her ear. The whine was soon replaced by her own pulse, thundering as she grew suddenly light-headed.

"I thought you were done trying to abandon me on the road," she said, trying to keep her tone light.

Xain did not so much as smirk. "I was," he said. "But now I have returned to the Seat, where I always meant to go. And I have my son. I could not come with you and bring Erin along."

She did not answer. She *could* not answer. *Of course not. And you know I would not ask it.*

"Moreover," Xain went on, "the High King has asked a duty of me, and I have agreed to it."

"No doubt you remember the dean of the Academy," said Enalyn. "Cyrus of the family Drayden. You met him briefly."

"I do remember," said Loren. She also remembered that Cyrus had not been there to defend the High King in the battle of the Seat, and rumors flew that he had abandoned his charges at the Academy as well.

"Cyrus has not been seen since the day the Seat was attacked. It may be assumed that he perished in the fighting." Enalyn kept her tone carefully neutral, but Loren saw the disdainful sneers that twisted the faces of both Xain and Eamin. She herself wanted to laugh out loud, but she kept her composure as Enalyn went on. "Now the Academy needs another dean, and I require an ally in that position. With Underrealm on the brink of war, I cannot choose a dean for political reasons, the way I did when I chose Cyrus."

"You mean that it would be foolish to appoint another Drayden," said Eamin lightly. "This is a small council, Your Majesty, and all upon it are trustworthy. You may speak freely, I think."

Enalyn gave him a cool stare, and then went on as though he had not said anything. "In any case, I require someone I can trust to remain loyal, and I have selected Xain. I asked him, and he accepted."

"Then it appears congratulations are in order, *Dean.*" Loren could not help the way her mouth twisted.

Enalyn must have sensed her mood. She put her hands flat on the table and said, "Very well. Those are the only matters I required you for. Your travel to Ammon will be seen to shortly."

The dismissal was clear. Loren stood from her chair and bowed. "Thank you, Your Majesty." But before she turned away, she saw Xain give the High King a quick glance. Enalyn nodded in response, and Xain stood to follow Loren from the room.

"I shall see you out," he said.

Loren shrugged. "If you wish."

In fact she did not want him anywhere near her, but thought it would be unseemly to recoil from him in front of the High King. Once they were in the hallway, however, she walked as far from his side as she could and stormed into the palace garden. Winter bit at her cheeks, and she drew her cloak close about her, thankful the first snows had not yet begun to fall.

"I am sorry," said Xain from behind her.

"You have done nothing that requires an apology," said Loren. "The High King commanded you."

"She did not command me. She asked, and I accepted. And I am sorry."

"Then take it back." She turned to him, blinking against the sting in her eyes. "Take it back and come with me."

"I . . . I cannot," he said, fists clenching by his sides. "Loren, my son—I cannot leave Erin again, and I cannot bring—"

"*I know!*" cried Loren, far louder than she meant to. But it felt good, and so she kept shouting. "I know you cannot take Erin into such danger. Why do you think I am angry with you? Because I cannot *be* angry with you at all. Nor could I be mad at Jordel, or Albern, when they—"

She stopped short and turned away, blinking harder. That had not been a fair thing to say, and she knew it. Why, then, did she not turn and apologize? But she could not, not when Xain meant to leave her alone the way he had often enough before.

"I thought the same thing," he said. To her shock, Loren heard the thickness of tears in his voice, and when she turned he wept openly. "The moment Enalyn asked me, I thought of how I was leaving you again, the way I had promised not to—and the way Jordel and Albern did. That thought has plagued me since. Yet I do not see another choice. Erin—I have my son, and I—"

"Be *silent,*" said Loren. She forced a smile. "Still your bleating tongue, wizard. You only repeat yourself, and we have said all we can say. And if there is one thing we have learned after all the leagues we have walked together, it is that you always wanted to be rid of me."

Before he could answer, she seized the front of his coat, drawing him in for an embrace as his tears fell upon her shoulder.

THREE

Chet did not take the news well.

He sat silent with his fists clenched as Loren spoke of the council. Across from their couch, Gem sat almost sideways upon his chair, swinging his legs back and forth over one of the arms, his eyes wide and his mouth slightly open.

When Loren finished, he straightened and gave a bright laugh.

"Wonderful! Helping to prevent a war will make a fine addition to the tales of you that already fly across the nine kingdoms."

"I think you greatly overestimate how far such tales have spread," said Loren.

"How can I? The High King herself had already heard of the Nightblade before she brought you into her service. What better bard could you wish for, than one who brings tales of your exploits to the highest of thrones?"

But Chet sat silent in his chair, picking at one fingernail with another. Loren could feel his sullen displeasure, and it worried her. The look on his face was not unlike the look he had worn in the Birchwood when her father threatened her, or hit her, and Chet had held himself back only at Loren's urging.

Gem, however, seemed oblivious to it. He sat forwards in his chair and slapped his knees. "And we will get to see Annis again! We have not received word from her in days. I wonder if she already knows we are coming? I should write her a letter."

"It can hardly get there before you will," said Loren. "It will not be long before we leave the Seat."

"Might Loren and I speak alone, Gem?"

Chet's voice was quiet and firm, and it cut its way into the conversation like a footman's sword. Gem's smile dampened, and he glanced at Loren. She nodded.

"Very well," said Gem. "I am famished anyway, and I think one of the cooks likes me, for she hardly tries to strike me at all any more when I steal food from her. I will return shortly."

He bounced carefree on his feet as he slipped from the room, but Loren did not miss the worried look he gave them. Once the door had closed again, Chet sat up on the couch and placed his elbows on his knees, folding one hand over the other before his eyes.

"Why do we not leave?" said Chet.

"I mean to," said Loren lightly. "For Ammon."

"Do not do that," he said softly. "Do not pretend ignorance of my meaning. Why do we not leave this war behind?"

"We have come this far," said Loren. "Why not see it through? And besides, I took the role of Nightblade."

"You did, and what of it?" said Chet. "What is the Nightblade, in truth? She has given you a title without a duty. It is meaningless. There has never been a Nightblade before, and so you cannot declare with any certainty what service you are expected to perform."

"I suppose, then, that it is for me to decide. I am able to determine the course of my life, the way I never could before."

"Hardly. You have put that control in the hands of the High King. Enalyn has my allegiance as well as yours, but do you truly think she holds your safety as her highest concern?"

Loren looked at him sharply. "Do you think that is *my* highest concern?"

She thought to shock him, but he only rolled his eyes. "Have you even decided how long you mean to serve her? Will you do so for the rest of your life?"

"I had not given much thought to it. But I will not leave the nine kingdoms to their own devices while the threat of war looms over them."

Chet stood and went to a side table that held a flagon of wine. He filled a cup for himself and arched an eyebrow at her. She nodded, and he filled a second.

"And what does the High King mean for you to do?" he asked, changing tack. "Obey Kal, of course, but what does that mean? Have you wondered what they intend to do with you? For I have an idea."

He placed the cup in her hand. Loren took a sip, but a light one, for she wished to keep her mind sharp. It felt as though they were sparring, and she did not like it.

She let some of her bitterness come through in her tone. "Let us hear it, then, oh wisest of advisors, for surely I would be lost without you."

"I think they mean to send you after Rogan."

That gave her pause, as he must have known it would. Just the brute's name was enough to strike fear in her. Suddenly the High King's palace seemed no safer than a flimsy woodland shack. Loren did not often dream, but in recent days, Rogan's dark face had plagued her sleep more than once.

Her silence had stretched long, and Chet wore a self-satisfied look that irked her. She sipped her wine again and shrugged. "Mayhap that is indeed their plan. If so, it is Rogan who should be afraid. When he found us in Northwood, he had the advantage, and we were the ones pursued. Now I walk with all the power of the High King behind me. Who does he have? The Shades? They lick their wounds in some unknown hole, likely hiding in the Birchwood and hoping we will forget about them."

"Dulmun backs him."

Loren snorted. "One kingdom against the other eight. And do not forget that the Mystics are on our side."

Chet frowned into his cup. "Rogan does not seem the type of man to begin a war without some hope of victory." But he could not put much strength in the words.

"Never would I compel you to walk a road you deem dangerous. I told you in Northwood that you were under no obligation to come with us."

"So you did, and I said then that I do not follow you out of obligation," said Chet. "I came because . . . well . . ." He trailed off, and his cheeks flushed with something other than the wine.

"We are no longer children, Chet," said Loren. "Speak plainly."

"Because I love you," he said, the muscles of his jaw twitching. "I know it, and you know it, though I may feel like a moon-eyed child when I say the words. I have only ever wished to keep you safe. When that meant fighting beside you, I did so willingly. But when it meant urging you to flee the troubles of Underrealm, I did that as well. You refused, and still I followed you, and I will again—but I will not stop warning you of peril when I see it."

"Do so if you must," said Loren. "Only do not forget, for both our sakes, that I will continue to ignore you and press on regardless."

His nostrils flared. "How can I forget, when you have never done anything else?"

She bit her tongue and turned her gaze away from him. She knew well that this was futile, and Chet likely did as well. "I should like to take a walk," she said.

"No, I am sorry," he said, slumping back and shaking his head. "You do not have to leave."

"It will give us both time to cool our heads—and to think upon this," she said. "Each of us knows what the other will say. Let us, then, have the argument separately, in our own minds, so that it need not drive a wedge between us."

She gave him a wan smile. He did not look up at her, and only put his hand to his forehead, as though he wished to say more but did not dare to. But as she passed him on her way out the door, he reached suddenly forth and took her hand, squeezing it. She returned the pressure, and at last their gazes met for a moment. She left.

FOUR

She did not return to the room until after nightfall, and Chet had gone to sleep already. She lay beside him, and he stirred without waking to wrap an arm around her. His warmth soon sent her to slumber—but then a dark dream seized her, dragging her mind into its depths and filling her with despair even in sleep.

Loren found herself standing beneath the boughs of the Birchwood. Somehow she knew it was the day she had left. But instead of the brown cloak she had worn on that day, in the dream she wore the black cloak Damaris had given her. Xain was nowhere to be seen. Dark storm clouds churned in the sky.

She panicked as a branch snapped behind her. Whirling, she saw her father. An arrow was buried in his chest, just below the collarbone, so deep that the head of it protruded from the flesh in the back. His body was covered in blood, and from the squelch he made when he moved, she knew it had run down to fill his boots.

But I did not shoot you in the chest! It was the leg!

She thought the words, but she could not say them aloud.

When she saw his face, she gasped. It was twisted in hate, and his flesh had begun to rot. Something had eaten away most of his left cheek, and his teeth showed through the hole. His eyes were sunken, for the meat around them had wasted away. A few fingernails had torn off. Dirt was caked deep beneath the ones that remained, dirt from his attempts to drag himself back to their village.

"You ungrateful wretch!" he screamed, so loud that she jumped. He spat at her feet. "You were never my daughter."

He lunged at her, and she cried out. But in midair he vanished, and the world around her dissolved to mist and shadow. Then the shadows took form, and the light turned silver. She looked up to see the moons peeking at her between the rooftops of Cabrus. The alley she was in seemed familiar. A figure in a deep green cloak stood only a few paces away. Loren stirred at the sight, and her breath quickened, for the figure's shape was familiar to her.

The green cloak rippled in the moonslight as she stepped forwards, hips swaying. Her movements were every bit as enchanting and seductive as the first time they had met, and Loren's heart fluttered just as it had then. In the waking world, of course, she knew that Auntie was a sadist, a murderer, and worse beside, but in the dream she knew none of these things.

Auntie stepped around and pressed up against her back. Delicate fingers traced along Loren's arms, and she shivered, her chest tight, her skin aching for the touch to linger. She could not force herself to move.

"It is the way you hold yourself," whispered Auntie, her breath brushing Loren's ear. A hand took Loren's hip firmly, and she released a shuddering sigh. "The way you put one foot before the other—just so."

She placed a foot before Loren's, so that now they were pressed even closer against each other. But then the foot moved quickly to the right, and Auntie pushed her hard. Loren yelped, tripping over the woman's ankle. She rolled quickly onto her back, but Auntie was atop her, her fingers grasping for Loren's throat.

"This is not vengeance," she hissed. "It is justice."

Loren fought, trying to wrestle herself away, but then the world dissolved to nothing again.

There was wood beneath her hands, and warm air blasted her face. She was on the deck of a riverboat.

Upstream, a ship pursued her, but no crew manned it. The captain, Brimlad, was nowhere in sight, and neither were Gem or Annis. But Xain sat against the wall of the riverboat's cabin, his hair thin and wispy, withered arms wrapped around himself. Loren shuddered as she saw the black glow in his eyes.

The ship had seemed at least a league away, but suddenly it appeared only a few paces behind them. Looking up, Loren saw a small figure in a red cloak. Vivien's eyes glowed with magelight, and she raised her arms.

"Abomination!" she cried. Black burns rippled along her skin, turning her into a twisted, mangled thing.

Loren turned to see Xain, but the wizard had gone. Had he gone below? But then she saw her own hands. They were wasted, the skin almost transparent, just as Xain's had been when he ate the magestones. She clutched at her hair, and it came away in her hand. A scream ripped from her throat, thin and feeble and blood-curdling.

She fell to hands and knees, and the world vanished again.

Now her fingers scraped on stone. Loren feared to look up, but something compelled her to.

Damaris stood before her.

They were in a cavern—Loren knew not where, for unlike all the places she had seen thus far, this was nowhere she had been in real life. The edges of the room were dark, with not a torch to be seen, and the only light fell from a hole in the ceiling far above to pool around Damaris in a perfect circle. Loren's body had returned to health, so that she could have stood, but fear shuddered in her limbs. Damaris' eyes were filled with an icy fury, and Loren cowered before it, certain that the merchant was here to take her revenge at last.

"Get up," said Chet. "We are with you."

His hands took her shoulders, and with his help she found her feet. He stood to her right, and looking to her left she saw Gem and Annis. Gem had his sword out and held forth, as though ready to do battle, while Annis' fists were clenched at her sides, as though she might try to box her own mother.

Then Loren's gaze drifted past Damaris, to a man standing just behind her. He had the brown-skinned, dark-eyed look of a Wadeland man. His black hair was cropped short, and a scar split his chin. He wore the blue and grey clothing of a Shade. She knew she had never seen him before.

"Who is that?" she asked Annis, but when she turned, the girl was gone. Gem and Chet, too, had vanished—and then she saw that they all knelt before Damaris, facing Loren. Chet was chained, and his eyes were mad with fear. Damaris held a dagger at his throat, but it was an old, rusted, twisted blade, nothing fine like Loren would have expected the merchant to have.

"You take my daughter?" said Damaris, her voice a harsh rasp. "Foolish girl. I will take *everything.*"

The dagger hissed as it laid Chet's throat open. His lifeblood splashed across the stones, and his mouth worked silently as he tried to cry out.

Loren screamed and fell on her knees before him, putting her hand to the wound, trying helplessly to hold it closed. But she could feel his life slipping away between her fingers. Her shouts could not save him. Nothing could.

"No!" cried Loren. "Gem! Annis! Help me!"

But when she looked up, she found that they were not chained after all. They never had been. A hungry light was in their eyes as they regarded her. Gem bared his teeth with an animal's snarl, and he pounced upon her. She felt his teeth sink like needles into her neck.

Loren woke at last, screaming and thrashing in her bed.

"Stop! Stop! Loren! Someone help!"

Hands seized her in the darkness. Loren swung a fist in the dark, screaming louder.

She struck Chet right where the dagger of a Shade had wounded him. He screamed in pain, and the sound of it was like agony in her heart. At last her mind was dragged to the present.

"Chet! No, no, no. I am sorry, I—"

The door to their room crashed open. Xain and Gem ran in, stopping just on the threshold. Xain's eyes glowed white with magic, and Gem brandished his sword. At the sight of the boy, fear seized Loren, her mind returning to the dream and his bared teeth.

"What is it?" cried Xain. "What is wrong?"

"I—I . . ." Loren shook her head, forcing herself to speak. "It is nothing. Nothing. A nightmare."

Xain's brow furrowed, and the light did not fade from his eyes. He ran to the balcony door and opened it, looking outside as though for a prowler. Then he rushed to the closet at the other end of the room and peered within.

"I am fine, Xain," said Loren, growing exasperated. "There is no one there. It was a dream." When he knelt and looked under the bed, she got to her feet and lifted him back up. "Stop. It is nothing."

"Nothing?" said Chet, still rubbing his chest where she had struck him. "It did not sound like nothing."

Xain stood, and at last he doused his magic. But his frown remained. "You sounded as though skilled torturers had you under their knives."

"Mayhap they did," said Loren. "But only in my mind. Look at me. Do you see any wounds?"

Without answering, he went to the wall, where two robes hung on hooks. He pulled one down and threw it to her, and she put it on gratefully. But no sooner had she covered herself than he seized her face, and she yelped as he pried at her eyelids with his fingers.

"Your eyes are wild," he said, ignoring her attempts to escape. "Gem, fetch an apothecary, and tell them to bring dreamwine."

"No, Gem," said Loren, finally forcing Xain's hands away. "Sky above, Xain, I tell you I am *all right.*"

The wizard's frown deepened. "I am not sure of that, though I will allow that you seem to be safe. Have you been eating?"

"The same as you."

"Have you been . . . how much wine did you drink?"

Loren forced a laugh. "I am no drunkard."

"So says every drunkard." But she could hear the tension leach from his voice.

"I could fetch *more* wine, if you wish," said Gem from behind him. "I feel I could use a cup myself, for your screams still ring in my ears."

Loren's spirits dampened at once as she looked at the boy. Gem looked the same as always, and the same impudent smirk tugged at his lips. Yet the memory of her nightmare would not leave her mind.

She shook her head and tried to smile. "No, Gem. I only need sleep, and I would wager you do as well. Off with you both."

Xain did not move, not until she took his shoulder and ushered him gently out. Gem went more readily, and was already yawning by the time he reentered his room. Once they were gone, Loren closed her door and turned to the bed.

Chet sat up, his bare chest glistening in the moonslight, one hand still on the scar of his dagger wound. He studied her in the dim silver glow through the window.

"Loren, what is wrong?"

"Nothing," she said lightly. She cast her robe on the floor and gave him a moment to take her in before sliding beneath the covers. But it did not distract him.

"You can fool Gem and Xain, but I know you are lying."

She was not so sure she had fooled Xain, for the wizard's eyes had been troubled. But still she kept her smile and ran a hand up his arm. "That is a strong accusation. How is your wound? I did not mean to hit you. I was not myself when I woke."

"It is all right," said Chet. "The pain is fading."

She bent to kiss the scar, and as her other hand squeezed his shoulder, she felt him relax. "Good. It is a mark of honor. I would hate for you to regret earning it."

Though his eyes were still grave, that forced a chuckle from him. "As though *that* is why I would regret it." His frown returned. "Are you certain you are all right? What did you dream of?"

Loren felt her smile grow strained. "I do not remember," she said. A sick feeling grew in the pit of her stomach at the lie. "Mayhap it was the battle of the Seat. That was no happy memory."

He hesitated, and for a moment she thought he would answer. But he only shook his head, and turned away to lie upon his side.

Soon he was asleep once more. But Loren lay awake all the rest of the night, until the silver of moonslight gave way to the pink blush of dawn. And she felt that eyes watched her in the darkness, the eyes of every enemy she had left behind her between the paths of the Birchwood and the palace of the High King.

— 39 —

FIVE

As they ate with Gem the next morning, Loren could sense Chet's concern for her. It fairly radiated from him, like heat from a flame. When she tried to reach for more food, he would offer to fetch it for her, and he kept asking her if she would like any more water to drink. She avoided his gaze all the while, and spoke lightly of small matters, but his worry remained—until a thought seemed to strike him, and he cocked his head.

"Where is Xain?" he said.

Loren glanced towards the wizard's room. "Sleeping, I imagine."

"Normally he rises earlier than any of us," said Chet.

Loren and Gem gave each other a dark look. That had not always been Xain's way, and had only begun after his battles with magestone sickness. Sometimes Loren wondered if the wizard slept at all any more. But now her thoughts were drawn to the night before, and her dream.

A chill went through her. She had recently consumed magestones—once, in Dorsea, when the Elves had forced her to do it, and then once again here upon the Seat when she sought an agent of the Shades. The fact that she had them, and had eaten them, was unknown to anyone but Chet, and even he only knew of the first time.

Could the magestones be linked to her nightmare? She could only find out by asking Xain, and that was not something she could do carelessly. If the wizard found out she possessed magestones—indeed, if anyone other than Chet learned of it—her very life might be in danger, for it was a dark crime under the King's law.

She shook off such thoughts and rose, going to Xain's room. Cautiously she tapped on the door, and when she heard no reply within, she pushed it open. Xain's bed was empty, the covers tousled, and his clothing from yesterday lay upon the floor.

"Gone," she said, shrugging. "Off on some business as the new dean, no doubt."

But she proved to be wrong, for Xain returned to them before they had finished eating. He stepped through the door wearing something that looked utterly foreign upon him: a full and beaming smile.

"What under the sky are you grinning about?" said Loren.

"I have a surprise for you," said Xain. "Or rather, the Lord Prince has arranged it, and he has allowed me to present it. Come with me."

Loren glanced at Chet, but he only shrugged. They rose, along with Gem, and followed Xain out into the hallway.

The wizard led them to a part of the palace they had rarely visited, where many of the High King's guards were stationed, as well as a great number of Mystics. Soldiers watched them pass with great interest. Loren's cheeks flushed as she realized that many of them were looking at her. She fought the urge to raise her hood and instead held her head high. As the Nightblade, she would have to grow used to this, she supposed.

Xain stopped at a heavy door, pausing before he opened it to ensure they were gathered behind him. He pushed it open to reveal a sort of barracks, with beds along the walls, each with a small chest at the foot. In the center of the room was a long wooden table, and around it sat several Mystics, their red hoods cast back from their faces. Loren stood in the doorway, wondering why Xain would bring her here. Then the Mystics looked up at her, and stood from their places at the table. A smile broke out on her face, wide enough to match Xain's, and she laughed.

"Weath! Jormund!" she cried.

The Mystics came forwards to embrace her, laughing—even large Jormund, who had hardly ever said a word to her. They had met her in Brekkur when Loren was fleeing east across Underrealm, and Kal had sent them to the Seat to help deliver his message to the High King. Now they clapped her on the back and shook Chet's hand, and Jormund even picked up little Gem, who squealed like a pup. But as she released Weath's wrist, Loren looked past her to the other Mystics at the table. They studied her with interest, but they had not risen, and she did not recognize their faces.

"Where are Erik and Gwenyth?" said Loren.

The room fell silent. Jormund looked at her solemnly, and Weath cast her gaze to the floor. Loren's breath caught in her throat.

"In the battle?"

"On the eastern docks," said Weath quietly. "We pursued the armies of Dulmun there, and pressed the assault as they tried to board their ships and escape. Erik fought like a madman and killed three of them on his own. But an archer, darkness take them, fired from the stern of a ship as it fled, and the arrow pierced his heart. Gwenyth fell later, as we tried to clear the Shades from the palace."

Loren bowed her head, blinking hard. "I wish I had been there."

Weath put her hand on Loren's shoulder. "Do not be sorry. From what we have heard, you were more sorely needed in the palace, and the nine kingdoms are grateful for your actions."

She forced a smile. The other Mystics stood from the table—three of them, and none looked alike. One by one they came forwards to be introduced. First was a short, slim woman of middle years, whose narrow eyes were quick and unsmiling. She was called Shiun. There was a tall, broad youth named Uzo, whose shaved head was darker even than Annis'. He squeezed Loren's wrist harder than he needed to, and she fought away a grimace as she tried to do the same. He smiled at that and clapped her shoulder. Gem gaped at Uzo, his mouth hanging open, and did not seem to hear when the young man offered him a hand to clasp.

The last Mystic was called Niya. Though she was only a finger or two taller than Loren, she was far more heavily muscled, so that Loren felt minuscule in her presence. Beneath a shirt of chain she had a leather jerkin with a high collar that covered her neck, but its sleeves were short, so that her thick arms were on display. She wore a secretive smirk as she approached Loren and held forth her hand. When their wrists clasped, her skin was smooth and warm, and the hairs on the back of Loren's neck tingled.

"The Nightblade," said Niya. "I suppose this is meant to be an honor. The High King holds you in high esteem. That is impressive indeed, for such a young woman.”

Loren’s cheeks flushed. “Not so young,” she said.

“Not *too* young, I suppose,” said Niya.

“Niya has been appointed the captain of our squadron,” said Weath. “She fought beside the former lord chancellor at the eastern gate, and took a wound in the battle.”

“It sounds as if you are a hero,” said Loren.

“Mayhap,” said Niya. “It was only a small cut, and it was not the High King who raised my station for it, unlike you.”

Loren realized that they had not released each other’s wrists. She did so at last, though her hand seemed reluctant to obey. “There is time yet.”

Chet eyed the woman as they shook hands. “I did not see you in the fighting,” he remarked.

The smirk she had worn for Loren vanished, and Niya raised her eyebrows. “And did you take count of every Mystic before the gate? You have a cool head for battle, it seems. What is your position, by the by? Other than bedfellow of the Nightblade, I mean.”

His jaw clenching, Chet opened his mouth to reply, but Loren barked a laugh despite herself. He turned his glare on her and held his tongue.

“Oh, come, Chet,” she chided him. “Do not be so serious. It was a joke.”

Niya grinned at Loren, and Chet forced a smile as well. “Well met, then,” he said.

"Indeed," said Niya, and returned to her table. Gem stood there looking crestfallen, his hand still outstretched to clasp hers, but she acted as though he was not there.

The other Mystics told Loren something of themselves. Uzo was a spearman, though he was quick to explain his spear was likely not similar to the ones Loren was used to; it was short and flexible, and he used it half as a staff. Shiun was a scout, and skilled with a bow, but when she heard that Loren had been learning the Calentin style of shooting, her brows lifted, and she extracted a promise that the two of them would trade advice the next time they were in the training yard. After a time, Xain put his hand on Loren's shoulder and gave her a smile.

"I am glad to see you reunited," he said, "but that is not the end of the news I have for you. I did not bring you to see your friends only so you could have a happy reunion. Ammon is in need of reinforcements, and these five will come with you on the journey there."

Loren's eyes shot wide, and she looked at the Mystics anew. Her expression must have shown her shock, for Weath smiled, and Jormund loosed his huge, booming laugh. Shiun and Uzo gave her a polite smile—but Loren looked past them, to the table where Niya sat. The Mystic woman had not taken her eyes from Loren, and for a moment they locked gazes. Loren's stomach did a pleasant turn, and she swallowed hard before turning away.

Her gaze met Xain's, who still smiled at her in delight of his surprise. A grin stole across her face to match his—but then she realized that this was his parting gift. A replacement, though a shoddy one, for his own company upon the road. That thought seemed to throw a dark cloud over her joy, and her smile faltered.

Xain saw it, and his own smile grew sad in response. "There is time yet before that bitter parting," he said quietly. "And I mean to fill it with happiness where I can. Tonight, you must let me take you out upon the Seat. We will eat and drink our fill, and pretend for a little while longer that no darkness waits beyond an ever-nearing dawn."

SIX

Loren returned to her quarters, along with Chet and Gem, and there Xain left them for the rest of the day. But he returned at dusk, bringing them fine clothes to wear. He handed the boys their outfits, but when he came to Loren he paused.

"I did not know which you would rather wear," he said. "I have brought you trousers of dyed black leather, to wear with a blouse and a vest, if you wish it. That is the sort of clothing I have always seen you in. But I also have here a dress. I am not sure if it is quite your size, and I had the clothier choose the cut. I am no expert in these things you understand, and—”

“Oh, sky above, Xain,” she said, laughing at his sudden awkwardness. “Let me look at the thing.”

Xain lifted it from his arm. Loren went still at the sight of it, her breath escaping in a soft sigh. Hesitantly she reached out and took it, marveling at the feeling of the cloth between her fingertips. It was as blue as the ocean, and worked through with thin threads of sea-green in delicate patterns like tree leaves. She had never seen a fabric that shimmered just so, reflecting the torchlight when she turned it over in her hands. Its sleeves ran all the way to the wrists, where they closed with small buttons of some cream-colored stone she had never seen before.

“It is a silly thing, I know,” he said at once, looking embarrassed as he pursed his lips at it. “Most likely you do not—”

“I do not often wear dresses,” said Loren. “The last one I owned was made by my mother, and she intended for me to wear it to a dance, the very night you and I met.” She pressed the dress to herself, smiling softly at him. “I ground dirt into that dress with my heel and spat on it, for I hated her. But this one I will keep. It is beautiful.” Then she frowned. “Though I hope you do not expect me to wear it often. I could not possibly mount a horse in this thing.”

He laughed and ran a hand through his hair. “Of course not. And you will find little occasion for dresses in Ammon, I assure you. But I am glad you like it, regardless."

When Chet saw her in the dress, he could not stop staring, and in the end she had to force him to continue getting dressed himself. Once they were ready, and Loren had donned her black cloak, Xain led them out of the palace and into the streets of the city, heading southwest.

Lamps burned from the corners of many buildings along the way, lending the city a cheery look despite the cut of the frigid air. The island was full of people about their business, and if there were more soldiers among the crowds than there had been a few weeks ago, still the mood was cheerful and boisterous, with much laughter, and songs that poured from nearly every tavern they passed. The rebuilding of the Seat had raised the mood of all upon it, and there was a sense in those who dwelt there that the war, if indeed it ever came, would be a short and simple affair, and no source of great trouble or worry.

Xain stopped before a tavern, and over its door Loren saw a stag painted in silver. Inside, a fire burned in the wide hearth, and the lamps along the walls strengthened its warm glow. Xain introduced them briefly to the matron, Canda, and she showed them to a table where they found well-cushioned chairs with intricate designs carved into the wood. When the food came, they found that it tasted nearly as delightful as the place looked. Seldom had Loren tasted any meat so finely spiced, even in the palace, and there were sweet roasted fruits the likes of which she had never seen before. The wine, too, was uncommonly good, and she wondered how much Xain had paid for it all. When she asked him, he shushed her with a wave of his hand.

"Tonight we are not concerned with such things," he said. "Tonight we think only of having one last happy memory together, at least until the next time we meet."

"Speaking of meetings," said Gem, who had snuck himself a cup of wine when Loren was not looking, "I have had a thought recently. How in all the skeins of time did the two of you meet each other? I have never heard the tale."

Loren blinked. She had told Chet the story, of course, but then they had spent far more time together since their reunion in Northwood. But she had never thought to tell Gem, for their journey together had consisted of one flight from danger after another.

So she settled back in her chair and told the story now, of how she had caught Xain running through the Birchwood and had begged him to take her with him. She skipped briefly over the description of her father and the reasons she wished to flee, and Gem did not press her for more details. But when she reached the part of the tale where they slept that first night on the riverbank, she scowled at Xain in mock fury and brandished her wine cup at him.

"And then this buffoon, darkness take him, *abandoned* me on the riverbank."

Xain's cheeks burned red, and he had to force a smile.

"I did. Though in my defense, I thought it would be safer for you."

"Oh, yes, very safe," said Loren, leaning over to Gem and muttering conspiratorially. "It only landed the constables hot on my heels, and then dropped me in the lap of Damaris of the family Yerrin, who, you will remember, has tried to kill me more than once."

The wizard barked a laugh. "And do you think I *planned* for that?"

They argued over that for a bit, and then Loren went on with the story, and by the time she had come to the part where Gem entered into it, the boy was so tired that he had nearly fallen asleep in his food. He perked up at the mention of his own name, but almost immediately his head began to sag again.

Loren looked towards the door, wondering what time it was. The common room was not so full as it had been when they entered, but there were more than enough patrons to keep it open for some hours more. Her heart sank at the thought of ending their night so soon, and she looked reluctantly at Xain. He gave her a sad smile.

Then Chet stood from his chair. "It grows late, and our urchin is almost asleep where he sits. I will see him safely to the palace and leave you two be."

Loren blinked at him. "You need not do that. I can come with you."

"Stay," said Chet, smiling and putting a hand on her shoulder. "You and I have all the coming journey together, and many days after that as well. But your time with Xain is nowhere near so plentiful, and should be savored. And besides, it would be a crime if you did not spend as much time in that dress as you possibly can, for I do not know when you shall get to wear it again."

Her sight grew misty, and she wondered if she had had too much wine. "Thank you," she murmured. Chet smiled and forced a grumbling Gem to his feet, and then walked the boy out into the night.

"He is worth more than his weight in gold, that one," said Xain quietly. "Do not forget it."

"I will not," said Loren. "All our lives he has cared for me, and some time ago that care grew into a love unlike any I have seen before. I only worry that it is too much, for if his feelings for me ever caused him harm, I could not bear it."

Xain cocked his head. "You speak as though you regret his feelings for you."

Loren shook her head quickly. "No, of course not. How could I, when I love him as well? Only sometimes I think he sees me as more than I am."

"Mayhap," said Xain. "Or mayhap you see yourself as less than you are."

She did not know what to say to that, and so they

sat for a while in comfortable silence. Loren finished her cup of wine, and Xain refilled it with the rest of the bottle. They sipped gingerly, and Loren could sense the same hesitance in the wizard that she herself felt—a reluctance to move on, to see this night end and the next step in their journey begin.

It was Xain who broke the silence. "Loren, I must ask you something. Do you still carry your dagger?"

She tensed. "Yes."

"You mean to bring it with you?" he said, studying her.

"I do. What else would I do with it?"

His eyes grew far away, staring over her shoulder. "I do not know. Once you asked me if you should throw it into the Great Bay. Mayhap you should do that now. I fear what might happen if Kal should learn that you have it. Jordel was worried enough about it, and he was a much more forgiving man. I wish I were going with you."

Loren frowned. "Kal was Jordel's master, and Jordel was the one who told me the truth of the blade in the first place. I had hoped to tell Kal of it, and seek his council."

Xain leaned forwards and shook his head, speaking in a low voice. "I do not think that would be wise. He seemed a man more prone to pragmatism than to kindness. Jordel did not press you to rid yourself of the dagger, because he trusted you. Though we met him only briefly, I do not know that Kal trusts anyone. If indeed you keep the dagger in your possession, you should not tell him of it."

She pursed her lips. "Very well. I shall keep it a secret."

"Promise me."

Loren rolled her eyes. "I promise you."

He smiled. "You are too confident in yourself by half. But it is one of your endearing qualities. I hope you will send my regards to Annis, by the by, as well as my apologies. That girl will never have much affection for me, I fear."

"Who would?" said Loren, raising her brows and drinking deep of her wine.

"Careful now," said Xain, scowling with mock severity. "Have you not heard I am a mighty firemage? I might catch you in my flame."

Loren chuckled. "It is good to see you happy, Xain. You have not had much occasion for joy since I have known you. And when Jordel . . ." She took a moment to swallow past a lump in her throat. "When Jordel told me how you used to be—before you fled the Seat, I mean—I could scarcely believe it. Now I see that he did not tell me even half of the truth."

Xain's eyes sparked with interest. "I never knew that. What did he tell you?"

"Do you wish to hear tales of your praise?" she teased. "He said that you were mayhap too quick to anger, but you were quick to laugh as well. He said that was how you earned yourself favor among the great, especially the Lord Prince. When I met Eamin, I could not understand why he would befriend such a dour man as yourself. But I have since seen a new part of you, and I am glad. If this is how you were before you left the Seat, then I would not take you away from it for all the gold in the nine kingdoms."

The wizard's eyes shone with tears for a moment. He cleared his throat, and then slapped the table abruptly. "Come. I wish to show you something."

Loren straightened. "What? Where? It is the middle of the night."

"All the better," said Xain. "Come."

She hesitated a moment more, but Xain had already stood and was making for the bar. There he spoke briefly to Canda and, after he placed a pair of coins in her palm, she handed him two more bottles of wine. One of these he placed in Loren's hand before drawing her through the room and out into the street.

SEVEN

The night was no longer young, and the first snow had begun to fall earlier that day—not enough to cause drifts in the streets, but enough that Loren drew her cloak tighter and blew into the side of her hood to warm her face. Xain led her west in the moonslight, and before long they approached a huge black building surrounded by a wall ten paces high, all in black granite with silver trim. Loren stopped short.

"The Academy?" she said, a shiver running up her back. "Xain, where are we going?"

"Inside, of course," he said. "Did you not know that I am the dean?"

He threw open the front door and strode in. Loren hastened to follow, looking nervously around. The front hall was wide, with two staircases leading up from it in different directions, as well as halls leading to endless rows of doors in all directions. Moonslight poured through the windows high above, though it weakened considerably before it reached the floor, and most of the illumination came from a chandelier high above.

She jumped as the doors slammed shut behind her, and turned to see that an old woman had closed them. The woman was short and wizened and had a mad look in her eye, but she ignored Loren entirely as she returned to her post by the door.

"Come," said Xain, making for a hallway off to the left. Loren followed, not daring to trail too far behind. She knew that anyone they met would likely be a wizard. It was a curious thought, for everywhere else in the nine kingdoms, wizards were a rare thing.

She need not have worried, for they did not see anyone until Xain stopped before another thick door, this one made of thick oak. Next to the door was a chair, and in the chair was a shriveled crone who could have been the sister of the woman at the front door. This woman's back was not so hunched, and her fingers not so gnarled, but her eyes held a mean and cruel sneer.

"What do you want?" she grated. Her nose turned up as she observed the bottle of wine Loren carried.

"I believe you meant to ask, 'How may I help you, Dean Forredar?'" said Xain. "And my answer, Carog, is that you may stand aside."

"Certainly," said Carog, giving him a nasty smile.

She hobbled out of the way. Xain stepped forwards and put his hand on the latch—but it did not budge. His shoulders heaved with a sigh, and he turned.

"Open the door, Carog."

Carog's eyes shot wide with mock innocence. "Oh, dearie me, is it locked? Now, where would I have placed the key? It gets so hard to remember these things at my age." She made a great show of fumbling at the pockets of her robes.

Xain glared at her. "If you have lost the key, then I have no choice but to declare you derelict in your duties and replace you. I am certain Mellie will recommend a suitable steward in your stead."

In an instant, Carog's face turned to a bitter grimace. Angrily she thrust a hand into her robes and withdrew a key, which she hastened to turn in the lock.

"Thank you, Carog," said Xain graciously, as he led Loren within. After the door slammed shut behind them, he smirked. "She has hated me ever since I was a student. I would sneak in here often without her knowing. She only caught me twice, but she never forgave me."

"She is horrid," said Loren.

"And age has not improved her. But I am the dean, and no longer need to care about such things. Come, and let me show you one of my favorite places."

Looking up, Loren saw that they were in a great circular tower—and then she realized that it was the Academy's bell tower. A wide staircase ran along the wall, built into the stone itself, and there high above them was the bell, massive even from this far down. Xain started up the steps, and she followed behind. His pace soon slowed, and she heard him pant heavily. But Loren had lost none of her hardiness from a lifetime in the forest, and she chuckled as she outpaced him.

"You are as slow as the day we met, wizard," she said. "Now that you are a man of books and learning, do not forget to leave your desk every once in a while, or I shall find you fat and lazy when I return to the Seat."

"Some would be glad to grow fat and happy in their later years," gasped Xain. But he quickened his pace to keep up with her.

They reached the top, and Loren marveled at the sight of it. The bell was surrounded by a wide platform, and at the edge of it was a rail. Beyond that was only open air, so that in all directions she could look out and see the city laid before her like a blanket, but shining with the light of torches and hearths. The wind was stronger here than it had been on the street, but Loren hardly noticed it, so taken aback was she at the sight before her.

"Xain," she breathed. "This . . . this is . . ."

"It is, is it not?" he said, his smile widening.

He guided her to the edge, and there he sat, draping his arms over the railing. Loren did the same beside him, laying her cloak beneath her so she did not dirty her dress. From within his coat Xain pulled his bottle of wine and removed the rag that sealed it. Loren took that as a signal, and she opened her bottle as well.

"To the High King Enalyn," said Xain. "Long may she reign, and her enemies be vanquished."

"To lengthy roads traveled together," said Loren. "May our memories of them never dim."

They clinked the necks of the bottles against one another and drank deep. For a while after that, Loren was content to enjoy the sights and smells of the city far below, and track the slow progress of the moons across the sky as they blotted out one star after another. The wine was the finest they had had so far that night, and half of hers was gone before she realized it. The edges of her vision had begun to grow blurry. She held up the bottle.

"How much gold have you spent on me tonight, Xain?"

Xain held up his own wine. "On us, you mean. Do you think I would spend a small fortune just to please you?"

She snorted. "I should say not. I have given you no end of reasons to be annoyed with me during our time together."

"And I have, in turn, made your life horrible upon occasion," said Xain quietly. He drank again from his bottle.

Loren shook her head. "Even at its worst, I would not call it horrible. Frightening, yes, and sometimes painful. But horrible was the Birchwood, and my father. Whatever else you have done, you took me away from that. And that would be cause enough for thanks. But I have learned, too, just how honorable you are at your core—that is, when you are not being a colossal idiot."

Though she spoke in jest, Xain looked at her solemnly. "And you, Loren of the family Nelda. How could I know, when first we met, the greatness in your own heart? Were you royalty, I do not doubt you would one day be the High King. Were you a merchant, your family would become the richest in the nine lands. And as things stand—well, what commoner could claim to be greater than you?" He raised his bottle in another toast, and then drank deep.

"You are drunk," Loren proclaimed. "And I mean to join you." She took another swig.

"Join me? You are further along than I am."

Loren looked up at the moons, which were close to vanishing behind the roof of the bell tower. But that brought thoughts of sleep, which brought thoughts of dreams. Her good mood dampened.

"Xain," she said carefully. "When you ate magestones . . ." She felt him stiffen beside her. "I am sorry. I should not have presumed to ask."

"It is all right," he said. "Only that is a tale I would rather not spread through the Academy. But none are near us to eavesdrop now. Go on."

"Did you dream?" said Loren. "I remember, when we carried you through the Greatrocks, that you would lie there twitching and moaning at night."

He arched an eyebrow at her. "What has brought you to such a question?"

Loren shrugged. "I do not know. It worried me then. There were many things I wondered during those times that I have never had the courage to ask you until now. You seem well recovered, but how can that be when you suffered so terribly?"

Xain gave a grim chuckle. "I did. But no, I did not dream, nor would I have. Magestones have other properties beyond strengthening a wizard's power. They quell the appetite entirely, for one thing. Do you remember how Jordel almost had to force me to eat? And they purge the body of other influences. The remedies of the apothecary have little effect upon a wizard who eats magestones, and the same is true for poisons. And as I said at the first, a wizard who consumes the stone does not dream."

"That is good . . ." said Loren absentmindedly. Then she realized how that sounded and hurried to correct herself. "I mean, it is a little sad, I suppose. But I am glad you do not have the nightmares I thought you did."

"Are you worried about last night?" said Xain, his

brows drawing close. "Loren, what under the stars did you dream of?"

"I told you I do not remember." She had made a mistake, and drawn his thoughts far too close to her secret. "I was only wondering if the sickness still troubled you at all. If you should fall back into darkness, I will no longer be here to box your ears and tie you up until you come to your senses." Pushing his shoulder, she flashed him a wide smile.

He returned it, and her fear left her. "You need not worry on that account. Those dark days are behind me, and will never return. I can hardly believe that you and I once conspired to sell those thrice-cursed stones. Do you remember?"

"Of course. It was not so long ago," said Loren.

Xain fixed her with a look. "Now that I think of it, that is a piece of information that may yet prove useful. If you remember, I had a contact in Dorsea who I thought might buy the stones. You may have need of such a man."

"But I no longer wish to sell magestones," said Loren, studying him carefully.

"Of course not, not any longer. But there are other goods beyond the King's law—and if you do not wish to sell them, or buy them, a spy should still know someone who deals in them."

"Oh?" said Loren. "Very well then. Where might I find him?"

"His name is Wyle, and he lives in the city of Bertram. It is in Dorsea, west of the King's road where it runs by the Greatrocks, halfway between their southern tip and the Moonslight Pass to the north."

"Very well," said Loren. "If I ever have occasion to visit him, I shall send him your regards."

"He will not take kindly to that," said Xain with a harsh laugh. "You might do better to pretend you never knew me. But now we have spoken overmuch of such things. It is a fine night. Too fine to spend it with talk of magestones and other dark matters beyond the King's law."

"I feel as though there are few matters these days which are *not* dark."

"That is true enough. This morning I gave my first speech to the Academy students. It was in the front hall, the one we passed through. They looked so young—and so frightened. And it was my duty to convince them not to be afraid, and that I would protect them."

"But you will," said Loren. "Is that not part of your duty?"

"It is, and I will not abandon it like that faithless steer, Cyrus," said Xain. "But I am one man—a wizard, and a strong one, I can say without boasting. Yet I do not know if I have it in me to keep them safe from all harm."

To her own great surprise, Loren squeezed his shoulder. *I must be more wine-addled than I thought.* "No one has that power, but few could come closer to it than you. Your only fault is that you are so stupidly serious about everything. If you can only shed the idea that you bear all the world's burdens, you will do much better."

Xain laughed. "Wise words from one so young. And I think you may be right. Besides, now that my son is returned to me, I need not worry half so much."

"I do not jest. You are a great wizard, Xain, and may even be a great man."

He lowered his gaze, looking down on the city again. "Jordel was a great man," he murmured.

For the second time that night, Loren swallowed past a tightness in her throat. "I thought you wished not to speak of dark matters."

"Even in death, Jordel is a light. That is what *you* must remember, Loren. If you think me great, know that I hold you in even higher regard. But you are young, and the nine lands hold grief enough to fill the lives of all within them. No matter how dark your road may grow, you must remember Jordel. If you live by what he would do, you will rarely go far wrong."

With another pang of guilt, she thought of the magestones. "I will remember," she said softly. "I have entered the High King's service because of him, after all."

Xain's eyes narrowed, as though that answer did not entirely satisfy him. But he gave no answer.

Another thought struck Loren. She took a deep breath. "Will we ever see each other again, you and I?"

She thought Xain might answer easily with a casual reassurance. Instead he shrugged. "Who can know? But I think we might. The answer lies more in your hands than mine. My duty will keep me on the Seat for the foreseeable future. Yet who knows what fortunes the coming war may bring?"

"I think the war will be over quickly, and easily, if it is not entirely bloodless," said Loren.

"Already it has claimed its share of blood," said Xain, quiet and solemn. "And I fear it has only begun. We are among the few who know the true enemy— not the kingdom of Dulmun, but the Shades' master. The Necromancer."

Loren shivered at the name. But she thrust out her hand to him. "A promise, then, between you and me. If we survive this war, I will return, and you and I will sit here together again, and here we will stay until all the tales of our journeys have been told."

Xain clasped her wrist in agreement. But Loren seized his and dragged him closer, until his nose was almost touching hers, and she scowled.

"And if you break your word to me *this* time, I will *drag* you to the top of this tower and throw you off of it. We will see if you can summon a storm to carry you safely to the ground."

The wizard burst out laughing, the longest, loudest, and clearest she had ever heard from him, and it was as if, in an instant, he had cast off all the cares that troubled him, all the way back to before the moment they had met in the Birchwood. She did not doubt that that laugh could be heard for a great distance in the city below.

"You have my word, Nightblade."

"I will hold you to it, Dean Forredar." Her mouth twisted. "It sounds odd upon my tongue."

"And mine," said Xain. "But now come. We have spent long enough up here already, and I grow cold. Besides, what would people think if they found the dean drunk at the top of his own bell tower?"

He stood and helped her up, and they stumbled down the stairs together. And for the first time in all their journey together, Loren thought that she could call Xain her true friend.

EIGHT

One day more passed, a day that Loren spent miserable after the wine from the night before. As the sun lowered in the sky, Xain came to sit with her in the common room between their chambers, and they discussed the road from the Seat to Ammon. The wizard looked even worse for wear than she did.

When night came and supper passed, they did not remain awake for long. Loren would have relished one more night spent together, but they would wake early the next day, and she would rather not be exhausted for the beginning of their voyage across the Great Bay.

A palace servant roused them before dawn, and Loren and Chet dressed together in silence. They shook Gem awake twice, and still he did not rise from his bed. In the end Loren lost patience and threw a pitcher of water on him. Xain awakened, too, and left with them so that he could say a final farewell before they set sail.

In the palace courtyard were the Mystics who would accompany them. Two carriages took them all quickly to the western docks. It was the same place they had landed just weeks before, as fugitives and refugees. They had risen far since then. Now the dean of the Academy was there to see them off—and, to their delight, so was the Lord Prince. Eamin awaited them in the dim grey glow just before dawn, and stepped forwards with a smile as they clambered down from the carriage.

"Fare well, Chet of the family Lindel, and Gem of the family Noctis. Fare well, Nightblade. I would have a promise from you, that the next time we see each other, you will tell me the tale of that time you met the Elves, eh?"

Loren bowed deep. "I give you my word, Your Highness."

Eamin's smile widened. Then he withdrew, and Xain took his place. He and Chet clasped wrists, with Chet regarding the wizard silently.

"I was not myself when first we met," said Xain. "You have shown yourself to be nothing but an honorable man, yet in the course of our travels I have given you no great cause to love me. I wish you well on the roads ahead, and beg that you think of me better than I mayhap deserve. Promise me that you will care for Loren."

"That I will do, promise or no," said Chet. "Fare well here upon the island, Xain. I may not love you, but you have proven yourself an honorable man as well, in the end."

When Xain went to Gem, the boy put his hands on his hips and sniffed. "Farewell, wizard. I suppose you have proven not to be such a poor traveling companion—though some times were better than others."

Xain chuckled. "I wish, my boy, that you were a wizard, for it would be my pleasure to oversee your instruction personally. As it is, my days will be emptier of laughter until we meet again."

Gem seemed to enjoy the thought of being a wizard very much, for his eyes shone. All pretense of bravado fell from him, and he leaped forwards to give Xain an awkward hug around the waist before scampering bashfully away and towards the ship.

Only Loren remained, and they looked at each other in silence. They had said all they needed to at the top of the Academy's bell tower. In the end she seized him in a great bear hug, and he squeezed her back, though his arms were far weaker.

"Fare well, Loren," he said. "Remember Jordel."

"And you. Fare well."

The captain set sail almost the moment they had boarded. Thus began their journey to Ammon, and a miserable journey it was. Winter had come at last to Underrealm, well and truly, and storms wracked their vessel all the way to the southern coast of Feldemar. Loren and Chet spent most of their time in their bunk, which could hardly have been less private, for it was only one bed of eight in the same cabin. Gem was in the room with them for the larger part of the journey, curled miserably under his blanket. He had not been overly prone to seasickness in the past, but this voyage was unlike either they had taken together before.

After six days of sailing, they docked at a town on Feldemar's southern shore, and there they rested overnight. Loren noticed a curious tension in the town that she did not understand at first. But then she realized that they were perilously close to the kingdom of Dulmun, the kingdom that had risen in treason against the High King. Though Dulmun had taken no military action since their assault on the Seat, most believed it was only a matter of time before the seafaring kingdom made war again, and coastal towns like this would likely be among their first targets.

The day after they landed, Niya purchased horses for all of them with a purse of coins that had been given to her upon the Seat. They had brought no mounts with them, for moving steeds by boat was most difficult with the strength of winter's storms. Loren was glad she had sent her horse, Midnight, to Ammon before her journey to the High King's Seat. Their reunion was one more thing to look forward to when Loren reached Jordel's home at last.

Their road north through Feldemar was hardly any more cheery than the ocean voyage had been. The kingdom proved to be a wet and marshy land, where the air was muggy despite the cold of winter. It did not snow here, but that was little comfort, for it rained heavily and always. Often the roads would be flooded, or covered by mudslides, causing long delays. Thus, a journey that should have taken them four days on horseback took seven instead.

When they camped for the night, or stopped for a midday meal, there was little conversation beyond what was necessary to build camp. But Loren did snatch some tidbits of information from the Mystics they rode beside, particularly the new ones. She learned that Shiun was a woman of Dulmun, an awkward fact considering that nation's treachery. But she had left that land when she was a young girl, and had spent the last many years in the southwestern reaches of Underrealm. Uzo hailed from Feldemar, and seemed the least uncomfortable with the heavy rains that pelted them. It was the way of winter in this land, he told them, and this was far gentler than the worst storms he had seen growing up. Jormund was a man of Calentin. That caught Loren's attention.

"Truly?" she said. "But you are a swordsman. Why do you not use the bow?"

"You know something of our archers, then," said Jormund, flashing his easy grin. "But a whole kingdom cannot stand back and fire upon their enemies from afar, for then they would be in grave trouble should those enemies ever get too close. And besides, I am too large to be an archer. When they put a bow in my hands as a boy, it snapped to kindling when I drew it." He laughed.

Gem's eyes went wide, but Loren leaned close and said, "He is joking."

She had meant to be quiet, but Jormund heard her. "I am not," he insisted. "Give me your own bow, if you do not believe me, and I will show you."

Loren declined.

Niya proved more reticent to speak of herself. When Loren asked the land from which she hailed, she said only "Wadeland." But she did not have the look of one from that kingdom, and she told them nothing of how she came to join the Mystics. Loren thought at first to press her for the tale, but soon realized that this was neither the time nor the place. She herself did not enjoy speaking of her childhood in the Birchwood, particularly when it came to her parents.

But that did not quell her curiosity about the Mystic woman—a curiosity, she admitted to herself, that was stoked to greater heights by the intense, smoldering look she often saw in Niya's eye when the woman thought she was not looking. Mayhap, Loren decided, she would be able to learn more once they reached Ammon.

Gem tried often to get Uzo to drill with him, for the boy still practiced the sword stances Jordel had taught him in the Greatrocks many months ago. He was much better at the forms now, and his arms had begun to fill out with his constant practice. But Uzo seemed to regard Gem as little more than an annoyance, and only joined in his training with great reluctance. Over and over again he trounced the boy, but Gem always sprang up off the ground beaming.

"You are a great warrior indeed," he said one evening, after Uzo had thrashed him thoroughly.

Uzo raised an eyebrow. "Greater than a boy with almost no practice? Stay your praise, for my pride cannot bear to be stoked any more."

Gem laughed as though that were a great joke.

One by one, Loren followed the landmarks that Xain had laid out for her on the route that would take them to Ammon. Sometimes they were easily found, and lay beside wide roads that were well kept. Other times they led her off into unbroken land, where there was nothing but thin goat trails to go by. But at last, after seven days, they came upon a wide plateau with a hill atop it, in the middle of a flat grassland, and upon that plateau was the stronghold of Ammon.

It was an impressive sight from the first, even when it was only a shape on the horizon that she could cover with her thumb. As they drew closer, they could see that it was built in three levels: first, a high wall that rimmed the edges of the plateau, from which there was only a single gate at the top of a ramp leading down; the middle wall, halfway up the hill, had two gates, and what looked like several structures built inside for the housing of troops; finally, the keep itself sat upon the hill's crown. It looked large enough to house half a thousand troops in comfort. As they neared, the plateau seemed to grow larger and larger, and the stronghold with it, so that Loren felt smaller the closer she drew.

Leagues away, they knew they had been spotted when they heard the clarion peal of horns signaling their approach. Soon after, they reached the bottom of the ramp, and felt eyes upon them all the way up. But when they reached the top, the gate was still closed. There, on the wall just above them, was an old man with a long white beard, wrapped in the red cloak of a Mystic. Loren recognized him, of course, for they had met only weeks before; he was Kal of the family Endil, and he looked just as severe as the first time she had laid eyes upon him.

"Who approaches the stronghold of Ammon, home of the family Adair?" said Kal.

"Loren of the family Nelda, Nightblade of the High King," said Loren. "But you know that already, and it is raining, so be quick and open the gate."

Kal scowled, but he turned to the men in the gatehouse and gave a nod. The drawbridge began to lower as they bent to the wheel, spanning the gap between the top of the ramp and the portcullis leading into the first level of the fortress.

"I would advise you be more careful with your manners," muttered Weath beside her, though Loren could see the wizard was hiding a smile. "I have known the grand chancellor for many years, and while he is not a stickler for ceremony, he sees great value in military decorum."

"I see greater value in a warm bed, especially now," said Loren. "I will not be kept huddling outside his fortress in the rain because I have not saluted to his liking."

After the drawbridge slammed into place, they walked their horses across it. Kal had descended to the courtyard and waited within, backed by a household guard of Mystic knights. Loren dismounted before him and gave a curt bow, pulling her gloves from her hands.

"Well met, Kal of the family Endil."

"And you, Nightblade. If you will follow me, there is much to—"

But a high-pitched squeal cut him off, and from between Kal's Mystics came a black and silver streak. It was Annis, in a dark dress that she had hitched up to run full tilt, and with a scream she flung herself into Loren's arms. Loren shouted in joy and hoisted her up in the air, and Gem launched himself from the saddle where he had been sitting behind Chet, tackling them both so that they all fell to the ground. He covered Annis' cheeks with kisses, and she laughed as she tried to hug him and Loren at the same time. Tears poured down the girl's cheeks, and Loren found it hard to keep her own restrained.

"Sky above!" barked Kal. "Are you servants of the High King, or children in truth? Get up, for though you may have all day to roll about in the mud like pups, I do not."

Loren rolled her eyes, but she got up and pulled the children with her. But Annis and Gem did not let go of each other.

"Very well," said Loren. "We are weary after our journey. If you will show us to our quarters, we will take our rest, and you may go about your business."

"Rest must wait," said Kal. "As I had begun to explain, you and I have much to discuss."

Stepping aside, he waved her on with a wide sweep of his arm. Loren sighed, hoping their discussion would be brief, for she was indeed weary and sick of the rain besides. But just as she stepped past Kal, she froze in her tracks.

In the group of Mystics who stood there, there was a man who looked to be from Wadeland. His hair was black and cropped close to the scalp, and a scar split his chin. He wore a red cloak now, but when last she had seen him, he had been dressed in the grey and blue of a Shade—and he had stood behind Damaris, in her dream.

"Loren?" said Chet behind her. "Is something the matter?"

The man was looking at her oddly—and did she catch a trace of fear in his eye? Loren tore her gaze away from him and looked to Chet.

"No. Nothing," she said. "Only I am tired, and my mind went far away. But I am sure the chancellor has no care for our weariness. Come, let us accompany him before he bursts with his impatience."

Kal growled something inaudible, and Chet snickered as they followed him onwards. But Loren stole a brief glance behind her. Mayhap she imagined it, but she thought she saw the man swallow with relief as she passed him by.

NINE

Kal took little notice of Loren's hesitation, and pressed quickly on until they had reached the keep atop the plateau. But Chet took her arm and drew her back a pace, and leaned in to whisper. "What was it? You looked as though you had seen an Elf."

Loren shook her head. "I . . . I am not certain. We should speak of it later."

Inwardly, she was not even certain what she would tell him. She knew nothing of the man she had seen. They had never met, so far as she could recall. All she knew was that he had been in her dream, dressed as a

Shade. Should she even try to do anything about it? A part of her wanted to believe it was a coincidence, but another part knew that was foolish. It was not exactly a common thing, to see something in a dream only to see it later in the waking world.

And then she thought of the rest of that dream—Damaris, and Chet's death, and Gem's teeth on her throat.

No. No, there was some explanation for this. There must be.

Kal stopped short, and Loren was so absorbed in thought that she nearly ran into him. He threw open a door in the hall and drew her into a small council room. Two Mystics took up positions of guard, one on either side of the door. Loren was relieved to see that neither of them was the dark-haired stranger from her dream. But when the rest of Loren's party started to follow them in, Kal waved his hands at them as if they were cats.

"Off with you—all except Loren. My men will see you to your lodgings, such as they are. You knights will receive your assignment in time. The rest of you may sit on the ramparts until the rain has pierced you through, for all I care. Go."

They went, with Chet giving Loren one last worried look before the door closed between them. But it was not until Loren turned to Kal in the center of the room that she saw Annis had remained. Kal acted as though it were the most normal thing in the world—

in fact he hardly seemed to notice the girl. He had eyes only for Loren, and he seized his long beard in his fingers as he narrowed his eyes at her.

"You certainly took your time to get here," he said.

Loren blinked. "I beg your pardon? I came here by the route that was given to me."

"Aye, and weeks after the attack upon the Seat," said Kal.

"When the High King ordered me."

Kal snorted. "If we all waited for orders, the nine kingdoms would already have fallen to ruination. Everyone moves too slowly, too slowly by half, and even the High King is no exception."

Unbidden, a flush of anger rose to Loren's cheeks. "You should not speak ill of your liege lord."

"Criticism should never be forbidden—least of all when it comes to kings," said Kal. "If a few more had been brave enough to speak against the Wizard Kings in their day, how many dark wars might have been avoided? But enough of this. I did not call you here to bandy words of politics and philosophy. Tell me of your journey, and what came before it upon the Seat."

"A moment," said Loren. "First, I saw someone in your courtyard. A young man, not much older than I, with dark hair and a scar that split his chin. Who is he?"

She was not displeased to see Kal frown in confusion, caught off guard by the question. Behind him,

Annis' eyes narrowed with interest. "Hewal? What of him?"

"He had . . . he looks familiar."

Kal snorted. "That is hardly possible. I have known him since he was a boy in Wadeland, and he has been stationed here since first he joined the Mystics. He was not with me when we met in Brekkur. If you have taken a fancy to him, that is not a matter I wish to give you any counsel upon whatsoever."

It was Loren's turn to be caught off guard, and she grew even angrier as she blushed anew. "I told you, I only thought he had an odd look." If she had thought for a moment to tell him of her dream, that impulse vanished.

"Forget my soldiers and their odd looks, and tell me of the attack upon the Seat," said Kal.

She did, at least in brief. When Loren spoke of some of the details of the battle, Annis' eyes went wide with shock and fear—especially when Loren told how she had brought the city gate crashing down to crush Rogan. Then Kal had her tell him of everything that had come after—when those who lived upon the Seat had fled to Selvan, and then returned, and finally when Enalyn had assigned her to Kal's service. She told him of the journey to Ammon as well, though he seemed to have little interest in that, and only studied the map that was laid out on his table, running his fingers through his beard in thought.

"Very well, very well," he muttered when she had

finished. "It is good you have come, even if it took you an age. I find myself with more duties than I can easily assume, especially after the High King named me Master of Spies. Hah! A useless title if ever there was one. She wishes for me to work for her in secret— yet because she names my position, I am known more widely than before, and secrecy comes scarce."

Loren felt that they must be coming to the heart of the matter now. "If you cannot act in secret, then let me act in your stead. What would you have me do?"

It was Annis who answered her, and once again Loren was surprised as Kal let the girl speak without interruption. "The answer to that is not entirely certain. Just now, the nine kingdoms are in a precarious position. The way that people perceive this war is even more important than the next battle. We have been trying to devise ways to sway the minds of the people, rather than outmaneuver our enemy on the field, for we are not generals. The High King's subjects, as well as her enemies, must see that she is resolved and capable, and that the kingdoms are unified behind her. None of the other kingdoms must be tempted to join with Dulmun."

That made Loren balk. "Would any of them do so? The treason of one kingdom is hard enough to believe. I cannot imagine that others would break their oaths."

To Loren's great annoyance, Kal and Annis looked at each other and rolled their eyes in unison.

"If that is true, why have the other kingdoms been so slow to answer Enalyn's call?" said Annis. "Oh, Selvan is with her, for she hails from that land. Dorsea was quick to bend the knee—no doubt they feared her reprisal after the Battle of Wellmont. Hedgemond, too, has pledged their strength—but that is an easy oath to keep, for they could not be farther away from the war itself. But where is Feldemar? Where are Wadeland and Idris and Wavemount? In days to come, their kings will no doubt claim that the High King's messengers were delayed by winter storms, or that their own messengers had been slow to return. Yet the truth is that they hesitate. And if even one of them joins Dulmun, the hesitation of the rest will only increase—and then we will have a true war on our hands, one that cannot be quelled easily."

All of this was a bit beyond Loren. In truth, she was shocked to hear Annis speaking of it so plainly, as though it were second nature. Her gaze lingered on the younger girl. Kal saw it, and a wry smile lifted one corner of his mouth.

"She is impressive, is she not? At first, I will admit that I was dismayed to be saddled with the girl. But she has proven herself to have an uncanny mind for strategy."

Annis' dark cheeks turned darker still, and she lowered her gaze demurely. But Loren saw the grin she could not banish.

"Very well," said Loren. "I will leave such lofty

matters to your hands, for the two of you seem more than capable of dealing with them. Yet my question remains: what shall I do?”

“If I have my way, you will be used to set an example,” said Kal. “Those who have acted against the High King must be brought to justice—and the more powerful the enemy we can lay low, the better. Do you know of any mighty enemy who might serve such a purpose?” His eyes narrowed.

Loren felt a chill steal up her back, and her heart turned to ice. “You mean to send me after Rogan.”

“Yes,” said Kal, nodding slowly. “No one knows where he is, but we must find him. Tales have spread throughout Underrealm of this warrior, the man no one can kill, who leads the armies that march against the High King.”

“He is not the only one of his kind,” said Loren. “We defeated another in the Greatrocks, one named Trisken. I would not doubt that there are more in the service of the Necroma—”

“Hist!” cried Kal, slamming his hand down on the tabletop. He looked at the door, almost fearfully. “Do not speak of such things where others may hear you.”

Loren arched an eyebrow. “I thought you trusted your soldiers, Kal.”

Kal scowled. “I do. And I am also responsible for their safety. Some knowledge is dangerous—something I know Jordel taught you, or tried to, though it is clear you did not heed the lesson.”

That hurt Loren more than she wished to show him, and so she lowered her head over the map. A thought came to her, and she pursed her lips. "It seems clear, then, what purpose you intend for me. Yet you seem to speak of dark deeds. I told the High King that I would not kill in her name, and she vowed never to command me to do so."

"Are you a fool, or have you not been listening?" said Kal. "I do not wish for you to murder Rogan. That would accomplish little. Our display of the High King's power must be as public as possible, and well within the law. We do not mean to kill him in darkness and shadow. He must be captured, and the King's justice brought down upon him in such a way that word of it will spread as fast as his exploits in battle."

That sounded far more palatable to Loren. And in fact, now that she thought of it, it sounded just like the stories of Mennet, the ancient thief of legend from whom Loren had drawn her first daydreams of becoming a thief. Mennet had never killed. But when a noble or great merchant was unjust and cruel to those who served them, Mennet would bring the King's justice down upon them without ever swinging the sword himself.

"Well and good," said Loren. "Then my oath is intact. When do I begin?"

"You are too eager by half," Kal grumbled. "And I have told you already that I do not know. If we knew where Rogan lurked, I would have acted already. I have learned what I needed from you. Go. Find your friends and settle into your lodgings. I will send for you again when I know our next step."

He bent over the map. Loren turned to make for the door—but she paused upon seeing a pained look on Annis' face. Kal noticed the room's silence after a moment, and he looked up, frowning. When he saw Annis' anxious expression, he sighed.

"Very well," he growled. "Spend this day in greetings and reunion if you wish. But I will expect you back on duty tomorrow."

"You shall have me," said Annis, barely restraining the glee in her voice. She ran towards Loren, seizing her arm and drawing her out into the hallway.

TEN

"Come!" said Annis, eyes bright as she clutched Loren's hand. "I want to see the others."

But Loren pulled her to a stop around the corner where no one could overhear. "In a moment. Annis, when did you become so wise in strategy that a grand chancellor of the Mystic Order would rely upon your counsel?"

Annis looked away bashfully. "Oh, that? That is no great matter."

"No great matter? He had you by his side the way the High King keeps the Lord Prince near her."

The hallway grew quiet as Annis searched for words. "Do you remember, long ago, when I told you of . . . of my mother, and what she would invite me to do?"

Loren's smile died as she nodded. Damaris of the family Yerrin, Annis' mother, was a cruel and ruthless matron. To achieve her ends, she had killed and tortured many. And when Annis was still a very little girl, Damaris had invited her to join in the violence. It was why Annis had been so desperate to escape her family when she and Loren first met.

"I remember," said Loren quietly.

"Well, she did not only draw me into her darker activities," said Annis. "I was there, too, for all the business one would expect in a merchant family—supply lines, and the movement of men from kingdom to kingdom, and things of that sort. Well, after I came here to Ammon, I was bored nearly to tears. I thought I would go mad for want of something to do. Then, mayhap a week after I arrived, Kal sent for me. He called me to his council chamber and asked me some questions of Yerrin activities in Dorsea. I answered him, and more besides, for he was asking the wrong sorts of questions."

Loren frowned. "What do you mean?"

Annis waved her hands as though she could pluck her explanation out of the air. "It would have been better if you were there. He wanted to know why our holdings in Selvan were so much stronger than in

Dorsea, since Dorsea borders more of the nine kingdoms than Selvan. He did not understand that Selvan, though it may be farther from the other kingdoms as the bird flies, is yet more deeply connected because of its wealth and its relationship to the High King, with whom all curry favor, and that trade routes are therefore more easily—"

Quickly Loren waved her hands. "Never mind. I am sorry I asked. Go on with your story."

"Well, I went on that way for some time, and when I paused to take a breath, I saw a strange look in Kal's eyes. I cannot think he has had many dealings with anyone from a merchant family before, for I did not tell him any great secrets of trade or commerce, but only the simplest truths we are taught as very young children. In any case, after that, he began inviting me to many of his strategy sessions. I think you spoke in jest before, but I suppose I *am* a part of his council."

A smile came to Loren unbidden, and she clapped a firm hand on Annis' shoulder. "Well, I for one am glad. You seemed at ease, and confident. Happier, mayhap, than I have seen you since after Cabrus."

Annis giggled. "I think I am. I have always thought of such things as a game—which my tutors did not favor, I can assure you, though they could not complain much, for I did well at my lessons regardless. And it has earned me some small amount of renown among the Mystics who dwell here."

Loren's smile widened—but mention of the Mystics made her think of the dark young man from the courtyard, who Kal had said was named Hewal. Her good mood evaporated. "As for that—do you know many of the soldiers in Ammon? Have you met them, or learned anything about them?"

"Not very much," said Annis, shrugging. "Why do you ask?"

Her dream flashed before her eyes. But how could she explain that? "No, nothing. Pay me no mind."

Annis' eyes narrowed, and the girl crossed her arms over her chest. "You asked Kal something of this, did you not? What is your interest in this Hewal fellow?"

Loren grimaced. She had forgotten how sharp and observant Annis could be, and always at the most inopportune times. "It is no great matter. Or, I do not believe so. But if it should become important, I will tell you before anyone else—other than Chet, of course. Does that satisfy you?"

"I suppose," said Annis. "Though you make it all sound very mysterious, and that is rarely a good sign with you. I could speak with Hewal if you wish, and try to learn what I—"

"No!" said Loren, far more sharply than she had intended. She tried again, softening her tone. "No, that is all right. But thank you."

Annis' eyes shot wide, and for the first time the girl looked truly worried. "Loren, what is it?" she whispered. "Are we in any danger?"

Loren thought of Chet's ruined throat, and the feral look in Gem's eyes as he attacked her. But she forced a smile. "No. Of course not. We are in a stronghold of Mystics, the greatest warriors in Underrealm. Where could we be safer?" She could see that Annis was not entirely convinced. But she took the girl's arm and led her on down the hallway. "Come. You have hardly had a chance to speak with Gem, and though you might not care overmuch, Chet, too, wishes to see you."

"Not so much as he wishes to see you, I am sure," said Annis with a sigh. "Are the two of you . . . is it much the same as when I saw you last?"

A furious red sprang into Loren's face. When last she had seen Annis, she and Chet had been chaste, but now . . . "Er, it is not—that is, not *quite* the same."

Annis must have taken her meaning, for her mouth formed a small circle. "I . . . I did not mean to . . . that is, forgive me for prying."

Loren could not help a laugh at that. "Still the modest merchant's daughter, I see. It is not prying that worries me—only I did not wish to embarrass *you*."

"Yes, well . . ." Annis looked thoroughly miserable through her bashfulness. "Might we speak of something else?"

"Mayhap our friends can distract us," said Loren. She took Annis' hand, and led her running and laughing down the hallway. Annis pointed the way to the stronghold's great dining hall, and there was Loren's party, seated and eating a meal from the kitchens.

Gem sprang to his feet at once and flung himself into Annis' arms, screaming with delight. Annis clutched at his shoulders, and then pushed him away to look at him—and Loren saw it. There, in Annis' gaze, was a pure and true love, even stronger, mayhap, than the way Loren felt for Chet. Tears came freely to the girl's eyes as she smiled and clutched Gem to her again. But Gem only smiled and laughed, and Loren saw no trace of the same feelings within him. Her high mood dampened for a moment.

Chet gave Annis a warm enough greeting, and then came to Loren. He took her hand in his and led her to the table.

"I will fetch you some food. What did Kal wish to discuss with you?"

Loren's mind returned to the council room, and the mission Kal had given her. Just as Chet had warned on the High King's Seat, she would soon hunt for Rogan. Her mood darkened, and he saw it. But she only shook her head.

"There is time to discuss it later," she said. "Let us wait until the happiness of this reunion has passed."

He frowned, and she feared he might press her. But then Annis sat beside her, and Gem on her other side, both of them talking animatedly. And in the face of their joy, Chet closed his mouth again, and went to fetch Loren her dinner, while Loren picked up a knife and began to pick at her nails with it.

ELEVEN

After they ate, Annis took Loren and Chet and Gem to the stables, where they found Midnight waiting. Loren gave a happy cry when she saw the mare, and scratched at her nose as Midnight whinnied in delight. But then the horse turned to Annis and pushed her muzzle against the girl's shoulder. Annis giggled and gave Loren an embarrassed look.

"We have become fast friends during our time here," she confessed. "I have visited her often, and usually bring a treat from the kitchens. Though I think that duty should now pass to you. Here." From a pocket in her cloak she drew an apple, and Loren fed it to Midnight, who gave a sharp nicker of pleasure.

They remained there for some time, and Loren brushed Midnight's coat, though it was already clean and shining. Then Annis took them out into the courtyard and atop the wall, where they looked out over the surrounding lands. It had stopped raining. Night approached swiftly, and the last of the sun's pale light dimmed through the clouds. From their high perspective, Annis pointed out this or that part of the fortress, sharing tidbits she had learned from the Mystics—who were growing more and more plentiful, the way she described it.

"Ever since the attack on the Seat, they have come in ever greater numbers," said Annis. "But they do nothing. There are no plans to engage in battle, at least not yet. They are only gathering their strength, and it is hard to escape reminders of the brewing war. I was only just starting to learn the names of those within the stronghold when all the newcomers started to arrive. Now I am nearly lost again."

"Are you? I can tell you where to find yourself, if you wish," said Niya.

They all gave a little jump and turned. The Mystic woman had appeared behind them as if by magic, and the others had come as well—Uzo, Shiun, Weath, and large Jormund. They each gave Loren a nod.

"You did not hear us coming?" said Niya, giving

Loren a wide smile. "You should keep a better look-out."

"I am in a stronghold full of allies," said Loren, rolling her eyes. "I thought I might let my guard down for half a moment."

Niya smiled at her, and then turned to Annis. A curious light shone in her eyes. "Well, if it is not the Yerrin girl."

Annis frowned. "I was not aware that we knew each other."

"But everyone in the stronghold knows you," said Niya, and her smile grew wider. "Those who dwell here already speak of you as though you are their little sister."

That mollified Annis considerably, and she held forth a hand. "I am Annis of the family Yerrin. Well met."

Niya clasped her wrist. "I already said I know who you are. I am Niya. These ones with me are Weath, Uzo, Shiun, and Jormund."

They greeted her one by one, and then stepped up to the ramparts beside Loren and Chet as Annis went on describing the lands that surrounded the stronghold. It seemed that Niya quickly grew bored, however, for she moved next to Loren and leaned on the ramparts just to her right. Loren saw that Chet took notice, and his mouth twisted in a frown.

"How went your council with the grand chancellor?" said Niya. She spoke quietly, so as not to interrupt Annis.

"Nothing very important came of it," said Loren lightly. She tried not to pay attention to how close Niya was, so close that she could almost feel the woman's breath on her cheek. "At least not yet. Though it seems the next leg of my mission might begin sooner than I had expected."

Niya straightened slightly, and forgot to speak quietly. "You are to ride forth? When?"

Annis' conversation halted, and the other Mystics looked to Loren. She shook her head quickly. "That has not been decided. Kal does not yet know where to send me. As soon as that changes, I am sure I shall be summoned."

The woman frowned. "But he will not send you out alone, I hope. We were charged with your safety."

"To see me here, yes," said Loren. "But after that?"

Niya's jaw twitched as she searched for words. "I would rest easier knowing you were in our hands than guarded by others in Ammon."

"Yes, and any excuse to march out the gate," muttered Uzo. "Already the air here cloys my nostrils."

They all went silent for a moment. Weath and Niya looked to Uzo, and from their expressions Loren felt that he had said something wrong, though she did not know what. But, too, she saw Annis look at Uzo, and Loren saw something in the girl's eyes—anxiousness? Mayhap even fear? But certainly a sense of warning.

Chet saw none of it, and it was his unknowing response that broke the moment's tension. "I am not eager to leave. Here we are protected, and beyond Ammon's walls I think we will find only danger."

Weath turned to him and smiled, her troubled expression vanishing. But Annis and Niya still wore dark looks, and both of them looked far away as though lost in thought.

"I would welcome some danger," said Jormund to Chet. "We have been idle since the attack on the Seat. I feel that if I do not do something soon, I may go mad."

"I have not seen as much battle as you, certainly, but I do not wish for more," said Chet.

"Mayhap you have no reason," snapped Uzo. "I was in the palace when they came. I knew a lover there, a courtesan of the High King herself, and some others as well."

"Meaning yourself?" said Niya, smirking.

Uzo's dark cheeks went darker. "In any case, I saw him during the battle. I was in formation, and we could not break through the lines of the Shades. I watched, helpless, as two of them dragged him from a side room. They cut him open there in the hall, and let his guts splash upon the marble floor. There was no reason for it. He had no weapon. It was slaughter for the sake of slaughter."

They were all silent for a moment after that. Loren saw Gem looking up at Uzo, his jaw hanging slack. The boy's eyes shone wet, and not from the light drizzle that fell from the sky.

One of Jormund's massive hands tightened into a fist. "I was stationed on the north wall, but I went running to the eastern docks as soon as the horns sounded. I saw the Dulmun fleet land, and the gate had already been drawn up against them. Some of the folk from the city had been trapped outside, but rather than flee north or south, they only pounded on the gate. We tried to get it open and let them in, but before we could, the Dulmun soldiers set upon them, piercing them with spears so that their bodies were pinned to the wall."

"We all saw dark things that day," said Weath quietly. "We all have reason to hate the Shades."

Loren thought of the part she had played in the battle of the palace, and found herself nodding in agreement. But then she thought of Xain—and that, in turn, made her think of Jordel.

"Vengeance," she said—but her voice broke. She cleared her throat and tried again, quietly. "Vengeance is a poor reason to ride into battle. Let us not make war for hatred. We should seek justice instead. A wise man—and a Mystic—taught me that."

Weath and Jormund bowed their heads. Loren knew that they had been Kal's soldiers for some time, and had known Jordel, at least in passing. But Niya gave Loren a wry look.

"Why should it matter if justice or vengeance swings the sword? A head will roll free regardless. I have fought before, and I have learned this: give yourself whatever reason you need to fight. But when you go to battle, fight to win. Then you may dream up whatever reason you wish. You cannot do that if you are dead."

Loren's ears burned. "I only mean that having a clear mind and a clear purpose may—"

Niya shook her head. "I know what you meant."

Somehow the reassurance left Loren feeling even more embarrassed. She knew that she had been naive when she left the Birchwood, and had thought that everyone she met could be held to her own rules of right and wrong. But that had ended in disaster more than once, and no more so than when Jordel had fallen in the Greatrocks. She could keep her own vow, yes, and never take a life—but she knew that if she led these Mystics upon their mission, and did not look upon the world with both eyes open, it would lead only to tragedy and death.

The Nightblade must have honor, she told herself. *But the Nightblade must also be wise—for who would call me honorable if I let others die?*

Her gaze drifted, and she looked down from the wall into the courtyard. The door to the stronghold opened, and a Mystic stepped out. The daylight was almost gone, but she recognized him from the scar that split his chin: Hewal. Her brows drew together.

"What?" whispered Chet, catching the look on her face. "What is wrong?"

Loren did not answer him, but turned to the rest of

them. "I am weary from the road and desire rest," she said. "I bid all of you a good night."

"I will show you to your quarters," said Annis brightly. "Follow me."

She led them down into the courtyard. The Mystics stayed atop the wall, with Niya giving Loren a final nod, along with a secretive smile that made Loren's heart flutter. As Annis scampered down the steps, Loren lagged behind to speak with Chet.

"You remember my dream upon the Seat," she said.

"I do," said Chet, frowning.

"I saw a man in my dream—a man dressed in the clothes of a Shade. And then, when we arrived at Ammon today, I saw him again. He was in Kal's guard. He had a scar on his chin."

Chet's eyes widened. "I remember the one. You are certain? He was in your dream?"

"I am. It was not a likeness—it was the same man."

"What . . ." Chet stopped and looked about, as though he expected to find eavesdroppers. "What do you suppose it means?"

"I do not know," said Loren. "You do not think I am going mad?"

"Why should I think that?" said Chet, shrugging. "I often dream of those I have met in the waking world, and sometimes I see people in my dreams who do not exist at all. But never have I seen someone in my sleep, only for them to appear in true life. And besides, you have spoken with Elves."

The memory made Loren shudder. "That was my thought as well. They are fey, and I never had such dreams before I met them. But even if this is some work of theirs, what does it mean? What should we do?"

"Who can we trust here?" said Chet. "Annis and Gem, of course, though I do not know if they will be of much help. What about Kal? Could you not tell him what you saw?"

"I do not think he would place much stock in a dream," said Loren. Her thoughts drifted to Niya, and she remembered how the woman often looked at her. "We might tell the Mystics who came with us."

"No," said Chet at once. "We barely know that Niya woman, for we scarcely met her a week ago. And though we have known some of the others a while longer, still we have not spent much time with them. I would hardly call them friends."

"Yet they are capable warriors, and Niya seems wise besides," said Loren. "She is a captain, as Jordel was. We need someone who knows something of the Mystics."

"If you must speak to one of them, speak to Weath, or Shiun or Jormund or Uzo," said Chet. "But not Niya."

Loren gave him a look, and she thought she heard what he was unwilling to say. Almost she took him to task for it, but now hardly seemed the time. "Very well," she said. "Let us mention it first to Annis—only I do not think it would be wise to tell her everything at once."

Chet gave a sigh of relief. "I agree."

They increased their pace to catch up with the children again. Soon they reached their quarters, and Annis stopped them before a wooden door. "I am just across the hall, in a room where some Mystics stay as well," she said. "Gem is in the next room over. Loren and Chet, your room is your own."

"Thank you, Annis," said Loren. She glanced up and down the hallway. No one else was in sight. "Would you mind stepping within for a moment? Both of you? There was one more matter I wished to discuss."

Annis and Gem frowned at each other, but they followed Loren into her room. It was a meager place, with only a bed, a single chest, and a bureau against the wall. There were neither chairs nor rugs nor drapes, as they had had upon the Seat, nor even a window, and only a small hole near the ceiling so that burning a lantern did not make the room too stuffy. Loren closed the door behind the children and stood before them, fidgeting with her hands.

"What is it, Loren?" said Annis. "Clearly something troubles you greatly."

"I must ask you to trust me," Loren blurted out. "But I cannot . . . I cannot tell you exactly why."

The girl's nostrils flared. "Is this about Hewal? *What* is the matter with you—or with him? Spit it out." She put her hands to her hips, and for a moment looked just like her mother as she scowled.

"Yes, it is Hewal," said Loren. "Is there anything—anything at all—that you know about him? The smallest detail might help."

Annis threw up her hands. "I have told you I know almost nothing. I believe he is a messenger, but I am not even certain of that."

Loren and Chet shared a look. A messenger? Who better to act as a spy for the enemy?

Gem was frowning at the both of them now. "What under the sky has you so worried?" he said. "I have not seen you this anxious since . . . well, since just before the attack upon the Seat."

"There is nothing for it," she said quietly to Chet.

"I know," he said.

Loren took a deep breath and spoke in a whisper. "I think he may be a Shade."

The room went very still. Annis and Gem both froze, as though they were afraid a movement might reveal them to some unseen enemy. At last Annis licked her lips.

"Why?" she said.

"I cannot explain that," said Loren. "But for my peace of mind if nothing else, we must look into it."

"How?" said Gem. "I do not think I could walk up to him in the dining hall and ask, 'Say, do you have another change of clothes that are blue and grey? Have you lost a friend named Trisken recently?' What do you mean to do?"

"I do not know exactly," said Loren. "But we can

start with his personal effects. The chances are small that we will find anything to prove what I suspect, but we have to try."

Annis shivered. "Very well. We can do it tomorrow. I will find out where his quarters are."

"Thank you," said Loren. "Now go to bed, both of you, and ready yourselves. Let us all hope that I am wrong."

TWELVE

ANNIS WORKED WITH REMARKABLE SPEED. WELL BE-fore the next midday meal, she approached Loren and Chet with Gem in tow. After bidding them to follow, she led them unerringly through Ammon's halls to the part of the keep where Kal's household guard slept. When she pointed out the door to Hewal's room, Loren led them all off down the hallway and around the first corner.

"Wait here," she told Chet. "Annis, you go down to the other end of the hall. If someone approaches, cough as loudly as you can, louder than someone struck with plague. We will slip out of the room as quickly as we can.”

Gem puffed out his chest. “Mayhap I should stand guard. I may have the loudest cough in all the nine kingdoms.”

“Who could doubt it?” said Loren, letting no trace of a smile touch her lips. “But you can read, where Chet and I cannot.”

The boy blinked. “I had not thought of that. Very well.”

As Annis ran down the hall to the next corner, Loren and Gem slipped into the room. *His bed is the first on the left,* Annis had told them. They found it at once. A small cupboard stood near the head, and at the foot, the customary chest. The chest had no lock, and at first Loren was glad. But then she realized that Hewal would not keep anything incriminating in an unlocked chest, and her heart sank.

Still, they had come this far, and it would be foolish not to look while they could. Within the chest they found some folded letters. Loren handed them to Gem, for she could not read them, but they contained nothing nefarious. Other than that, it held only several changes of clothes and a second pair of boots. Loren turned the boots upside-down and shook them, but there was nothing hidden within. The cupboard at the other end of the bed was no better, holding only a few tunics. Loren probed them with her fingers to see if something was folded inside, but they were only harmless cloth.

They left the room as quickly as they had entered, and walked away with Chet and Annis in tow. Loren scowled as they walked, slamming a fist into her palm.

"Nothing," said Loren. "Not that there was any great hope. But I thought I might find some sign—a pendant with the Shades' mark, mayhap."

"I mean you no offense," said Gem, "but if this Hewal were careless enough to keep such a thing in his possession, I think he would have been discovered long before we arrived."

"If he is even a Shade in the first place," said Annis. "And since you will not tell us why you think he might be, I cannot offer any other ideas of how we might learn whether it is true."

"Mayhap it is nothing," said Loren. "This was likely a foolish idea in the first place. Forgive me for bringing you into it."

Chet stopped short, forcing the rest of them to do the same. "You did not summon us on some lark, Loren," he said quietly. "I think you should tell them. Then they may understand why this is so important—and why we should not stop our search here."

Loren looked about. The hall was empty, but still she felt out of place, as though there might be spies eavesdropping around either corner. "Very well. But not here."

Annis raised an eyebrow. "You said only yesterday that this was a stronghold filled with allies. Are you so fearful of being overheard?"

"I said that to the Mystics, who no doubt believe it themselves," said Loren. "I myself am not entirely convinced. Come. We are not far from our rooms, and can speak more privately in my chamber."

"*Our* chamber," muttered Chet, but he smiled as he said it to soften the words. Loren led them onwards, and soon they had enclosed themselves in the room. When Loren had checked twice that the door's latch was secure, she turned to the children. But looking upon their expectant faces, she suddenly balked, and turned to pace the room instead.

"Spit it out, Loren," said Annis. "Whatever you have to say, delay helps nothing and no one."

"I do not myself understand it," said Loren. "Therefore I am leery of trying to explain, for it is a mad tale."

Gem scoffed. "And we are all of us strangers to mad tales, after all the leagues we have ridden together."

That made Loren smile, and her worry eased slightly. "I see your point. Very well. I . . . . saw Hewal in a dream. While we were still on the Seat. You remember, Gem, how I awoke in terror one night." Gem nodded, frowning. "I saw many things in my dream, but among them, I saw your mother, Annis. And behind her stood Hewal—but he wore the blue and grey of a Shade, and not the red cloak of a Mystic."

"Wait, what do you mean you saw him?" said Annis. "That is, do you mean that you saw *him?*"

Gem blinked at her for a moment before he said

carefully, "I think she means to ask whether you saw some man who looked *like* Hewal?"

"No," said Loren. "It was no likeness. It was Hewal. He looked into my eyes, and he smiled. He had the same scar on his chin, the same hair, and . . . it was him."

"That is . . . odd indeed," said Annis. "I have never heard of anything like it. I would say it is some sort of spell, except that I have never heard of a wizard who could do such a thing."

Chet spoke quietly from where he was leaning on the wall. "Tell them why the dream matters."

"Yes. There is more," said Loren. "One night, when we traveled across Dorsea, I woke while the moons were still high. When I rose, I saw Chet had been charmed into slumber, and a party of Elves surrounded our camp."

The room went silent, and the lamp flickered, as though a chill breeze had blown through to freeze them all solid. Gem seized Annis' sleeve in fear, and Chet's hands balled to fists at his sides. But then the moment passed, and Loren let loose a quiet sigh of relief.

"Elves?" squeaked Gem. "They came upon us? How did you make them leave?"

"She did not," said Annis, her voice shaking. "You cannot *make* an Elf do anything, no more than you can send away a winter gale by scolding it. What did they want, Loren? What did they *do?*"

"They wanted nothing, and they did little," said

Loren, speaking carefully. She had no intention of telling Annis about the magestones that she held, even now, in a pocket of her cloak. Not even Chet knew that secret. "But one of them touched my skin, and when it did, I could . . . I could *see* everything, inside and out, and the threads that bound it all together. It almost drove me mad. Mayhap, for a moment, it did. But this dream . . . it came after I met the Elves. And in the dream, I felt the way I did when they stood before me."

Gem snapped his fingers and pointed at her. "When the Lord Prince met us upon the Seat, he said it. He said you were Elf-touched. That is why."

"Yes," said Loren.

"And he is right," said Annis quietly. "I did not see it so clearly before we parted, but I see it now—whether because I am searching for it, or because it has grown more pronounced in the weeks that have passed. But there is a light in your eyes that was not there before, Loren, and a . . . a sort of *sharpness* to you. Are you certain the Elves did nothing else?"

Nothing but the magestones, thought Loren. But she already knew from Xain that that had nothing to do with it, or with her dreams. "Nothing," she said. "It must have been their touch."

"But even if this is true—no, do not look me that way, you know what I meant," said Gem. "But how can we be certain of your dream's purpose? None can know the thoughts or intent of Elves. They may not have even meant to do . . . whatever it is that they did to you."

"Whether they meant to or not, Loren saw what she saw," said Chet. "I do not think that is something we can easily dismiss."

"I think you are right," said Annis. "This paints everything in a different light. Even if Hewal is not a Shade, such a vision cannot be cast aside without careful thought. Mayhap the dream was only a message, leading you down the right path to find them. Hewal could be the link that leads you to the Shades, without being one himself."

Loren had not thought of that. "It is possible. But how can we know?"

"By watching," said Chet. "It seems the only thing we know about him for certain is that he is a messenger for Kal. Thus, when next he delivers a message, we should watch him—even follow him, if we can."

"Will you know when he leaves, Annis?" said Loren.

"I can find out," said Annis. "And I will tell you at once."

"Very well," said Loren. "Let us hope I am not wrong about this, and that we do not waste our time on some useless flight of fancy."

THIRTEEN

Beginning the next day, Annis kept a careful watch on all messengers entering and leaving Ammon. But Hewal was not one of them, and days passed while they waited impatiently. The longer the waiting went on, the greater grew Loren's frustration. Before a week had passed, she had begun to fidget incessantly with her hands, and often caught herself picking at her fingernails with a knife, though they were already immaculately clean.

Chet tried to be patient with her, but after she snapped at him on the fourth day, he loosed his own irritation. "If this bothers you so, why do you not bring the matter before Kal? You are the Nightblade. Word of your suspicion should be enough for him to take at least some action—or, at the very least, he might tell you when he next plans to send Hewal out on some errand."

"And what, exactly, should I say? 'I saw your messenger, Hewal, whom you have known since he was a boy, in a dream, and he was dressed as a Shade.' Kal seems to place *such* great faith in me; he will likely clap Hewal in irons straightaway."

They did not speak the rest of that day. Loren managed to bring herself to apologize the next morning. But the situation only grew worse, and not least because Kal himself did not seem to need Loren for anything at all. When she tired of lurking around the stronghold, hoping to catch Hewal in some wrongdoing, she would often make for the chancellor's council chambers. But every time she entered after a timid knock, Kal would send her away, saying that he knew no more than the last time he had seen her, and that she must be patient. He kept Annis close, however, and so at meal times Loren would ply her for information—yet Annis knew precious little, for she and Kal still spoke only of logistics and supply lines, and these bored Loren almost to tears.

After a time she accepted her fate, and she began to spend most of her days on the stronghold's training grounds. There, wrapped in her black cloak against the persistent rain, she practiced her archery. Albern had not had enough time to teach her the finer points of Calentin archery, but she remembered his lessons clearly, and over and over again she went through the forms he had shown her. By now she had advanced to the point where she could draw an arrow and fire it in the space of a heartbeat, but her aim often suffered. If she wanted accuracy, she had to revert to the way she had learned to shoot growing up: placing the arrow on the left of the bow, and holding it steady with her forefinger.

Sometimes Chet came to join her. At first she tried to pass on what Albern had taught her, but he gave it up after only one afternoon. "I prefer shooting the way I have learned," he said. "My father taught me to shoot that way, and it was how I put game on the table for many years. Why should I need to learn another style?" Loren wondered if he would say the same thing if he had had more opportunity to see Albern shoot. The Calentin man had been able to empty a quiver in the time it took her to fire only two arrows; every shot found its mark, and could puncture chain mail besides.

Chet did not spend nearly so much time in train-ing as she did, however, for he spent most of his days within the stronghold. He and Weath had become fast friends on their journey north to Ammon, and now she had taken it upon herself to teach him to read. He told Loren that it came to him slowly, but that he was learning the way of it.

"That is well," said Loren. "I have little time for such learning, and so you can read my letters for me." He gave her a mock scowl.

Many of the Mystics in the fortress spent their days in the training yard as well—and Niya was among them. Though Loren often bundled up against the weather, Niya took no such measures, and she still wore her high-necked leather shirts with no sleeves. Loren lost count of the number of times she found herself standing and staring at the Mystic's thick and muscular arms. They bore no scars; either Niya wore armor when she went into battle, or she was a far better fighter than any opponent she had yet faced. The Mystic often caught Loren staring at her, and Loren would blush as she hurriedly returned to her archery.

Once, Niya approached her while she was shooting. Loren paused and looked at her expectantly, one arrow halfway to the string. But Niya only shook her head and waved her hand, prompting Loren to continue. Loren nocked and fired, drew, nocked and fired. But with Niya watching, she tried too hard to make the motions look smooth and fluid, and her aim was even worse than usual. One arrow missed the target entirely, and snapped in two against the stone wall behind.

"Who tried to teach you the Calentin style?" said Niya.

"You recognize it," said Loren. "I thought you were from Wavemount."

"I am, and yet I have fought beside soldiers from

all the nine kingdoms. And I have seen enough Calentin archers to know that whoever instructed you was a poor teacher—or, mayhap, they did not have as much time for your lessons as they should have."

Loren thought of Albern with a stab of heartbreak—and of guilt. "It was the latter," she said quietly. "My instructor was . . . well, he is lost now."

Niya let a silent moment pass. "He taught you the forms all right—but only from the waist up." She came over and, before Loren knew what was happening, Niya was right behind her, with one hand on her waist and the other on her left shoulder. "You lean the way you should, and you have your left shoulder lower than your right, the way you ought to. But your legs are the problem."

"What about my legs?" said Loren. It was suddenly hard to speak around the quickening of her breath.

If Niya noticed how flustered Loren had become, she did not remark upon it. She knelt and took Loren's right knee in her hands, pushing it gently so that it bent. "You learned the more ordinary type of shooting, and so you lock your knees when you fire. But your back leg should be coiled, like a serpent ready to strike, and you must use it when you loose." Her hands slid over, and then down Loren's left leg to her ankle. She pushed it forwards, almost causing Loren to lose her balance as it slid on the ground. "This should be extended forwards, so that your body can move over it when you shoot, like a hinge."

"I . . . I do not entirely understand," said Loren. One hand rose to draw her hood a bit farther around her face, to hide how red she had become.

With a chuckle, Niya rose to stand behind her once more. She put her left hand on Loren's waist, and her right on Loren's torso, just under the pit of her arm. "You use your whole body to fire, not just your arms. Act as a lever to propel the arrow forwards. Like this." She pushed her hands together, so that Loren leaned forwards. "That sort of motion, every time you shoot. It adds only a little more power to each arrow, but that little bit of power can be the difference between a killing shot and only a deep wound—and in the meanwhile, it adds a motion to your body that gives you better control over the arrow."

Loren could feel the woman's breath on her cheek. She had to force herself to speak. "You did not learn all of this only watching Calentin archers."

"I did not say I only watched them. Try it. Loose an arrow."

Her fingers fumbling, Loren drew as Albern had taught her, and loosed towards the target. But the motion of her legs was unfamiliar, and the arrow clattered off the cobblestones before skittering past the base of the target.

"Your training has gone amiss. That was my worst shot yet."

"My advice is sound, but you are too well practiced at doing it the wrong way," said Niya. "Keep at it, and mayhap one day you will shoot like a true Calentin."

She stepped back, and Loren loosed a long, low breath—but then Niya slapped her rump, and she jumped into the air, barely restraining a scream. Whirling, she readied herself to give Niya a tongue-lashing—but the Mystic was already striding away, and had soon vanished into a door leading into the stronghold.

Loren tried to still her racing pulse as she drew her cloak around her again. She surveyed the training yard to see if anyone else had been watching—and felt sick to her stomach as she saw Chet standing nearby. He was under an awning, one hand still on the door through which he had emerged, and for half a moment Loren hoped he had only just come out—but the look on his face told her that he had been there long enough, at least, to see the moment when Niya left. Loren forced a smile and waved to him, and slowly he made his way over to her.

"Who could have known that Mystic training was quite so involved?" said Loren lightly. She knew at once that it was a foolish thing to say, but she could not remain silent against the smoldering anger in his eyes. His expression was not unfamiliar to her; she had seen it often enough in the Birchwood, but then it had been directed at her father, every time he would lay his hands upon Loren.

Chet ignored her poor attempt at a joke. "I do not like that Mystic woman."

"You are being ridiculous."

His nostrils flared. "Do not do that. Do not dismiss what I say, as though it has no foundation—as though we both did not witness what just occurred."

Loren sighed. She stepped up to him, and placed a hand upon his cheek. "You should not worry over such trivial things. We have been sent here to Ammon for a purpose. Whatever game Niya plays at is nothing compared to that."

He glowered in the direction the woman had gone. "We were sent here for a purpose, yes. What was she sent here for?"

Now Loren was beginning to grow frustrated. "Are you angry at her, or at me?"

"I . . . why should I be angry with you?" He blinked twice, clearly flustered. "She is the one who behaves poorly."

"Then do not show anger when I am around and she is not. Let her act how she wishes. Why should we care? I am my own person. Do you not trust me?"

Chet looked at her for a long moment. She studied his chestnut eyes, never flinching. "Very well," he said at last, quietly. "You are right. Of course I trust you."

Loren smiled at him. But in the back of her mind, she could not quite quell her own doubts. She still felt a flutter in her chest when she thought of Niya's hand on her waist, and she could still smell the woman's breath on the edge of her cowl.

Without warning she snatched Chet's hand and

dragged him towards the door that led in to the stronghold. "Come with me."

He nearly stumbled as he trotted after her. "Where are we going?"

"To our bedchamber. I mean to prove myself still further."

FOURTEEN

Trisken stood upon the stone bridge, menacing in his armor. One massive fist clutched his spiked war-hammer near its head, and its butt rested upon the stones near his feet. The feathers of one of Albern's arrows protruded from his eye socket, but through the blood that streamed down his face, white teeth gleamed in a grin.

"You brought me the Yerrin girl, an abomination, and a Mystic to kill," he said. Sick laughter poured from his throat, dragging rotten fingernails of terror up Loren's back. "I could have asked for no finer gifts."

"I brought you nothing!" she screamed, for the storms had started, and she could hardly hear herself over the thunder. "We killed you!"

"How can you kill that which will not die?" he said, throwing his head back and cackling. "How can you kill that which serves death itself?"

Then she saw that he stood on a cairn. She remembered it well. They had built it over Jordel's body. She fell to her knees, weeping as she had when first they buried the Mystic—and then she fell back, shrieking in terror, as a hand covered with desiccated flesh burst from the mound of stones.

She landed hard on her rear end, wincing from the impact on the stone bridge—except that she was no longer on the stone bridge. Instead she lay upon a soft and silken bed, and fine cloth of many colors was draped upon the walls of the small room. Two torches were mounted in sconces, but to Loren they seemed far too large, and their flames licked at the drapes. Her sharp intake of breath brought the scents of fine perfume and wine, and she realized that she was in a house of lovers. Blushing furiously, she pushed herself up, intent on leaving. But she went stock still as the room's door opened.

The lover entered—a woman Loren had never seen before. She looked like an Idrisian, and her long black hair was worked into a single fine braid. Though she was clothed, the fabric was sheer enough to deepen Loren's blush considerably. The lover's gaze locked on

Loren, and she swayed as she made her way towards the bed. When she reached the foot of it, she did not stop, but crawled forwards on hands and knees.

"I . . . I did not mean to come here," said Loren. How *had* she come to be here, anyway? She could not remember. "I must go. Chet awaits me."

"Not for long," said the girl. "Stay with me. You have paid, after all."

"I assure you I have not," said Loren. She tried to leave, but her body would not respond—as though it knew she did not truly wish to go. Her eyes went to the torches on the walls. Their flames rose ever higher. How had they not already caught the silks in a blaze?

The lover was close now, too close for Loren to escape without pushing her away. Her lips pressed against Loren's ear. "Would you like to meet my parents?" she whispered.

The question was so unexpected that Loren was shocked out of the moment. "I . . . what?" she said. "Who are your parents?"

"He wonders," said the lover. All of a sudden she drew back and curled her knees up to her chest, wrapping her arms around them, like a child huddling against the cold. "He wonders, and I cannot tell him."

Loren nearly asked who the lover was talking about—but then she cried out, for the torches had caught the walls on fire at last. She leaped from the bed, trying to pull the lover with her. But the lover merely lay on the bed, curling further in on herself, and began to weep. And now the door was wreathed in flames. They could not get out. The smoke burned her eyes, forcing her to shut them as she coughed and coughed and fell back to the bed—

—only she did not land upon the bed, but in a foul-smelling flow of filth and refuse. She fought to get clear of it, and her hand struck stone. It was the edge of the channel, and she knew that she was in the sewers of Cabrus. Coughing and spluttering, she emerged from the stream, falling breathless upon her back.

Snik.

Cold steel pressed against her throat. Loren froze.

"Sweet, simpering little tart," hissed a familiar voice. It was Auntie. Crouching, she held Loren's own dagger to her throat. "Why did you come back here? You should never have returned."

"I did not mean to come here," said Loren, unable to stop the tears that poured from her eyes. "Please, forgive me. I will leave, I will never come back, I will—"

"It is the way you hold yourself," said Auntie, lifting the dagger. Loren thought she was free, but then Auntie's other hand seized her throat. "The hip juts out slightly."

With a shriek, she plunged the dagger into Loren's heart.

Loren screamed.

"That might be a stance of rest, but this hand you hold a bit farther from your body than the other."

She withdrew the dagger, but only to sink it into

Loren's heart again, and then pull it out, and then again, and again, and now Loren could not even scream, for only blood came bubbling up from her lungs.

"It is ready to leap to the hip and draw forth the knife, the knife, *the knife, the knife, the knife!*"

The world slowly went black, and Auntie's furious screams faded to nothing. Then, in the blackness, Loren heard the sound of rushing water. She opened her eyes—when had she closed them?—and saw that she stood in a city of gold. It was built around a waterfall, the source of the sound she had heard. The city was built in two levels—one at the bottom of the falls, and one at the top. The buildings all glistened and gleamed with gold trim, which shone all the more in the light mist that pervaded the air.

She was on a balcony not unlike the one she had had in the High King's palace, one that afforded her an excellent view of the city and the lands all around—a landscape similar to the one surrounding Ammon, with strange trees that hid dark pathways.

"Welcome to Dahab."

The voice made her jump. She turned to see Hewal standing beside her on the balcony. He did not look at her, but only leaned on the railing, looking out. Again he wore the blue and grey of the Shades. Without warning he sprang up on the railing, and then his mouth became a beak, his feet claws, and his hands wings. He had turned into a crow. With a raucous cry he took to the air, soaring higher and higher as he spiraled up into the mists coming off the waterfall. Her mind flashed a word: *Weremage.*

Loren watched the bird soar for a moment—and then she found that she was no longer upon the balcony. Now she stood on a huge pillar of stone in the midst of the river near the bottom of the waterfall. Its roar deafened her, and she could barely keep her footing upon the slippery rock.

Then she saw that Damaris stood there, just out of arm's reach. And behind Damaris was Gregor, and now the bodyguard was truly giant-size, with hands as large as Loren herself. He reached out for her, and though she wanted to flee, there was nowhere to go. His fingers wrapped around her, and she barely managed to squeeze out between them. But they wrapped around her again, and again, each time dragging her closer.

"I will take *everything,*" said Damaris.

Gregor seized her at last, and he lifted her to hold her suspended over the waterfall. Between his fingers she could only just glimpse his face, and his cheeks that were sliced open, and the bloody ruined mess of his mouth, the stab wounds all over his body that seeped blood through his clothing and chain mail.

His hands fell away from her, and she thought she would plunge into the river far below—but she landed on the pillar again. She looked up, wondering why he had released her, only to find that he now held Gem, Annis, and Chet, and that they now hung over the water in her stead. Loren rose to her knees before the giant and clasped her hands to beg.

"Please, let them go," she cried. "Let them go. You want to kill me—since the beginning, you have only wanted to kill me."

"I told her to kill you, yes." Gregor's voice was like thunder. It struck her like a fist to the chest. "She would not listen, and her love for you made a corpse of me."

"Everything," whispered Damaris in her ear.

Gregor released her friends, and they fell into the water. But at the last moment, Chet reached out and grabbed an outcrop of the pillar Loren stood on, and the children clung to his arms. He tried to lift them all, but the weight was too much. Screaming, Loren fell to her stomach and reached for him, trying to help him up. The children climbed over him and took her hands, and she got them to safety. At last she reached Chet, but she could not raise him—he was too heavy.

Chet looked into her eyes for a long moment. Then his arms slipped, and he fell into the abyss—for it was not the waterfall, but the stone bridge again, and his body fell to lie, broken, beside Jordel's forever. Even as Loren's screams redoubled, she felt hands seize her cloak. She looked up, expecting to see Gregor again. Instead, she found Gem and Annis. They had ruined mouths just like Gregor's, and they laughed as they pitched her over the edge of the bridge.

She came awake screaming again.

Chet was fighting to hold her down. This time she had just enough presence of mind not to strike him. But she could not still her panicked screams, and guards in red cloaks came bursting into the room, swords drawn.

"It is all right!" cried Chet. "She is all right. Just help me hold her!"

One of them came, taking Loren's arm and holding her in place as she slowly got her bearings. Her gaze roved all over the room, and she could not force it to stay any one place for long.

"Loren. Loren!" said Chet. He took her face in his hands and forced her to look at him. "Loren. It is me. You are here, with me, in Ammon. It is all right. There is no one there. Come back to me."

At last her hands stopped trying to find purchase on a bridge that was not there. A long, shuddering breath escaped her. "I . . . I am all right. I am all right."

"Yes, you are," he said, and pulled her close. She clutched him to her, staring over his shoulder into nothingness.

"Is she ill?" said the guard who had remained by the door. "Should I fetch an apothecary?"

"No," said Loren at once.

"Are you certain?" said Chet. "Mayhap some dreamwine . . ."

"No, Chet," she said, pushing back to look at him. "I am all right. It was only another dream."

A look of recognition crossed his face. He heard

what she had not said—that once again she had seen visions. He turned to the Mystics and shrugged. "As she says. Thank you."

The guards did not look eager to leave. But Loren seemed to have grown calm again, and so they stepped out of the room.

Chet turned to her and whispered, "Did you—"

"Shush," said Loren, putting a finger to his lips. She listened hard. Finally, after the space of several heartbeats, she heard the quiet footsteps of the Mystics slipping away. A sigh slipped from her. "They are gone."

She fell back upon her pillow. It was the eve of Yearsend, some days after Niya had given her instructions in the training yard, and they had learned nothing more in the meanwhile. Hewal still had not been sent from the fortress, and they had seen him do nothing nefarious within it. Why, then, had she had this dream now? Was it a sign of something soon to come?

"What was it?" said Chet. "Did you . . . did you *see* anything? Was Hewal there?"

"He was," said Loren. "And he was dressed as a Shade again. But this time there was more—he turned into a bird, and flew off into the sky."

"A . . . a bird?" said Chet. "Do you mean that he is a weremage?"

"I do not know that, any more than I know for certain that he is a Shade," said Loren. "But that is what I saw. And . . . and I saw a golden city built on a waterfall. It is not a place I have ever seen before, and yet . . . and yet it was so *real.* I think it must be a real place—just as I first saw Hewal in a dream, and then found him in the waking world."

Chet frowned. "But why were you screaming? None of this sounds very terrifying."

Almost she answered him. Almost she told him of Trisken, and Jordel's grave, and Auntie, and what had happened to him and Gem and Annis. But at the last moment, words failed her, and she shrugged. "I saw nothing else. Or at least, I remember nothing else. Whatever frightened me, it slipped away as I awoke."

He looked at her for a long moment. She could see in his eyes that he did not believe her. "Loren," he said at last. "I have told you that I trust you. Do you not trust me in turn?"

A pang of guilt struck her, and she pushed herself up on her elbows. "I . . . I do, of course, Chet. And yet there are things I do not wish to say. Not because I fear for you to know them—but because I fear to say them aloud, and give strength to the thought behind them."

"You cannot truly believe that."

Loren shrugged. "How can I know what to believe? I see things in my dreams only to find them in the waking world. And there . . . there are things I see that I could not bear if they ever to pass. Do not force me to say them out loud. I beg you not to."

He did not answer her. After a long moment's silence, he lay down again and turned his back to her, drawing the blanket tight around himself against the cold.

She waited until his breath had deepened with sleep. Then she went to her cloak and reached within one of the pockets for her brown cloth packet. From it she drew a magestone. For a long while she looked at it.

A wizard who consumes the stone does not dream, Xain had said.

She was not a wizard. Yet mayhap it would help.

Loren broke the stone in half and slid one piece onto her tongue. It dissolved into nothing, and she swallowed. The room did not grow brighter, for she did not have her dagger close to hand. But she felt a calm slip through her. She lay back down beside Chet, and was soon asleep—a dreamless sleep at last.

FIFTEEN

Four more days passed in cheerless rain. Loren told Gem and Annis of her dream—as much of it as she had discussed with Chet—but they had no more inkling of its meaning than she herself had. The four of them were more watchful after that, but Hewal was just as inactive as he had always been, and nothing of interest happened within Ammon's walls.

The last day of Yearsend arrived, and the stronghold held a feast to celebrate the new year. It had been more than two weeks since Loren arrived at Ammon, and her frustration had now dwindled to a pervasive apathy. She rarely went into the training yard anymore, and spent most of her time either in the stables visiting Midnight, or in her own chamber, from which she emerged only for meals. But the Yearsend feast drew her out of hiding at last, if only because Annis was very excited about it. Somehow, the girl had convinced Kal to let her arrange the whole thing, and it promised to be a merrier affair than Ammon had seen in years.

Just after dawn on the day of the feast, Loren rode with Chet to a nearby river to bathe, and she also laundered her clothes. When at last they went to the dining hall after midday, they were not disappointed. The smell of the food struck her from a good ways off, well before she walked in the door. Most of the tables had been moved to the edges of the room, except for a line of them down the center. Upon these were placed all manner of fine foods, from meats and vegetables to sweet treats baked with honey, and still other dishes made with spices that smelled wholly unfamiliar to Loren. They found not only the usual wine and ale waiting for them, but brandywines and meads and other, clear liquors that Loren had never seen before, but which smelled stronger than anything she had ever tasted.

There were minstrels as well, a small party of them clustered off to one side of the room. They did not wear the red of Mystics, and so Loren guessed they must have come from one of the towns that lay not far away from Ammon. They plucked and pounded and blew upon their instruments enthusiastically, if not particularly well, and Loren saw many of the Mystics around the room stamping their feet and pounding their fists or mugs upon the table in time with the music. But from his elevated table at the head of the hall, Kal often glared at the minstrels, and tore more savagely at his meal the longer they played.

After Loren had taken her plate down the row of tables and loaded it high with food, she found a place at a table with Chet and Annis and Gem. Gem looked to be nearly done with his first plate by the time she reached them, and he soon rose to go fill another. Annis ate more delicately, but she savored her bites, moaning gently at each morsel and dabbing at the corners of her mouth with the edge of her sleeve.

"Having planned the feast myself, I was able to instruct the kitchens in preparing all of the dishes just the way I like them," she said. "I have not enjoyed so many of my favorite treats since I left my family's home upon the Seat."

"However did you convince Kal to let you do this?" said Loren. "This is a fine celebration. One might almost call it joyous, and that is a word I would never have used to describe the grand chancellor. I am surprised he did not flay you when you presented your plans to him."

Annis giggled. "I offered my expertise in planning the feast, and Kal accepted easily enough. Then, when he saw the list of things I intended to procure, he al-

most boxed my ears. But then I showed him my figures, and how this feast would cost him just over half
of what he normally spent, for I did my duty and se-
cured the best prices for the wares I required. He fell
silent quickly enough after that, and left me to handle
the rest of it." She leaned over the table and dropped
her voice to a murmur. "Though I waited until *after*
that to hire the minstrels."

Chet laughed aloud, and Loren joined in. They began to eat, and she swiftly discovered that she and Annis shared similar tastes, as it was the best food she had
had in some time, and even compared favorably to the
meals she had been served in the High King's palace.

After some time, and more food, and more wine as
well, some Mystics pushed tables against walls to clear
a section of empty floor. Then the minstrels redoubled
their playing, and the drummers took the lead, and the
dancing began. Loren had never dreamed she would
see these warriors, who were always so grim in their
red cloaks, laughing and prancing upon the stone floor
like the villagers from her home in the Birchwood. The
comparison seemed especially apt when Chet got to
his feet and drew her up after him, pulling her into a
dance that she laughed all the way through.

"We have never danced together. Do you realize
that?" he said, as one song finished and they waited for
the chords of the next to begin.

She smiled at him—but then the smile dampened,
for his words brought her parents to mind. They, after

all, were the reason Chet had been forbidden to approach her at the village dances.

"I am sorry," he said quickly. "I only meant that I am happy to do so now."

"And so am I," she said. "I wish we had had years of this. We should not let that fate befall others."

She pointed back to their table, where Gem and Annis still sat. Annis had begun to fiddle with her fingers, and every so often she looked nervously over at Gem. The boy did not seem to notice her, for his gaze wandered the room, lingering on the table where their Mystic friends sat. Chet's gaze met Loren's, and he nodded as he took her meaning. As the next song began, they ran up to the table. Loren seized Gem's hands and drew him up, while Chet did the same to Annis.

"Come, master urchin," said Loren. "I know you are a scholar and an expert thief. Let us see if you are a dancer as well!"

It soon became apparent that he was. The minstrels struck up a tune as old as the mountains, to which Loren had learned the words of a song of the moons, Enalyn and Merida. But half a hundred voices in the hall broke out into nearly as many songs, for bards in all the nine kingdoms had written different poetry for the same notes. That made the dancers laugh, and Gem's feet danced lightly upon the stones in time with Loren's as they whirled around each other. Loren was almost as surprised at his practiced ease as she was at Annis' awkwardness, for the girl's feet fumbled as she did her turns with Chet. But then the middle of the song came, and Loren and Chet gave each other a look. They took the children's hands, and spun them off to each other, an effortless trade that reunited them at the same time it pitched Gem and Annis together.

Loren leaned in close. "That was well done."

"You had an equal hand in it," said Chet, and kissed her cheek. They kept on with the dance, sneaking glances at the children all the while. Gem danced as easily as he had with Loren, laughing and smiling at Annis, whose cheeks had gone darker as their hands clasped. Her steps were still staggered and halting, but Gem led her easily enough, making up for her stilted movements with his own liquid grace.

The song ended. Chet and Loren bowed to each other. Gem stepped back to do the same, but Annis was slow to release his hands, and he laughed as he pried his fingers free and bowed. Then he ran over to the table where the Mystics sat, extending his hand towards them. Shiun waved him off. Weath, too, shook her head, and he went to Uzo. The dark young man gave Gem's outstretched hands a bemused look, his eyebrows rising slowly. Then he shrugged and got to his feet, following Gem away from the table as the next song began. But Annis still stood in the middle of the floor, looking after the boy.

"May I?" came a voice. Loren turned to find that it was Niya, who had risen and approached them. She held one bare, muscular arm forth, hand extended in an invitation. Loren's cheeks burned, and she saw Chet glare.

"I have tired myself out, I am afraid," said Loren. "Mayhap Chet would accept your offer."

"Mayhap I would not," said Chet, crossing his arms.

"That is just as well," said Niya, shrugging. "I do not think his spindly frame could withstand me. Another time, then."

Chet's scowl deepened, and he took a half-step forwards. But Niya turned and left them, striding straight past her table and out of the room. Loren returned with Chet to their own table, for indeed she had grown weary with dancing, and drank deep of the cup of wine she had left there.

When they had rested, they danced again, and then they drank again, and after they had done that a few times more, they fetched themselves more food to eat. The feasting had begun soon after midday, and would continue until everyone in the hall had gone to bed or fallen senseless beneath their tables. At some point Loren lost track of Annis, and then of Gem, and then Annis reappeared, and then she stopped looking after either one of them at all. She had just taken it into her head that she might retire to her chamber with Chet—mayhap for the night, or mayhap just for half an hour—when a hand clutched at her sleeve.

She turned to find Gem standing before her, wide-eyed and breathless. At once she sensed that something was wrong.

"What is it?"

"I went to relieve myself," he said. "When I was walking back through the courtyard, I saw someone standing there. At first I paid them no mind—until I saw that it was Hewal. He looked to be readying a horse for travel."

Loren and Chet looked to each other. Travel? On the final day of Yearsend? "Kal could have sent him on some errand," said Chet, but even he did not sound as if he believed the words.

"Any message could surely wait until tomorrow." Loren looked to the head of the room. There sat Kal. Wine had not appeared to improve his mood, for he scowled ever more heavily at the minstrels and the dancing. She could go and ask him . . . but he looked to be in no mood for questions. And if something *was* wrong, the delay meant Hewal would likely vanish before she could follow. "We must go after him."

"We should be quick," said Gem. "He will leave at any moment."

Together they flew from the dining hall. Loren was thankful she had worn her cloak to the feast, but Chet and Gem had no such protection, and they huddled into themselves against the sudden, biting cold. At least there was no rain. The day had waned on, and the sun was only a finger's breadth above the horizon, but night's chill had come early.

At once they saw him there in the courtyard: Hewal, fiddling with the straps of his saddlebags. He paid no mind to them, nor to the few others who milled about the courtyard or the walls. And why should he take notice? It was well known that he was a messenger for Kal. Anyone would assume that he was on the grand chancellor's business.

"Go and fetch cloaks for travel," said Loren. "I will ready horses for us."

Chet nodded and turned to obey—but the door opened behind them, and he stopped short. Framed in the light of the doorway was Niya, and beside her stood Weath. Weath merely looked confused, but Niya's eyes were narrowed, and her brows drawn together.

"What is it?" she said. "What is wrong?"

Loren hesitated only a moment before replying, "It is nothing. I only wanted a moment of fresh air."

"That is a lie," said Niya flatly. "I saw the three of you when you ran out of the dining hall. Something is the matter."

Loren looked uneasily at her friends. Chet was glowering at Niya, while Gem balanced on the balls of his feet, hesitant to leave now that the Mystics had arrived. But what should she say? She had known Weath for some time, and had traveled a ways with Niya—but how would they react if she told them she meant to chase down one of their own?

"Out with it," said Niya. "I shall not leave it be, and so you had better tell me now, lest I keep you from whatever mischief you are about to get up to."

"A messenger is about to leave the stronghold," Loren began.

"Loren," said Chet, a warning tone in his voice.

She pressed on, ignoring him. "We believe he may be up to something. I cannot explain why, and I may be wrong, but we mean to follow him and find out for certain."

A long moment of silence stretched. Weath looked to Niya, but Niya did not take her gaze from Loren. At last she nodded.

"Weath, fetch Shiun. We may need her to track him."

"I . . . what do you mean?" said Loren.

"We are coming with you, of course," said Niya. "Or have you forgotten that the Lord Prince himself assigned us to your service?"

Loren had pointed out before that the Lord Prince only bound the Mystics to bring her to Ammon, but she did not repeat the point now. They had wasted too much time already. Glancing over her shoulder, she saw that Hewal had already left the upper courtyard. "Very well," she said. "Get ready to ride as quickly as you may—and Chet, fetch those cloaks *now*."

He frowned for a moment, looking distrustfully at Niya, but then ran to do as she said. Loren looked at the Mystics and tossed her head towards the stairs.

"Let us get on with it, then, and hope that we are not already too late."

SIXTEEN

Loren led Gem and Niya to the stables at a dead run, going straight to Midnight's stall. As she began to ready the blanket and saddle, the mare nickered and tossed her mane, sensing the excitement on the air.

"After so many days of idleness, I am relieved we have something to do at last," said Niya from across the stable.

Loren could not help smiling at her, though she quickly masked it as she noticed Gem eyeing her. "I must admit I feel the same."

They had almost readied the horses to ride by the

time Chet returned, and with him came Weath and Shiun. He had already donned his own cloak, and he threw another into Gem's hands. The party brought their horses into the courtyard and mounted quickly, with Loren dragging Gem up to sit behind her in the saddle. They rode out of the gate and through Ammon's two levels to the final gate that opened upon the ramp. There they stopped, and Niya hailed one of the gate guards.

"The messenger who just left through here," she said. "Which way did he ride?"

"South," said the guard.

They did not pause to answer, but rode out at once. Loren spurred Midnight to the head of the group, but Niya slapped the reins of her horse until the two were neck and neck. At the crossroads they pulled to a stop again, looking down the south road. But they saw no sign of Hewal upon it, nor of any rider.

"Shiun, take the lead," said Niya. "If he diverts from the road, you will see it better than any of us."

"Chet should ride beside her," said Loren. "He is a hunter."

Niya raised her brows. "Of rabbits, mayhap. I doubt he has often stalked men on horseback." Loren frowned, and Niya sighed. "Very well. Shiun and Chet, ride in front."

The Mystic said nothing, but only nodded and nudged her horse. Now they made their way more slowly, for Shiun could not keep a good lookout at a gallop. The reduced pace grated on Loren's nerves, but she knew from her own limited experience at hunting that they could not press on any faster, lest they lose the way.

After a time, Shiun stopped her horse and pointed off the road. "There. Fresh tracks leading that way."

Loren gave Chet a glance. He rolled his eyes and shrugged at her, and she smirked.

Niya nudged her horse forwards beside Shiun's. "Can you follow him more quickly now?"

Shiun nodded. "Yes. He has cut through the land heedlessly. He does not think anyone is following him."

"That is his folly. Lead on."

They rode on at a light canter, with Shiun giving her horse only the slightest nudge to keep on track, until they reached the edge of a forest. The last sliver of sun just barely showed above the horizon, and the way ahead was dark beneath the trees. Shiun looked to Niya and raised her brows.

"The trail will soon be hard to see, at least until the moons rise," she said. "But if he continues to ride straight, I think we might follow him easily enough. From here, though, we should go on foot, or we might alert him to our presence sooner than we would wish."

Niya frowned. Then she looked to Loren. "Night-blade? Should we press on?"

Loren blinked. Niya had seemed forceful enough so far. Why now did she wish for Loren to give the orders? "I . . . we should. If my suspicions are correct, we cannot be too stringent in our pursuit."

With a nod, Niya turned to Shiun again. "As she says."

They dismounted, and Shiun led them between the trunks. Very soon, sunlight vanished from the sky that was just visible through the branches above, and they had to make their way more slowly, with Shiun leading them straight down the same direction they had already been traveling. Eventually the moons appeared, and then they were able to increase their pace once again.

"How does he know where he is going?" said Gem.

Loren glanced back at him. "We are following his tracks."

"I did not ask how we are following him," said the boy. "I know we can see his tracks—or at least, that woman can, because I feel blind as a bat in this forest. What I mean is—how does *he* know where he is going? There is no path here to follow. How does he pick his way so unerringly?"

Chet shrugged. "Paths are not always necessary. If one comes to a place often enough, the feet begin to remember the way, better than a sailor steering by the stars."

Weath raised her head to look at the rest of them. "Then he comes this way often. This is not his first time—nor, likely, his second or third, but one of many."

That cast a solemn silence over them all. What purpose could Kal's messenger have for coming so often to the middle of this wood?

Soon Shiun bid them all to halt with an upraised hand. Drawing Loren and Niya to her side, she pointed ahead through the trees.

"What is it?" whispered Niya. "I see nothing."

"I see it," said Loren. There, a few hundred paces ahead, was a horse tied to a tree. She could not be certain it was Hewal's from such a distance, but it was black, as his had been. "It seems his horse is there. But where is Hewal?"

"Close, no doubt," said Shiun. "We should leave our own horses nearby. Hidden. Then the three of us—or, better, only two—should go on alone."

"Three," said Niya. "He would not come out here to be on his own. He is meeting someone. If it comes to a fight, I would rather outnumber them."

Shiun nodded. Loren handed Midnight's reins to Chet. But when she turned to go, he caught her hand. "Be careful," he whispered.

"I shall," she told him. "And besides, Shiun and Niya will be with me."

Chet eyed Niya. "Forgive me if I am not greatly comforted."

Loren smiled and touched his cheek. "Take the horses and the others and get out of sight, in case Hewal should circle around and return for his steed before we can come to warn you."

She turned to follow Shiun. The Mystic led the way through the woods, bow out and an arrow half-drawn. Niya had not had time to fetch her sword, but she had a knife. Loren had only her hands—and the dagger hidden on the back of her belt, though she would not draw that unless it was a matter of life and death. They moved as silently as they could. Loren knew how to muffle her steps, and Shiun was quiet as a mouse. Niya did her best, but the woman was clearly not well practiced in woodcraft, and Loren winced at her every footfall. A light drizzle began to come down upon them. Loren put up the hood of her cloak and brushed the hair from her eyes.

Shiun stopped and held out a hand for them to do the same. She pointed ahead to where two figures huddled together against the rain. The one in the red cloak was clearly Hewal. The other, a Feldemar woman, was unfamiliar—and Loren was a little disappointed, though mayhap not surprised, to see that she did not wear blue and grey.

"Do you recognize her?" said Loren.

"I do not," said Niya. "But that means little. This whole kingdom is strange to me."

"Hist," said Shiun, and drew them back into the shadows of the forest—for Hewal had turned away from the other figure and begun to walk back towards them. After he passed them by, Loren leaned forwards and peered towards the other figure. In her hand she held a piece of paper—a message from Hewal.

"There," she whispered, pointing.

"I see it," murmured Niya. "Wait a moment longer for him to get out of earshot. Then let us take her."

"The two of you go," said Shiun. She raised her bow. "I shall watch from here, and prevent her from escape if she should slip from your grasp."

Niya rolled her shoulders, casting her red cloak off her bare, muscular arms. "That is unlikely."

Loren struck out to the left, circling around through the woods as she approached the figure. The woman, whoever she was, made her way through the trees in the opposite direction from where Hewal had gone. She moved slowly, clearly not expecting any threat in the darkness. Loren shadowed her steps several paces to the left, while Niya drew closer and closer from the rear.

When Niya was almost close enough to charge, Loren made her move. She ran forwards a few quick paces, letting her feet fall heavy and loud, and then slapped her hand on a tree trunk for good measure.

The woman came to a stop at once and froze, her eyes searching the darkness. Niya pounced from the shadows and bore the woman to the ground. She fought like a wildcat, but Niya wrestled her facedown into the loam, holding one arm twisted behind her back and jerking it upwards until the woman grunted with pain.

"Give us the message," hissed Niya through gritted teeth.

"I have no message," said the woman.

Shiun appeared from the darkness nearby, her arrow trained on the woman. Loren pulled her cloak aside and dug through its pockets. In a moment she heard the crinkling of parchment, and soon she had the letter. She pulled it out, broke the seal, and unfolded it, leaning far over so that her body shielded it from the drizzle. The words meant nothing to her, but she did not need to see them. There, at the bottom of the page, was a symbol she knew well—a twisted, spiked design, like a vine that wound in and around itself, but covered with thorns. The symbol of the Shades. She sucked a sharp breath in between her teeth.

Niya looked up. "What? What does it say?"

"Enough," said Loren. "We may return to Ammon now. Bring this one with us."

But the woman on the ground gave a great heave, and Niya lost her balance for just a moment. The woman's hand darted to her belt and drew forth a dagger. Loren cried out a warning, diving at Niya and bearing her backwards to take her out of the dagger's reach—but the woman plunged the dagger into her own heart. She collapsed, hunching over the blade, and her lifeblood splashed upon the dark mud to turn it darker still.

SEVENTEEN

"Darkness take her!" snarled Niya.

She flipped the woman over, mayhap hoping to keep her alive. But it was far too late for that. Loren seized her shoulder and drew her back. "I am sure the darkness below will indeed take her, but we have more pressing business. Hewal has gotten too far already—mayhap he will return to Ammon where we can find him, but mayhap he will not. We must catch him at once."

"Very well," said Niya. She gave the woman's corpse a final glare before turning to go. "Let us chase him down. I will take my anger out upon his hide."

As quickly as they could, they ran back the way they had come. When they reached the place where Hewal's horse had been, they found it already gone. Chet and the others emerged from the jungle, the horses in tow. Gem's eyes were wide, while Chet's brows had drawn together in concern.

"What happened?" said Chet. "Hewal came back this way, mounted, and rode off. We were just about to go and find you, for we feared something had gone wrong."

"Not for us, but for someone he met with," said Loren. "We must catch him, and quickly. Gain your saddles and ride!"

They did, spurring to a fast trot, for they could not safely go any faster between the trees. As soon as they emerged from the forest into open ground, Shiun stopped them. They all scanned the horizon, but could see nothing in the moonslight.

"Blast it," said Niya. "He could have ridden south, or he could have gone north, back to Ammon."

"We could divide ourselves," said Weath. "Let me take the boys back towards Ammon, while the rest of you ride south. If you find him that way, you will need more strength than we, if we should find him returned to Ammon and in the midst of our brothers."

"How can he have gone so far in so short a time?" said Niya, as though Weath had not spoken.

"We search by moonslight," said Shiun, shaking

her head. "No doubt I could see him if the sun were still up."

Loren thought quickly. In her cloak she had her magestones, and upon her back she had her dagger . . .

She jerked in her saddle, looking back towards the forest. "A moment. I dropped the letter."

Without waiting for an answer, she turned and galloped Midnight back into the trees. Gem clung to her back at the sudden movement. Once he had righted himself, he leaned forwards to peer at her.

"Why did you lie to them? I can hear the crinkle of the letter in your cloak pocket."

"Because there is something else in my cloak pocket, and I would rather they not see it," said Loren. "Gem, you have proclaimed many times that you are my man, and loyal to me. You must prove it now—for you can never tell anyone what you are about to see. Promise me, and quickly."

"I—I promise," he said, though he looked even more confused.

She steeled herself, and then reached into her cloak to draw forth the brown cloth packet. From it she drew a shard of magestone—a remnant of a piece she had already broken in half—and quickly put it between her lips. It melted upon her tongue, utterly tasteless, and slid down her throat with ease.

Gem's eyes shot wide. "I . . . Loren—"

"Shush," she said. "You promised."

Her boots dug into Midnight's ribs, and they came

riding back to the others. Niya looked at her with a scowl.

"That has wasted even more time," growled the Mystic. "I have decided that Weath's plan is best, and that we should—"

Loren let Niya's voice fade to the back of her mind. She reached within her cloak, placing a hand upon the hilt of the dagger on the back of her belt.

The night grew bright as day, for in her sight the moons glowed like suns. She saw all the landscape around them in brilliant, vivid color. Even the darkness between the trees was illuminated, as though each leaf was a small lantern casting a silver glow upon the ground. She scanned the horizon in all directions, and her eyes caught upon a movement. There he was—Hewal, riding upon the road, making his way south and away from Ammon. He rode at an easy pace, a light trot his horse could maintain for leagues at a time.

"There!" she cried, shooting up straight in her saddle and pointing. "I see him!"

Niya stopped talking abruptly and frowned. She looked in the direction of Loren's outthrust finger. "What? I see nothing."

Neither did Loren, for she had loosed the grip on her dagger. But she feigned surprise. "What? He is just there. A good distance away, and small, but it is him. I am sure of it. Come!"

She set off without waiting for an answer, sending Midnight into a headlong gallop upon the road. The others had little choice but to follow her, and so they did, and soon the lot of them were riding hard. Loren could almost sense the shock that went through the others when they, too, spotted Hewal at last.

When they had closed the distance to half a league, Hewal heard them and pulled his horse to a stop. In a few moments they had reached him, and they fanned out to create a semicircle facing him. Hewal did not seem particularly alarmed, but only bemused. After surveying the group, he focused upon Loren.

"Nightblade," he said, inclining his head. His voice sounded as it had in her dream: smooth and bright, fresh with youth but heavy with the weight of duty. "Has Kal sent you? Is there some news concerning my errand?"

"No one sent us," said Loren. "Though, I wonder what masters have sent you upon your ride this night, Hewal. I do not think it was Kal of the Mystics."

She reached into her cloak to draw out the letter, and held it up so that it fell unfolded in the moonslight. The symbol of the Shades was plain to see, even from the few paces that separated them.

Hewal stared at it for a moment as though he did not comprehend what she had said. Then, brow furrowed, he climbed down from his horse. He took a step forwards.

"Stay where you are," said Niya, drawing her knife and pointing it at him. Shiun drew an arrow and nocked it. Hewal stopped in his tracks. "You will return with us to Ammon, and if you make no trouble, you may even survive the journey."

Hewal raised his hands, and a small smile crossed his lips. "I do not think any friendly reception awaits me at Ammon. Therefore I do not think I shall come with you."

An image flashed into Loren's mind—Hewal in her dream, when his eyes had glowed white and he had transformed into a crow.

"Wait!" she cried. "He is a—"

She was too late. Hewal's eyes filled with light, and his body erupted into a mass of flesh, muscle and fur. A black bear stood where he had been a moment before, and around its feet pooled the shredded scraps that had been his clothing.

Hewal roared and lunged at them. A massive claw took Weath's horse in the side, and the beast screamed as it died. Weath fell from the saddle and rolled away from the road.

"Back away!" cried Loren, wheeling Midnight around and dancing a few paces off. "Shiun!"

The Mystic had already sprung into action, drawing and firing an arrow. The shaft pierced Hewal's side, and his bestial roar took on a note of pain. But he sprang towards her, and Shiun had to spur her horse away before she could fire another shaft.

Leaping from Midnight's saddle, Loren threw the reins into Gem's hands. He caught them on instinct and opened his mouth, but before he could speak, Loren cried, "Get to Ammon!" and slapped Midnight's flank hard. With her nostrils filled with the scent of bear, the horse brayed in fear and rode north for the fortress, with Gem desperately clinging to her back.

Loren thought of reaching for her dagger, but what good would it do her? Its short blade would not save her against a bear. It was proof against magic, yes, but did that mean it could stop a weremage's claws? She had never had a chance to test it. Now did not seem the best time to do so.

Shiun was dancing back and forth, giving Hewal no clear way to charge. Niya stood a few paces off, brandishing her knife, but it seemed as impotent as the dagger. Chet had dismounted and stood beside Loren. His face was grim.

Loren took his shoulders. "It is a bear. How do you hunt a bear?"

"Go into its cave with spears," said Chet.

"We do not have a cave, or spears," said Loren. "And we are not dealing with a savage beast. Hewal has a human's wit."

Chet shrugged helplessly. "What do you want me to say? I have never hunted a weremage before."

Loren gave a frustrated growl—but then the ground shook beneath their feet, and she heard Niya shout. She flung herself to the side, seizing Chet's cloak and dragging him after her. Hewal barreled past them in a flash of black fur, roaring his anger as his terrible claws passed through the air where they had just stood.

Niya and Shiun seized them and pulled them to their feet. Shiun had another arrow nocked, but she did not draw. Weath stumbled over to them, shaking her head dizzily.

"Shoot him!" said Niya, looking to Shiun.

"I am not a good enough shot to strike the eye, and nothing else will be a worthwhile strike," said Shiun. Loren saw that Hewal had turned back towards them, and was edging to the right, presenting only his front. "The skull is too thick, and the shoulders are useless."

"Not if we can drive a knife into them," said Weath. "But that is a dangerous job, to be sure."

"I will do it," said Niya. "Only I will need a distraction."

"If I had a spear . . ." Weath shook her head, and then reached to her belt and drew a knife. "I will do my best."

"And I," said Loren. "But I have no blade. Does anyone have a knife to spare?" She feared to reveal her dagger with all of them so close to her.

Niya knelt and took a blade from her boot. "Here."

Loren followed Weath, who approached the bear slowly at a half-crouch. Behind her, Loren heard Chet mutter, "No one offers *me* a knife."

There came a *snikt* from Shiun, and soon Chet crept up beside Loren and Weath with a blade in hand. The three of them moved slowly forwards while Shiun stepped to their right to flank Hewal.

Hewal let out a low growl. It rumbled from his

chest and thrummed in Loren's boots. She breathed deep to steady herself. "I doubt he will charge again," she muttered, hoping the weremage could not hear her. "He has seen we can evade him too easily. Likely he will stand his ground and swing at us. He does not need to press forwards into our midst, for he knows he can wait for us to step within reach."

"What should we do, then?" muttered Chet, speaking from the corner of his mouth. "We need to get his attention."

"Feint at him," said Weath. "I will do it."

"You have been hurt already," said Loren. "Let me."

She did not wait for an answer, but took two quick steps forwards. She slashed at the empty air, three paces from where Hewal stood. He lurched backwards and swiped at her, growling. But quickly he turned his focus to Shiun, for she had raised her bow and begun to draw. Loren took another half-step towards him—but he lunged suddenly, forcing her to dance back.

Just then, she saw movement over his shoulder. There was Niya, creeping forwards through the grass, little more than a shadow in a red cloak. She lifted one hand, her dagger held ready to bring down in a stab. Hewal paused. He raised his muzzle into the air, sniffing.

With a wordless cry, Loren lunged and slashed at him. He jerked away, just as an arrow from Shiun flew forth and lodged in his foreleg. Chet, Loren and Weath pressed forwards, brandishing their knives. Hewal bellowed and reared up on his hind legs, and then Niya struck. Leaping forwards, she wrapped one thick arm around Hewal's neck and plunged the knife into his shoulder. He cried out anew—but this time the sound was pure fear.

Loren's elation lasted only a moment, for whether by accident or intent, the weremage toppled backwards. Niya had to throw herself clear and roll away, taking the knife with her. Hewal rounded on her, swiping at the air, but Niya rolled again, distancing herself. No sooner had she risen to her knees than she flipped the knife into her fingertips and threw it. Hewal only just raised a paw in time, and instead of driving into his throat, the dagger buried itself up to the hilt in his foreleg. A low whine issued from the bear's throat, and white light came from its eyes once again.

Slowly Hewal shrank, his thick coat of fur sinking back into his body. In the shrinking of his frame, Niya's knife slid free. It fell to land in the dirt, coated in red. At last Hewal stood before them, naked and panting in the moonlight, blood pouring from his wounds.

For a moment, all was still. Then, though nothing had been said, Hewal began to laugh.

"Oh, you are a clever one indeed, Nightblade," he said. "I do not know how you learned the truth about me, but once again you have shown your worth as a foe."

His familiar tone made her pause. "What do you mean? I have never seen you before, and you know nothing of me."

"You are the Nightblade. Everyone knows of you,"

said Hewal, and now his smile turned cruel. "Rogan and his undying brutes. My brothers and sisters. And sweet Damaris of the family Yerrin. She, in particular, sends her regards. And she looks forward to her reunion with you—which, now that I am exposed, will certainly be soon in coming."

"What reunion?" said Loren. "Tell us what the family Yerrin is planning, and you may yet escape with your life."

"Do you think I believe that?" he snarled. "I have played at being a Mystic for years. I have seen how they treat those they put to the question. No, such a fate is not for me."

His eyes began to glow. Beside Loren, Niya straightened with a start, and then lunged. "He is healing himself!"

Hewal jumped straight up—and in the air, he grew a beak, and black feathers sprouted from his skin. The crow's wings flapped desperately as Shiun's hastily-loosed arrow pierced the air below him. He flew off through the sky, giving a raucous, braying caw.

The sight of the beak erupting from his face, indeed his whole transformation, made Loren weak. It threw her mind back to her dream, and she saw Chet's opened throat—but then she turned to see him standing beside her, alive and whole. Her mind could not reconcile the images from her dream and the sight before her eyes. Her knees gave out, and she sank to the ground.

"Loren!" cried Chet. He knelt beside her. "Are you all right?"

"I—it is nothing," she said, shaking off the vision. "A moment's dizziness, that is all."

He frowned at her. "Did he hurt you? I did not see him land a blow . . ."

She shook her head quickly. "He did not touch me. I am all right." With his help, she fought her way back to her feet. Niya, Weath, and Shiun all stood there, looking at her. "I am fine. Except that he has escaped, and we have nothing."

"We have enough," said Chet. "You have the letter. That is proof enough of his guilt."

"And what use is guilt?" snapped Niya. "He could lead us to those who commanded him, and now we have not the faintest clue where to find them. Who cares if we know the dog misbehaved? I wish to find the masters who told him to bark."

"Well, we have not done that," said Chet. "Scowl about it if you wish."

Niya opened her mouth to reply, but Loren cut her off. "You said he healed himself? What did you mean?"

The Mystic glared. "Weremages. They transform their own bodies, and therefore many are able to close their own wounds and stop themselves from bleeding to death."

"That is a useful talent," said Loren.

She had not meant it as a joke, but Niya gave a grim smile anyway. "Mayhap—but it is almost as painful as suffering the wound again. I take some small comfort that I caused him that much pain, at least."

Loren sighed. "I find little to give me comfort just now. Come, let us mount our horses. We have a long ride back to Ammon, and we do not bear good news."

EIGHTEEN

Two horses were gone, so Loren rode with Chet and Weath with Shiun. They made their way back to Ammon quickly enough, but Loren did not press them too hard. There seemed little need for haste, since it would not change what they would find at the end of their ride.

As they rode up the ramp to the front gate, Loren stole a glance at the Mystics beside her. She had not thought of it until just now, but if there were any consequences to face for their actions that night, the Mystics would likely suffer worse than she would. She was the

Nightblade, and it was not entirely clear whether Kal was her master or not. But these were Kal's soldiers, and they had ridden off in Loren's company without orders. Kal did not seem the sort to take such things lightly.

"It might be best if we do not mention your involvement tonight," said Loren. Niya looked over at her. "In coming with me, I mean. I can tell the grand chancellor that it was only Chet and I, and eschew any mention of you at all."

Weath pointed up ahead. "Though I appreciate your selflessness, I doubt that that would work."

Loren looked up. There, at the top of the ramp, the drawbridge had already been lowered. Standing just inside of Ammon's gate was a party of Mystics on horseback. At their head was Kal, and beside him was Gem, who still rode Midnight. Loren felt her stomach do a turn. They reached the top of the ramp and stopped.

"Nightblade," growled Kal.

"Grand Chancellor," said Loren.

"I had meant to ride out to your rescue, for I gathered that it was necessary. It seems that is no longer the case. I imagine you have some tidings for me."

"I do, though I fear they are ill news."

"What other kind is there these days? Very well. Come."

He turned and led her—not quickly, but at a walk even slower than if they were on foot—all the way back up through Ammon's three levels. In the space of a few heartbeats it became monotonous, and then tedious, leaving Loren's mind free to wonder about the tongue-lashing he no doubt had in store for her. As she considered it, she realized that that was likely the point—this plodding pace was meant to give her as much time as possible to contemplate her impending fate.

When they reached the stronghold's keep, Kal dismounted and handed his horse off to a stableboy. Loren quietly asked Gem to see to Midnight, and then followed Kal into the fortress. As they approached his council chamber, they found Annis waiting in the hallway. The girl paced back and forth, hands twisting together anxiously in front of her, as though she awaited news of some close relative lying upon their deathbed. When she saw Loren approaching, she came running up.

"Are you whole? Gem said—"

"I am safe," said Loren. "We all are. I must speak with the grand chancellor."

"Indeed you must," said Kal. "But the girl comes, too. The rest of you, however, may leave us—I have no wish to move the entire Yearsend feast into my own chamber."

Chet looked to Loren—and to Loren's surprise, so did Niya. She steeled herself. "The rest should be present as well. Our tale is . . . unusual, you might say, and I would rather that you did not hear only my account of it."

Kal glared, but he did not argue with her, and the

whole party followed Loren into the room. They all stepped back towards the room's edges, away from Kal and the council table—all except Niya, who stood just beside Loren, but a half-step back, the way a soldier stood by their commanding officer. But Loren pushed that comparison out of her mind at once, and began to tell her story. She left nothing out, save for the moment she had eaten magestones. Soon she came to the end of her tale.

The moment she finished speaking, Kal snorted. "A weremage? I told you I have known Hewal since he was a boy. I have known his father. He went through the trials. There was no trace of magic within him."

Loren looked at the others in the room. Weath and Shiun shifted on their feet, not meeting Kal's gaze. Only Chet and Niya looked straight ahead, unflinching.

"It is true, Grand Chancellor," said Chet. "We were all there."

Kal looked at Niya. She gave him a small nod. His scowl deepened.

"Hewal made mention of how long he had been a Mystic," said Loren. "He called it a charade, one he had been forced to play for a long time. Mayhap he was entered into your service for just this purpose— in which case, his father may not be so close a friend as—"

"Be silent!" said Kal, slapping his hand on the table. "If what you say is true, do you not think I can come to that guess on my own? The High King's favor has given you too high an opinion of your own wit—high enough that it spurs you to foolish courses of action, like pursuing one of my own men into the wilderness without orders."

Loren had to restrain a grim smile. Her tone had mayhap been too condescending, but in truth, it felt good to throw Kal off-balance after the way he always grumped at her. "You call that foolish? Had I gone to you, we might have missed Hewal altogether, and you would know nothing."

"I know little enough now," said Kal. "Had you done things properly, Hewal might not have escaped."

Loren's hand tightened where it held her belt. "I serve the High King," she said, quiet but firm. "I will do what I think is in her best interests."

Rather than answer, Kal turned to the rest of them. "You are all dismissed."

The Mystics began to move for the door, but Chet tried to speak up. "We have told you already why we—"

"You are here to corroborate Loren's tale," said Kal, his voice rising. "Now that that is done, you are as useful as a second nose. Get out! You are neither in the High King's service, nor mine. You are nothing more than the Nightblade's bedfellow guest."

Chet's whole body tensed. Loren saw the muscles working in his jaw. But she put a hand on his arm and turned him to face her. "It is all right," she murmured. "Go."

He did, but only after giving Kal a final dirty look.

Niya held the door until he was through, and then, as she closed it behind them all, she locked gazes with Loren for a moment. She gave a small nod and a smile, and then she was gone. But Loren noted quietly that, again, Annis had remained in the room, and Kal still paid her no mind.

Loren braced herself, certain that now Kal would loose the full strength of his wrath. He looked like a pot about to boil over, his anger frothing just below the lid. But rather than shout, he held out a hand. "You said there was a letter. Give it to me."

Tension bled from her, and Loren reached into her cloak with relief. After she handed it to him, Kal whipped the letter open and looked it over. Loren wished she had had someone read it to her before she returned to Ammon, but there had been no time. Kal frowned. "Darkness damn this place. Girl, fetch me that lamp."

At first Loren thought he meant her, but he waved his hand at Annis. She started, as though she was surprised to be called upon, and then hastened to obey. Kal sat down in his chair and held the letter close to the light, his eyes skittering back and forth across it. When they reached the bottom of the letter and the symbol of the Shades there, his frown deepened.

"This is, in part, a report," said Kal. "A report of your arrival here at the stronghold, and a brief account of your actions, few though they have been. It seems you have attracted someone's interest."

"You mean Damaris," said Loren. "It must be her."

Beside Kal, Annis' expression grew solemn, and she dropped her gaze to the table. But Kal raised his brows and leaned back in his chair. "That seems quite a guess."

"Hewal mentioned her. He said we would be re-united soon."

"If . . ." Kal paused, and his mouth twisted as though he had just bitten into a piece of spoiled meat. "If Hewal is indeed an agent of the enemy, he may have spoken only to throw you off the trail. We can put no stock in any of his words."

Her recent dream flashed back into her mind. The city where she had seen Hewal, and what he had told her there. *Welcome to Dahab.* She braced herself, and then she took the leap.

"There was something else Hewal mentioned before he escaped. A place called Dahab."

The room fell utterly quiet. Annis looked up, her eyes wide with wonder, and then she and Kal traded glances. Loren had feared she might get only blank looks from them, but this was somehow worse. Was Dahab indeed the city she had seen in her dream? And if so, *how* had she seen it?

What was happening to her?

"That is quite a detail," said Kal. "Why did you not tell us that when you first mentioned the tale?"

"It has been a long night," said Loren. "It slipped my mind."

"Is there anything else that 'slipped your mind?' Surprise is not healthy for the elderly, and tonight has turned the last of my beard grey."

Loren shook her head quickly. "That is all."

Kal studied her for a moment, and then he threw the letter down. He began to pull at his beard, while Annis leaned surreptitiously over the table, trying to see the letter.

"I think that Damaris is in Dahab," said Loren. "I think that this letter was for her. I wish to go there, and capture her."

A loud snort erupted from Kal as though by accident, so loud that for a moment he dissolved into a fit of coughing. "Do not be ridiculous. You propose a perilous mission, led by little more than a far guess. Damaris is of no interest to us now. Rogan is the greater threat. You do not even know anything of Dahab."

She had gone this far, and so there seemed little sense in restraining herself. The visions in her dream had proven correct. "A city of gold. It is built around a waterfall, is it not?"

Kal rolled his eyes. "Very well. You have heard of it. But the rest of what I said holds true."

"This is the best chance we have seen," said Loren. "Damaris is there. I can . . . I can *feel* it. After our confrontation in the Greatrocks, she went to ground, and there she has remained ever since. She *must* be in Dahab. And furthermore, it makes sense to pursue her.

She worked with Rogan, and with the Shades. When the attack on the Seat failed, Rogan and his soldiers would have needed somewhere to hide, and someone to help hide them. Who better than the family Yerrin, and Damaris in particular? Finding her could lead to him. It seems to me that this is but the first step in the mission you set before me."

"Pardon me if I do not trust in your *feelings,*" said Kal. "I have only ever trusted information from reliable sources, and I will not change that now."

Loren shook her head and leaned over the table. "Where do you get such information? From your spies. You have them across all the nine kingdoms, do you not? Let me be one of them. It is better than sitting here idle, as I have since I arrived. Enalyn did not raise me up so that I could languish away here."

But she had gone too far at last, for Kal shot to his feet and slammed both hands on the table. "Do not bandy the High King's name about here as though you are her kin, you upstart little sow. She appointed you the Nightblade so that you could follow *my* orders, and that is what you will do."

His fury almost made her quail, and for a moment she saw not Kal, but her father, and his meaty fists clenched by his sides. She shook away the image. Her father was not here. He was dead. And she would never flinch before an angry old man again.

"Before the High King brought me into her service, I always acted on my own. It is what I did during that time that made me valuable enough that she desired my assistance in the first place."

Kal roared so loud and with such force that a fleck of his spit splashed upon her cheek. "No, what you did during that time led to the death of Jordel!"

She froze. Kal had made no move towards her, had not made to hit her, as her father had. Yet she felt as though she had been struck in the gut, and a far harder blow than she ever suffered at home in the Birchwood. She felt a stinging at the back of her eyes, and she fought it away. Kal would not get the satisfaction of seeing her weep. But he seemed to know how deeply he had hurt her. Though he did not smile, she thought she saw a grim satisfaction in his eyes as he leaned back.

"Did you ever consider that mayhap Enalyn brought you into her service so that she—or *someone,* and I suppose the duty is now mine—could keep an eye upon you? Left to your own devices, you helped Xain escape the law, and then escape Jordel. By your side he fled halfway across Underrealm. Because of you, Jordel was banished from his order—*my* order, I should say. And then he died for it. You do not need to be left to run free. You need someone who knows what they are doing to instruct you—and darkness take you, you must heed those instructions. It is even in the name you have been given. You call yourself Nightblade. A blade is a tool. A knife in the hand, to be wielded—not some thrice-damned hero of legend."

Loren wanted to answer him. Nightblade was no one's tool. Mennet had never been a tool, he had been his own man. And had she not always desired to be Mennet? But words would not come—not because she could not think of them, but because they would not emerge past the tightness of her throat, and if she forced them to, they would come with tears. She would not allow that in his presence.

In the silence that had consumed the room, it was Annis who saved her by speaking up at last. "If she is a tool, then use her. That is a tool's purpose, is it not? To be used. Honed. I have walked beside Loren almost since the beginning of her travels. I know her as a girl far more capable than many give her credit for, when first they meet her. You sent her to the High King's Seat with little more than a message to deliver. In turn, she saved the Lord Prince, the High King, and all the nine kingdoms. She may surprise you again. But she will learn nothing, and serve no purpose, if she stays here in Ammon."

Kal glanced at her. "Nor will she learn anything if she gets herself gutted in some back alley in Dahab. You may have your uses, girl, but that does not mean I hold you in much higher regard than the upstart here."

"Yet you need a spy to investigate this information," said Annis. "And by sending Loren, you may solve two problems at once, for she will need a party of Mystics to accompany her."

She looked at him steadily as she said it, and when

he looked to her, they shared a long moment of silence. It seemed to Loren that something passed between them, something she could not understand. Finally Kal gave a frustrated growl and turned back to Loren.

"Very well," he said. "But there will be rules. Vow to obey them, and I will send you. Refuse, and you can stay locked in your bedchamber until you rot."

Loren lifted her chin. "What rules?"

"You will do nothing foolish," said Kal. "That means you will not take any action—real, meaningful action, I mean—without consulting me first, by letter. You will go to Dahab to see if Damaris is there. If she is, you will send word—and you will *only* send word. You will take no action against her in Dahab without my express approval and guidance."

The thought of finding Damaris there, and then not capturing her, grated on Loren's very soul. But if she did not agree, she would be forced to stay here.

"Very well," said Loren. "I vow I will obey you, to the letter."

Kal snorted. "'To the letter.' Very well. We are done here, and you may take your dramatics elsewhere. It is late. Girl, I shall not need you any longer." He waved Annis off and turned to his desk in the corner. Annis came to Loren, and they left the chamber together.

NINETEEN

No one waited in the nearby hallways. Once they were out of earshot of the guards, Loren drew Annis aside.

"I am sorry," she said. "I should not have asked to pursue Damaris without speaking with you first."

Annis shook her head slowly. She looked as though she were gazing at something behind Loren, but there was nothing there to see. "There was no time. And besides, I think you are right to do this. I think my mother is a worthier target of the King's justice than Rogan would be. I have had my reservations about pursuing him for some time. Even if we should catch him, and execute him, I do not know how much it will accomplish. Yes, there are rumors of his exploits, of course, but to most of the kings and nobles he is utterly unknown. But my mother . . . yes, if my mother was brought low, that would truly give pause to the mighty across the nine kingdoms. Of course, Kal may not wish to anger my family even further than they already—"

Loren put a hand on her shoulder, and Annis stopped abruptly. Her gaze focused on Loren, as though she were just waking up.

"I am sorry. Was I babbling?"

Loren smiled sadly and gripped her shoulder a bit tighter. "No one could blame you for being hesitant to pursue her. Damaris will be treated fairly, Annis—mayhap not mercifully, but fairly."

"Yes, I . . . yes," said Annis. Tears welled in her eyes. She stepped closer to Loren, who put an arm around her shoulders and held her tighter. Annis did not return the embrace, but she put her head on Loren's shoulder. "I know. And I know that I must sound like a monster, saying these things of my own kin. Yet this—is this not why I wished to escape with you in the first place? I have known since I was a child that Mother's ways were evil, and that she must be brought to justice. But that has only recently become a possibility. I suppose I have been trying to steel myself for it to happen. I fear I have done a poor job."

"You have done marvelously," said Loren, rubbing her arm. "I am with you, and will help see you safely through this."

"I know," whispered Annis. One shaky arm came up to wrap around Loren's waist. "Thank you."

Loren pushed her back a bit. "All of that having been said, I should warn you—this will likely be perilous. It may make sense for you to remain in Ammon while we pursue her. Kal will certainly want your counsel."

Annis shook her head at once. "No. I must be there to face her when she is brought down—the same way I was there in the mountains to confront her. I did not ask to be a Yerrin, but still I am one of them, and it is my duty to see their evil put to rest."

Despite herself, Loren chuckled. "And Kal says I am one for dramatics. But very well. If you can convince Kal, I would be happy to stand by your side. Thrice we have been separated, and each time I have missed you worse. I will never by my own choosing part ways with you again. I swear it by the sky."

"And I," said Annis. Then she put her hands on her hips. "But as for convincing Kal—why should I need to? I am not in his service."

Loren gave an uneasy look back in the direction of Kal's council chamber. "I wonder if he would agree."

It turned out that Kal did not agree. When Annis came

to him with her proposal to accompany Loren on her mission, he raged for almost an hour at her foolishness. From the way Annis described it to Loren afterwards, she bore it all patiently until it seemed clear that Kal was only ranting to hear himself shout. Then she stamped her foot, and when the noise shocked Kal to silence, she said, "I have never entered your service. I have never entered the High King's service. I am pledged to no one at all, in fact. And though I have taken your room and board, I think I have provided counsel enough to pay that back several times over. So unless you wish to tie me up and throw me in one of your dungeons, I will accompany Loren of my own free will."

Kal scowled and complained a bit more. But in the end, she spoke only the truth. And his anger may have been mostly for show, because he gifted her a horse from his stables for the journey.

The morning after they pursued Hewal from the stronghold, Gem came to find Loren. At first he only acted as though he was bored and looking for something to do, but he hovered around, and often she caught him studying her with worry in his eyes. Therefore she found an excuse to send Chet away, and when they were alone she fixed the boy with a look.

"What is it, Gem? You are hovering about me like a fly over rotting fruit."

"An insect, am I?" said Gem, sniffing. "I thought I had earned better than petty insults."

Loren rolled her eyes. "I am sure you will survive the slight to your honor. Tell me what troubles you."

"It is . . ." Gem glanced at the door to Loren's chamber nervously, and then leaned forwards to whisper. "It is the magestone I saw you eat."

Loren blanched. Of course. She should have known he would come to her. "I asked you not to speak of that," she said.

"Not to others, of course. But Loren . . . I have seen what they can do—"

"To wizards," she said quickly. "I do not have the gift of magic."

"And so I thought the stones would have no effect upon you at all," said Gem. "But it seems that that is not the case."

Loren sighed and cocked her head, thinking for a moment of how to explain it best, and also how to do so quickly, for Chet would soon return. "You know that Jordel and I often took counsel together, alone, yes?" she said.

"I remember," said Gem softly.

"And you know also that my dagger has been something of interest to me since before you and I met."

Gem snorted. "If by 'interest,' you mean you treasure it enough to nearly get yourself killed."

"Well, in our time together, Jordel taught me some of the secrets of the dagger. I cannot tell them all now. But then when I met the Elves, they showed me one more of the dagger's secrets. When I eat a magestone, and place my hand upon the hilt, I can see in the dark, as though it were day—mayhap even better."

The boy's eyes went wide, until she thought they might pop from his head. An eager grin stole across his face. "Really?" he whispered. "That is astounding. What a tool for a master thief!" But then his expression fell to doubt. "Yet if it means you must eat magestones . . ."

"I have eaten them ever since that night in Dorsea," said Loren. "Not very often—four times in all, and each time only half of a stone, broken and dissolved on my tongue. Have you seen me descend into madness? I am not a wizard, Gem. They do not do me any harm, the way they did to Xain."

Eagerness claimed him again. "But then this is wondrous!" he cried. "This is fantastic! What a thrilling addition to the tale of the Nightblade! A dagger that lets you—"

"No!" she said sharply, silencing him at once. "No one must ever know of my dagger. No one. Not even Kal and the Mystics, not even the ones who travel with us. That is another tale I cannot tell you now, but you must trust me in this—and you must never mention the dagger."

To her surprise, Gem narrowed his eyes and nodded conspiratorially. "Very well. Mayhap that is even better. If they do not know it is because of the blade, that is all the more impressive. A girl—a woman, I should say—who can see in the dark, and . . ." He paused, frowning. "What else did you say it could do?"

"Sky above," she muttered, shoving him by the shoulder towards the door. "That is enough for now. Off with you, and forget all that we have discussed here—except that you must not speak of the blade."

"Secrecy is my specialty, my lady," said Gem, giving her a bow at the door. He threw the latch, but paused just before he left, grinning at her. "And, it seems, it is yours as well—Nightblade, master of the shadows."

Loren reached for a boot to fling at him, but he ran off down the hall, cackling. He did not even close the door behind him.

TWENTY

To Loren's immense disappointment, it took them days more to ready for the journey. As she had done with Xain on the Seat, she spent her time studying maps and learning the routes to reach Dahab. She did her planning with Annis, rather than Kal—the grand chancellor did not see fit to provide any advice, nor compel Loren to spend any more time with him than necessary, and for that she was grateful.

Dahab was an old city in the south of Feldemar. It had once been the kingdom's capital. It was also the ancestral home of the family Yerrin, and had been as far as anyone could remember, or discover in tomes of history. Fat with wealth and power, Dahab exerted its influence over all the nine kingdoms, though ostensibly it still served the king of Feldemar, who dwelt in the city of Yota farther to the west.

At this time of year, the roads there would be hard. They would be crossing the heart of Feldemar, a dense jungle where bogs and marshes could trap the unwary. Indeed, throughout the nine kingdoms, Feldemar was thought of as a particularly wild place. Its kings through the centuries had built and maintained roads as best they could, but the land fought them at every turn. And without many wide stone roads to carry troops, supplies, and the King's law, the "kingdom" was more akin to a collection of provinces scattered across the wide and wild landscape. Sometimes lesser lords would claim rule over one part of it or another, disregarding royal decree or birthright. As long as taxes still made their way to Yota, the king rarely put forth much effort to suppress them. Thus small conflicts of territory and dominance often raged across Feldemar, fought in bitter skirmishes of only a few dozen soldiers at a time, in the wet and marshy underbrush that covered much of the landscape.

But the wealth and power in the city of Dahab kept it free from such infighting. War was only good for business when it was fought on a grand scale, and Feldemar's petty border squabbles contributed little. The family Yerrin had enough coin to maintain order by any means necessary. Their own guards were above such work, but whenever bandits grew too bold, the Yerrins would hire mercenaries to root them out of their jungle holes for the slaughter, and all in the name of commerce.

Therefore the roads Loren would take would be mostly free of bandits and highwaymen. Loren and her party would face only natural dangers on their journey, and those were none too perilous.

As for the party itself, Annis informed Loren that she would be sent out with the same Mystics who had accompanied her to Ammon in the first place. That reminded Loren that Annis had said something to Kal about solving two problems at once, and she asked what it had meant. But Annis avoided her gaze and equivocated.

"Ammon was never meant to hold so many soldiers at once," she said. "It is a constant chore to keep it supplied, and every hungry mouth removed from it makes the job easier." But Loren knew that when they left the fortress, they would take enough food with them for the journey, and so that seemed a poor explanation. Yet Annis would say nothing more.

On the morning of the second day after their confrontation with Hewal, Loren awoke early and could not return to sleep. After tossing and turning for some time, she sighed and gave it up. She was thankful at least that she had not been woken by one of her dreams. While Chet snored peacefully, she put on her clothes and made her way to the stronghold walls.

She had no particular aim in her wandering, but soon she found herself on the southwestern end of the fortress, looking out at the lands that fell away until they reached the jungle on the horizon. The sky grew lighter with every passing moment, and would already have turned from grey to pink if it were not for the thick clouds overhead that threatened rain. Loren studied the lush green before her. Soon she would ride out across those lands, in the very direction she was looking now, until she reached a city that she had seen only in her dreams.

She heard footsteps on the wall behind her, slow and easy.

"What wakes the Nightblade so early in the day?"

Niya's voice made Loren swallow and take a moment to compose herself. But even as she hesitated, the Mystic came and leaned on the wall just next to her, so close that their elbows pressed against each other. Through the thin fabric of her sleeve, Loren could feel the warmth of the other woman's bare arm.

"I do not know," said Loren. "I awoke for no reason."

"Not another dream, then?" said Niya. "I heard that a nightmare came upon you recently."

Loren shook her head. "No. No dreams today. At least none I remember."

Niya nodded. Loren glanced at her, but the woman kept her gaze trained on the landscape.

"How did you know about Hewal?" said Niya.

Loren floundered. "I . . . what? Why do you ask?"

"Because I do not know the answer," said Niya, smirking. "At first I assumed that Kal had had you watch him. But when we returned to Ammon, and the grand chancellor did not believe your tale, I realized that Hewal's betrayal was a surprise even to him. So then I wondered: how did you know, when Kal suspected nothing?"

Loren shrugged, but that made their arms rub together. She thought about shifting so that they were no longer touching, but she held her place for the moment. "Hewal had a suspicious look to him."

Niya smirked. "Do not most people look suspicious? Many would say that I have an odd look to me."

"I have not decided about you, yet. But I have seen nothing to make me suspect you. Should I?"

The Mystic's smile grew broader, and she nodded as though conceding a point. "Very well. But there is another reason I came to speak with you, after I saw you brooding here on the wall. I have been told that I, and the other Mystics who came here to Ammon with you, have been assigned to accompany you on your next mission."

"Yes," said Loren.

Niya sighed—it sounded like relief. "That is good. As I have mentioned, I feel you are safer in my hands than in others'."

A deep flush crept up Loren's neck. "You mistake the way of things. I am the one leading the expedition."

"Can you tell me where we are bound?"

"Kal did not tell you?"

The Mystic snorted. "Kal did not even tell me that I was assigned to you. That news came down through the chain of command."

She could see no harm in it. "We make for Dahab, to gather information for Kal's plans."

"I see," said Niya, nodding. "And did Kal assign me to you, or did you request my presence?"

The red had begun to seep from her cheeks, but now Loren felt it return anew. "I do not know what you mean."

Niya rolled her eyes. "Very well, if you wish me to couch my meaning behind other words: did you request *my squadron* of Mystics?"

"I requested nothing," said Loren. "In either direction. I did not request for you to come with me, or to remain here. The decision was Kal's."

"You do not care either way, then?" said Niya, smirking again.

"I . . . have not spent much thought on it."

The smirk turned into a grin. "When will you stop pretending that you do not think about me, just as you know I think about you?"

Loren flushed a deeper red, but she held the woman's gaze. "I have not pretended anything of the sort. Yet you, in turn, know that Chet loves me, and I him."

Niya did not look away. She only edged a little closer. "And what do I care about love? This is war time, and I am not looking for a wife. Only a pair of green eyes, and everything beneath them."

Neither of them moved for a long moment. Loren was not sure which way she *wished* to move. Or rather, she was torn between what she wished to do, and some sense of . . . duty? Obligation? She was not certain. But in the end, she stepped away from Niya. The spark in the air faded to nothing.

"No," she said. "What you seek is not important. What Chet and I have agreed to, is."

"Oh?" said Niya, who did not look put off in the least. She folded her arms—*Those thick, thrice-damned arms,* thought Loren—and cocked her head. "And what have you agreed to? You have discussed such things?"

"I . . . not in such detail," said Loren. "Yet I know what would hurt him, and what would not."

Niya growled in frustration and looked away. "Do you think he knows anything of hurt? I suppose I should expect such foolishness from youth. You will learn, eventually, that young love rarely ages as well as either of the parties involved."

The words came surprisingly harsh and bitter. But the vicious look on Niya's face melted away as quickly as it had come, and she summoned a sad smile—though it seemed forced.

"I speak from passion, and not wisdom," she said. "Forgive me. It is your decision, of course, if you wish to limit yourself to a boy who . . . well, he can hardly know what he is about, can he? But now I must return to my duties. Fare well, until our journey together begins."

She turned and ambled off down the ramparts towards the western tower. Loren felt confused, and more than a little restless. She looked out across the landscape again, but it no longer held such attraction as when she had first arrived. So she made her way down the stairs instead, and through the hallways back to her chamber.

Chet sat at the edge of the bed, looking as though he had just woken. His hair was mussed, and he rubbed sleep from one eye with the back of his hand. "Good morn."

"Shush."

Loren threw her cloak upon the floor and pushed him back down upon the bed, and they did not speak for some time.

Afterwards, he lay breathless beside her. "Sky above," he muttered. Loren smiled, but it quickly faded. He saw it, and propped himself up on one elbow. "What is it? What is wrong?"

What could she tell him? He had said often enough what he thought of Niya. Anything Loren could tell him that was close to the truth would only turn his distrust to anger, and just before they all set out on a journey together. It would not do to have them battling with each other the whole way to Dahab. And if their tempers got the better of them once they reached the city, that could be disastrous.

One thing, at least, was close enough to the truth. "I am worried about the road ahead," she said. "Just as with Hewal, I saw it in my dreams. It is unsettling, to say the least."

"Mayhap your dreams are trying to guide you," he said. "Though I know it comes at a price, for the terror of your visions is plain to see, this could yet be a gift."

Loren looked away. "A gift. Hardly."

"Not all of us can see what is to come in days ahead."

She looked up into his eyes. "I do not see our fate. Do you understand? Sometimes I see things from the past, only they are twisted and horrible. Other times, I see things that do *not* come to pass, and could not. This is not prophecy. No one has that power. I only see . . . clues. Hints. Things that can help guide me in what to do—and, mayhap, what to avoid doing."

The sight of his slit throat flashed through her mind, and she craned her neck as she felt the phantom pain of Gem's teeth at her neck.

Chet had gone solemn. Loren feared he might ask her again about her visions, even after she had asked him to trust her. But he only said, "And what must you avoid doing?"

She gave him a smile and leaned forwards to kiss him before pushing him onto his back once more. "Not this, certainly," she said, as she climbed atop him.

TWENTY-ONE

No trumpets blared when they set forth from Ammon, and there was no assembly of troops in the stronghold's courtyard to see them off. In fact they received even less of a parting ceremony than they had had upon the Seat. Only Kal was there to bid them farewell, his hood drawn up against the rain. He wore his cloak of red, unlike the Mystics with Loren, who had stowed their own cloaks in their saddlebags and wore plain brown. The success of their mission relied upon secrecy, and it would not do for a party of Mystics to be seen making their way across the kingdom.

As Loren gained the saddle atop Midnight, Kal gripped her ankle. She looked down at him, bracing herself for a final biting remark. But he only said, "Remember your vow to me, girl."

She softened somewhat, and nodded. "I will."

"I believe it." Then he stepped closer, and his voice dropped so that Loren had to stoop to hear it. "Forgive what I said in anger and after too much wine. Jordel's death was not your doing. He was his own man."

Loren could not reply for a moment, and she blinked hard as she drew her hood up against the rain. "He was that," she said at last.

A single guard at the gatehouse observed their passing, and before midday Ammon was lost from sight behind them. Niya and Loren led the procession. Chet followed just behind Loren and to her side, almost as if he was ready to spur his horse between her and Niya at a moment's notice. Loren saw, but she made no mention of it. The last thing she wished to do was call attention to the rapidly growing divide between him and the Mystic.

They stayed on the main road all that day and camped within sight of it that evening. But early on the second day they split off onto a less-traveled path that plunged straight into the heart of the wilderness. If they were lucky, and the weather not too harsh, the side roads would only cost them two days on the journey, and it would be that much harder for the family Yerrin to observe their approach.

But the sky did not cooperate. On the third day they were blasted by the heaviest rainstorm Loren had ever seen in her life. It forced them from the road to ride beneath the trees, and even that did little to shield them. Niya called them to a halt long before the sun had gone down.

The storm did not pass the next day, or the next. They had underestimated the fury of Feldemar's winters, and the journey became a cheerless affair.

After the second night camping in the rain, Shiun let them build a fire against the weather. "No one will be able to see its glow through this storm, unless they have almost stumbled upon us already," she said. "And secrecy will do us no good if we freeze to death."

Loren was surprised that they even *could* build a fire in such weather. But Uzo set about with sticks and leaves, and built a little shelter against the rain. He did it effortlessly, and though it looked a flimsy thing, it did not rock in the wind, and it kept the rain from dousing the wood.

"We learn this trick as children," he said, the first time Gem praised him for it. The boy had scooted up close to the fire, practically sticking his frozen hands right into it. "These storms come every year, and there is nothing to be done about them. The world cannot stop to appease the sky's anger, and so those who travel in such weather must learn how to endure it."

One morning, when the storm was particularly fierce, Niya commanded them to remain camped there for the day. When Loren objected, Niya shook her head firmly. "We are at your command, Nightblade, but it would be foolhardy to press on through this. The winds might pick us up and carry us away. And besides, the horses will tire themselves to death against such a battering. We must hope that one day's rest will not make any great difference."

She found a place in the jungle where the trees kept off the worst of the rain, and there she commanded the Mystics to drill. Uzo and Jormund practiced against each other. Loren marveled at how Uzo, though he was by far the smaller, was able to keep up by using his speed and skill as much as his spear. Though young, he seemed a most capable warrior. She was not surprised that he had survived the battle on the Seat.

Gem followed along with the two of them for a while, off to the side, until Weath took pity and practiced his sword forms with him. Shiun stood apart from the rest, practicing her archery against a tree. Loren stayed with them for a while, but she had no interest in training. Instead she returned to her tent, which Chet had never left, and fumed to him.

"Here we sit, helpless against the weather," she said, trying without success to wring the water from her clothes. "Some agents of the High King we have proven ourselves."

"I do not know that I think this is so terrible a thing as you seem to," said Chet, grinning at her. "I can imagine many fates worse than being trapped in a tent with you for days on end."

Loren scowled and slapped his shoulder.

The sixth day was the worst yet, but at Loren's insistence, Niya commanded them to press on. They had already lost too much time, and a day of rest had filled them all with an urgency to keep moving. But the road grew worse and worse, and their horses kept slipping in the mud. They had to ride upon a riverbank for almost two hours straight, and the footing was so uncertain that they almost lost Jormund to the floodwaters. Niya called them to a halt hours before sundown, and the frustration in the camp was palpable as they all built their tents.

Soon afterwards they sat around the fire, staring into its licking flames, saying nothing. Out of all the party, Weath had seemed the least affected by the sour mood. Now she looked around the fire and gave a low chuckle. "A sorry lot we all look, and all for the sake of a little unpleasant weather."

"I would call this more than a little unpleasant," said Jormund. The big man's broad shoulders were hunched over his bread and meat to keep them dry. He tore another chunk off his loaf with his teeth.

But Gem seemed to appreciate Weath's attempt to lighten the mood, or else he was still grateful for how she had practiced swordplay with him, for he smiled at her. "I do not know about that. I grew up in a city that would become filthy in the summer, so that the smell of it pervaded the countryside all around. During those times, I would have welcomed a storm such as this to clean out the gutters and the back alleys."

"As you say," said Weath, smiling in turn. "I think the kingdom of Idris would welcome a storm to soak their lands. They have lain dry and barren for generations beyond count."

"Indeed!" said Gem, puffing out his chest. He raised his voice, shouting into the storm that still pelted them. "In fact, I am glad to be in such a storm as this, and not back in Ammon, where I could be warm and dry!"

But across the fire, Uzo snorted. "I do not love the storm, but I *am* glad to be gone from that place, darkness take it. Better these wildlands than all the old guard staring down their noses at us."

A cold snap seemed to rush through the camp. Weath and Shiun went stone still, looking at Uzo in shock. Niya sat up straight from her place by the fire and slammed her wooden plate down upon the ground. Loren tensed, though she was not entirely sure what was wrong.

"Enough of that talk, Uzo," said Niya. "We are all of us Mystics, old and new. I will not have you bring division to our ranks."

Uzo avoided her gaze. Beside him, Loren saw that

Jormund was scowling, though he did not speak in Uzo's defense.

"Am I understood?" said Niya.

"Yes, Captain," said Uzo, though no one could miss the tinge of defiance in his voice.

Niya stared at him a moment longer, as if daring him to look up. Weath looked ashamed on Uzo's behalf, which was well, Loren supposed, since Uzo did not look ashamed in the slightest. Jormund's face had gone a shade darker, as though he barely restrained himself from an outburst.

At last Weath cleared her throat. "I spoke in jest before, of course. This storm can take itself back to whatever pit in the darkness it crawled out of."

Jormund let loose a long, low sigh. He looked up and forced a smile, as though determined to forget the discomfort of a moment ago. "And do you notice how it only started after our journey began, and grows stronger the farther south we travel? It is like this mission is Elf-cursed."

Weath chuckled easily. "I doubt the Elves care one way or another about a party such as ours."

But Uzo's scowl deepened, and he shook his head. "Elves. Do you all believe in such tales?"

"Uzo," said Niya in a warning tone.

Loren looked at him in confusion. "What do you mean?"

He met her gaze, unflinching. "You mean you believe in Elves as well?"

"Uzo!" barked Niya.

His eyes flashed as he met her gaze at last. "Can I not speak my mind on something so trivial, Captain? Or does your order for silence extend even to my disbelief of superstitious tales?"

Niya was about to answer, but Weath spoke first, cocking her head. "Do you mean to tell me that you do not even think Elves are real?"

Uzo turned to her, his glare softening somewhat. "Of course not. No one but the witless would think so."

Loren did not even know what to say to such a thing. She looked at Chet and Annis beside her. They both raised their brows and shrugged. But Gem looked between Uzo and Loren, his brow furrowed, as though he were suddenly unsure.

Niya spoke, a contemptuous smile playing at her lips. "Uzo is a farm boy from here in Feldemar. From the north, are you not?" Uzo stared at her and gave a slow nod. Niya shook her head at the rest of them. "He is practically an outlander. Elves rarely trouble that part of the world, and as a result, many of their elders have begun to forget."

But Uzo rolled his eyes. "They have forgotten nothing. They only stopped believing campfire stories. Do you ever notice how every time a story is told about Elves, it is always a tale of someone far away? And always, too, it happened a long time ago. Who has seen an Elf in living memory? Have you, Captain?"

Niya did not answer. Uzo looked around the camp, but no one spoke up. Loren felt a curious burning in her breast, a heat that crawled its way up the back of her neck. She realized suddenly that her hands were clenched to fists. Chet put a hand on her arm in warning, but she ignored it.

"I have," she said.

That sent the whole camp into silence. Gem and Annis looked at each other nervously, while Chet ducked his gaze. It sounded like a boast, and she had not meant it to. The Mystics all stared at her in wonder—even Uzo, who clearly had not expected to be challenged. But he recovered quickly, shaking his head.

"What do you mean?" he said. "You cannot mean that *you* have seen them. You heard from someone else—"

"I saw them," said Loren. "With my own eyes. As close as you and I are now. Closer, in fact."

His nostrils flared in anger. "Then tell the tale of it. Explain yourself, if you are so wise in the way of such things."

"I do not know that I need to follow your orders, Uzo," she said.

Uzo's anger became a smirk. "I thought not. By all the tales that are told of Elves, if you had seen them, you would be dead."

But Weath shook her head. "That is not true. There are all sorts of tales about Elves, and the only thing they agree upon is that you never can tell what they will do.

Sometimes they will kill everyone in sight. Sometimes they will walk straight into the middle of a campsite—or even a city, if some tales can be believed—and kill one person. Just one. A king, or a peasant, or even a babe. Once they decide you must die, you die. Other times they leave you be. That is the great terror of the Elves: that no one can know their intentions, and that there is no escaping their wrath if they turn it upon you."

She turned to Loren then. "This explains much," she said. "I knew there was something odd about you from the moment we met, on that ship in Brekkur. It is something in your eyes. I have never seen its like before, but I have heard it can be a sign of those who are Elf-touched."

Loren frowned. "Others have said much the same thing. The Lord Prince even remarked upon it. I thought it was only their color—that seems to catch most people's attention easily enough."

Weath shook her head quickly. "It is not only that. Wizards like me can see it more easily than most, but it is clear to all, if you know what to look for. Look at her, Uzo. You can see it, can you not?"

Uzo stared at Loren for a moment, and she saw recognition dawn upon him. He turned sullenly away. "I see only a pair of green eyes," he muttered.

But Weath looked at Loren and gave her a little smile. Loren tried to return it, but she felt suddenly out of place. Everyone around the campfire returned to their meals, studiously avoiding looking at her. Only a moment ago, Loren had felt like a member of their company—if not a Mystic herself, then at least a friend to this group of them. Now, though, other than to Chet and Gem and Annis, she felt like an outsider—somehow apart from the rest of them, and someone to be avoided.

But one pair of eyes lingered. Niya still looked at her, and the Mystic's face was a curious mix of trepidation and wonder.

TWENTY-TWO

Loren rose with the dawn the next morning and left the camp to relieve herself. When she had finished, she straightened and drew her trousers up again. Just as she finished tying the drawstring, Niya stepped out from behind a tree, making Loren jump.

"Good morn, Nightblade."

"Sky above!" cried Loren. "What were you doing there? Were you *watching* me?"

Niya only rolled her eyes. "We are on campaign, at least of a sort. There is little room for modesty in a war party. Do you think the rest of us cannot your hear the grunts you and your lover let out when the moons are high?"

Loren could feel herself turning a deep shade of red. "I . . . I thought the sounds of the storm—"

But Niya cut her off with a sharp wave of her hand. "Enough. I only came to ask you if it is true, what you said last night about the Elves."

"I am no liar."

They studied each other for a long moment, Niya searching for something in her eyes. At last she gave a small nod. "Very well. I meant no offense. But it is a most unusual tale. Then again, much about you seems unusual, and mayhap this explains why. When did you see them?"

Loren shrugged, a little put off. "Some time before I came to the Seat, when I traveled east across Dorsea."

Niya's shoulders slumped, as though she had hoped for a different answer. "I see. It was after the Greatrocks, then? When Jordel fell?"

Loren cocked her head. "Yes. Did you know him?"

"No. I have only heard stories. Who does not know the exploits of the Nightblade, after all?" Her look of burning curiosity faded, to be replaced by a familiar small smirk. "In particular, they speak of the hatred between you and the merchant Damaris. Is that why you are so eager to pursue her to Dahab?"

"I do not hate Damaris. I only wish to see her brought before the King's law."

"Oh, but she is worthy of hate, is she not?" said

Niya, her smirk taking on a feral quality. "Many in the Mystics have tales of the family Yerrin, of their cruel dealings and the corpses that may be laid at their feet. Yet we only mean to capture Damaris. Would it not be easier to kill her? Does she not deserve it?"

A chill went through Loren. "That is not my duty. No doubt the King's law will deliver whatever sentence is just."

Niya snorted. "Mayhap. Yet if the end result will be her death, why should we not do it ourselves?" She studied Loren's face for a moment, but found no agreement there, and so she sighed and looked away. "Oh, do not look at me so. I am half jesting, after all. Though it *would* be cleaner, certainly."

Loren peered at her, a thought slowly forming. "What did Damaris do to you?"

Niya's nostrils flared. "I do not take your meaning."

"Whence came this thought? You have known from the start that we did not set out to kill her."

"I have never seen the woman before in my life." Niya shook her head and turned away—but not angrily. Rather she looked like a woman who had just remembered something she had not meant to forget in the first place.

"The family Yerrin, then," said Loren. "What are they to you?"

Niya turned back, and it was as though she had never been angry at all. "Nothing, Nightblade. Nothing more than an obstacle in our mission. Only sometimes I think the King's law is too slow, and in the name of justice it allows injustice to live too long. But though you may wish to believe differently, the Mystics are not above assassination to achieve our ends."

Loren suppressed a shudder. She supposed it was no great surprise, but still it was not pleasant to hear. "That is hardly honorable."

"Nor are those we are sometimes forced to kill. Yet if Kal wished Damaris dead, he would not have sent us. He would no doubt employ a Drayden. Then the whole affair would be taken care of with little fuss."

The name of Drayden made Loren pause and study the Mystic more closely. "What do you mean?"

"Have you never heard of them?" said Niya, raising an eyebrow. "That is odd. They are well known throughout all the nine lands."

"I have heard of them, certainly. But I do not understand . . . why would Kal employ one of them? Theirs is a dark name."

"So is the family Yerrin's, and yet we Mystics have many dealings with them. Do you know nothing of the Drayden killers?"

Loren shook her head.

"They are assassins without peer. They work in the shadows, and they never fail to eliminate their mark. Mostly they work for the benefit of the family Drayden itself. But sometimes they can be hired, though it takes a hefty weight of gold."

"But surely Kal . . ." Loren let her words trail off.

She had almost said that Kal, at least, would not employ assassins, even if the Mystics would. Yet before the thought could reach her lips, she knew it was foolish. Mayhap he would not do so lightly, but if he thought it was the only way to achieve an end, she did not think he would hesitate.

She realized that Niya was studying her face as these thoughts raced through her mind. "Poor little Nightblade," said the Mystic. Her voice had gone quiet, and held none of its usual veiled barbs. "You are surrounded by dark deeds, and darker times."

"Yet not all is darkness," said Loren, lifting her chin. "And the darkest night is still lit by the moons. I knew a Drayden—Qarad, your former lord chancellor. He proved his loyalty when he died, battling the Shades within the High King's palace."

Niya turned to the tree beside her and picked at it with her fingernail. "Yes. I never met him myself, and I had always heard he was a terror to the soldiers who served him. But he knew his duty."

They let a long silence stretch between them, a respectful moment for the dead. Then Loren cocked her head, remembering the night before.

"What did Uzo mean last night, when he mentioned the old guard?"

"Nothing," said Niya at once. "He is young, and newer to the Mystics than some. Such a combination rarely breeds temperance."

"I have never had much temperance myself," said

Loren. "But what did he mean? He said something else, when we were in Ammon—something that turned your mood dour, as it did last night. I will have an answer."

"Oh you will, will you?" A spark of mischief shone in Niya's eye, the jibe returning to her voice. But then she sighed, and her expression grew more somber. "Kal is of the old guard, and he assembles Mystics to his side who share in his beliefs. For hundreds of years, the Mystics have had one purpose: to preserve the King's law, and through it, the nine kingdoms."

"Of course," said Loren. "That *is* their purpose, is it not?"

"It is. But some Mystics have grown weary of that being our sole pursuit. Our order holds much power now over the nine lands—not only because of our soldiers and the great number of wizards within our ranks, but because of our many connections to the wealthiest and most powerful families across the nine kingdoms. Only in the Order of Mystics will you find Yerrins and Draydens working side by side, as well as many members of the nobility. In our oaths, we forsake all ties to the families whence we came. But in truth, blood is not so easy to cast aside. If all the Mystics with powerful connections were to act in concert, united by some common purpose, we would be powerful indeed. Have you never heard our order called the Tenth Kingdom?"

"I have not," said Loren.

Her mind went racing back to the village of Strapa, where Mystics had pursued her and Jordel as they searched for Xain. Derrick, the leader of their pursuers, also thought of the Mystics as being of two kinds. He had even slain one of his own soldiers. *This one was a poison within our ranks,* he had said. But Jordel had been furious with him, for he believed that all were equal who wore the red cloak.

"But still I do not understand," said Loren, shaking her head. "You say that they are not happy with their duty. But what else is there?"

"Nothing," said Niya. "There is nothing else."

"Do not be coy with me," said Loren. "What do they *wish* to do? You say they have influence, and could wield it. To what end?"

"There is no end," said Niya. "They are aimless. Unhappy with their state of affairs, but with no plan to improve upon it. And do not worry, Nightblade: you will never find me being coy with you."

That made Loren's cheeks burn—but, too, she could sense that Niya still withheld something. It made her suddenly nervous to be traveling in this grim company of red-cloaked soldiers. She felt as though for some time now, she had been swimming with the flow of a river, and had only just become aware of a dangerous undercurrent that she could neither see nor predict.

Niya must have seen her anxiety, for she gave a sad smile and stepped forwards. With two fingers she reached up and brushed a lock of hair behind Loren's ear. "These are far too many worries for a woman so young. Free your mind of such troubles, Nightblade. They are for the red cloaks, not the black."

Loren stared into her eyes for a moment. Then she pushed past the Mystic, making for the camp.

Two days later, they awoke to a grey morning with rain lighter than they had seen in some time. They were nearing the journey's end, and the sight of better weather brought their spirits up.

"This is a good omen," said Shiun. "If this holds, we could reach Dahab before sundown."

"Then let us press on as quickly as we may," said Annis, rubbing at her arms through the sleeves of her shirt. "And when we have concluded our business in Dahab, let us remain there a while, or mayhap forever. I mean never to spend another night in the wilderness battered by rain, if I can help it."

After a meager breakfast they set off. And whether because of the prospect of reaching the end of their road, or the weather, their mood was now almost cheerful. There were snatches of conversation as they followed the winding paths through bogs and marshes, and once, Gem offered to sing Uzo a song, though Niya quickly told him to be silent.

"We have seen nothing to tell us that we are being watched, but still we should be cautious," she said. "And by no means should we go singing through the woods and call our foes down upon our heads."

Shortly after midday, they heard swift hoofbeats ahead of them. Niya and Loren shared a glance. They had sent Shiun ahead to scout the way, and if she was returning now, she was coming quickly. Niya waved them all off the road, and they retreated into the trees.

"Swords," muttered Niya. She and the other Mystics all drew. After a moment, Gem fumbled his own blade from its scabbard.

"If it is not Shiun, let them pass us, and only fight if we are spotted," said Loren.

But it was Shiun after all. As soon as she reached the spot on the road where the rest of them were hiding, she pulled to a stop and waved to them. Loren walked Midnight out into the open.

"If you meant to conceal yourselves, you did a poor job," said Shiun. "The marks of your passing are like signal fires."

"Enough of that," said Niya. "What is wrong?"

"There are soldiers," said Shiun. "Yerrin guards, up ahead."

Loren frowned. "Where our path meets the main road?"

"No," said Shiun. "Upon the road we travel."

That cast a grim mood over all of them. They had taken this way specifically to avoid detection, believing Yerrin would only be watching the major routes.

"So we have wasted days in our journey, and for little purpose," said Chet.

"No," said Loren. "The main road would have been

little better, and there would be no way to keep their watchmen from spotting us—which is what we must try to do now."

"Why would they have guards posted, unless they knew we were coming this way?" said Niya.

"There could be any number of reasons," said Loren. "It could be a precaution, or they could be on the lookout for another foe entirely."

"Do you not think Hewal has arrived ahead of us?" said Weath. "If he has warned them that we are coming . . ."

Loren and Chet shared a look. Hewal would not have given such warning, because Loren and the Mystics should not have known he was in Dahab. They had only come because of Loren's dream, which only Chet, Gem, and Annis knew about. She could not explain it to the rest of them, not now at any rate.

"Of course Hewal could have told them we might come, but he could not have known we would take this route," said Loren. "And regardless, we cannot turn back now. If anything, we should take this as a sign that Damaris is in Dahab for certain. We must not let her slip away."

"There might be a way past the guards," said Shiun. "The path we ride now leads to a log bridge. That is where the Yerrin guards have placed themselves. But the river beneath the bridge can be crossed another way, bypassing the guards—with Weath's help."

Loren frowned, but Weath only nodded. "Say on."

"The river runs through a small divide in the land, several paces below the bridge. If we walk through that divide, there is a place close by where the water grows shallow and somewhat calm, despite the flooding from the rain. There, Weath could turn the water to stone, giving us a bridge to cross over. If we are silent, we should be able to avoid the guards' attention."

"Why not cross the river somewhere else?" said Annis. "We should do it far from the bridge, so that there is no danger of the guards seeing us." She looked more nervous than the rest of them. Loren realized that, if they were spotted, word would surely fly to Damaris that her daughter had been seen near the city of Dahab. If that happened, Loren doubted that all the Mystics in Underrealm could keep Damaris from hunting them down.

But Shiun shook her head. "There is nowhere else, at least not that I have seen. Upstream and down, the river moves too quickly. I could search for another calm section, but that would take time—mayhap days."

Loren looked to Weath. The alchemist nodded. "Shiun and I have known each other a long while. I trust her judgement in this."

"Very well," said Loren. "When only one path presents itself, the wise take their first step. Lead the way, Shiun."

But the Mystic hesitated, looking at Niya. Loren turned to find Niya studying her own hands.

"Why do we not simply take the bridge?" said Uzo. "We could dispatch the guards and be on our way in no time."

Niya looked up to meet Loren's gaze. "It would be faster."

"No," said Loren. "There is no need for fighting if subterfuge will serve."

"Yet speed is imperative to our mission," said Niya. "And we have wasted days already."

"You speak of saving less than an hour's time," said Loren.

Niya turned to Shiun. "If we *are* discovered while we try the more difficult crossing, what will be our position?"

Shiun's expression remained carefully neutral. "It will be difficult. They will have the high ground, and we would have to climb the riverbank to engage them."

"There. You see?" said Niya. "If anything should go wrong, we will all be at far greater risk."

Loren felt as though the argument were slipping away from her. "If we kill their guards, our advantage will be lost. Speed is important, but so is secrecy. Do you wish to warn all of the family Yerrin that we approach Dahab?"

"If we do our job well, no guard will escape to bring such a message."

"Yet if they do not hear from their guards at all, they will be suspicious regardless. And we will move more slowly than before if one of us is injured in the fight."

"That is unlikely," said Jormund with a grim smile. He pressed his fists together until his knuckles cracked.

"You risk all of our safety, for the sake of some guards you have never met," said Niya, brows drawing together.

"While you are willing to wantonly sacrifice the lives of strangers," said Loren. "I am in command here. We go by the river."

Niya's face turned a shade darker. But at last she jerked her horse's reins to the side, nudging it away from the rest of the group. Weath let out a low *whoosh* of breath. Shiun studied Loren for a moment, and then turned to lead them off the road.

TWENTY-THREE

They were closer to the river than Loren had thought, and soon reached the bank. Looking down, she saw at once what Shiun had meant about the difficulty in crossing. Its surface was a roiling mass of angry white foam.

"We will remain atop the bank for a ways," said Shiun. "There is no place to safely climb down closer to the water."

They had to ride in single file, for the trees pressed close to them on the right hand side. Loren rode just behind Shiun, with Chet behind her, and behind him,

Niya and the rest of the party. Once or twice, Loren glanced behind her, excusing the motion by peering around the jungle first. She caught a glimpse of Niya's face, but the Mystic's anger seemed to have faded—or else she was suppressing it. But at least her complexion was no longer so red, and she was not glaring as she had been before.

Finally they reached a place where the ground grew a bit more solid underfoot. There was a little shelf not far below them. Shiun led them down, so that now they walked on the river's very edge. Loren guided Midnight to the right, so that the horse did not risk losing her footing in the river's soft mud. Midnight hardly needed the urging. She eyed the water nervously and nickered. Loren stroked her mane.

They reached a curve in the river. Before they turned it, Shiun stopped them and bade them to dismount. "On foot from here," she whispered. "Keep yourselves quiet, and mind the horses." Loren passed the command back down the line.

As they made their way around the curve, Loren saw the bridge at last. It was made from a single thick log, taken from a tree so massive that four people could not have wrapped their arms around its girth. The trunk had been shorn in half down the middle, so that its top formed a large platform almost three paces wide. It lay across the river, one end on each of the banks, which were now six paces above their heads.

Shiun stopped and pointed. Loren peered in the direction of her finger. After a moment she saw it: a figure in a dark green cloak, concealed in a tree on the other side of the river. One of the Yerrin guards. But the guard was looking the wrong direction—across the river and up—and was half hidden by branches besides, so she could not see the party making its way along the bank.

Raising two fingers for silence, Shiun led them onwards. They crossed beneath the bridge in dead silence. Just after she passed under it, Loren heard a loud sniff from above. She froze, standing stock still for a moment. Cautiously she glanced up. But she could not see who had made the noise, and there was no other sound. Shiun pressed on, and Loren hastened to follow.

At last they saw the place Shiun had mentioned. A tree had collapsed, smaller than the one that formed the bridge, but still sizable. It lay directly across the river as though human hands had laid it there. It turned the water upstream into a still pool, which gently flowed over the top of the log before turning into the raging floodwaters they had walked beside all this time.

There was not enough space for Weath to press forwards to the front of the group, so they all moved down until the alchemist had reached the still waters. Loren glanced back down the river the way they had come. The log bridge was a ways off, but still too close for comfort. Now would be the most dangerous part of the whole affair.

Weath took a deep breath. She knelt at the water's edge and put her hands into it. Loren could only imagine how cold the water must be, but the alchemist did not complain. From behind her closed eyelids, a gentle light spilled forth.

As they all watched in wonder, the water around Weath's hands began to change. It swirled and then solidified. For a brief moment it looked to Loren as though it had turned to ice. But then the ice went grey, and turned harder until it had become stone. The stone rippled farther and farther out into the river, at first in a perfect semicircle, but then, as Weath found her focus, it became a straight line, little more than a pace across. It edged forwards slowly, ever so slowly, and each moment seemed an eternity under the threat of the nearby bridge. At last the stone touched the bank on the other side. There it sank into the silt and mud, creeping into the earth like the roots of a tree and anchoring itself to the shore.

Weath's eyes opened, and the glow in them brightened. "All right," she gasped. "I shall have to hold it here while the rest of you cross."

"What about you?" said Loren.

"I can hold it up for myself at the end, but the rest of you must go first. One at a time—I cannot bear the weight of more."

Niya pressed forwards without answering and led

her horse across the stone. She walked a bit too slowly for Loren's liking, but the stone bridge was wet from the splashing water, and Niya had to pick her way carefully. When she had reached the other side, she pressed herself and her horse up against the riverbank and waved the rest of them on. Jormund stepped forwards and placed one foot on the bridge. Weath gave a wry smile.

"You should eat less, big man."

Jormund grinned at her and pressed on. After him went Chet, closely followed by Gem, and then Shiun and Uzo. Only Weath, Annis, and Loren remained to cross. Annis looked to Loren, but Loren waved a hand at her. "You first."

Annis gave her a wan smile and stepped forwards. Loren's smile vanished the moment Annis turned her back. The girl looked terrified. As a merchant's daughter, she had never engaged in as much physical activity as the rest of them. Across the river, Loren caught Chet's eye and tossed her head at Annis. He nodded and stepped to the end of the bridge, holding forth a hand, ready to help Annis once she was close enough.

The girl moved step by step, each one more cautious than the one before, each one agonizingly slow. When she reached the halfway point, her shoe slid on the wet stone. For a panicked moment, Loren thought she would fall over. But Annis recovered, throwing both her arms out to steady herself. On she pressed, but now she moved even more slowly, frightened by her near miss. Chet leaned farther forwards, grasping for her outstretched hand.

Annis slipped again. Almost within reach of the riverbank, she teetered on one foot. Chet lunged for her, seized the back of her collar, and flung her to the riverbank. But Weath's concentration wavered, and when Chet's foot came down, it slipped right through the stone. He did not cry out as he fell into the river, but that did not matter—for Annis' horse fell, too. It struck the water with a thunderous splash and a loud whinny. After their quiet sneaking, Loren nearly jumped out of her skin at the sound.

Shouts came from downriver, and two figures in green cloaks appeared on the bridge. One of them pointed at the party.

"Darkness take us," said Loren. She flung herself onto Midnight's back. The mare plunged into the stream under Loren's heels and struck out, swimming hard for Chet, who was fighting to reach the shore. The cold river clutched at her legs, making her gasp, and she had to force herself to push Midnight on through the water.

Weath sprang up, the glow in her eyes intensifying, and led her horse forwards. Stone rose up from the bridge to meet her hand, maintaining her connection as she held it up for herself and crossed. Behind her horse's hooves, the bridge began to dissolve away, turning to water again and sweeping away downriver. Niya, Jormund, Uzo and Shiun mounted their horses, and with a battlecry they charged up the riverbank. Gem gave his own thin scream and ran after them, though he had no horse and could not keep up.

Chet's head bobbed under the surface of the water until he struck the dam. Loren thrust out a hand and seized his shoulder, and he pulled himself onto Midnight's back behind her. The horse's hooves found purchase on the bank at last, and she emerged from the river, scattering water in all directions.

"Watch after Annis!" cried Loren, as Chet jumped from Midnight's back.

"I will, but where are you—?"

His question was lost as she spurred Midnight after the Mystics.

The fight had already begun. One Yerrin guard lay on her back. Her hands clawed futilely at an arrow in her throat. Jormund had two more occupied, keeping them at bay with great sweeps of his sword. Niya and Uzo had one each. *Why are there so many?* thought Loren.

But all thought fled her as she saw a green cloak rippling. Unseen by the Mystics, another guard ran from the fighting.

A messenger. They would ride for Dahab and warn the family Yerrin.

Loren sent her heels into Midnight's side and went after the guard with a cry.

She caught up to the Yerrin soldier and tried to leap from the saddle, tackling him to the ground. But

Loren was still not as practiced on horseback as the rest of the party. Her foot caught in the stirrup, and she fell atop him without any control. Her ribs struck a rock, driving the air from her lungs. Dazed and gasping, she rolled away.

There came a *hiss* as the guard drew his sword. He and Loren fought to their feet almost at the same time. Her bow was unstrung and on Midnight's saddle. She only had her dagger, but she hesitated to use it. What if the guard recognized it and escaped? Or what if one of the other Mystics came upon them and saw it?

The guard lunged forwards, thrusting his sword. Loren back-stepped and almost stumbled. He swung to the left, and then down. Loren did not let him draw close enough to reach her, but it seemed he was guiding her in some particular direction. She glanced behind her and saw only trees.

He swung again, and she ducked behind a trunk. Too late, hasty footsteps told her his aim: he ran away from her, straight for Midnight. Loren went after him.

No doubt he had hoped to gain the saddle and ride off before she caught him. But he wore chainmail and heavy boots, and Loren had always been a fast runner. She tackled him in the knees just before he reached Midnight. To her relief, his sword slid away on the grass. But he surprised her with a kick, and she fell back with explosions of light dancing before her eyes.

If he had pressed his advantage, he might have choked the life from her before she could stop him.

But he went for the sword instead, and that gave Loren time to regain her feet. He charged wildly, swinging without skill, hoping to catch her by surprise. Loren danced back again—but this time he gave her no room to glance behind her. One haphazard swing sent her leaping away, only to strike her head on a low branch. Loren fell to hands and knees. The guard attacked, sword raised.

A knife came flying. It sank into the Yerrin guard's side just below the arm. He cried out and dropped his sword. Niya appeared and tore the knife out. The Yerrin guard sank to his knees. She seized his hair, placing the blade to his throat.

"Is Damaris in the city?" she hissed.

The guard spat at her but missed. "Darkness take you and your kin."

Niya drove a knee into his side where she had stabbed him. He screamed. "I will not ask again. Some other of your fellows survived. Only one must live to tell me what I need to know. Tell the truth, and it could be you."

Loren rose, her shoulders heaving with deep gasps. But when she saw Niya, she paused. The Mystic's clothes and hair had become badly mussed in the fighting, and the high collar of her jerkin had come undone. There, where the leather parted, Loren could see a mass of scar tissue from some old and terrible wound.

The jungle had gone too silent, and Niya looked up at Loren with a frown. Her skin went a shade paler when she saw Loren looking at her scar. With a savage twist, she plunged her knife into the Yerrin guard's throat. As he fell to the ground, coughing his life into the soil, Niya buttoned up her collar again.

The forest went very still for a moment, except for the thrashing of the dying guard. Loren felt that she should say something. But then they heard the sound of hooves in the underbrush, and Shiun came riding into view with Chet. They both pulled to a halt. Chet was still dripping from his dunking in the river.

"Where is Annis?" said Loren.

"S-safe," said Chet, shivering. "We won the fight. W-Weath and Gem are w-with her."

"We must get you dry," said Loren. "You will catch your death of sickness." She brought Midnight to him, and as he dismounted, she fetched a dry cloak from her saddlebags to wrap around him.

"The Yerrins?" Niya's voice was thick with some emotion hastily hidden, though whether it was anger or embarrassment, Loren could not tell. The Mystic woman was still looking at her. Indeed she had not removed her gaze since Loren saw the scars at her throat.

"All dead," said Shiun. Chet's expression grew dark. "The Yerrins in Dahab will know something is amiss, but no one remains to tell them just what it is."

"Very well," said Niya. With her gaze still locked on Loren, she bared her lips in a fierce grin. "It appears we might as well have charged the bridge after all, Nightblade."

Loren flushed with anger. She tilted her head towards the corpse on the ground. "Mayhap—but then this one might have gotten away, for he would have had time to escape while you were fighting."

That gave Niya pause. At last she turned away, staring at the man on the ground. "Mayhap. We cannot change what has happened. Only now we must move with haste, and accomplish our aims in Dahab before Yerrin notices their missing patrol. The moment they do, they will send someone to search for them."

She reached up a hand, and Shiun pulled her into the saddle. They rode off back towards the others while Loren rubbed Chet's arms to warm him.

"They k-killed the Yerrins," said Chet quietly. "All of them."

Bowing her head, Loren wrapped her arms around him, trying to pass her warmth to him through the cloak. "I know. They are warriors. This is what they are trained to do."

"Y-yet you are s-supposed to be in c-command of them, and you told them you did not w-wish—"

Loren released him, climbed onto Midnight's saddle, and met his gaze. "I am not their master. They are my guards, not my servants."

Chet turned away from her to look ahead through the jungle.

"I did not wish for this," she told him quietly.

"I know."

TWENTY-FOUR

They had to hide the bodies, so that if the family Yerrin came to investigate why their patrol had not returned, it would take some time to find them.

"We might drag them off into the trees and hide them behind cut branches," said Jormund.

Loren was uncomfortably reminded of when she had first met Damaris, who had slain a squadron of constables and forced Loren to help her men bury the bodies. As she studied the grim look on Annis' face, Loren wondered if the girl was thinking the same thing.

"Too easy to find," said Shiun. "They will see the hewn trees, and then they will know what to look for."

"Throw them in the river," said Uzo. "No doubt the bodies will wash up on the bank, but it will be a ways downstream. It is fastest, and will not be any easier for searchers to discover than anything else we might do."

So it was agreed. The Mystics took care of the grisly work. Chet donned a new change of dry clothes and huddled off to the side under three cloaks, trying to dispel his chill. Loren wanted to be with him, but he was still dour after watching the Mystics slay their foes. It seemed distance was what he needed now, and so she gave it to him. The ride would warm him anyway, as well as the heat from his horse's body. As the others dragged the corpses to the log bridge and threw them off, Shiun rode back across the bridge and downriver a ways. She soon returned with Annis' horse. Its recovery seemed to be the only bit of good news from the whole affair.

All of them readied to ride on. Loren saw that Annis was staring down at the ground and went over to the girl. "What is wrong?"

"It is my fault we were discovered," said Annis. "If I had not slipped, they would not have seen us."

Loren shook her head. "No. Any one of us could have done the same. You should not blame yourself."

Annis looked around at the rest of the party and frowned. "I should not have come. It was the foolish notion of a foolish girl. I am no warrior."

"I would call you many things before I called you foolish," said Loren, putting a hand on her shoulder. "Strength of arms is not the only worthy quality in this world. A great enough wit will not only triumph over might, but make it look a fool. I value your mind far more highly than a simple swordsman."

That drew a small smile from Annis, though the girl did not look entirely convinced.

They rode hard once they set out, with Shiun scouting the way again. Gone was their high mood of that morning. No one spoke, but only watched the road as it passed beneath the horses' hooves.

They drew upon Dahab just before twilight. The clouds had mostly dissipated from the sky, and half the sun showed above the horizon to light the land. When they crested the last rise, the whole party stopped in awe.

North of them, the river they had crossed met an even greater waterway that ran south. But almost immediately, it reached a high shelf in the land and fell off into a great waterfall. "There is the Nelos," said Uzo, pointing to the river. "It flies away south until it reaches the Skytongue, which flows into the Great Bay many leagues away."

But Loren could not speak. As beautiful as it was, she had no eyes for the river, or even for the waterfall it formed. She could look only at the shelf, upon which was built the city of Dahab.

Just as she had seen in her dream, it was built in two

levels. Both held palaces and mansions aplenty, and all of them with gold trim. The dying sun upon the gold made the whole place shine like a jewel in firelight, so that they could not long observe it without having to shield their eyes. Upon the higher level were built grander mansions, and ones fairer to look at. Many of them were made of white marble that gleamed nearly as bright as the gold, and Loren was reminded of the High King's palace. But even a stranger could see that the true power rested in the city's bottom layer. There the buildings were more solid, more sinister—and far older, from the look of them.

It was not only the sight of the city that struck Loren dumb, but the fact that she beheld it, in truth, for the second time. She could not be sure, but she thought she even saw the pillar of rock where Gregor had held Annis, Gem, and Chet over the abyss. Suddenly she was struck with terror at the thought of bringing her friends here. She wanted to turn back, to spur Midnight into the jungle and hide away, never to return.

Instead she nudged the horse's side. "Onwards," she said. "We should try to reach it before the moons rise."

Your dreams are not the future, she told herself. *You are not so important that the Elves would give you that gift.*

But that did nothing to quell the fear in her heart.

As they neared the city, three buildings in the lower level caught their eye. They were massive, flat on top, but with sloping sides so that they almost resembled pyramids. They were wrought all in black granite, and the style looked familiar to Loren. Then she realized that they looked very similar to the Academy of Wizards on the Seat. But while the Academy stood tall and proud, these mansions sat like spiders in the shadows. Even their bronze trim looked like crooked legs, coiled before springing forth to snatch some unwary prey.

"Those buildings are the homes of the family Yerrin," said Uzo. His jaw clenched. "If there are answers for us in this city, they will be there."

"A great many of your kin must dwell here," said Gem, looking over to Annis. "Have you not visited the city before?"

"No. Before the journey that brought me to Cabrus, I had never left the Seat." Annis straightened suddenly in her saddle and turned to Loren with a curious expression. "I have only just now realized that that was my first journey away from home, and I am still upon it. It has been eight months since I saw the place where I was raised. What a long and wandering road it has been."

That gave Loren pause as well. Had it really been so close to a year since she left the Birchwood? Her birthday had passed some time in Octis, unmarked. She had been in the Greatrocks then, and Jordel had been alive. But that had never held great importance for her, since her parents had never celebrated it.

Not far from the city, they had to rejoin the main road. It was close enough that Yerrin would have little warning, even if they were spotted, but still they did not wish to be noticed. Therefore they split up and entered the city in twos and threes. Chet and Loren rode in together, and reached the city's gates just as the last of twilight faded from the sky. The guards did not even seem to notice them riding alongside the trading carts and wagons.

Once inside the city walls, they passed a few streets and then regrouped with the rest of the party. Then Uzo led them on through the winding streets.

Despite the ominous presence of the Yerrin mansions, which were visible over the neighboring buildings, the rest of the city seemed a far less sinister place than Loren had expected. The knowledge that Dahab was the ancient home of the family Yerrin had made her think it would be some dark den of evil. But in fact, the buildings looked much the same as they did anywhere else, except that here they were often walled with a reddish-brown plaster and had roofs of red tiles made with clay. The people talked and laughed and joked as in any city Loren had visited so far, and she saw many street performers here, which had been a rarity in Cabrus and Wellmont. Even upon the High King's Seat they were not so plentiful. She saw dancers swinging wide staves that were set on fire, and two duelists performing an elegant dance with blunted swords. One woman beckoned to wide-headed snakes on the ground, and at her command they bobbed and weaved into intricate patterns like whirlpools.

As they neared the black mansions, Loren saw that not only were they built close to one another, but they were in fact in a sort of compound, with a single great wall that surrounded all three of them. Uzo led them in a wandering path around the wall, as though they were merely travelers taking in the city's sights. But they all studied the place surreptitiously, eyeing the few gates, which were closed, and the many guards that patrolled the ramparts.

When they had finished their circle, they stopped at a tavern. There was no stable, but there was a long post outside where they could tie their horses, and a servant girl there who Loren paid to watch the steeds. Inside they found a cheery room full of many patrons. The tables were low, and each was surrounded by cushions placed directly on the ground. Loren smelled wine and ale, but also a sweet, spiced scent she could not place.

"Tea," said Uzo, lifting his nose and taking a deep sniff. "Sky above, it smells wonderful."

At a table near the back of the room, they ordered ale and wine, and tea for Uzo. They waited for the drinks to be delivered before they spoke. When they had all had a few sips, Loren leaned forwards.

"What can we expect inside the Yerrin walls?" she asked Uzo in a low voice.

Uzo shrugged. "I have only visited this city twice before," he said. "And I have never been inside the Yerrin dwellings. They permit no outsiders to come within, except for important guests on official business—usually nobility."

Loren thought of how she and Jordel had infiltrated the Shade fortress in the Greatrocks. "Mayhap we could disguise ourselves as guards. That might get us inside."

But Niya shook her head. "We could never pass for Yerrins. Did you not see the guards' helmets? The fronts are open, so that their faces are plain to see."

"At least Uzo could get in," said Loren. "He comes from Feldemar, and has the look."

Niya rolled her eyes. "You must listen better. *None* but Yerrins are permitted inside the wall. Uzo's skin is not enough. They are a family. They know each other. He would be recognized—or rather, he would not be, and therein lies the problem."

Loren's face flushed with embarrassment, which she tried to pass off. "What, then?"

To everyone's surprise, Gem spoke up. "Are there other buildings inside the wall?"

They all looked to Uzo, but he shrugged. "I do not know for certain."

"But there would have to be," said Weath. "We see only their great manors, where the family's important scions live, as well as the people who serve them. Yet the Yerrins would need more than that—storage for food, granaries for horse feed, and even cleaning sheds for the groundskeepers."

Gem's face broke into a smile, and Loren guessed

at his idea just before he gave voice to it. "There will be rooftops, then. There is no one better on rooftops than I. If we can climb the wall, mayhap we can travel across the smaller buildings to reach the manors, and without anyone seeing us."

Niya's nostrils flared, and she snorted. "Good on rooftops, are you? Mayhap in the city you called home. But you do not know this place."

"Loren can pick her way through any forest, even if she has never been there," said Gem. "I am the same with cities."

"He does have a sense for such things," said Loren. "With him to guide me, mayhap I can slip into the Yerrin dwellings."

"You?" said Chet. "You speak as if you mean to go alone."

"I am the spy," said Loren, shrugging. "Surely you do not think that all nine of us can sneak in together."

"Two may conceal themselves better than nine, yet three are not much more noticeable, and may be much safer if it should come to a fight," said Niya. "I will come with you, for you will need someone by your side who will do what is necessary to get back out alive."

Loren thought she heard the meaning behind that: *who will kill, if need be.* She met Niya's gaze, but the Mystic did not flinch.

"I should like to come as well," said Chet. "Surely one more will not make a difference."

But her dream flashed into her mind, and she saw

Chet in Gregor's clutches. "No. You must remain here. Each person added to the mission only increases the danger."

"Then let me come instead of Niya," insisted Chet. "I can look after you as well as she can."

"That is not what I said I would do," said Niya. "I said I would get her—and *all* of us—out alive. You might look after her, but you will not drive steel into a guard's gut if they stand between you and escape."

Chet gave her a glare, and she returned it. But before either of them could speak again, Weath put her hand on the table to draw their attention. "The plan all sounds well," she said. "But what do you mean to *do* once you are inside? That is still unclear."

"We must learn if Damaris is in the city," said Loren. "Surely someone inside will know."

"You mean to interrogate them?" said Uzo. "You will hardly have the time."

"I do not require much time," said Niya. Her hand dropped to the knife at her waist.

"If a corpse is found, Damaris will know someone is after her, and may flee the city," said Weath.

"I said nothing of corpses," said Niya. "But if Damaris should learn that we are here, and if she then tries to flee, then so much the better. We can follow her while sending word back to Kal, and the Mystics will bring her to bay—removed from the proud manors of her family where her defenses will be strongest. It is harder to shoot a bird in flight than when they are roosting—but when a swallow hides within the earth, it cannot be shot at all, and one must draw it into the open."

Annis looked at Loren across the table. Loren thought she knew the girl's mind: this was somewhat beyond the orders Kal had given them. Yet Loren knew of no other way to learn whether Damaris was in the city, and they were running out of time. If Yerrin had not already discovered their missing party of guards in the jungle, they soon would.

"It is decided, then," said Loren. "The rest of you will wait here for our return. And if anything should go wrong, and the three of us do not return, you must send word back to Ammon at once."

Chet glared into his cup of wine. Loren had barely touched hers, but now she threw the rest of it back all at once. Niya smirked.

"Bolster your courage however you must, Nightblade, and then let us carry out your plan."

Loren thought to herself that in fact, the plan had been Gem's. But she said nothing, and only returned Niya's smile.

TWENTY-FIVE

Loren, Gem, and Niya left the tavern soon afterwards. Chet and Weath came with them, to provide as much help as they could before the three of them passed beyond the wall.

Now that the moons had risen, Dahab was like an explosion of light. Its many lanterns and torches caught on the gold trim that adorned every building, so that the whole place shone nearly as bright as during the day, but warmer, a soft orange glow that wrapped them within itself. Yet everything was edged by the blue glow of the moons, and it blended with the firelight to give the buildings an ethereal, magical look. As she marveled at the sight of it, Loren realized that every torch and lantern was placed to cast its glow on as much of the gold as possible, as if each structure had been built for just that purpose.

"Now the whole city glows like a gem," said Gem. He looked up at Loren, grinning. "I call that a good omen for us—or for me, at least."

Loren smiled back—but then her mind turned to her dream, and she saw his face turn savage, his teeth bared as they tore at her throat. Her smile became forced. "I hope so."

The streets had begun to clear with the day's end, and they found a section of the wall with almost no one nearby. Just before they climbed up, Chet took Loren aside for a moment.

"You must promise me to return," he said, looking into her eyes.

"I can make no such promise," said Loren. "But I promise to try."

"That is hardly comforting." Chet glared over her shoulder, and even without turning, Loren knew his ugly look was for Niya.

"Whatever your feelings towards Niya, do not let them blind you." Loren had to fight to keep her irritation from her voice. "She has proven herself loyal so far."

"So far," said Chet.

Loren put a hand on his cheek. "Dear, dear Chet. Look after Annis. If all goes well, we shall return soon, but if it does not, she will be in greater danger than the rest of you."

"I hardly agree," said Chet. "If they catch us, we will be killed. I do not think she faces that fate."

But Loren remembered when last she had faced Damaris in the Greatrocks, and she remembered the merchant's wrath. "Yet she faces her own sort of horror. Look after her."

He gave a slow nod. Then he laced his fingers together and knelt. Loren glanced up the street. Weath had cleared the few passersby from sight, and she gave a nod. Loren placed her foot in Chet's grasp and her hands upon the wall. They looked at each other, and he nodded three times in quick succession. After the third nod he heaved upwards, and Loren jumped. Her fingers seized the top of the wall, and she gripped it tight, bracing her feet against the surface to steady herself. Then, slowly, she pulled herself up to the edge.

Cautiously she raised one eye over the lip of the wall, and then ducked back down at once. There was a guard not three paces away, walking in Loren's direction. But the guard's gaze was turned up and outwards, over the city, and she took no notice of Loren's fingers as she passed.

Once the footsteps drew away, she pulled herself over. No other guards stood nearby, and so Loren waved down to Gem and Niya. One by one they followed her. Chet did not look happy to heave Niya up the wall, but he did it, and soon they were all up. There was a rooftop within easy jumping distance, and another beyond that. Indeed, just as Gem had predicted, there seemed to be a route that ran all the way to the bottom of the first manor far ahead.

"Better and better," whispered the boy, grinning at them in the moonslight.

"Stop prattling and jump," growled Niya.

Gem rolled his eyes. He scampered off and made the leap to the first roof, landing catlike upon the tiles. Loren feared the sound he would make when he landed, but she heard nothing at all when he came down. When she followed him, she found that the rooftop was very solidly built. They could not have made a noise upon it if they tried.

"Stay close, and stop when I do," said Gem, and ran off.

He jumped from one rooftop to the next, always lurking in the shadows of higher buildings when he could. Sometimes he would turn left or right, though Loren saw no reason for it, and then a moment later she would see that they had avoided an obstacle they would not have been able to climb over. The boy's skill was marvelous. Truly he looked at a city the way she did a forest: each one different and yet all of them sharing a common set of rules.

Suddenly Gem stopped. Ahead of them was a building with a second story, though there was another roof on their level to the left.

"Why do you halt?" said Niya. "This is no time for nerves, whelp."

Loren glared at her before speaking to Gem more patiently. "What is it, Gem?"

"I think we must climb this way," said Gem, pointing at the taller building ahead.

"That is a waste of time," said Niya. "We should go around."

"It is too heavily lit," said Gem. "This way keeps us out of the torchlight from the walls."

Niya scowled at him, but Loren spoke first. "Very well. Up it is."

"It is a waste of—" Niya began.

"We will waste more time arguing," said Loren. "If Gem says this is the way to go, I believe him."

The Mystic snorted and turned away. Loren could not understand her frustration with Gem. She had never seemed fond of the boy, but now it was worse. It seemed fear of discovery was wearing on the woman's nerves.

The two-story building was not made of the same granite as the manors, but plaster like the other smaller buildings. There were window ledges and wooden beams to take hold of, and Gem scaled them easily enough. Loren was not quite so quick, but she followed close behind, and Niya's powerful arms propelled her up easily. At the top, Gem reached up and gripped the edge of the tiles, using them to pull himself to the roof. He lowered a hand and took Loren's arm as she did the same. But Niya did not wait for Gem's help, instead grabbing one of the tiles on her own.

With a *clink,* the tile came away in Niya's hand. She lurched away from the wall. For an instant it seemed the Mystic would fall to the cobblestones far below. But Loren had just gained the rooftop, and she threw herself flat to seize Niya's hand. The Mystic slammed back into the wall with a grunt, while Loren clung desperately to the roof, trying to keep herself from sliding over. The tile that had come off spun away, shattering as it struck the cobblestones far below.

"Hurry!" gasped Loren. Niya got her hand atop the roof, and with Gem's help, Loren pulled her up. No sooner had they ducked out of sight than they heard a voice on the ground below. They all froze—but it was no shout of panic or alarm. Peeking back over the edge, Loren saw a solid-looking man in fine green clothes step out the front door of the building atop which they lay. He looked at the tile on the ground for a moment, and then turned his gaze skyward. Loren retreated just in time. There was a long moment of silence. After her pulse had resumed its normal pace, Loren risked another peek. The man had gone, and no alarm had been raised.

"A stroke of luck, that," said Gem.

Loren looked to Niya. The Mystic woman did not look chagrined at her mistake; if anything, she only seemed angrier at Gem. But when he led them to the other end of the roof and helped them climb down,

Niya waited patiently, and followed his lead as he took them farther along the rooftops.

At long last they reached the closest manor. Now that they were up against it, it was even more imposing than it had been when viewed from the streets. The buildings pressed close here, up to its very walls. There was a window just in front of them, and inside was an empty room with no lights. Loren reached out to the window, but it would not budge under her hand. "Locked," she muttered.

There was another window just a few paces down, but it, too, was locked. They tried one after another, but without success. Niya muttered a curse. "The family Yerrin, it seems, are not all fools. Likely it is one duty of the manor guards to ensure all windows on this level are secure."

"The higher floors might be open," said Loren.

"That is my thought," said Niya. "Boy, climb to the next floor and try one of them."

But panic seized Loren's breast, and she shook her head. "No. I will do it."

Niya frowned at her. "He is a better climber."

Loren hesitated. In truth, she was already nervous to have brought Gem this close to the manor. Certainly she did not want him to come inside with them. She did not truly believe that her dreams showed her the future, but the thought of Gem in Gregor's hands—or, worse, the thought of the boy going mad and attacking her—would not leave her mind.

"He should remain here, on guard. If anything goes amiss, he will serve as a lookout, and can come to warn us. His purpose here was only to help us reach the manor, after all."

To her relief, Niya shrugged. "Very well. But we have tarried too long here already. If you wish to lead the way, then lead."

Loren nodded and looked up. There was a window there, and a granite ledge below it, just a pace out of reach. She stepped back and then took a running leap, feet scrabbling on the wall. Her fingers just reached the ledge. From there she was able to pull herself up enough to grip the bottom edge of the windowsill, and then it was a simple matter to stand upon the ledge. She tried lifting the window. It swung open easily, without a sound.

"It is open," she whispered down.

"Very well," said Niya. Without a glance at Gem, she jumped up and caught the ledge. Loren slipped into the room, and Niya was not a moment behind her.

Loren leaned back out the window. "Wait here for us," she said to Gem. "If you hear sounds of alarm from within, ready yourself to run. If you think for a moment that you are in danger, flee, and do not look back."

"I will not leave you here," said Gem.

She glared at him. "You will. You have pledged yourself to me, and this is the most solemn order I have ever given you. Do you understand?"

He matched her scowl with one of his own, but in the end he nodded.

"Good. We will return as quickly as we may."

Loren drew back into the room. Niya stood facing her, a curious expression on her face. The moment's silence stretched a bit too long, and Loren looked out the window. From this vantage point the city was laid out before them like a blanket of stars, mirroring those in the sky, except that its light was orange to match the silver-blue from above.

"A fine sight," said Niya in a careful tone.

"I suppose so," said Loren.

In truth the city only filled her with dread, for she could not see it without seeing her dream. Niya inclined her head, inserting herself into Loren's field of view.

"I meant to say . . . earlier, during the fight in the jungle. You saw my wound."

Loren blinked at her for a moment, uncomprehending. Then she remembered the terrible scars at Niya's throat. "Yes."

The Mystic searched her eyes. But then she shrugged with a humorless smile. "I hide it behind this collar. I think it is hideous to look at, and some others have agreed."

"Few of us go through life without wounds, and many of them scar. I am only amazed that you survived such an injury. It looks as though your throat was cut more than once."

Niya's face turned a deep, angry red, and Loren balked.

"I am sorry. I did not mean to bring forth a grievous memory."

"Grievous indeed," said Niya, though she sounded more angry than mournful. "And impossible to forget."

"You should not let it trouble you," said Loren. "You cannot help the scar, and anyone who remarks upon it is not worth worrying about."

"That is more easily said than believed."

Loren frowned and turned her gaze out the window again. She wished she were anywhere but in this city. Her fear seemed to grow with every passing moment, and as much as she longed to find Damaris lurking within this place, at the same time she dreaded the thought that she might.

"Niya, there is something dangerous here."

Loren paused. She had not meant to speak at all. The words had come out almost against her will. But as Niya looked at her, she pressed on heedlessly. "I think Damaris is here. I am almost certain of it. And worse, there is a man, her bodyguard—a man named Gregor. He is dangerous, mayhap more dangerous than anyone I have faced in my travels, and—"

Without warning, Niya seized her shoulders and kissed her. The second their lips met, Loren's worries vanished into sparks of bliss. Her own hands rose to Niya's waist, though she did not mean to move them. More than a month of desire was now finally real, and she only wanted all the city to fade away, and all the world beyond it as well—

And then she remembered Chet, waiting for her in a tavern just beyond the wall. She pulled back, pushing Niya away.

"No," she said quietly. "Clearly I have not spoken plainly enough. I love Chet."

"And I have told you I do not care for love, nor desire it," said Niya, wearing a self-satisfied smile. "And you seem far less convinced of your words than the last time you said them. I do not regret it. You deserved a kiss, and likely needed one as well."

I did, thought Loren. But she shook her head. "You could hardly have chosen a worse time."

Niya sighed and rolled her eyes, though her smile did not leave her. "Very well. Until another time, then. In the meanwhile, let us go and find a merchant."

TWENTY-SIX

They listened at the room's door for a long moment, but could hear no sound in the hallway beyond. Loren opened it cautiously and poked her head outside. There was no one in sight. She slipped out of the room, and Niya followed. At the end of the hall they found a stairway and took it up to the next floor. Loren waved Niya back and peeked down the hallway, but it was as empty as the first, and the rooms looked all the same.

"Not here," she said. "Let us go up another floor."

"Why?" said Niya. "What are you looking for?"

Loren thought back to Damaris' room at the Wyrmwing Inn in Cabrus. It had fairly glowed in its opulence, a wide and spacious place with drapes and fine furniture. "We seek Damaris, or someone of similar stature who would know where she is. These floors are filled with small drawing rooms and apartments, doubtless for the servants, or mayhap only for storage. If I know the family Yerrin, the higher we go, the more important will be the people who dwell there."

So they ascended. At each landing, Loren inspected the hall beyond. Her guess was right—upon each level, the doors lessened in number, and soon they were worked with fine designs in gold. But they had not climbed much higher before they heard the tramp of heavy boots coming down the stairs towards them.

"Into the hall!" whispered Loren.

They ducked around the corner of the stairwell door just in time. After the steps passed, Loren and Niya poked their heads back out. They saw four Yerrin guards, who soon vanished around the next curve in the stairs.

"We should expect to see more of them from this point on, I think," said Loren.

But Niya smiled at her. "Did you not see them? Within the manor, they have closed helmets."

At first Loren did not understand. But after a moment, she matched Niya's grin with one of her own.

The next hallway up was not empty. They saw a pair of guards within it, walking together away from the stairwell. They had little time to lose before the guards would be out of sight. After nodding to each other, they ran silently up behind.

Each threw an arm around one of the guards' necks. Niya bore her opponent to the ground and squeezed until she fell unconscious. But Loren's guard almost slipped from her grasp. He struggled mightily, reaching for a dagger at his belt.

Loren caught his wrist, struggling to twist his arm behind him. Niya rose and drove a fist into the guard's stomach. He doubled over. Snatching his helmet away, Niya brought it crashing down on the back of his head. Finally he collapsed to the floor.

"Easy enough," said Loren, panting.

Niya snorted.

They found an empty room and left the guards trussed up within, tied with some drapes they tore from the windows. Loren used her hunting knife to cut two strips of the cloth into gags. They had already stripped the guards of their uniforms, and put them on over their own clothes, including the helmets. The guards had gloves, too, so that no bit of their skin was exposed.

"Your clothes are a better fit than mine," said Niya, squeezing her hands into the gloves.

"I cannot help my lithe figure," said Loren with a smirk.

Niya eyed her. "Nor should you."

That turned Loren's cheeks a deep red, and she

chastised herself. She must try to control her tongue, and not encourage Niya in her advances.

Loren folded her black cloak and shoved it underneath her chain mail and leather shirt. It gave her the appearance of a paunch. Niya abandoned her own brown cloak in favor of the guard's green one. They made their way back to the stairwell with more confidence and climbed two more floors without seeing anyone else.

On the third story up, they ran into another pair of guards escorting a merchant. At first Loren thought to walk straight past them, pretending to be about their own business. Then she saw Niya draw aside. She did the same at the last moment, and they stood at attention as the merchant passed them by. The other guards gave them a brief glance, but the merchant did not even appear to notice they were there, and soon he was out of sight around the corner.

"Remember that we are guards, and therefore servants," said Niya.

"I will not forget again. You have some skill in subterfuge."

Though she could not see it beneath the helmet, Loren heard a fierce smile in Niya's voice. "I prefer a knife, but deception will serve in a pinch. Should we pursue the ones we just passed? He was a merchant. Mayhap he would know something."

Loren considered it for a moment, but then shook her head. "We would have to fight the guards, and would be too exposed while we did so. We should look for one in the hallways, not the stairwell, and follow them to a room where they may be subdued without witnesses."

They began to inspect the halls more carefully. They walked the entirety of each floor, striding with impunity as though they were on an errand. Their surroundings began to grow more elaborate. Now even the side tables in the halls were well-carved, and the sconces for the torches were wrought with intricate designs. No one else, guard or merchant, spared them so much as a glance. Loren was reminded again of when she and Jordel had pulled this very trick in the Greatrocks. For a painful moment, she wished he was here now. Though Niya was a competent enough companion, she was no replacement.

On the next floor, they passed by someone alone—a wizened merchant in a fine green dress. As soon as she saw the woman coming, Loren started, and only just managed to keep herself from coming to an abrupt halt in the middle of the hallway. Once they were alone again, Niya stopped and turned to her.

"What is wrong? Who was that?"

"Her face . . . I remember it from somewhere." And then it came to her in a flash. "Her name is Gretchen. She kept Damaris' accounts. I saw her when I first met the merchant, and Annis as well."

"We will not find a better target than that," said

Niya. "And we have spent too long in this place already. Who knows but that the guards we subdued have awoken, and are struggling free from their bonds even now."

They turned and went hastily back the way they had come, and soon they could see Gretchen just ahead of them. The woman reached the stairwell and went up to the next floor. Niya and Loren followed close behind. In the hallway, Gretchen entered the second door on her left, closing it behind her with a soft *click*. Loren and Niya stopped just outside it and looked at each other.

"There might be guards inside," said Loren.

"There might not," said Niya. "And we are out of time."

She opened the door before Loren could answer and strode confidently inside. With little other choice, Loren followed—but inside, they both froze.

They were in a sitting room. In the center was a small table surrounded by plush chairs, upon one of which Gretchen now sat. There were no guards in the room, but there was one other person—a young man with dark hair and a scar that split his chin. Hewal.

Gretchen and Hewal looked up the moment the door opened. When Loren and Niya paused, Gretchen frowned.

"What is it?" Her voice was a shrill bark, like a small dog that thought itself a mastiff. "Are you lost?"

Loren could not think of what to say. Thankfully Niya's wits were quicker. "No, my lady," she said, deepening her voice to disguise it. She pushed the door shut and took a step into the room. Loren followed. "Only we have been sent with orders. It appears the two of you may be in grave danger."

The old woman's brows flew skywards. "Us? This is the Golden Manor, you twit. What possible danger could there—"

But Loren saw Hewal's eyes go wide, and he shot to his feet. Niya was quicker, lunging forwards and tackling the man to the ground. Loren went for Gretchen, clapping a hand over her mouth and seizing her arm as she tried to rise. Niya and Hewal wrestled for a moment, but she was stronger, and held him down while she drew her knife. She held the point of it under his chin.

"Be still, weremage," she said. "If I see the slightest glow in your eyes, I will plunge this into your brain. I know you cannot heal that wound away."

Keeping one hand over Gretchen's mouth, Loren reached up to remove her helmet. When it came off, Gretchen's eyes narrowed, and then in a moment they shot wide. She screamed something, but the words were muffled under Loren's hand.

"Yes, Gretchen." Loren gave her a grim smile. "It has been a long time. We have questions for you, and you would do well to answer them."

Hewal was nearly spitting with rage. "How?" he said. "How did you find me here?"

"You can never escape the Nightblade, weremage," said Loren. "Remember that well." *He does not need to know that we did not come here looking for him,* she thought. It would have made her laugh out loud, if the situation had been less serious.

Hewal snorted. "I suppose Kal's spies are not so incompetent as I had believed."

Struck by a thought, Loren raised her brows. "Oh, do you think you deceived Kal? You are mistaken. He has known of your deception a long time, and played you for a fool all the while."

Joy coursed through her as she saw his face grow pale—but then he calmed himself and snorted. "You lie. Kal knew nothing, or he would have been more careful with his secrets. If you could hear only half the things I know about him and his precious order . . ."

Despite her best efforts to remain calm, dread seized Loren's heart at his words. But Niya pressed her dagger harder against his skin. He went quiet. Loren saw a small drop of blood appear at the tip of the dagger.

"Be silent, wizard," said Niya. "We seek Damaris. If you wish to live, you will tell us where she may be found. In fact, I offer the two of you this chance: whichever one of you tells us where Damaris is hiding may live. I will take great pleasure in bleeding the other one all over this fine rug."

Hewal glared at her, but Gretchen's eyes went wide with terror. "Do you wish to volunteer?" said Loren.

She took her hand away from Gretchen's mouth, but dropped it to her throat. "Speak. But if you try to scream, I will throttle you."

"I have nothing to say to you, ungrateful wretch." Gretchen tried to spit at her, but the saliva only splashed out on her own chin. "I told Damaris she should have killed you."

"Mayhap she should have," said Loren. "But now she never shall, for I mean to bring her before the King's justice. Tell me where she is, and I will see that that justice is lenient upon you."

"She is far away from you!" hissed Gretchen.

Loren frowned. "She is not here in Dahab, then?"

Gretchen snapped her mouth shut at once, but Loren could see the fear in her eyes and knew it for the truth.

What, then, had her dream shown her? She had seen Damaris here—*here,* in this very city. If that was a lie, then why was Hewal here? Why had she been allowed to see that he was a weremage, or that he would be in this city at all?

Her thoughts were drifting, and she forced herself back to the present. She would have to worry about these things later. Now Niya put her face closer to Hewal's, sneering at him. "The old woman has been the most helpful so far," she said. "You had best contribute something to the conversation, lest I grow bored of you."

Hewal only glared. Niya shrugged and turned back

to Gretchen. "Very well. He does not seem forthcoming. Say on, old woman, and my friend and I will leave you be."

Loren saw Gretchen hesitate, her throat working. "Do not scream," warned Loren.

"She is far away," said Gretchen. "Far from here."

"You have said as much already," said Niya. "Tell us more."

"A fortress. Far to the west. Too strong for you fools to break into."

Niya clutched Hewal's throat tighter and turned the dagger on Gretchen, holding it just under the woman's eye. "What is it called? Where may it be found?"

Gretchen squirmed under Loren's hands, trying to edge away from the knife. "Yewamba! It is Yewamba, it—"

A moment too late, Loren saw the flash of light in Hewal's eyes. He slapped Niya's hand away and sprang, and as he moved, great claws of bone shot from his hands. But he did not attack Niya, nor Loren. He plunged the knifelike claws into Gretchen's throat and chest. One of them sliced open the back of Loren's hand, and she recoiled in pain. Hewal did not press his attack, but jumped back and away from them both.

Niya flipped her knife around, but Hewal flung a chair at her just as she threw it, and the blade went wide. Gretchen collapsed on the couch, blood spurting from her throat to cover Loren's chain mail.

"The window!" cried Loren.

But she was not fast enough. Hewal turned and flung himself into the window, curling his body into a ball. The glass burst outwards with a great crash. The glow of Hewal's eyes grew brighter. In a heartbeat he was gone, and a crow flew away into the night, cawing madly. Loren seized Gretchen's shoulders, trying to sit her up so that she did not drown in her own blood.

"Leave her," said Niya. "She is dead already."

It was true. A spark of life remained in the woman's terror-filled eyes, but already it was fading. Loren gritted her teeth and stood back, pressing her sliced hand hard into her sleeve to stanch the flow of blood. Niya went to the window and looked down.

"Guards heard the window breaking," she said. "It is time we left."

"But we do not know where this Yewamba is," said Loren.

"We can discover that later, or so I hope."

"I am covered in blood. I cannot walk out of here like this, for they will know that something is amiss."

Niya's eyes grew narrow as she studied Loren. For a long, curious moment, Loren felt that she was being judged, as though Niya weighed one grim option against another. Then the Mystic's face relaxed.

"Well, I hope you do not expect me to leave you here. We have a mission to find Damaris, you and I, and I will not let you abandon it so easily."

That forced a laugh from Loren. "Then I hope you have an idea."

"Mayhap we can follow our quarry," said Niya, tossing her head towards the window. "Only we cannot fly, and shall have to climb."

Loren went to the window and leaned out to look down. "It is a long way."

"Not so long as the stairwell, if we must fight our way down. And I do not think you will be much use if it comes to swords, which it surely will."

"You are correct," said Loren. "Very well. These outfits will no longer help us." Quickly they shed their guard uniforms, and Loren donned her black cloak once more. From Niya's discarded cloak she cut a strip of cloth and tied it around the cut on her hand. She lifted the window to climb out.

"A moment," said Niya, seizing her cloak and drawing her back. "You have proven to be something of a lure that summons luck. You found Hewal when we did not even seek him. We shall need more of that luck if we are to escape. I think you should give me another kiss."

For a moment Loren could not believe her own ears. "Before was not the time for such idiocy, and now is even less so."

Niya only widened her eyes in mock fear. With two hands clasped to her heart, she simpered, "Without your luck, I fear even to attempt the climb."

Loren wanted to strike her. But in her mind's eye she could almost see the guards who even now must surely be rushing up the tower towards them. She darted forwards and gave Niya a brief kiss, and then slapped her shoulder, hard. "For your stupidity."

"A small price to pay," said Niya, and climbed out the window.

TWENTY-SEVEN

The way was slow, and Loren felt horribly vulnerable on the outside of the building. As she climbed, she kept a careful eye out for Hewal. In bird form, it would be easy for the weremage to spot them and warn the Yerrin soldiers. But no crow wheeled in the sky. Hewal must have flown to the ground and entered the Golden Manor from there, hoping to catch them on the stairwell.

As luck had it, they came down not far from where they had left Gem. The boy jumped across two rooftops to join them before they reached the bottom. By that time, the whole compound rang with shouts of alarm and the sound of tramping boots.

Gem stared at them both in wide-eyed wonder. "By the sky above, what did the two of you do in there? You have mustered an army."

"Time enough for that later," said Loren. "Now it is time for running."

Run they did, with Gem leading the way across the rooftops once more. This time he did not suggest they climb the higher building. He took them in a dead sprint around it—and then he cut right, running straight for the wall.

Loren skidded to a halt. "Gem, this way is exposed."

"Every way is exposed now. You have kicked the anthill."

He was right. Guards ran all along the wall. They were mustering to move through the compound in rank and file, searching for the intruders. The quickest way was safest now.

The wall was close. There were two guards straight ahead. Just before the three of them reached the last rooftop, the guards spotted them. Loren slowed in her run. But Niya sped past her.

"No time," said the Mystic, and she made the leap.

One of the guards raised his sword, but she caught his wrist, wrenching him to the side and clearing a space for Loren and Gem to land beside her. With her other hand she struck the guard hard in the throat, and as he choked for breath, she pushed him back over the wall. He fell to the street beyond with a scream, which ended abruptly as he struck the cobblestones.

The other guard came for Loren, who sidestepped the woman's wild swing and shoved Gem away. They were pressed close together now, giving no time to think. Loren lunged and slammed the crown of her head into the guard's nose where it was exposed by the helmet. She felt it snap with a wet *crunch*. The guard fell upon her back, stunned. Loren shook away the spots in her eyes.

"Over!" she cried, and nearly flung Gem off the ramparts. But she caught his hands and stooped over the edge, lowering him as far as she could before she let go. He landed well and rolled away, and Loren hopped over after him.

An arrow sailed through the air above her, and she flinched, losing her grip before she meant to. She almost landed straight on her ankles, and only just managed to roll with the impact. Her tailbone came down hard, and she groaned as she regained her feet. A moment later, Niya came crashing down beside her, turning over and over as she rolled across the street.

"Get up," said Gem, pulling on her arm. "They are almost upon us."

He dragged Loren to her feet and tried to flee with her. But Loren went to Niya and hauled her up. The Mystic's ankle had twisted, and she limped when she tried to walk.

Loren threw an arm around her and half-dragged her away from the wall. They passed the body of the guard Niya had thrown over. Loren tried to ignore it. Mayhap he was still alive, but Loren thought she would feel better if she did not know for certain.

They ducked into the first alley they saw, and Gem led them around two different turns before they came upon a well-populated street.

"Which way to the others?" said Loren.

"This way," said Gem. "At least, I think so."

"You do not remember?" growled Niya.

He frowned at her. "Do you? Then follow me." And off he ran. Loren pulled Niya after him, trying to ignore the woman's grumbling.

Gem was right in his guess after all, and soon they reached the tavern. Chet and Uzo were waiting outside, and Chet's face was nearly chalk-white. But it flushed with color again when he saw Loren, and he ran forwards to help with Niya.

"What happened?" he said in a low voice. "Half of the city seems to be in an uproar."

"Why does everyone want an explanation while danger still looms?" said Loren. "Get the others out of there. We should ride as far from this place as we can. Let us find an inn on the other side of the city."

They all made ready to leave. Loren went to help Niya up on her horse. "I am not badly hurt," said Niya, scowling at her. "It was only a little turn."

"Do not act so surly when I am only trying to help

you," said Loren. "It would seem I am not so lucky as you thought."

"Yet I am alive. And I have the memory of you kissing me by your own choice."

Loren's eyes went wide, and she looked over her shoulder. But Chet was a few paces away, tending to his saddle, and had not heard. She leaned in closer. "I would rather you did not speak of it."

Niya grinned at her. "Is that an order, Nightblade?"

"It is. You can mount your horse on your own." Loren went to Midnight and climbed into the saddle. She took no small pleasure in seeing Niya struggle to do the same.

They rode off, south and away from the Yerrin manors. No one gave them a second glance, yet still Loren felt as though eyes were upon her. She drew up her hood to hide her face, and kept a wary lookout for anyone wearing green. When they had almost reached the city's southern wall, they found an inn with a sizable stable, and there they pulled to a halt.

"See to the horses and meet us within," Niya told Shiun and Jormund. Then she turned to Loren. "I could use a drink, and you deserve one."

Though Loren was still irritated with the Mystic, she could not deny that a cup of wine sounded like the finest thing in the world. Once inside they ordered food and drink and had it brought to a table near the back, out of view of the front door.

The moment they found their seats, Weath leaned

forwards. "Did they recognize you?" she said. "Will they follow you, or trace this back somehow?"

"Yes," said Loren. "Hewal was there. He saw me plainly, and must have guessed who Niya was under her helmet."

Uzo smirked. "I am sure you have heard this before, but your green eyes leave you ill-suited to life as a spy."

"It was not Loren's fault."

Niya and Chet said the words at the same time. They glared at each other for a long moment before turning away.

"Very well," said Weath. "What did you learn?"

Loren looked around, conscious that there could be ears listening in any corner. "The one we seek is not in the city. She resides in a fortress—a place called Yewamba, far to the west of here."

"Then we have what we came for," said Weath. "We should make ready to leave. I suggest we spend one night here, for we are all weary from the road, and the three of you need rest even more. But we should ride before first light. Uzo and Jormund can buy us supplies for the journey back to Ammon."

"Thank goodness," said Chet. "Even on this side of the city, I cannot shake my fear that we could be found at any moment."

But Loren remained silent. Then she realized that Niya, too, had yet to answer. Their gazes locked across the table.

Gem looked back and forth between the two of

them with wide eyes. "Oh, darkness take us," muttered the boy.

"We are going to Yewamba," said Niya.

Chet gawked at her. "We certainly are not. We are going back to Ammon to bring our news to Kal."

"Kal will receive his news," said Loren quietly. "We will send someone with a letter. Jormund, I think."

For a moment it seemed Chet thought she was joking, for a grin played at his lips, coming and then fading again. It was the face of someone trying to understand a joke, and it pained Loren to see it. But when she did not smile in turn, he shook his head slowly.

"You cannot be serious. Loren, you are not this foolish."

"She is far from foolish," said Niya. "She is wiser than you are, at any rate. We have waited for weeks—months, in fact—for an opportunity to bring our enemies to heel. Now we have such a chance. But it will not last long, for Hewal will surely send word of what has happened here tonight, and then our target will hide herself in another dark hole. I will not waste our opportunity, and neither will the Nightblade."

Chet and Weath both began to speak, but Loren cut them off with a raised hand. "Niya is correct. We left Ammon to accomplish a purpose."

"That purpose was information," said Chet.

"Information leading to a capture," said Loren. "But if we do not act on what we know, that will never happen. If we had learned that the one we seek was in some outland kingdom, some place like Hedgemond, that would be one thing. But this fortress, wherever it is, lies far to the west. If we ride the long distance back to Ammon to tell Kal what we have learned, and then devise a plan, and *then* set out after her, weeks will have passed. Even if winter ends tomorrow and not a single storm troubles us the whole while, the chance to catch Damaris will have vanished."

"So you would rather ride west without any plan at all," said Chet. "You understand, I hope, why I see little wisdom in that."

"We will devise our plan upon the road," said Niya. "That is how commanders in the field are supposed to act."

Chet seemed to sense that he was losing, for his frustration grew more plain with every word. "But you do not even know where you are going," he said, spreading his hands into the empty air. "This fortress you speak of could be anywhere."

Loren looked to Annis. The girl had remained silent through the whole argument, staring into her own lap. "Annis."

The girl jumped. "What?"

"You know where it is."

"I . . ." Annis' eyes went wide, and she looked around at them. "I do not know *precisely* where it is. Yet there is—that is, when I was with Kal, and we studied the maps and the records, there was a place. Something I took note of. It *was* to the west of here, and it was like—

like a sort of hole, but for coin. No roads passed through it. There were no cities, only mountains. Yet all around it, numbers disappeared from ledgers without explanation. Garrisons marched from fortresses to reinforce some other stronghold, but that place was never named. Food and other supplies—all went missing. And I have heard the name of Yewamba before. It was spoken in the halls of my family. It is a place we called home in the past, a long-abandoned fortress of great power."

At the words *long-abandoned fortress,* Loren felt her hackles rise. She saw the image from her dream again: Damaris standing in a vast cavern, bathed in a single pool of light. Quickly she pushed the image away.

Chet was at a loss for a moment. But he recovered, planting a hand on the table and shaking his head. "No. This is madness, all of it. You made a vow to Kal. Will you break it?"

"I vowed that I would take no action against our target in Dahab," said Loren. "And I will obey that vow to the letter."

"You know that is not what he meant."

"I must agree with Chet," said Weath. "Riding out on our own seems foolhardy."

"It is," said Loren. "And I will not ask you to come with me. I am no fool. I know this goes directly against Kal's wishes. You risk his wrath if you accompany me. Neither, Chet, would I ask you to follow me into darkness and danger. I did not do so in Northwood, and I will not now. But I am going to Yewamba. Always I have done what I thought was best. Sometimes that brought great sorrow, and not just for myself. But it is also the only reason we know as much as we know. It is the reason the High King is prepared to fight this war in the first place. Before we left the Seat, she told me that the nine kingdoms were more important than any of us. I still believe that. And this is what I must do to preserve them—and to mete out justice for a friend who fell before his time. Were Jordel here, I think he would do the same."

That cast most of them into silence. But Chet glared into his lap and shook his head. "You speak of justice, but I hear revenge behind your words."

"Then go to Ammon," said Loren. "Indeed, I would feel better if you did. There is no doubt that I ride upon the more dangerous path. Turn your road from mine, and take the children with you."

"Not likely," said Gem. "I go where you go, as I have always done. Well, since we met."

"I will not turn away either," said Annis quietly. "I cannot say with honesty that this is a wise course. But I think . . . I think it is the right one, and I must follow it. For the same reason I came with you this far already. Though I do not know what help I will be."

"You have been tremendous help already," said Loren. "We would not even know where we were going, were it not for you. Do you see? Wit above might."

Annis smiled at her. And beside the girl, Chet shook his head and sighed, even as his scowl deepened.

"Of course I will not abandon you now, Loren," he murmured. "Not ever, not while I draw breath. But my fear is not for myself, nor for the others. It is for you, Loren. I do not wish to follow you only to witness your doom."

Weath looked as though she wished to say a great deal more. But when she gave Niya a searching look, the captain's expression remained unmoved.

"Very well," said Weath, lowering her gaze. "I will send the others out for supplies. We can be ready to ride by first light."

TWENTY-EIGHT

They slipped through the city's gate in a grey morning, passing through a wet chill that hung in the air but did not fall as rain. The guards at the gate seemed more attentive than they had before. Loren guessed the uproar at the Yerrin manors had something to do with that. But she traded her black cloak for a plain brown one, and they rode out in twos and threes, the way they had entered the city, and no one marked their passing.

Just out of sight of the city walls, they sent Jormund away to ride east. Loren gave him his instructions and bid him farewell, a little apart from the others.

"This holds all of the information we were able to gather," she said, placing a scroll in his hands. She had dictated the message upon it to Gem. "It also tells him that we ride west for Yewamba. He will no doubt be angry. You must make it clear to him that it was my decision, and that you had nothing to do with it."

Jormund gave her a wry smile. "Do you think I would distance myself from you so? I will tell him it was my counsel that sent you west, and that I begged to come with you."

Loren smiled at that. "I wish that you could ride with us. We shall miss your sword."

"I hope you do not need it. Fare well, Nightblade."

"Fare well."

He bade good-bye to the rest of the party and then mounted to ride away. Loren and the others watched until he was out of sight, and then they rode west.

From the first day they left Dahab behind them, they noticed a change. Winter's storms no longer battered them as they had before, and while the air was still frigid, at least it was free from rain. The roads west of Dahab were nowhere near so ill-kept as the ones to the east, so their journey was almost pleasant. The month of Martis was nearly past, and winter was just beginning to give way to spring.

When they made camp on the first day, Loren waited until Chet had gone to fetch firewood, and then she went to Niya. "You did something in the manor that I meant to ask you about."

Niya smirked at her. "I did, and I will do it again. Or more, if you but give me half a chance and half an hour."

Loren's cheeks flamed. "Not that. I meant the knife. You threw it at Hewal—just as you did the first time we faced him. You are very good with it."

"As I said, deception and knives are my two great loves. But still you have asked me no question."

"Can you teach me? To throw a knife like that, I mean."

Niya cocked her head slightly. "I thought you were against killing."

"I am. But a knife may be used for other things than death, even when thrown. Or has it escaped your notice that you yourself have not killed Hewal with it?"

That forced a bark of laughter. "It was not for lack of intent, I assure you. But very well. I can teach you to throw, if you wish to learn a fancy trick to entertain your friends. Only you must promise me something."

Loren frowned and spoke in a low murmur. "I will not . . . that is, I will not do again the thing you made me do in Dahab. I should not have done it the once."

"*Made* you do?" said Niya, smiling. She dropped her voice to a murmur as well, as though respecting Loren's wish for secrecy, but it only made her tone more inviting, more electric. "I have given and received enough kisses that I know when a woman is enjoying herself."

Once again, crimson rushed into Loren's face. "If you do not wish to teach me to throw, then just say so."

She turned to leave, but Niya put a hand on her arm, gently holding her in place. "Calm yourself, Nightblade. I did not say anything of the sort, and that was not the promise I meant to extract from you—though I find it interesting that your thoughts went there so quickly. Here is your vow: that you will never throw a knife at me."

That took Loren aback, and she frowned. "Of course not. Why would I?"

Niya grinned. "I am sure I will give you reason. But no, it is only something I was made to promise by the person who taught me."

Loren allowed herself a tiny smile at that. She supposed such a tradition was no evil thing. "Then I give you my word, and easily."

The Mystic led her to a nearby tree and produced a hunting knife from her belt. "You must hold the knife by whichever end is lightest. The weight on the other end will give your throw power. Here."

She placed the blade into Loren's hand, and Loren felt the weight of it. "I would hold this one by the hilt." *But my dagger, I would hold by the blade,* she thought. Her fingers wrapped around Niya's knife.

"Just so, but you must hold it differently," said Niya. She pried Loren's fingers apart—Loren did not miss the heat of the woman's skin upon her own—and adjusted the grip. "Hold it with only your thumb and the first two fingers—three, if the knife is larger. The hardest part is ensuring that the knife does not spin in the air, so that the blade strikes your target, and not the hilt. Do your best, but do not be surprised if it does not work."

Loren drew back and threw. The blade wobbled slightly, but it sped true, and the first finger's breadth of it sank into the bark of the tree. Niya drew back, eyes wide with astonishment.

"It comes to you naturally. And to think, in Ammon you doubted my skills as a teacher."

An urge gripped her, and Loren obeyed it without thinking. She looked the Mystic in the eyes and smiled. "Mayhap in Ammon I was distracted from the lesson."

Niya's smile turned feral. "And what, I wonder, distracted you?"

They paused like that for a moment. Then Loren shook her head and took a step back. "I should not have said that. I did not mean to be untoward."

"I know what you meant, girl. I have told you before, I know when a woman is enjoying herself." Niya went to the tree and removed her knife before walking off. Without looking back, she called over her shoulder, "You have talent, but you need practice to turn that into skill. Use your hunting knife."

Loren watched her go until she felt someone's gaze upon her. She turned quickly, expecting to find Chet.

But it was only Gem, watching her with a curious expression.

"It seems I have some ability when it comes to throwing knives," said Loren.

"I have always wanted to learn to do it," said Gem. "Mayhap you can teach me."

Loren arched an eyebrow. "Me? Niya should instruct you. She is a master at it."

Gem looked the way the Mystic had gone. "I suppose so, but she is . . . an intimidating woman. I do not think she likes me, and would rather learn from you in any case."

"It would be my honor—only let me practice a bit myself, so that I know better how to instruct you."

She threw the knife for an hour before she went to sleep that night. When she stood her watch in the early morning hours, she practiced with her dagger instead of the hunting knife, for no one was awake to see it. Not every throw was as true as her first, but she found herself getting better and better at it. She kept practicing as the days passed, and very soon she could easily land her throw within a hand's breadth of the spot she aimed for.

It was good to have the distraction, for the road was otherwise monotonous. It gave her something to do when they stopped to eat, or to make camp for the night. Though the road was far easier than the one they had taken to Dahab, it was not well traveled, and they would sometimes go two or more days without seeing someone passing by. When they did, they avoided speaking, or giving any greeting more than a nod.

The landscape they traveled was fair enough, Loren supposed, but she preferred the drier, taller trees of the Birchwood to the jungled land they rode through now. The vegetation always seemed damp, and the trees were knotted with great vines that clutched their trunks as if to strangle them. When they did come upon clear, green lands, it felt as if the air grew lighter, and they drank it in with deep breaths. But always the road took them back into the jungle again, where they would spend days at a time beneath a canopy of leaves so thick that they never saw the sun.

They came often upon smaller side roads that led off deeper into the jungle. Many were marked on their maps, and ran in the same direction they traveled. But when Shiun suggested they use those roads, Niya shook her head.

"It is no use trying to use back ways and lesser-known paths," she said. "Now more than ever we require speed. If we can reach Yewamba fast enough, Hewal will not have enough time to warn Damaris of our coming."

"Could he not remain in bird form, and fly there in only a few days?" said Loren.

"I do not think he is strong enough for that," said Weath. "To hold a shape other than their own, a weremage must keep their concentration, and the greater their change, the harder it becomes. Changing his form so that he looked like another person would be one thing. That requires only the smallest use of power, and many weremages learn to hold such a transformation even as they sleep. But it would be a powerful weremage indeed who could maintain the form of a bird, or any beast, for days on end. And if Hewal were so strong in his magic, he would likely have turned into something far more fearsome than a bear when last we fought him."

"How do you know these things?" said Gem, eyes alight with curiosity. "I thought you were an alchemist."

"Weremagic and alchemy are mirrors of each other," said Weath. "Indeed, they can sense each other, so that I can tell when a spell of either branch is used near me, unless the wizard has learned to conceal it."

"Can they do so?" said Annis, arching an eyebrow. "I have never heard of this."

"Magic has many secrets," said Weath, shrugging. "The children of merchants rarely learn them unless they are wizards themselves, for what would be the purpose? As for your question—yes, a wizard may conceal their spells after much practice—and the smaller the spell, the easier to hide it."

"I am surprised to hear you call them alchemy and weremagic," said Loren. "Xain insisted the branches had different names. He called himself an elementalist."

"He is a noble," chuckled Weath. "I am a farmer's daughter from Dorsea. I never cared for the frivolities that the Academy tried to force upon the students."

Loren looked at her again, raising a brow in surprise. She had met few enough Dorseans, other than the taciturn villagers they had met for one terrible night as they fled east across that kingdom. They had been reserved and easily offended, much like the people in tales Loren had heard of Dorseans all her life. But Weath was kind and generous to the point of fault, and always the one to calm tensions among the party. She was curious if Weath knew that Loren was from Selvan, and for the first time she found herself wondering if Dorseans grew up with tales of Selvan's people as well.

The days passed quickly, if quietly, for the jungle sometimes made them nervous to speak too much. It was as though the verdant growth itself was listening to them, and was none too pleased by what it heard. The wildlife was as colorful as the vegetation. They learned from Uzo that they must not touch any of the brightly-colored frogs, for some of them had poison in their skin. Most snakes, too, were venomous. In fact it seemed that so many animals in this place were venomous that Loren wondered what people ate.

But while the creatures around them bore little resemblance to the animals of her home, they were often breathtaking in their beauty. Uzo, however, hardly spared them a second glance. Loren soon realized that to him, these were as commonplace as starlings in the Birchwood. She wondered if he had ever been to one of the southern forests, and if so, whether the squirrels and rabbits were as wondrous to him as these animals were to her.

"I think we are upon the right road," said Gem, when nearly a week of travel had passed. Some of the others gave him odd looks. He grinned at them from his seat beside Loren. "The sky itself has stopped hampering our journey. Why else would it spare us its storms, except as a sign that we are going where we are meant to go?"

That drew a chuckle from most of them. Even Uzo smiled, though he often seemed annoyed by Gem's antics and never-ending optimism. "This journey has taught me that Elves are real. I suppose I can believe in your signs and portents as well."

Gem did not stop beaming at that for the rest of the day.

But though the mood of most of the party had risen considerably, Chet's only grew worse the farther they rode. He would not acknowledge Niya at all unless absolutely necessary, and then he would say only one or two words at a time. He was curt with the rest of them as well, and would often make snide remarks. When asked to help gather firewood, or hunt, he would sometimes mutter, "We would not need to do so if we were riding in the right direction." When they made camp each night, he made a point of sleeping out of Loren's reach within their tent.

For the first several days she bore it silently, for she thought his ill mood might fade after a time. Gem kept trying to entice him into conversation, though Chet never seemed willing. Then, on the tenth day of their ride, Gem asked curiously why Chet and Loren and Shiun did not keep their bows strung while they rode.

"Because we know how bows work," snapped Chet. "And we do not want to break ours. If you wish to learn about archery, find an instructor."

Gem balked. Loren fixed Chet with a steely glare, and then looked over her shoulder at the boy. "Gem, ride with Annis for a while. I must ask Shiun a question about the road ahead. Chet, come with me."

Chet had gone sullen. He could no doubt sense her anger, and must have known this was no ride for pleasure. "She is not far ahead," he said lamely.

"Come," she said, and nudged Midnight into a canter. She heard the hoofbeats of his horse behind her a moment later.

When they were out of sight of the others, she turned from the road down a side path. It led up a hill, and Loren slowed to a walk. He followed behind her silently, for which she was grateful—if he had made some snide remark about their course, she might have struck him. The path soon took them up to a crest that looked over flatlands to the north, running to a great lake in the far distance. She stopped and turned Midnight so that they faced each other.

"You must stop undermining this mission."

"It is a fool's errand. It is not safe, Loren."

"Of course it is not safe," she said angrily. "Where is safety to be found in this time? Nowhere in Underrealm, that is for certain."

"So your intent, then, is to seek danger? How does that seem a wise course?"

"My intent is to help stop this war. Unless the High King and those who serve her stop the Necromancer—"

"Then let the High King stop them," said Chet. "You have done enough."

"Nothing is enough until the danger has passed," said Loren, shaking her head. "The threat only grows."

"And so does the threat to *you,*" said Chet. "I could bear it when you entered Enalyn's service, for if you were determined to join in this battle, it seemed better to have the power of the Seat at your back. I thought you would be safer in Ammon, far from all the battles that have yet been fought. But this . . . this is not just foolish, it is foolhardy beyond reckoning."

"You thought," said Loren, rolling her eyes. "When will you learn that your thoughts are your own? They are not mine. I never planned to seek safety."

"Why did you even leave the forest, then?" said Chet, shouting now. He nudged his horse forwards so that they were within arm's reach of each other. "You *said* you left because of your parents. They are gone now, Loren. You can do anything you want to—"

"Of course I can do anything I want!" she cried. "I *always* could, without any need for your permission. And this is the life I choose."

Chet went stock still. He stared at her for a long while as she sat there, her shoulders heaving, barely restraining the urge to throw him from his saddle and pummel his foolish head. And in the silence, Loren saw the dawning realization in his eyes. It was the look of a man who had been speaking to someone in a mask, only to have the mask ripped away and the person beneath look nothing like he thought.

"It is," he said, his voice suddenly small. "It *is* what you choose."

And suddenly Loren felt that she, too, saw someone entirely new to her. In her eyes, Chet again became the young boy who had made her promise to dance with him, the boy who had followed her with doe's eyes around their village. She did not know what she had seen him as only a moment before. That image of him was wiped away so completely that it was as though it had never existed, and now he was little more than a child again.

Of course he is a child, she thought. *You both are, if you would only be honest with yourself.* But pride kept her from giving voice to the thought.

"Do you enjoy this, Loren?"

Her fury had burned a bit lower in the long silence, but she was still angry as she shrugged. "I—of course I do not *enjoy* it. I do not enjoy danger, or the deaths of those I love. Jordel died, and Albern, and Mag with Sten by her side. Yet that is why I can do nothing else. That is why I must go on—because they cannot. You have told me often of your plans, or at least your desires, to run away from all this. You say you want to hide away in some forgotten corner of Underrealm and let this great war pass us by, like hiding in a hollow tree against a raging storm. I can never do that, Chet."

"I thought you wanted to, once," said Chet. "I thought we both wanted to run away together."

"Because that was better than the life my parents deigned to give me. But now I could not live with myself. I could not abandon the nine kingdoms or the people I love. And that is *because* of my parents, Chet. That is what they would do—run away, look after themselves, never giving a thought to anyone else. I have roamed too far and seen too much, and I love too many. A merchant's child, a city urchin, a fallen wizard, and yes, even you, you great idiot. I love you all, and more besides, and all of you will suffer if darkness is allowed to win."

Chet looked at her a moment longer before turning away. "I cannot live my life for others. Not anymore. I want to live in safety, as long as I can, and I want you to be safe. That is all I want, Loren. I do not care for Underrealm, but only for you. The nine kingdoms mean nothing to me. Not next to a pair of green eyes."

"That is some bard's sentiment, Chet," said Loren. "It is not anything useful."

He did not answer, or even look at her. Slowly he turned his horse and rode back towards the others, leaving her alone on the hilltop.

— 288 —

TWENTY-NINE

They reached Feldemar's western lands three days later. Annis told them they were close. Loren had often consulted with her during the journey, huddling together over their map, and she had pointed out the place where she thought Yewamba must be located. As she had said, there was nothing marked there. The closest thing was a small town nearby, a place called Sarafu. It was little more than a village, but it was one of the areas from which much coin and many soldiers had vanished.

"If there is a road to Yewamba, we may find a sign

of it in Sarafu," said Annis. "At the very least, the area around it will be our best hope to start looking."

They could not ride into the town, for it would not do for the Yerrins to learn that a party matching their description had come there. Instead they set up camp in the jungle an hour's walk away. They sent Uzo and Shiun into the place to buy supplies and ask after information. Hewal had never met either of them, other than during their brief fight south of Ammon. Loren hoped he would not recognize either of them by their description, if he heard any word about two strangers arriving to the town.

The Mystics returned with no information that would help. They had not asked after the fortress by name, of course, but no one in town seemed to have heard of any military movements, and they had spied no Yerrin activity at all. If the family Yerrin was indeed operating in Sarafu, they did so in secret.

They began their search the day after they arrived, splitting the party in two. Loren led Chet and Weath riding north along the foot of the mountains, while Niya took Uzo and Shiun south. They followed roads when there were roads to follow, and dove off into the countryside when there were not. Gem and Annis remained at the camp, looking after their possessions.

Once again, Loren found herself at the foot of the Greatrock Mountains. These were the northern reaches of the same range, after it turned northwest and cut across Dorsea. Here they formed Feldemar's western border, just as they formed Selvan's in the south. As they had ridden west, she had feared that the sight of the mountains might call to mind painful memories of Jordel. But these peaks were so different from the ones they had traveled together that she could hardly believe they were the same range. In the south, the peaks were tall but gentle, peaked with snow atop the grey and brown of rock and soil. In Feldemar, the jungle ran straight up the sides of the mountains to the very top, even now, in winter, and their silhouette was like a row of upraised knife blades against the sky.

The first long day's search revealed nothing, and they returned to camp defeated. Niya came back shortly after Loren, and from the slump of her shoulders Loren thought she could tell how successful they had been. But she rose from her place by the fire and went to them, regardless.

"Did you see anything?"

"Nothing," said Niya, shaking her head. "We will ride farther tomorrow."

"As will we."

And so they did. Loren led the others galloping north on the best road they could find, passing in a rush the landscape that they had searched in detail the day before. When they reached lands they had not yet searched, they slowed once more to renew their hunt. But that day proved just as fruitless as the first, and their heads hung still lower by the time they had returned to the camp. This time Niya came back first. She, too, had been unsuccessful.

They were a morose party that night. As they sat eating a meager meal around the fire, they rarely looked at each other. Niya spit a bit of gristle into the flames, and the sound was so loud that Annis jumped.

"We might think of moving the camp," said Niya.

"But which way?" said Loren. "If we move north, it may take us farther away from Yewamba—but the same is true if we move south."

"We know it is not here," said Uzo. "I say we flip the coin."

"It is fourteen days since we left Dahab," said Loren. "Surely word has reached Yewamba by now. We are giving Damaris too much time to prepare."

"And what do you suggest, Nightblade?" said Niya, raising her hands in exasperation. "If you know of a wiser course, then tell us, and we will follow it."

Loren frowned and looked into the fire. Of course she had no better idea, and they all knew it. But if they took the camp in the wrong direction, their whole mission here might end in disaster.

After a moment's silence, Weath spoke quietly. "Mayhap this is a matter best left to daylight. During the night, all roads may look dark, and choosing between them becomes more difficult."

"That seems wise," said Gem brightly, smiling at the rest of them. The smile was not returned.

Gregor stood before her.

As before, the man was giant-sized, larger even than he was in life. His hands looked as though he could crush her to a pulp between his fingers; his massive legs were like oak trunks. He was so large that the trees around him seemed dwarfish, though the tops of them still stretched over his head. Now his face was not wasted, as it had been before. And his eyes were not sunken, but smoldered with a dark light, as though he were a wizard who had eaten magestones.

"I told her to kill you," he said. His voice was not thunder now, but the roar of the ocean, the inexorable tide that in time tore down even mighty mountains.

Loren wanted to turn and flee, but her feet were rooted in place. She looked around in a panic. It was Feldemar, the very land she had been searching for the past two days. Gregor stood between two peaks, peaks that stretched impossibly far above them both, yet seemed small and insignificant next to the giant.

Then, Loren saw that they were not quite alone. Behind Gregor, making its way down a little path between the peaks, was a caravan. It was small, only three wagons—but she recognized them as belonging to Damaris, from the caravan she had led when Loren first met her. Awestruck, Loren watched as the wagons vanished one by one.

Her attention was drawn back to Gregor as the

man reached into his cloak. He pulled something out, holding it up before her—and then Loren saw that it was not one thing, but three. Three small, black stones that shone in the moonslight. Magestones.

Gregor flung the stones at her, and she flinched. But in midair they twisted and turned, growing as they moved, lit from within, and when they had finished they had become the bodies of Chet, Annis, and Gem. Her friends fell lifeless at her feet. Now she could move, and she fell to her knees beside them, crying their names. Chet's throat was cut, the same as always. Gem would not attack her now, for his body was broken in a thousand places. Annis had dark bruises around her throat where she had been strangled.

Someone dragged her up by the hair.

"*The knife,*" hissed Auntie's voice. But it was not Auntie who held her—it was Damaris, and the merchant held the same knife as before, an old, rusted, twisted thing, far below her station.

Loren woke just as the knife parted the skin of her throat.

The sound of her scream escaped her, but she came to herself just in time, and stopped it there, so that she only gave a little yelp. Her hands grasped in the darkness, but she did not strike out, did not hit Chet by accident. She only found his arm and gripped it, squeezing it tight, afraid to let go.

Chet shifted in his sleep and rolled onto his back. But he did not wake.

She lay there a while, letting her pulse slow, letting the panic and the fear seep from her, like water from a rag hung up to dry. It was somewhat of a relief to know that the aftereffects of these dreams were easing. Mayhap, in time, she would even wake without feeling the terror they always left behind.

When her pulse had stilled, she sat up and dressed herself before slipping from the tent. Outside, their little clearing was fairly well-lit, for both moons hung directly above them in the sky. She looked up at them and loosed a long breath, feeling the last of the tension leave her.

"Did you dream?"

The voice startled her. It seemed the shock of her nightmare had not entirely fled, for fear went coursing through her limbs again, making them shake. She looked across the camp to find Niya sitting against the base of a tree, on watch.

Of course it would be Niya on duty, she thought.

"I did."

Niya rose and took a step forwards. "And what did you see?"

Loren blanched. "See?"

"In your dream. I heard a brief cry. Did you not have a nightmare?" Niya was studying her face, her head cocked slightly, curious.

"I . . . yes. I did. But I cannot remember it."

"Hm."

She strode forwards, and Loren tensed, though she

did not know why. But Niya went straight past her and towards the trees. Just before she vanished from sight she stopped and turned.

"Will you stand for me, while I relieve myself?"

"Yes, of course," said Loren. "I will take the watch, if you wish it. I do not think I will sleep again tonight."

Niya nodded and vanished.

Loren went to where the Mystic had been sitting and put her back against the same tree. The ground still held some of Niya's warmth, and Loren sighed.

Her thoughts returned to her dream. The peaks of the Greatrocks she knew well enough—they were visible even now, a darker black against the backdrop of stars in the sky. But the path she had seen, the two peaks in particular . . . those were sights she had not seen with her waking eyes.

She thought back to Hewal and how her dreams had shown him in Dahab. Could this be the same? Was Yewamba *in* the mountains themselves? If so, she was correct in her reluctance to move the camp, for they would not find the fortress in the lands surrounding the Greatrocks.

Niya soon returned and entered her tent without a word. Loren stood watch the rest of the night, and when dawn came, she waited impatiently for everyone to rise.

"I have had a thought," she said. "We should not move the camp."

"What, then?" said Niya.

"I wonder if we have been looking in the right place. We have been searching the lands near the mountains. But those lands are open to all, even casual passersby. If Yewamba had been built in such a place, surely it could not have escaped notice all these years. It would be on the maps. But it is not. What if it is *in* the mountains?" Loren looked at Annis and Gem. "We know full well how cleverly a stronghold can be concealed in such a way."

Their expressions grew solemn, and Loren knew they were thinking of the Shade stronghold where Jordel had met his end.

Niya looked to Shiun. The scout shrugged. "It is possible. We could easily have missed a path into the mountains in our searching, for we did not look for such a thing."

"It would make sense," Annis interjected. "I told you that much coin and many supplies had vanished in this area, enough for a mighty stronghold indeed. I had been wondering how so large a place could escape notice of the High King's mapmakers."

With a sigh, Niya shrugged. "Very well. It seems as good a guess as any."

They ate hastily after that. Loren could feel it in all of them—a sense of nearing the end of their journey, that this time, surely, they would find what they sought. They mounted their horses and rode off. But this time they rode together, making as far west as they could, and did not split into two groups until they had reached the feet of the mountains. Then they went in the same groups of three as they had the past two days.

This time the going was far slower, for they had to ride around and over ridges, and the land itself seemed to try to halt their progress. Soon Loren began to grow frustrated, and with her frustration came doubts. This was taking more than three times as long. What if it was all a waste of time? What if another day went by, and they were no closer to their goal? That was only another day for Damaris to prepare for their coming, or mayhap flee Yewamba before they arrived.

She looked up and froze. Her hands jerked on the reins, and Midnight came to a sudden stop. Chet and Weath wheeled around, staring at her.

"What is it?" said Chet.

But Loren could not take her eyes from the mountain peaks. There were two of them, and she recognized them. She had seen them the night before, in her dream.

"Weath, ride south," she said. "Tell Niya to come at once."

Chet and Weath looked at each other, and then they followed Loren's gaze.

"What is it?" said Chet again.

"I am not certain."

Weath hesitated, choosing her words carefully. "Then what should I tell Niya, when I find her?"

"Tell her I have found something. Bring her to the foot of those two peaks there."

She showed Weath, and then the Mystic rode away south. She and Chet pressed on ahead.

"Did you see it?" said Chet. "In a dream?"

"Yes," said Loren. "It came to me last night."

His brows rose. "I did not hear you."

"They are growing less terrible." *At least after I wake,* she thought.

They soon reached the place, and Loren saw what she had already known they would find there: a small wagon trail that vanished between the foot of the mountains. She could almost imagine the caravan wagons making their way into the Greatrocks—but then her imagination conjured Gregor before her, and she shuddered, feeling the blood drain from her face.

"Are you all right?" said Chet.

"Yes," she said quietly. "We should get out of sight and wait for the others."

They took the horses off into the trees, but before they did so, Loren turned to look at where the trail ran off in the other direction. At once she saw the reason why they had not spotted the trail in the last two days' search: it ended abruptly just before a small gap in a ridge. It was natural, but as perfect for concealment as if it had been built by human hands. On the other side of the wall, she did not doubt that the trail resumed— but if they had seen it from there, they would only have seen a trail that led to a flat wall, and would not have tried to follow it.

They dismounted and tied their horses to a tree

out of sight of the path. There they sat in silence as they studied the peaks, fixing themselves a light lunch. Loren thought of taking her bow and trying to hunt, but she did not wish to be out of sight if Niya and the others should return.

Some time after midday, there came a steady *clop-clop* of horses' hooves through the trees. Loren stepped into the open and hailed them as soon as they came into sight. They gathered around her on the path, looking over the peaks and the faint trail that led between them.

"A fortunate find," said Niya. She looked at Loren and arched an eyebrow. "I find it incredible that you should have stumbled upon this by chance."

Loren kept her expression carefully neutral. "What other explanation is there?"

Niya's nostrils flared, and she looked away.

"You think this is the way to Yewamba?" said Uzo. "That seems a narrow track to supply a fortress as large as the Yerrin girl made it sound."

"We have found no better sign," said Loren. "Let us investigate it."

"Lead the way, Shiun," said Niya. "And be wary. If we are indeed upon the right trail, there will be guards before long, if they have not seen us already."

"We should proceed on foot," said Shiun. "For the noise, and so that we may pass more easily between the trees."

Niya nodded and dismounted, and the rest of

them followed suit, tying the horses in a place of concealment from the road. Then Shiun went on ahead of them, running at a half-trot into the trees, where she disappeared. Loren and Chet strung their bows, and the rest of them set off after her at a slower pace.

"It is fortunate after all that we did not move the camp," said Niya, giving Loren a careful look.

"Fortunate indeed," said Loren, not returning her gaze.

Not even an hour passed before Shiun returned to them, stepping out from behind a trunk as though she had appeared from thin air. The party came to a halt, and Niya's hand went to the hilt of her sword.

"There are guards," said Shiun. "They are many, and they are Yerrins."

Loren and Niya went on ahead with her. She took them silently through the trees, and Loren made very sure to place her feet just as Shiun did—she had some gift with woodcraft and stealth, but Shiun was a master of it. They stopped, and the scout pointed to the top of a ridge on their right. Loren saw two little bumps, and as they watched for a moment, one of them moved.

"Two up there," said Shiun. "And three there."

She pointed back down the slope they were on, towards the path, which curled and curved its way through the jungle. A motion in the trees beside the path caught Loren's eye, and she saw three more figures. They wore green cloaks—not the light green of

Yerrin merchants, but a deep green meant to blend into the jungle.

"Something is close by, that is certain," said Niya.

"There are none higher up the ridge we stand upon," said Shiun. "We can press on that way."

They followed the ground up until they had almost emerged from the trees and into the daylight. But Shiun stopped them, keeping them hidden, and they followed the course of the ridge as it ran farther west. Soon they had passed the guards on the opposite ridge. Below them and ahead of them, they saw that the path took a long turn around the spurs of the mountain that stretched down on either side of it.

Ahead of them, the sun had neared the peaks. Soon it would be dark, and Loren was growing somewhat impatient. But she did not say anything, for who knew if other guards might lurk in the jungle around them?

At last, just as the sun began to sink out of sight, they rounded the spur to follow the path's curve. And there, at last, they found what they were looking for.

They walked upon the foot of a mountain, but a smaller peak stood pressed up against it, and that peak ended in a flat top. Within the mountain itself was built a mighty stronghold that Loren knew at once must be Yewamba.

It stretched out towards them into a great point, like the prow of a ship or the head of an arrow, and all along the top of it ran a great wall. The land that sloped up towards the fortress was rocky and treacherous, and only a single road had been built leading up. From where they stood, they could see arrow slits in the walls of the stronghold as well as in the slopes. Yewamba had been hollowed from the rock, descending into the earth, so that the mountain was the fortress and the fortress, the mountain.

The image of a wide cavern flashed into Loren's mind, the cavern where she had seen Damaris in her dream. She suppressed a shiver.

"Yewamba," said Niya, her voice a fierce rasp.

Loren nodded. "If Damaris of the family Yerrin is anywhere in Underrealm, she is here."

THIRTY

They did not speak of what they had seen while they made their way back out of the valley, for they did not know for certain if there were any more guards around. It was a long walk, made longer by the fact that the sun had now gone down and they had to pick their way through the darkness. Loren's mind raced all the while, wondering what they should do. When she had first heard of Yewamba, she had not imagined it would be so grand a place, so impregnable. The thought of trying to conquer the fortress with only six of them— eight, if they counted Gem and Annis—now seemed laughable. But what was their alternative? Returning to Ammon? Kal would be furious with her, and she would not even have accomplished what she came here to do, which was the only thing that might stay his wrath now.

At last they reached the place where Chet and the others waited for them. They all came forwards and gathered in a group, but Loren held up a hand to forestall their questions.

"There will be time enough to tell you what we saw, but now we must return to camp. Gem and Annis are likely worried sick, and we should not leave them alone overnight in any case."

And she would not say another word until they had all mounted their horses and begun to ride east. Shiun had them remain quiet until they were out of the valley mouth and back near the main road again, but then Chet turned to Loren.

"Did you find Yewamba?"

"Yes," said Loren. The others looked to her with interest. "It is a mighty fortress, and from what we could tell, it is well garrisoned. Even if Kal brought all the Mystics in Ammon, I doubt he could take it by force."

Niya looked at her sharply. "It is good, then, that we mean to use subterfuge instead."

"I do not see how," said Loren.

"Then you intend to give up?" said Niya. "We have come too far for that."

Loren shook her head. "Let us discuss this when we have returned, and we can think upon it properly."

"Then ride faster." Niya obeyed her own command at once, savagely nudging her horse into a canter in the moonslight.

Gem and Annis came to meet them with palpable relief when they reached the camp at last. "We were worried," said Annis. "We feared you had been discovered and taken."

"I am glad to say we were not," said Chet. "Not yet, at any rate, though I think Niya has some mad scheme to ensure that is how we meet our end."

"Do not make snide comments at me, boy," snarled Niya. "If you have counsel to give, then let us hear it."

"Enough," said Loren. "All will be heard in turn."

They sat around the fire Gem and Annis had built. Loren and Niya described Yewamba, with Shiun interjecting every so often with some description of the place and the guards placed around it. When they had finished, Chet spread his hands.

"It seems plain to me that there is little hope of entering the fortress," he said. "We should return to Ammon and let Kal deal with it."

"I do not doubt that he will already have sent a host this way," said Loren. "Jormund will have reached him by now, and Kal will have wasted no time assembling his forces. But it is as I said before: even all the Mystics at his command cannot hope to besiege the place, not without tremendous loss."

"But neither can we hope to conquer it on our own," said Chet.

"We do not need to conquer the fortress," said Niya. "We only need to capture Damaris. That is why we have come all this way. Loren and I have proven our worth already. The two of us can drag this merchant from her hole."

Loren frowned as she looked into the fire. It was possible, she supposed. But Yewamba was not the Golden Manor. It was not in the city, for one thing. Escape would not be so easy. And neither would their entry, for she had no faintest idea how to sneak into the place. There were no rooftops for Gem to lead them across.

"We cannot pass the main gate without detection," she said slowly. "That is the first obstacle."

"You speak as though this is something you are considering," said Chet, incredulous. "Do not tell me you have begun to agree with this mad course."

But Niya ignored him and nodded eagerly at Loren. "Shiun can scout the place tomorrow. She can find us a back entrance. The stronghold is built into a mountain—there must be more than one way in, even if we must tunnel through the rock."

"I could help you there with magic," said Weath. "But I cannot withhold my own concerns. Even once we gain entry, it seems to me that we have but a slim chance of success. Damaris will be well guarded, and extracting her will be no easy task."

"Who agreed to come because they thought this would be easy?" snapped Niya. "If you wish to turn back once you have gotten us inside the stronghold, I will not stop you. The Nightblade and I can manage on our own."

"You advocate for madness," said Chet. "The wisest course would be to make for Ammon. At the least we should remain here, waiting for Kal's arrival, and watch the stronghold in case Damaris should try to escape it."

That did seem wise to Loren, and for a moment her heart leaped. It was safer, certainly, and she could not deny the pit of fear that formed in her stomach at the thought of sneaking into Yewamba. But Niya shook her head scornfully.

"There must be other ways out of Yewamba, just as there are other ways in," she said. "If Damaris learns that a host from Ammon has arrived in the area, doubtless there is some tunnel in the mountains that she can use to evade it. Our only hope is taking her by surprise."

"Hope," scoffed Chet. "I do not see hope in any part of this."

"Do you not? Then let me explain it more clearly, *boy*. Underrealm stands on the brink of war. Damaris' capture and execution could quell the flames of rebellion. The High King could declare open war tomorrow. She may have done so already, and word of it has not reached us yet. But we here, now, just we six, can put an end to it."

Niya's words awoke a flame in Loren's heart. She

remembered what Enalyn had told her upon the Seat: that the preservation of the nine kingdoms was the greatest purpose there was. Niya spoke the truth now; ending Damaris' string of crimes could help bring that about. Loren could do it. And if Niya guessed correctly that Damaris had a means of escape, Loren might be the only one who could.

But more than that, she could end the nightmares, or at least remove the power of them. Mayhap the cavern from her dreams awaited her in Yewamba. Mayhap Gregor was there, too. But if they succeeded, if Damaris was captured and brought before the King's law, Loren need no longer fear the visions that came in her sleep. For a moment her mind quailed at the thought of Chet's corpse, and the corpses of Annis and Gem. But she had seen them die in Dahab as well, and that had not come to pass.

You do not see the future, she told herself once again. *And you were a self-important fool if you ever believed it so.*

"We must do it," she said quietly.

They all stopped and looked at her. Chet's expression fell into despair, and she knew he could see her determination.

"If there is more than a fool's hope of success, we must try," she went on. "Niya is right. All of Underrealm is papyrus awaiting only an ember to ignite it. We can douse the flames before they erupt. That is the duty of the Mystic Order, and it is my duty as the Nightblade."

"But we cannot do it on our own," said Chet. "Kal's force—"

"Is not enough," said Loren. "And even if it were, how long would it take? If he set out from Ammon with his whole host the very day that Jormund reached him, still the march would take more than a month. It might take two. Then they would lay siege to Yewamba. Another two months. Mayhap more. The place looked as though a dozen could repel an army for a year."

"It would become a symbol for the traitors," said Weath quietly. She stared into her hands, her shoulders slumped, as though she had just realized a terrible truth. "Our mission, our true mission, would be a failure, for it would only drag the war on."

"Yet if we succeed, we few?" said Loren. "What if the tale should spread throughout Underrealm that one small band of the High King's spies captured Damaris from her impregnable home and brought her to justice? What traitor would dare to stand against the crown then?"

The camp was silent. The answer was obvious to them all.

Niya's bright teeth shone in the firelight. "Then we are agreed. Loren and I will infiltrate Yewamba and bring Damaris forth. Once we have escaped with her, the rest of you—"

"No," said Chet.

"Chet—" Loren gave him a warning look.

"Let me speak," he said sharply. "I know—or I have learned, on our journeys—that you will not be swayed once you have decided something, Loren. But in some matters, I will not change my mind either. If you are determined to do this, I am coming with you."

"And I," said Gem at once. He beamed at Uzo as though he expected the young man to chime in with agreement. Uzo raised his brows and remained silent.

Annis gave a nervous titter of laughter. "I hope it is understood by all when I do not volunteer, for I would only get in the way."

"Of course, Annis," said Loren. "And as for Gem, and Chet, I will not deny that a part of me wants to forbid you to go. Your lives are dearer to me than my own. But I cannot command you to remain behind in good conscience, when you have urged me so strongly not to go in the first place."

"Chet urged you, you mean," muttered Gem, so quiet that Loren barely heard it.

But Niya shook her head. "That is unwise, Loren. If we should be caught in the fortress, these boys will not keep us from death. We should not risk any more lives than we must."

"You speak as though I am yours to command," said Chet. "I am not. Nor am I yours, Loren. I obey only myself, and if you do not wish for me to come with you, you shall have to tie me to a tree."

"Do not tempt me, boy," growled Niya.

Loren glared at her. "Chet speaks the truth. He is no Mystic, and so he is not yours to command."

Niya drew back, agape. "You cannot tell me you wish to endanger him."

"My wish is not important," said Loren. "I know him well enough to know that he will not hamper the success of our mission, and so if he wishes to come, he can. Or am I no longer in command?"

The Mystic's nostrils flared, and her chest heaved with quick, angry breaths. When she spoke, the words came terse and angry. "Very well, Nightblade. But might I have a word alone?"

Without waiting for an answer, she stood and walked away from the campfire. Chet watched her go, still frowning.

"You do not need to go with her," he said.

"We gain nothing by being angry and divided," said Loren. "If I can soothe her temper, it will be better for us all."

So saying, she rose and went off in the direction Niya had gone. She found her a ways off, when the fire had receded to little more than a glow in the distance. Niya was pacing back and forth before a wide mahogany tree, and when she saw Loren approaching she slammed a fist into the side of it.

"You let that boy sway your mind too easily," she said. "Few appreciate a good lover more than I. But it is a girl, and not a woman, who makes decisions with her loins instead of her head."

Fury seized Loren, and she spoke without thought. "Is that so? I think you have done nothing else since we first met."

Niya stopped dead, eyes narrowing and fists clenching at her sides. For a moment, Loren was afraid to move. She half thought that Niya meant to attack her. But then a smile split Niya's scowl, and she snickered.

"Mayhap you speak fairly," she said. "I can admit to my own distraction. But when it comes to our mission, I put such thoughts aside. I worry that you have not learned to do so."

"And I grow tired of hearing that," said Loren. "You, Chet, Kal—it seems everyone thinks I am a little girl, swaying this way and that like a willow in a gale. Just because I was silent while all gave counsel does not mean I was waiting to find something to agree with. I listened, and when I came to my own decision, I gave it."

Niya studied her for a moment. Then she took a step closer, her demeanor changing entirely. Loren no longer feared the woman's temper, but grew nervous for an entirely different reason.

"I had not thought of that," said Niya softly. "And it was wrong of me. I did not give you enough credit. You *are* young, and sometimes I forget that an old soul lurks behind those eyes."

The Mystic reached up and brushed away a lock of Loren's hair. Loren fought to keep her knees from shaking. "I accept your apology," she said, keeping her tone reserved.

"For a long while now, I have sought to be entrusted with a command," said Niya. "Now that one has been given to me, even one so small, I suppose I sometimes forget you are the one in charge here. I was a fool to call you a little girl. You are a woman grown, of course—that is why I cannot stop desiring you."

"Yet you should stop, as I have told you often enough before." Loren tried to sound indignant, but she could not even speak forcefully enough to convince herself. "At least you should make up your mind about it—I feel as though one moment you scorn me, and the next you whisper honeyed words."

"That is because the distance between here and Dahab has increased both my impatience and my hunger."

"It has not increased mine."

"That is a lie."

They both knew it was true. Niya took another step forwards, so that they were almost touching. They were out of sight of the camp. Loren knew no one would come to disturb them. Almost she surrendered to her instincts; almost she reached out for the woman. She even lifted her hands to do it.

And then at the last moment she regained control. She put her hands on Niya's shoulders instead, gently pushing her away.

"I love Chet," she said. "You must stop this."

"Why?" said Niya. She cupped Loren's cheek. "Neither of us wants me to."

"Because you are trying to make me do something that I know I would regret. He has suffered enough because of me. I will not cause him more pain."

"Then say nothing of it to him," said Niya. "I will not."

But those words doused the fire in Loren at last, and she reached up to pull Niya's hand away. "No. That is not who I am. I value honor."

Niya scowled. "So says the former thief."

"Former," said Loren. "And even then, I never meant to steal anyone's affection."

"If that were true, then you would never have looked at me the way you did when we met," said Niya. She pushed past Loren and made for the camp. It was a long while before Loren's heart had stilled enough that she could follow.

THIRTY-ONE

The next day they sent Shiun back into the mountains to scout Yewamba and see if she could find another route inside. The rest did not wait idly, but moved the camp. They took themselves west, across the main road and into the jungle at the mouth of the valley. There was a sort of cleft in the mountains there, where behind a rise there was a wide clearing. There they erected their tents once more, though Niya commanded them to light no fires.

Shortly after midday, Shiun returned with good news. "There is a path," she said. "It runs up the back side of the mountain, and it is perilous. The last part cannot be climbed without Weath. But it will bring us straight to the top of the walls, and from there we can enter the stronghold with ease."

"That is our party, then," said Loren. "All but Annis and Uzo, who will stay to guard the camp."

"And happily enough," said Uzo. "If you succeed, I confess I will be jealous of the glory you will have earned yourselves. But I have never found anything onerous about guard duty, especially when the alternative is to thrust my head between the very jaws of death."

Loren smirked, but the expression quickly died. "If we do not succeed, you must return to Ammon as swiftly as you can. Take Annis with you, and keep her safe. Her information about the stronghold will be of immense help to Kal."

Uzo nodded. "Of course. And . . . I should say, in case I do not get another chance, that I am sorry if I have been coarse with you during the journey. I thought I rode with a young girl who had been raised above her station by fortune alone. I see now that I traveled beside a brave warrior instead."

She flushed and shook her head. "No warrior, but only a spy. As luck would have it, however, that is just what was required. They say that even a dull knife is better for cutting than a golden spoon."

His teeth flashed in a smile. "They do not say that in this kingdom, but it is true enough."

Their meal that night was a somber affair, made more so because they could not cook and so had to eat the salted rations from their packs, which had begun to run low.

"If we return, you and I should go hunting," Loren told Chet. "It will make our journey to Ammon much easier."

Chet looked at her oddly. "You say 'if.' Are you that doubtful we shall come back?"

She shook her head at once. "Of course not. I only meant . . . I was not thinking."

He looked away and did not answer.

Uzo volunteered to stand watch the whole night, since he would be able to sleep the next day while the rest of them could not. Loren was in the midst of readying for bed, and wondering how she would be able to sleep, when Annis approached her.

"Loren," she said quietly. "Might I speak with you?"

"Of course. What is it?"

Annis looked around the camp, her gaze lingering longest on Gem. "Alone?"

Loren frowned, but she let herself be led off away from the camp. Annis took her out through the cleft in the mountain, into the open jungle and to a small stream that ran south not far away from the main road. The sun had long passed from sight behind the mountains that loomed over them, but its light still filled the sky. Here in the foothills, they had a clear view of the land to the east, and just near the horizon, Loren could make out the edges of the mountains' shadow. The glow of sunlight there was like a soft golden blanket being drawn back and away from her, over the edge of the world and out of sight.

Together they stood and watched it slowly creeping away, until Annis cleared her throat. "Let us sit on the bank of the stream," she said, her tone too airy, too light. "I want to put my feet in the water. I can hardly believe how long it is since last I bathed."

"Very well," said Loren. She was more curious than ever about what troubled Annis, but it seemed the girl would not speak of it until she was ready. So they sat together upon the bank beside the stream and pulled off their boots. The water was not too very cold, despite the winter. Uzo had told them that it never snowed in Feldemar, and all of the south-flowing rivers carried water from the north, where it remained hot and sunny all year round.

"This is a strange land, but I find it very beautiful," said Annis, looking out into the gathering darkness between the trees.

"I prefer the Birchwood, but I am happy to have seen it," said Loren. "Together you and I have wandered forests, grasslands, great rivers and jungles, and even the ocean. All that is left now is to visit a desert together."

"Mayhap one day we could journey to Idris," said Annis, her eyes all alight. "I have heard it is an exotic place. When all of this is over, I should love to go there with you." But then her expression fell, and she looked away. "When all of this is over."

"Annis, what is it?" said Loren. "I wish to hear what troubles you, but I must rise before the dawn."

"Of course. Forgive me." Annis drew a deep breath. "I do not want Gem to go with you. I want you to command him to stay."

Loren's heart sank. "I cannot," she said. "Or rather, I will not. I have tried it before—with both of you, in fact. You each made it plain how much you hate it."

"But you are all wandering into danger, danger that could overcome even grown warriors. He and I are both still children, and though he practices his swordplay, he is no fighter. I worry that he will try to join a battle, if one should break out, and then something will—"

"We both know why you are worried, Annis," said Loren irritably. "You worry that if he does not return, then you will never have told him how you feel, and will never know if he felt the same. The solution is simple: *speak* to him. You are an eloquent girl, when you do not let your tongue run away with your mind. You know that I love you as my sister, but frankly I have grown tired of how reluctant you are to even broach the subject with him."

To her surprise, Annis' eyes brimmed with tears, and she gave a sniff. She bowed her head and turned away. Mortified, Loren sat up and placed a hand on her back.

"Annis, I am sorry. I spoke too harshly, I—"

"No, you spoke true enough," said Annis, voice trembling. "Only . . . it is not that I am afraid to tell Gem. It is just that I wish I did not have to."

Loren frowned. But as she thought upon it, she understood, and her expression softened. "He has never fawned over you the way you have over him."

Annis fixed her with a glare, but her brimming tears robbed it of any bite. "I do not fawn, but otherwise you are right. He has never looked at me . . . in that way. I keep hoping to see it in his eyes, the way I see it when Chet looks at you. He looked that way from the first moment I met him, and I was there as the two of you fell deeper and deeper into love. It was effortless."

"Of course it was, you great fool," said Loren gently. "Chet and I have known each other our entire lives. He loved me even before I left the forest, before I met you. Everyone is different. Every love is different. He never told me how he felt, for he never needed to. But he is not Gem, and you are not me. So free yourself from both our misery, and speak to him."

Annis' eyes shone, but not with tears. "You are right," she said, quiet as a prayer. "I will. I *will* tell him. And I will tell him that if he does not return from Yewamba, I will storm in there and drag him out myself."

Loren laughed. "Good. Then go."

The girl shot to her feet, but paused when Loren remained sitting. "Are you not coming?"

"I will in a moment," said Loren. "But my feet are enjoying the water too much. I wish to relax a little while longer, for I think I shall not have another chance in some time."

Annis smiled at her and set off into the trees. Loren face fell the moment the girl's back was turned, and she looked down at her feet as they dangled in the stream.

He loved me even before I left the forest.

Loren had said the words without thinking. But why had she not said *We loved each other?*

She loved Chet—she knew that she did. But she had known for some time, in the back of her mind, that it was not the same as his love for her. If it were, she could never have manipulated him so easily on the day she left her home. If it were, she would not think of Niya the way she did now—and the proof of that could be found in Weath. Weath and Chet had become fast friends, and Loren could see how attractive the woman was, with her short copper hair and lithe, supple figure. Loren could remember one or two occasions when Chet's gaze had lingered upon her a moment longer than was proper.

Yet never once had Loren suspected that Chet might harbor any intent towards Weath beyond friendship. But Chet seemed to have more than an inkling of the connection between Loren and Niya. It made him jealous, and no matter how Loren denied it, she knew it was for good reason.

Even now, Loren could not stop thinking of how easy it would be to secretly draw Niya out of the camp. They could be alone for one night. Mayhap the last night of both their lives.

What had she told Annis? *You worry that if he does not return, then you will never have told him how you feel.*

The same could be said for Loren herself. Always she had denied what she felt for Niya, no matter how the Mystic goaded her. And now she had told Annis to be bold, to act as fear had always prevented her from acting before. Yet she would not do the same, even though she might never have another chance.

She remembered her heated argument with Niya just two nights before. Again she saw Niya standing just before her, almost pressed against her. When her mind played across it, the memory of the woman's scent flooded her nostrils.

A stone lay by Loren's hand. She picked it up and flung it hard into the water, where it broke the surface with a loud *plop.*

"Darkness take the woman," she muttered. "And darkness take me as well."

She drew her feet from the water and pulled her boots on, making her way slowly back to camp.

THIRTY-TWO

SLEEP DID NOT COME TO LOREN FOR A LONG TIME. Chet had rolled over into the corner of the tent before she entered, and he did not move as she undressed and crawled beneath their blanket. She rolled back and forth, trying to get comfortable and drift off. There was a lump beneath the tent, and she kept trying to shift around it to find flat ground again. But at last she had to admit that the lump was only an excuse, for she had slept on far worse terrain during her journeys.

"Close your eyes, woman," grumbled Chet.

Loren sighed. "I am not the only one who cannot sleep, then."

He turned over, and in the pale moonslight through the tent, she saw his eyes glinting. "Of course I cannot sleep. I am terrified of what tomorrow could bring. Do you not feel the same way?"

"I suppose so," she said with a shrug. "But on the other hand, I am somewhat used to that feeling."

"If that were true, sleep would come easy. Yet I think I understand your meaning. I do not feel as though I should be frightened. I was there for the fall of Northwood, and you and I faced Rogan more than once. I was there when assassins came for the Lord Prince, and I was in the battle on the Seat. Yet somehow this feels different."

"It is different," said Loren. "All of those times were a surprise. The danger came from nowhere, and then it ended. This might be the first time you have planned to march into mortal peril."

Chet snickered. "I suppose that is right enough."

Loren felt herself relax at his laugh. She had not heard it in some time. Cautiously she scooted closer to him, and he did the same, placing his head on her shoulder. She curled her arm around him, fingers idly stroking his arm, and he laid a hand across her stomach. The feeling of his skin loosened her taut muscles even more. It felt natural between them again. It felt right. Suddenly the doubts she had had upon the bank of the stream faded away, and they seemed silly in her memory. This was how it had been when she first came to know that she loved him—beneath the boughs of the Birchwood, and then when their trysts began upon the Seat.

Then she remembered Niya, and the light in the woman's eyes when they looked at her. Comfort fell away, and she felt like a fraud with Chet in her arms.

"Chet, you have not been wrong about Niya," she said quietly. "I know you have suspected her for some time. And I dismissed it, but I should not have. Niya would have me, if she could. She has said as much, subtly and in ways that were less so."

He was still for a while, and then he pushed himself up on his elbow. In the midst of his silhouette, his eyes searched hers. "And? What came of it?"

"Nothing," said Loren. But then she realized that that was not strictly true. "She kissed me. Twice. In Dahab."

She could feel him tense. "You . . . why would you—"

"I did not," said Loren quickly. "She did it without asking."

He pushed himself up still farther. "What? Loren, that is only a step away from taking someone against their will, from breaking the High King's harshest law."

"That is not the way of it," said Loren. "I know how it must sound, but . . . do you remember the first time we kissed, on the shores of Dorsea, just before we sailed for the Seat?"

"Of course," he said quietly. "That memory will never fade."

"I did not ask you before I kissed you," said Loren.

"Yet you knew," he said. "You knew I loved you."

"How? You had never said the words, nor had I. We had never spoken of it at all. And when we began to—that is, when we became . . ." She flushed, and wondered if the moonslight would reveal it. "Even when we did more than kiss, we did not speak of it then. You told me you loved me for the first time just before we left the Seat. We had shared a bed for weeks before then."

He thought about that for a moment. But then he shook his head. "I do not understand, Loren. You knew my desires, and I knew yours. And so the only way I can think that what Niya did was no crime, is if she also knew your desires, and she was right."

She stared up at him. Shame burned in her breast, but she did not look away.

"I see," he said quietly. He began to turn away, to roll towards his side of the tent again.

"Stop, Chet," said Loren, pulling him back. "I do not want to be with Niya."

"You just said otherwise. So what is the truth?"

"The truth is that I am here. With you."

"That is not an answer."

"Yes. Yes, I would lay with Niya if it were not for you."

It thrilled her to say it out loud. Her skin rose to

gooseflesh at the words, and she grew quick of breath. But then she raised a hand to cup his cheek.

"But that is something I would merely enjoy. A momentary pleasure, like drinking a cup of wine. Between such a fancy and what I want—what I truly desire—a wide gulf stretches. Much would have to change in this world before I would attempt to leap it."

He did not answer for a moment. Loren realized she was holding her breath, and slowly she let it out. And then, when he spoke, she heard a small smile in his voice.

"So you do not fancy me, then?"

She gave a frustrated growl and slapped his arm. "Be silent, you idiot. I love you, Chet. I will not lay with anyone else, but that does not mean I can promise I will never have desires. Can you tell me, in truth, that you have never thought of another? Mayhap Weath?"

"Anyone can see that she has a fine figure," said Chet. "But there my thoughts remain. I will never lay with her."

"And I will never lay with Niya," said Loren. "It is not precisely the same, for I feel a way about her that you do not feel towards Weath. But I have chosen love over desire. I hope you know that."

"I do," he whispered. "I only wish that my love was enough for you. That it did not leave you wanting another, or feeling this deep need to pursue the aims of the High King."

"That is another matter entirely, and you know it."

"Of course it is, but it comes from the same place in your heart. I believe you when you say you will be true. Yet even so, I am not enough. There is your quest—your mission. Can you not give that up for me as well?"

"No," she said flatly. "And you should not ask it of me. Not if you love me in truth."

He paused to consider that. "I understand your sense of duty," he said at last. "It is a quality I admire, in others as well as yourself. It is only that I do not see anything for you beyond this war. If I were in your position, I might do the same as you have done. But always I would dream of a quiet home in the woods, where I might spend my days after the war—if indeed it becomes a war at all. Do you want that, Loren?"

"I do not know. It sounds fine enough, I suppose. But when I think of it, I do not feel the yearning for it that is plain in your voice."

"That is what I thought," he said, sighing. "Is there even a time after the war, in your mind? And what do you see there?"

She sat up, and he rose from his elbow to sit beside her. She took his hands into her own and traced a finger along the back of his hand. "I have no easy answer for you. I cannot say what I know you want me to say. How can I know what the distant future holds when I cannot even know what will happen to you and me tomorrow? But right now, I love you. And your love is dearer to me than any honor the High King could bestow. Can that be enough? At least for now?"

He turned his hand over to grasp hers, and lifted it to his mouth to kiss her fingers one by one. "It can," he murmured.

Loren kissed him, and they lay down again together, still and content. Soon she was asleep, a dreamless sleep more sound than any she had had since leaving Ammon.

THIRTY-THREE

Uzo went about the camp to wake them all before dawn. One by one they came out of their tents and stood stretching in the crisp air. Loren caught herself looking at each of her companions. Often they returned her gaze, but no one spoke a word.

They were silent, too, as they readied themselves for the journey. The Mystics buckled their swords at their waists and donned their shirts of chain. Loren left her bow—Albern's gift—for it would be of little use in the fortress, and only by terrible misfortune would she need it before then. Niya had her sword and a brace of knives at her belt. She caught Loren staring and winked. Loren smiled and shook her head.

Annis rose to see them off, though of course she would not be coming with them. Loren noticed at once that Annis and Gem would hardly look at each other, and each flinched when the other spoke. They kept a wide distance between themselves as well. Loren groaned inwardly. Whatever Annis had told Gem the night before, it did not appear to have gone well. But she could waste little thought on that now. She would have to ask what happened after their journey to Dahab, if indeed there was an afterwards in which they could speak with each other.

She went to Midnight just before they left and stroked the mare's muzzle. "You will be safe here," she said. "If I do not return, I am sorry, but that only means you will belong to Annis. You like her."

Midnight blew a wet snort into Loren's face, making her laugh.

Shiun led them from the camp and into the jungle. They paused at the mouth of the valley while she went ahead to search it, making sure no new guards had been posted there since last they came. She soon returned to wave them on. The sky had only just begun to turn grey.

For a long while she led them on the same path they had taken the last time, but when she reached the place where they had seen the guards, she took them in another direction—right instead of left, up the face of the northern ridge rather than the south. Loren wondered at the change, but she did not speak. Shiun had been out all day scouting the path, and the woman was like an Elf in the woods, silent and sure. She would not lead them astray.

At one point they stopped dead, and Shiun gestured them into a crouch. Loren looked around for the reason, and then she saw two forms moving a little bit below them on the ridge. They wore the green cloaks of Yerrins, and they appeared to be eating. Shiun turned to Loren and leaned close, whispering into her ear.

"Do we remove them now?"

Loren blinked at her. "Remove . . .?"

Niya pressed forwards, her breath hot on Loren's cheek. "We may have to escape at great speed. Every guard we kill on the way in is one we will not have to fight on the way out."

"No," said Loren. "When are the patrols replaced? Do you know?" Shiun shook her head. "Then we could raise the alarm while we are still inside, and not even know it. The family Yerrin prides themselves on not killing needlessly—we should endeavor to do the same."

Shiun glanced over Loren's shoulder. From the corner of her eye, Loren saw Niya shrug. Shiun turned away without a word and pressed on.

The grey had lightened considerably when they reached the base of Yewamba's sudden cliffs. Dawn's approach filled them all with urgency. The route up looked to be a difficult one, but Loren knew from long experience that climbing up would be much easier than climbing down.

Their path began to wind back and forth, and Shiun would pause every few moments to check that the rocks gave her another path up. But then they reached the top of the slope, and it turned into a sheer wall at least thirty paces high.

"Where do we go from here?" said Loren.

"Up," said Shiun, arching an eyebrow.

"That is why you brought me," Weath said, smiling. She stepped forwards and pulled off her leather gloves. Her eyes began to glow. "I may not be much of an alchemist, but I *am* an alchemist."

She put forth her hand at about the height of her knee, and her fingers sank into the rock like it was made of water. Soon she had carved a little depression there, and she placed her foot inside it. She made another for the other foot, and then she reached up to create her handholds. Hand over hand and foot over foot she began to climb, creating new handholds each time.

"Sky above," whispered Gem. "I would have given much to have known a girl like her when I was the best thief in Cabrus."

Niya snorted. "I will go next," she growled.

"I will follow," said Loren. "Then Gem, Chet, and Shiun. You can cover our rear best with the bow."

Shiun nodded. Niya was already climbing up just behind Weath, gripping each handhold almost as soon as the alchemist's foot left it. Loren came after her as soon as there was room, and soon the whole group was on the cliff face, making their way slowly up, like ants ascending the leg of a table.

The sun rose at last while they were halfway up, and eastern light poured upon them from the left. Loren paused for a moment to look back down. Yewamba's little valley was in view, but nothing beyond, for the mountains blocked the landscape from sight. It was the very reason Yewamba was so well hidden. She could not see any guards from her vantage point, and she hoped that none looked their way, for surely they could not miss the sight of five small figures crawling their way up the light grey stone of the cliff.

A wind had begun to blow. Loren shivered and reached up for the next handhold.

Just then, Niya's foot slipped from the wall. She gave a grunt as she slid down, reaching desperately for something to hold on to. With no time to think, Loren braced her feet and reached up to try and halt Niya's fall. It did little to slow her, but Niya gripped a handhold in time, stopping with a jolt. Loren realized suddenly that her hand was on Niya's rear.

The Mystic looked down at her with a savage grin. "Time for that later, Nightblade. We are working."

"Get on with it," said Loren, removing her hand. She looked down towards Chet, trying to send him a silent apology. He rolled his eyes and shook his head. She hoped that meant he was not upset.

Looking up again, she realized they had finally neared the top. Weath was already out of sight over the wall, and Niya was scrambling over as well. They all quickened their pace, Loren nearly leaping from hand-hold to handhold, and Gem following so fast that his fingers scraped on her boot more than once. But just before she reached the lip, Loren heard a muffled cry and the scuff of leather boots on stone.

We are discovered, she thought. A moment's panic seized her as she wondered if she should keep going. But then she realized Weath and Niya were in danger, and she lunged up—only to recoil again, as a body sailed over her head and fell into the open air. She caught a glance of it—and saw Weath's pale face, her red hair fluttering, bone jutting from her neck. In silence the Mystic fell, and in silence struck the rocks far, far below, too far away to hear the impact.

For a moment, horror froze them all. Then Loren vaulted over the top of the wall to land on the rampart just beyond. Niya was there, kneeling over the body of a Yerrin guard. The blade of her knife was still buried in the woman's throat. Niya looked up at Loren, her eyes wide with grief.

"She came—she surprised us, we—Weath, she did not see her, and—"

The words died in her throat, and Loren could only stare. Slowly she turned to the top of the wall again, her breath catching in her throat, as the others came over one by one and joined her in silence.

THIRTY-FOUR

After a long moment of mourning, Shiun broke the quiet. "The sun is up. We are far too exposed here."

"Yes," said Niya. She wiped something—sweat, or tears—from her eyes with the back of one hand, while the other wiped her knife clean on the dead guard's cloak. "Help me get her out of sight."

"We have no time to find a hiding place," said Shiun. She looked at the corpse disdainfully. "Throw her over the wall, where she may join Weath in death."

Niya nodded, and together the two of them lifted the guard to toss her into the open air. There was a bloodstain on the floor, but that could not be helped. Chet and Gem still sat where they had climbed up. Chet stared blankly in the direction Weath had fallen.

"Chet!" whispered Loren. His head jerked towards her. "Come."

The boys edged forwards slowly. There was an inner wall opposite the ramparts behind which Loren and the others had ducked, and now Shiun poked her head over it, looking about. When she crouched again, she spoke to Loren and Niya. "I cannot see very well, for the wall blocks vision, but I see only another half-dozen Yerrins atop it. That is a light guard, for I would guess that the wall is many hundreds of paces long. Below us, the courtyard is entirely empty. If we are fortunate, they will not notice this one missing for a long while."

"How can you think we are fortunate when Weath is dead?" said Chet harshly.

"Chet," said Loren, meeting his gaze. He lasted only a moment before looking away. "Go on, Shiun."

But Niya spoke first. "We should leave one lookout here, and the rest of us will enter Yewamba. We will find Damaris and bring her up, then carry her down the way we came."

"Carry her down the cliff?" said Loren. "How can we manage that?"

"I have rope," said Shiun, patting a large leather pack that hung at her hip. "We can bind her and gag her, and with one on the ground to guide her descent, the rest of us may lower her down."

"Good enough," said Niya. "Chet will remain here, while the rest of us—"

"No," said Chet. "I will go with Loren."

Niya glared, but Shiun nodded in agreement. "I will remain. The boy only came to keep her safe, and he is no warrior. He will be useless here if he is discovered."

"That is why he should not be here at all," snarled Niya. "But very well. If we are resigned to this foolishness, then let us carry it out."

With Shiun remaining behind, Niya led the rest of them down a stairway and into the empty courtyard. Not far from the bottom of the steps was a door. Niya paused there for only a moment, pressing her ear to the wood to listen. Then she pushed it open and stepped through, with Loren only a pace behind her, and Chet and Gem at her heels.

They were at the top of yet another staircase landing, except that this one descended to both the left and right. Both directions turned almost immediately, deeper into the mountain. Loren ran down to the corner of the one on the left, and saw that it turned away from the other.

"This one turns to the right."

"And this one to the left," said Chet, who had gone in the other direction. "Two paths in two directions, but which to take?"

Loren thought hard. Yewamba was a fortress built from a mountain shaped like an arrowhead. Yes, an arrowhead, or the prow of a ship. And on a ship, where did the captain reside? Always their quarters were towards the rear—or in this case, deeper into the mountain.

"This way," she said.

"How do you know?" said Chet.

"It is a guess, but I think it is a good one. We can argue about it if you like."

He grimaced, but Niya ran down the steps after Loren. "Listen to her. If she says she knows where to find Damaris, I believe her." She vanished almost at once around the corner and was lost from sight.

Chet and Gem ran up to Loren, and Chet's face was full of concern. "Did you see this in your dreams as well?"

"No," said Loren. "It is truly a guess. And my dreams do not show me the future."

"They have guided us well enough so far," said Gem. "We would not be here without them."

"They are—" She stopped short. Chet's corpse flashed in her mind, and Gem's madness. "I know nothing of this place. I only think that we will find Damaris in its deepest, darkest hole. Now let us hurry, for Niya has already left us behind."

They took the steps two at a time until they caught the Mystic. She had paused where the stairs ended, opening into a hallway that branched left and right while also running straight ahead. Torches lit the place, just as they lit the stairwell. Niya glanced over her shoulder. "Nightblade?"

"Straight ahead," said Loren, and took the lead.

The craftsmanship of the fortress was nothing so opulent as the High King's palace, and yet in its own way it seemed grander, more powerful. There were some pillars and beams that looked as though they had been brought here, but much of it was carved out of the rock of the mountain itself, and they did not appear to have taken much effort to make it beautiful. It was as though whoever built Yewamba had done so long before the decorative refinement that gave birth to the Seat. The stronghold had a sense of lurking, of ominous presence and malice, a long-forgotten and long-sleeping threat that only waited for the right time to wake and sweep all its enemies away into the darkness below the world.

That menace weighed more heavily on them the deeper they drove. The halls all turned exactly left and right, so that Loren was able to remember the way she was going easily enough, and led them always west, deeper into the heart of the Greatrocks. But all the while, they never saw another soul, nor any sign of one—save for the lit torches on the walls. But those made the air oppressively hot, and stuffy besides, so that soon they were huffing and wheezing even though they were not running.

"It is like being wrapped in a blanket on a summer day," said Chet, his forehead glistening with sweat.

"Where are they?" growled Niya. She stopped and ducked through the open doorway of some of the rooms as they passed. "There are tables in some of these, and dishes, and weapons in others. But where are the people?"

"Mayhap they heard us coming," said Gem. "Mayhap they fled. They must have heard I was with you." But even his customary bravado could not withstand the creeping silence, and his smile faltered.

"Hush," said Loren, stopping suddenly. They all froze where they stood. Loren listened harder, and then she heard it again—the clink of metal on pottery.

She turned to the rest of them. "A kitchen?"

"Food," said Gem, licking his lips.

"Be silent, Gem."

"I do not smell anything," said Niya.

"I think sound carries farther in this place than scent," said Loren. "And worse, I cannot tell where the sound came from."

"Then what do you propose to do?"

"Press on. Only be more careful, now that we know others are near."

They moved slower after that, careful to let each step fall silently. And then, at long last, they heard a sound. Shuffling footsteps, the sound of soft leather on stone, and moving towards them from the right.

Loren pointed to one of the rooms, and they lunged through the open doorway to hide themselves on either side of it. Loren risked leaning out slightly to look back into the hall. A young woman in a plain brown dress, her skin as dark as night, walked past them. She carried a broad silver tray in two hands, and upon the tray were several platters of food with gold covers.

Niya looked at Loren after the girl passed. "Did you see it?"

"I did," said Loren. "Fancy food for fancy people. Let us follow our little songbird."

They waited until the girl had turned the next corner out of sight, and then ran after her. Two more hallways they followed her, until she rounded the final corner and ducked into the first doorway in the hallway there. Peeking around the corner, Loren saw a guard at the door. She looked to Niya.

The Mystic pounced silent as a striking wolf. Her hand caught the guard by the throat, choking his cry of alarm to silence. Her dagger was in her hand, and Loren quailed—but Niya only brought the pommel crashing into his temple, and he collapsed. Loren ran past them both and into the room, where the servant stood looking at the door, her eyes wide with alarm. When she saw Loren, she tried to scream, but Loren covered her mouth with a hand and seized the tray to keep it from falling. Chet took it from her and set it on the ground while Loren pressed the girl back into the wall.

"Silence! Be silent," said Loren. "We will not hurt you."

But the girl's gaze went over Loren's shoulder, and she screamed into the hand that kept her quiet. Loren turned to see that Niya had dragged the guard into the room and, now that he was out of the hallway, was slitting his throat with her hunting knife.

"Niya!" cried Loren in a harsh rasp.

The woman glared up at her. "Every one I kill now is one I will not have to fight when I escape. I say that for myself, since it seems plain you will not fight at all."

"I will not kill," said Loren. "Darkness take you, Niya. Get into the hallway and keep watch. Warn us if you hear anyone coming."

Niya's nostrils flared, but she did as she was bid. Loren turned back to the girl and shook her by the shoulder to get her attention.

"Where are you taking this food? I am removing my hand so that you may talk. Do not scream."

Cautiously she lifted her hand, no more than a finger's breadth from the girl's lips. But the girl shook her head. "I will tell you nothing."

Loren sighed. "Tell us, girl. Do not make this difficult."

"Who are you? What do you want? Why did you kill him?"

Glancing over her shoulder at the dead guard, Loren remembered what Uzo had told them in Dahab: the Yerrins were family, and none but the family were allowed inside. Doubtless the guard was some cousin of the girl's. She cursed Niya again in her mind.

"My companion killed him because she is a madwoman," said Loren. "We are seeking someone. Help us find her, and you will not be harmed. I swear it. But if we take too long in our conversation here . . . well, my companion will grow impatient, and then she will speak with you herself."

Fresh terror filled the girl's eyes. "I am only a servant. I know nothing of the stronghold."

"I would wager you know enough. Where are all the soldiers stationed?"

The girl only shook her head. Loren glanced back over her shoulder.

"Gem, fetch Niya."

"No!" cried the girl. "No, no, please. The soldiers are all in the eastern chambers of the stronghold, far from here."

"And who resides here?" said Loren.

She looked all around, desperate for some escape, but there was none. "The wealthier members of the family. The caravan heads and accountants, the higher scions."

"To whom do you bring this food?"

The girl's throat bobbed up and down as she swallowed. "The . . . the lady of the fortress."

"Is it Damaris?"

Though the girl did not answer, her eyes grew wider with fear, and her skin went a shade paler. It was all the answer Loren needed.

"But there is no one in this room," said Loren. "Where is she? How did you mean to bring the food to her?"

Gem ran up beside them, where there was a small door built into the wall. He turned the latch and opened it outwards into the room. "This way, I would wager."

Chet pressed in behind him, and Loren leaned over to look. There was a small wooden platform there, affixed to a rope that ran up and down in the pitch blackness beyond.

"What is it?" said Chet.

"I think . . ." Gem leaned in and pulled on one of the ropes. The wooden platform moved down slightly. "Yes, I think this is some device that brings things up and down in the fortress. If the kitchens are up on this level, this would be how they send food down to those on the lower levels."

"She is below us then," said Loren, focusing on the girl once more. "How many floors down?"

"Please, no," said the girl. "You cannot reach her. She is well guarded. And if it is known that I helped you . . ."

They heard footsteps at the door, and Niya reappeared in it. "What is taking so long?" she snarled. "Will she not speak? Give her to me."

Loren turned back to the girl and raised her brows.

"Fifteen," squeaked the girl. "Damaris is fifteen floors down."

"You have done well," said Loren. Then she shoved the girl back so that her head slammed into the wall. She fell unconscious at once, and Loren caught her before she reached the floor.

THIRTY-FIVE

"I WILL GO FIRST," SAID GEM.

"Let me," said Niya. "If there are foes on the other side, you will be of little use."

"I am smaller, and if there are foes, I will see them first," countered Gem. "I will be able to tell you, so that the situation may be resolved with stealth rather than by alerting the whole kingdom to our presence."

Loren looked up from where she and Chet were tying up the servant girl in the corner using the cloak of the slain guard. "Let Gem go first. He is craftier than any of us." With her dagger Loren cut a strip of cloth from the girl's dress and shoved it in her mouth, and then tied it in place with another.

"I do not doubt it," sneered Niya, glaring down at the boy.

Gem slipped into the dark hole in the wall and crawled over the edge of the wooden platform, clinging to the rope in the darkness. "I cannot see how far down it goes," he said. "But the rope is sturdy, and there are many rough patches on the wall where you may place your feet. It will not be too difficult a climb."

"Still, you may wish to rid yourself of the chain shirt, Niya," said Loren. "Doubtless that will only make things harder."

Niya arched an eyebrow. "I will keep it, though your concern is touching. I think it will come to fighting before we leave here, and I would not be defenseless when it does."

"Suit yourself, then."

One by one they entered the darkness behind Gem: first Loren, and then Niya, and finally Chet. The rock pressed in close, with only a few handbreadths to either side of them. Gem had said the climb was not difficult, but that was because his tiny body fit far more easily than any of theirs. The air grew stuffy and hard to breathe, and it was worse the farther down they went, so that Loren guessed the only source of fresh air must be above them.

"Sky above, it stinks here," said Chet.

"Can you imagine how terrified Annis would be if

she had come with us?" said Gem. He snickered, but then went silent. "Still, I wish she had."

"Still your prattling," said Niya. "There could be foes less than a pace away from us even now."

Indeed, they passed several more doors like the one they had used to enter the shaft. There did not appear to be one on every floor, but almost, and from the edges of each came thin shafts of light. It was the only illumination they had, and barely enough for them to see by. Loren wondered what would happen if another servant came to use the dumbwaiter and pulled on the rope. Would they all go plummeting into the darkness to land in whatever hole lay below them?

"Go faster, Gem," she hissed.

She guessed that they had passed seven floors now. But then, as they kept going, the air grew sweeter. They could breathe more easily, and she felt a draft upon her arms. And far, far below them, there came the sound of rushing water.

The stream, thought Loren. It must be the same stream that ran out to skip beside the main road. It ran out of the mountain itself. Of course. What better way to dispose of the stronghold's waste? No doubt there was some station upriver where they could collect fresh water, which would let Yewamba withstand a siege for almost any length of time. By using this shaft, and others like it, they could dispose of their rubbish, their unused food, and even the contents of their chamber pots.

But Gem had stopped, and she almost stepped on him as her thoughts wandered. "Fifteen," whispered the boy. "This is where she meant to send the food." He paused there a moment, listening. "I do not hear anything on the other side."

"Then give it a push," said Loren.

He tried, but in the dim light she saw him shake his head. "It is shut."

"Climb down a bit farther," she said. "Let me try."

Gem slid farther down the rope, and she took his place at the door. From her belt she drew her dagger and slipped it into the crack between the hatch and the wall. She probed up and down, searching for the latch. At last she found it and lifted it, and the hatch jerked open. It sounded loud as a thunderclap after the long silence, and they all froze. But from the other side there came no sound.

She stuck her head through the opening. The room beyond was another servant's room, and it was empty. Carefully, silently, she slipped out. Niya followed her quickly, and then came the boy, and then Chet.

"The air is even worse here than it was in the shaft," said Chet. "I think I might choke."

"We can but hope," said Niya. Quickly she stole to the room's door and looked both ways down the hallway outside. "No one. But I hear sounds from that direction."

Loren went to the door and heard them, too— voices, far enough to be only a low murmur, but still close enough to be heard. They were to the left, which was west, and deeper into the mountain.

"It seems the right direction," she whispered. "Let us go, but be cautious."

The hallway now was more natural rock than cut stone, and every surface was rough to the touch, so that they could not brush too hard against the walls without scraping their skin. It was harder to muffle their footfalls, and so they had to move even slower than they had before. There was a channel cut into the rock below them, and an iron grate was laid over it flush with the floor. In the channel there flowed a thin stream of water, hardly enough to dip a hand in, though there was room for much more. Another strange feature of the stronghold, though Loren had not even a guess as to its purpose.

At last the hall turned and opened into a wide room beyond, with a domed ceiling carved in sweeping designs. Loren caught a glimpse of horses and men cut into the stone, but her attention quickly went to the soldiers in the room instead. She and the others dove behind the edge of the room's doorway before they could be seen.

There were not many soldiers, mayhap only two dozen, but that was far more than they had any hope of taking in a fight. There was a long row of tables against either wall, and there the soldiers sat, eating a meal. All of them wore shirts of chain and greaves of iron plate, and they all had helmets, though they had removed those to eat. Loren took a second glance and cursed—the helmets were open-faced.

Niya had spotted it, too. "No disguises this time," she whispered.

"What shall we do?" said Loren.

"Turn back?" said Chet. But even he did not sound hopeful that the idea would be accepted.

"There," said Gem. "Look."

He pointed to the floor. The same channel that had run beside them ran through the center of the mess hall and out the other side. And it was far removed from the tables where the soldiers sat.

"It will be a tight fit," whispered Chet.

"And filthy," said Niya. "Mayhap we can find a way to sneak around."

"When did you care about a little dirt?" said Loren. "It is the fastest route for certain, and already I worry that the servant may be discovered at any moment."

They could not argue with that, and so together they stole back down the hallway. Once they were far enough away from the mess hall that they did not need to fear being heard, Loren and Chet stooped together and lifted up a section of the iron grate. It lifted easily enough, though the iron scraped on the stone with a noise that made them all nervous.

"In, quickly," said Loren, placing the grate to the side. Niya took off her sword and, holding it in one hand, she crawled into the channel. Gem was just behind her. Chet motioned to Loren.

"I will go down first and lie on my back. Push the grate on top of me as quietly as you can, and I will do my best to hold it up while you crawl in. I can lower it down from below."

In a moment they had done it. From beneath the grate, Chet held up one side of it so that it slanted, and Loren slid in beside him. As they pressed up against each other for a moment, she kissed his cheek.

"For luck," she said.

He grinned and slowly lowered the grate, following her as she slithered along the channel. The water they crawled through was dirty, but it seemed an ordinary sort of dirt, from the earth and not from human waste. Loren was grateful for that—she had half-feared that the trough might be a secondary method of disposing of the chamber pots.

"At least this gives some relief from the heat," whispered Chet behind her.

Loren realized that might be the channel's purpose—to somewhat cool the air, here in the bowels of the fortress where it was so warm. But she looked back at Chet and put a finger to her lips, urging him to be silent.

They came to the turn in the channel where it entered the mess hall. Niya paused for a moment and looked back to make sure they were with her. She placed two fingers to her lips for silence, and then crawled forwards again, much more slowly this time.

Half a pace at a time, they made their way through

the room. Above them and to either side of them, the chatter of the soldiers seemed like a shouting throng, and they flinched at every raised voice and sudden laugh. Loren's nerves nearly failed her every time she had to put one of her hands or her knees back down in the water, for she feared to make even the smallest splash. She looked up again, trying to guess how far they had gone. She might have been halfway through the room, or only two body lengths in. She could not be sure, and her view was blocked to the front by Niya and Gem, and to the rear by Chet.

Then a soldier crossed the room, and stepped loudly on the grate just over Niya's head. Startled, the Mystic dropped her sword in the water with a *splash*.

Loren looked up through the grate as they all went perfectly still. She counted the thudding of her heartbeats. *One. Two. Three. Four. Five.*

No one came into view. The sound of talking all around them did not pause for so much as a moment.

A long, shuddering sigh escaped Loren, though she fought to keep it silent. Niya looked back over her shoulder and grimaced.

They went a little faster, no longer worried about the small sloshing sounds that came from their progress. Soon they had crossed to the other side of the room, and then the channel took a turn down another hall. Still Niya pressed on, until they were well away from the mess hall. Then the Mystic woman flipped over and lifted the grate above herself, setting it gently on the stone to the side. She climbed from the channel and stole into the first room in the hall. Gem hopped out after her, but he waited for Loren and Chet to emerge and replace the iron grate before the three of them followed Niya into the room.

It was an office of some sort. There was a large ledger on the desk in the corner, though it was closed, and the opposite wall held shelves of scrolls. Thankfully the room was unoccupied, at least for the moment.

"This looks more like the sort of place we seek," said Niya.

"Yet Damaris is not here, either," said Loren. "Let us move on, and quickly, for now I expect the place will be well populated."

They began to steal from room to room, pausing at each one to ensure there was no one around to see them dashing by. Only when a hall was lined by doors that were all closed did they dare to run, and even then they did it at a crouching sort of shuffle to keep quiet. But they only found more offices, and rooms of accounts, and once a study, with a fine upholstered chair and many books upon its shelves.

They passed a grand staircase, with bannisters of wood embedded in the stone walls to either side, and the entire length covered by a woven stair runner. It was patterned like a fine rug, and the edges looked new, but the middle was worn and dirty. Gem stopped and stared at it for a moment, but Loren took his shoulder and pushed him on.

Finally Niya rounded a corner and stopped dead before immediately backing up into Loren again. They pressed themselves to the stone wall, and Niya met her gaze. She held up two fingers, and then pointed to the sword at her hip. *Two guards, both armed, in the next hall.* Loren nodded, and then slid around Niya to see for herself, peeking around the corner. They stood together on the left side of the hallway, hands on the grips of their weapons, staring straight ahead at the opposite wall.

From within the room where they stood guard, Loren could hear voices. Some were deep, some were shrill, but they did not speak over each other, and she could make out each of them with crystal clarity. And she heard one that she knew better than most in Underrealm: a powerful, velvety voice, almost melodic, rich with power and well used to it. The voice of Damaris of the family Yerrin. She drew back again.

"Come," she whispered, motioning towards an empty room they had passed. The door was open, but Loren had seen that it had a bolt. They entered the room and closed the door behind them, and Loren slid the bolt into place before turning to the others.

"We have found her," she said. "Damaris is in that room. Now we must figure out how to remove her from this fortress, even if we must drag her screaming the whole way."

THIRTY-SIX

"I FEEL AS THOUGH WE HAVE TRAVELED ACROSS A KING-dom to find a door, but no one told us the door would be locked and bolted and protected by magic besides," said Chet. "Tell me I am not the only one who sees this as hopeless."

"Keep your voice down," said Niya.

"And take heart," chirped Gem. "I have always seen this entire affair as hopeless."

Chet glared at him. "That is not comforting." He wiped one sleeve against his forehead. "I might not mind if it were not so hot down here."

Loren ignored them. "We must subdue the guards before we can capture Damaris. I think the two in the hall will not be much of a problem. But if I know Damaris, there will be other guards within her council room. And I heard other voices within besides, voices I do not recognize. Also, though I did not hear him, Gregor will be here." Even saying the man's name sent fear coursing through her very soul. Gem's cheerful smile vanished in an instant. He, too, had met the giant bodyguard.

But Niya sliced her hand through the air, as though banishing Loren's warnings. "Darkness take the guards. We can rush the room and take the ones at the door—I trust that you three can subdue one, while I kill the other?—and slay whoever we find inside as well."

"You do not know Gregor. He is a beast in human form," said Loren.

Niya spat, sending a thick glob of saliva to splash on the open pages of a book on the desk beside her. "Say what you wish of him, but I will gut him regardless."

Loren only shook her head. Chet spoke up. "But that is not all we must do," he said. "Once we have Damaris, how do you mean to get her out of the fortress? She will not cooperate just because you have her in hand. And we are fifteen floors below our only means of escape."

They all went quiet at that. But in a moment Gem

looked up with a bright smile. "The shaft. The same one we came down in. Why do we not use the platform to bring her up, like a tray of food?"

A slow smile overcame Loren, and she nodded. "That could work. And I will admit that the idea of escorting her out of here in such an . . . *undignified* manner amuses me no end. Yet the way to that shaft is back through the mess hall."

"It cannot be the only one, not in a place this large," said Gem. "We have come through many passages on our way here. I am certain I can find another."

"Go, then, and search," said Loren. "Only be careful, and do not let yourself come to harm."

"Yes, my lady," said Gem. He gave her a quick half-bow and vanished. Niya rolled her eyes.

"That leaves us with the council room," said Loren.

"We can take the—" Niya began.

"We cannot take the guards," said Loren, shaking her head. "Not with any degree of certainty. You are a powerful warrior, Niya, I will not deny that, but I will not hinge all of our success upon your skill with a blade."

"Unless you have a better suggestion, you have little choice," said Niya, folding her arms.

The room fell to silence, for of course Loren had no answer. Chet shook his head and tugged at the collar of his tunic. "Darkness take this place," he muttered. "The air is so *thick.*"

At his words, an idea came to Loren in a flash.

"Fire," she said. "We can build a fire of wood, cloth and parchment, so that it fills the hall with smoke. The smoke will drive them out of the council room and make it hard to see besides. In the confusion, we can snatch Damaris right out of the hands of her guards."

Niya frowned, but Loren could almost see the idea taking root in the Mystic's mind. "Mayhap. But they will move fast once they smell the smoke, and could slip past us before we can act. We should block their first means of escape."

"The stairwell we passed," said Loren. "The rug was new, but its fibers have already been worn down. It sees much use. That is the route they use to come and go from this floor."

"We must block the stairwell, then, and we should do the same to the hallway at its feet," said Niya. "That way the guards in the mess hall will not be able to come and help their lady."

"But if we fill it with furniture, we will be spotted before we can set the flame," said Chet.

Loren thought hard. "The floor above. If there are not so many of them up there . . ."

Niya straightened. "Why wonder? Let us go and see."

They slipped out and went back the way they had come, quickly reaching the stairwell. They stole up it and looked down the hallway in both directions. At once Loren thought she must be right in her guess, for only every other torch was lit, and they saw no one in any direction. A quick search of the rooms confirmed it: this floor was used little, if at all, though it still had furniture aplenty for their purpose.

"We will build a small mountain of chairs and tables at the top of the stairs," said Loren. "When we are ready to begin, Chet, you and Gem shall send the furniture crashing down. We will return to the room where we just were. Damaris and her guards will pass that way, but they will find the hall blocked. By the time they return in our direction, the smoke should be too thick to see. That is when Niya and I will snatch her away and take her down the hall in the other direction. We will take the first stairway up that we can find. You will meet us there. Then Gem will take us to the shaft leading up, if he can find one."

Gem burst around the corner just then, bouncing on the balls of his feet. "He can," he said. "I found it only a short distance away. I poked my head inside just to be sure—it does not have a door for the level Damaris is on, which is why they did not use it to send her food."

"Good work," said Loren. Despite the gravity of their situation, her mouth split in a grin. "We have our plan, then."

"As far as schemes go, it seems less than simple," grumbled Niya.

"Simple schemes are more easily countered," said Chet.

"Elaborate ones have more chances to fail."

Loren stifled a laugh and clapped one hand each on their shoulders. "Enough. This plan will work. I can feel it. Ready yourselves, for now we snare a merchant."

⸻ 362 ⸻

THIRTY-SEVEN

Loren and Niya ran hurriedly from room to room on the lower level. They built stacks of books and drapes beneath tables in half a dozen offices. At any moment Loren feared a guard would come wandering down the hallway, and the plan would be foiled. But soon they had their little pyres built, and Loren ran quickly to the stairwell. On the floor above, she found Chet waiting for her. Beside him was a huge pile of chairs and couches, all of them stacked atop a pair of tables at the head of the stairs.

"Are you ready?" she asked breathlessly.

"Yes," he said. Then he seized her shirt and drew her in to kiss her. "Be safe."

"And you." She kissed him back.

"Ahem," said Gem. He did not clear his throat so much as he simply said the word aloud.

"Oh, be silent, Gem."

She fled back down the stairs to Niya, who had been watching them. As they ran down the hall towards the first room to set their fires, Niya arched an eyebrow. "Do I get no such consideration?"

Loren ignored that. "Here." She took a torch from a sconce and placed it in the Mystic's hand before seizing another for herself. They split off and ran to separate rooms

In the first, Loren thrust the torch into the pile of books. The dry parchment caught at once. The smoke was even thicker than she had thought it would be, and she quickly ran to the next before it grew too heavy to breathe. Two more fires she set, and at the last one she threw the torch into the flames. She and Niya met each other in the hallway and ran back to the room where they had concocted the plan. To ease their breathing, they held the edges of their cloaks over their noses and mouths.

Scarcely had they shut the door before they heard shouts from Damaris' council room, and they quickly pressed themselves to either side of the door to wait. Many boots came tramping towards them, and Loren tensed. The party passed them by, the guards rushing their lady towards the stairs. Any moment now, Chet and Gem would throw down their barrier . . .

A crash shook the walls, ending with the sound of splintering wood, shards of it scattering upon the stone floor. A renewed cry sprang up from the guards, and the sound of running came back towards Loren.

"Now!" she cried, and she and Niya threw their shoulders into the door. It flew outwards like a battering ram, and she felt it strike bodies. Three guards were bowled to the floor, two of them unconscious and the third stunned. Loren blinked against the smoke that flooded her vision, trying to see the figures ahead of her. She spotted one in a dark green dress pressing a green handkerchief to her mouth. Loren seized an arm and dragged the figure forwards. The face came into view, and her heart skipped a beat. Damaris of the family Yerrin stood before her, in Loren's clutches at last.

"We have her!" cried Loren. "Go!"

She dragged Damaris off down the hall. The merchant's eyes were still pressed so tight against the smoke that she had not realized who had taken her arm. But Niya did not follow them at once. Behind Damaris there were several other figures—some in the fine clothes of merchants or noblemen, and others in guard uniforms.

Niya slew them all.

Loren paused for a moment, horror-struck. First Niya cut down the unarmed figures in the fine clothing. Then she attacked the guards. The smoke had begun to work on her by then, but the guards were nearly poisoned from it, and they all fell beneath her blade. She hacked them down as though she had gone mad, leaving them mangled on the floor in their own blood.

Loren could not stop it. She could not help them. So she turned and ran.

It was a long way before she found another stairwell. This one was plain stone, and it was crumbling, so that she had to take care with her steps. But as she started her ascent, Damaris began to recover from the smoke at last. She swiped desperately at her eyes with the sleeve of her dress.

Her eyes focused on Loren's face.

Damaris recoiled, trying to snatch her hand away.

"You!" she cried. "Guards! *Guards,* darkness take—"

Loren wrenched the woman's arm around and behind her back, and with her other hand she covered Damaris' mouth, taking care that the merchant could not bite her.

"Be silent, Damaris. You know that I will not kill you, but I can make your path out of this place more painful than it has to be." She shoved the merchant up the stairs, and Damaris had to walk or fall flat on her face. Whenever she tried to break free, Loren wrenched on her arm again, until the woman cried out beneath her hand.

But all the while, Loren looked fearfully back over her shoulder as they went. Suddenly the thought of

Niya coming up behind her was terrifying, for she did not know what strange war-lust had seized the Mystic. It reminded her of when Mag had fought the Shades in Northwood. She had entered some sort of battle-trance, and become something inhuman. Only that had been a cold and dead-eyed fury, and Niya's seemed born of pure rage and hatred. It frightened Loren to her core, and she only wished to get as far away from it as possible.

At the top of the stairs, she headed back towards where Gem had shown them the shaft leading up. The smoke had begun to rise to this level, but it was nowhere near as bad, and she found the place easily enough. But when she found the room, only Gem was there. Loren looked behind him, and then inside the room, but Chet was nowhere to be seen.

"Gem," she said, panic seizing her limbs. "Where is Chet?"

"Some guards spotted us just after we threw down the furniture," said Gem. The boy panted heavily, as though he had just run a great sprint. "We split up and said we would meet here. He has not returned yet."

Loren spun, dragging Damaris with her as the merchant cried out in protest. She looked both directions down the hallway, and then ran to the next intersection to look there. Chet was nowhere in sight.

She did not know what to do. She had been willing to leave Niya behind, at least while the woman was in her bloodlust. If worst came to worst, Niya could find the shaft and escape on her own. But Chet . . . how could she go on without him?

You cannot, came the answer in her mind.

Damaris took advantage of her distraction and opened her mouth to bite down on Loren's forefinger. But Loren felt the motion at the last moment and dragged her hand away. The merchant's teeth cut into her skin, but not the flesh. She seized the back of Damaris' hair and slammed the merchant's whole body into the wall, screaming with rage.

"Still yourself, you noxious witch!" she cried. With another great heave, she crushed the merchant into the stone again. "I swear by both the moons that I will end you."

Damaris only laughed. "We both know that that is a lie, *Nightblade.* Tales of you fly all across the land, of the mercy of your hand. And I know you still better than those stories."

"Gem, find rope," said Loren. "Or cord, or anything to bind her with—the more painful the better."

The boy ran off to obey her. Loren shoved Damaris into the room with the hatch and then drew her dagger. She hacked a long strip from the back of Damaris' dress, heedless of the large hole it made there. Her knife slipped for moment and drew a thin line of blood from Damaris' shoulder blade, and the woman hissed with pain.

"My apologies, *my lady,*" said Loren. "Mayhap if you struggled less, that would not have happened."

She balled up most of the cloth and shoved it into Damaris' mouth, tying it in place with the rest. Damaris grunted as Loren pulled the knot as tight as she could. Gem returned in a moment with a thin rope that looked as though it had once belonged to fine drapes, though Loren could not imagine why there would be window coverings in this place, so far from the sunlight.

"Loren!"

She whirled. Chet stood there in the doorway. His clothes were so scorched that she hardly recognized them, and he was covered in soot, but his skin was unmarked by blade or burn. Loren's eyes filled with tears in an instant.

"Chet," she said. "Thank the sky. I thought you were lost. I meant to go and find you, I—"

"That is all right. I am here." He went to her and put a hand on her arm. "You have Damaris. I can scarcely believe it."

"It worked," said Loren. "Now come, quickly, and help me get her into the shaft." Gem already had the thing open, and was hauling on the rope to lower the wooden platform so that they could put Damaris onto it.

"Of course, of course," mumbled Chet. "Only forgive me . . . the smoke . . ." His eyes wandered, taking her in, and then looking to the door of the room. He seemed dazed, half senseless.

She looked at him with concern. "Are you all right? What is wrong? Are you hurt?"

But before he could answer her, Loren heard footsteps from the hall. They all froze, even Damaris, and Loren watched the doorway with wide and fearful eyes. The footsteps stopped just out of sight. Then, with two great staggering steps, Niya appeared in the door.

Loren's first instinct was to loose a sigh of relief, but then she tensed again. The Mystic had taken a wound in the fighting. It looked to be a stab wound from a knife, but it was high on her shoulder and did not seem fatal.

That was not what gave Loren pause. It was the look in Niya's eye—still furious, still filled with a lust for blood and death. Loren felt that she must do something, but she did not know what.

"Niya," said Chet. "You are here, too. What a relief." It did not seem that he saw any sign of the woman's dangerous mood.

"You . . ." growled Niya. She staggered into the room, and Loren saw that the stab wound was not her only injury. Her left arm was badly burned near the shoulder. *"You."*

The sword fell from her hand, and relief washed through Loren. But then Niya strode into the room and seized Chet by the front of his shirt. Before anyone could react, the Mystic drew her dagger and slit Chet's throat.

THIRTY-EIGHT

"No!"

Loren fell to her knees beside Chet as he slumped to the ground. She seized his throat, trying hopelessly to staunch the blood as it poured out over her fingers. Her dreams played in her mind, the dreams where Chet always died, always, just as he was dying now.

Gem gave a scream and launched himself at Niya. But the Mystic struck him a heavy backhand blow, and he landed hard on the floor. Damaris struggled against her bonds, trying to fight to her feet. Niya kicked her back down, and she lay still. Then Niya seized Loren by the back of her cloak and hauled her up.

"Stop your fretting, Nightblade," she growled. "Look."

Loren struggled against her, fighting to reach for Chet again. She knew she could not save him. But darkness take her if she would not be with him as his life slipped away, if she would not give him at least that comfort.

Then she froze.

From Chet's eyes poured a glow she knew well: magelight. And as she watched, his form began to change.

His skin darkened, and his sandy brown hair turned black. When the glow faded from his eyes, he was Chet no longer, but Hewal. He raised a hand, reaching for her, but she could not know whether it was in anger or in fear, for the blood that bubbled up around his teeth was all she could see.

Life fled him at last, and his hand fell to the stone floor.

Niya let go, and Loren jerked away from her.

"You . . . how did you . . ."

"Sky above, girl." Niya's voice was a low growl, still holding some of the fury of her battle-rage. "Look at him. He wears different clothes. Chet wore boots into the stronghold, but Hewal has shoes on."

She spoke the truth. Hewal's clothes were burned and torn, but they were clearly different. In her relief at seeing Chet again, Loren had not seen the details of his appearance.

"I . . . I thought . . ."

"I know what you thought," said Niya. "But we are out of time. All of Yewamba will soon be mustered against us, and we must escape before that happens."

"But Chet—the real Chet, I mean, where is—"

"Loren!" Chet's voice rang out from the hallway. A moment later he appeared there in the doorway, gripping its edges with his hands. Loren ran to him with a cry, but she stopped a pace away, hesitant.

"Sky above, *listen,* girl," said Niya. "Look at his boots."

Loren did, and they were Chet's, and she ran forwards to embrace him. He started, surprised, but then his arms folded around her.

"What is it?" he said. "What is wrong? Gem and I became separated, and—"

He froze, and she knew that he had seen Hewal's body. Loren pushed away from him and followed his gaze.

"He took your likeness, and when I saw him I thought you . . ."

And then she recalled her dream. Chet in the depths of Yewamba, before Damaris, his throat cut. Even Auntie's appearance, over and over again, every night.

Weremage, she thought.

All at once she understood, and she began to laugh. It rang from her clear and loud, mayhap her first true laugh since that final night with Xain upon the Seat. She laughed until her knees were weak, and she had to hold Chet to remain standing.

"Loren, I do not understand what has happened," said Chet.

"You will," she said, touching his cheek. "Everything, I promise you. I will tell you all. But after we have escaped."

"That may be a problem," said Gem. He had thrust his head into the shaft with the wooden platform, and now he withdrew it. "The way is shut."

"What do you mean?" said Loren. She went to him and looked for herself. Far above, she could see a large metal grate. It had been placed to block the way up, with only a tiny gap in its middle so that the rope could run through it.

"It looks to block the top five levels, if I guess the distance correctly," said Gem. "A measure to prevent escape by the very route we had planned to take."

Loren turned to Damaris, who sat against the wall now. Though the merchant's mouth was covered, Loren could see the smile in her eyes. She knelt and pulled off the gag.

"How can we escape?" she said.

"You cannot," said Damaris. Her voice was calm, measured, and utterly in control. "You will die here, slain by my soldiers. Your only possible consolation will be taking my own life before that happens—and I call that a small price, for your end is assured."

Loren saw no doubt whatsoever in the woman's face, and it sent a chill through her. But Niya seized the front of Damaris' dress and dragged her to her feet, slamming her back into the wall.

"Do not toy with us, wretch," said Niya. "There is a way out. A way that you would use to escape, if Yewamba were besieged beyond hope of victory. Tell us where to find it."

Damaris cocked her brows. "I do not know you, woman."

"You will know me before the end," hissed Niya. "Tell us how to get out."

"Never," said Damaris. "Not in a lifetime could you understand the depths of my loathing for this girl, with her simpering eyes and stolen cloak."

"I have stolen many things, but not this," said Loren, smiling fiercely at the merchant. "The cloak you gave me freely. And, too, you drove your daughter away from you and into my company. You may blame yourself for that as well."

Damaris jerked without warning in Niya's arms, breaking free and flinging herself at Loren. But with her hands bound behind her it was a feeble lunge, and Loren caught her by the shoulders. Damaris thrashed and struggled, screaming in Loren's face.

"Never speak of her to me, you mewling sow! You will beg me for death before I am through with you. I have spent a lifetime plumbing the depths of pain. I will plunge you into them again and again until you have forgotten your own name, until you have forgotten everything but agony!"

Loren pushed her slightly away. She drew back her hand and gave Damaris a calm, measured, crushing slap across the face.

"No. You will not."

Chet put a hand on her shoulder. "We have remained here overlong," he said. "If we cannot use the shaft to escape, we should find a better place to hide."

Niya seized Damaris once again and spun her around before driving a knee into her gut. The merchant gave a thin grunt, wheezing as she tried to suck air into her lungs. "Tell us," said Niya. "Tell us before I end you."

Damaris only laughed.

The Mystic squeezed her by the throat, cutting off the laugh and pressing her windpipe until her eyes bugged out. "I give you one final chance. Speak. I have killed many here today, and I will kill more before the end. Speak, or you are next." She drew her knife and pressed the point against Damaris' jugular.

"Stop it," said Loren. She seized Niya's wrist and pulled it away. "That is not the mission."

"The mission?" snarled Niya. "The mission now becomes escape—and if we cannot capture Damaris, better to kill her."

"Our situation is not hopeless. We saw on the way in how sparsely populated this place is. We may still make our way to the top." Loren's hand tightened on

Niya's wrist. "And we may need Damaris as a bargaining chip. Without her, our chances dwindle."

Rage still burned in the Mystic's eyes, plain for all to see. But a spark of cunning flashed within them, and Loren felt the tension in her arm fade away. "Very well," she said in a low voice. "Because we need her."

Loren nodded, and then turned to Damaris. "That is twice now when I could have killed you and did not. That is in repayment, for you have done so twice for me."

"And never a greater mistake," hissed Damaris. "But you have no power over me, girl. You have only ever called off the trained dogs who march by your side—the wizard who became a dean, and now this Mystic."

"You are a fine one to talk," said Loren, arching an eyebrow. "When have you ever held a blade yourself, rather than commanding the one in Gregor's hand? Gag her."

She turned away as Chet did as she asked. But then a thought struck her, spurred by her own words. Gregor.

"Hold a moment," she said, and turned to Damaris. "I did not see Gregor with you below. Is he here in Yewamba?"

The merchant froze. Above the gag, she studied Loren with narrow eyes.

"You seem fairly obsessed with this Gregor fellow," said Niya scornfully. "Is he another lover, mayhap, whose affections you scorned?"

Chet glared at that, but Loren ignored it. "He is her guard. And he is loyal to her beyond measure or reason. Her other guards obey her to the letter, for their duty is to their family. If Damaris ordered them to kill us at all costs, even if it meant her own life, they would obey." Loren smiled at Damaris. "But not Gregor. If we offered her life in exchange for our escape, Gregor would accept in a heartbeat."

Niya's hand tightened on Damaris' shoulder. "We will not surrender her."

"Of course not," said Loren, her smile broadening. "But Gregor will believe that we will. He knows I am . . . an *honorable* thief."

Damaris screamed into her gag and lunged for Loren again, but Niya dragged her back. Loren looked over to Chet and Gem, who wore hopeful smiles for the first time since they had all entered the room.

"Find us some Yerrin guards, my friends. It is time we got out of this place."

Damaris struggled all the while they dragged her down the hallways. Niya held her arm across the woman's throat, placing her in front of the party as they sought for guards to bargain with. They had to find a staircase down to the next level, for the one they were on was still abandoned.

Eventually they neared the mess hall they had snuck through earlier. Around the corner from it they stopped, and Niya looked to Loren. With a nod, Loren ushered her around the corner.

"Guards of Yerrin!" she cried.

The room went utterly silent, and everyone within froze.

The guards had mustered in groups around the tables on either side of the room. It seemed that two captains had gathered their men around to inform them of what had happened and to issue orders. Loren saw that many of the men had burns on their bodies or their clothing, and wondered how long they had been fighting the flames, trying to find their lady among the smoke and the blaze. Now they edged away from the tables and towards the center of the room, hands going to the hilts of their swords.

"That is enough of that," said Niya, tightening her grip on Damaris' neck. "Stay your hands, or see her body broken."

They froze, looking at each other uneasily. Then one of them stepped forwards, a barrel-chested fellow with a thick beard flecked with grey. "Unhand our lady, or things will not go well for you."

"We will not," said Loren. "Not until we have spoken to Gregor."

At that the man paused. He glanced at Damaris. From beneath her gag she shouted, and with her eyes wide she shook her head back and forth. But her words could not be understood, and the guard captain frowned.

"Run and fetch Gregor," he said to one of the men.

"Captain—"

He lifted three fingers. "Do as I say, and do not return without him. Am I understood?"

The guard gave Loren and the others a worried look. "Yes, Captain."

The guard ran out the room's other exit at once. The captain turned back to Loren. "What do you want?"

"Assurance of escape," said Loren. "Once we are safely on our way out of Yewamba, your lady will be freed."

"I cannot allow that," he said at once.

Loren smiled. "We will see, once Gregor arrives. Where is he?"

"Not far," said the captain.

"Good, then," said Loren. "If it is all the same to you, we will be in the hallway with your lady, to ensure that none of your men think to try their luck with an attack."

The captain took a quick step forwards. Niya jerked Damaris up until the merchant was forced to stand upon her toes. The captain froze. "Do not take her out of our sight," he said.

"Very well," said Loren. "She and my friend will stand in the doorway where you may see her."

They backed away slowly, with Loren and Chet and Gem taking up position just to the left of the door. Niya stood in sight of the guards, holding Damaris before her. The merchant continued to struggle and fight, flinging her hands back and forth where they were bound before her.

"Be still," snarled Niya. She drove a fist into Damaris' side, causing her to groan and sag.

"Niya!" said Loren. "Enough. If you harm her too badly, they will not help us at all."

"I will do more than harm her if she does not stop her squirming," said Niya.

Chet looked up and down the hallway. "What is taking the guard so long?" he said. "I thought Gregor was nearby."

"If I know him, he searches high and low for Damaris," said Loren. "He might have gone farther than the captain knew." But she understood his anxiety—she, too, felt more ill at ease the longer they remained here.

"*Still* yourself, witch!" said Niya. Her arm constricted on Damaris' throat just a bit more.

"I think you squeeze her too tight," said Gem, frowning. "She is twitching."

Loren glanced over. Though they were still bound before her, Damaris' arms were indeed spasming back and forth—or rather, her hands were, in jerky little motions. Then Loren's eyes shot wide. The merchant was not struggling against her bonds—she was signaling to the guard captain.

"Niya, run!" she cried, but too late. A door down the hall burst open, and with a great shout of battle cries soldiers in mail shirts and green cloaks stormed into view. Niya froze in shock, and Damaris jerked away from the woman's grasp, then ran stumbling into the mess hall before she could be reclaimed. Loren ran to help, but only in time to see Damaris turn beside the captain and rip the gag away from her mouth with a triumphant grin.

"Kill them!" cried Damaris. "Burn this place to the ground if you must! Bring me their corpses!"

With a snarl, Niya drew her sword. But Loren seized her arm and dragged her back.

"You cannot take them all!" she cried. "Run!"

They did, turning and fleeing down the hallway as an army surged after them.

THIRTY-NINE

"We cannot leave without Damaris," said Niya as they ran.

"We cannot capture her and live," replied Loren. "If you turn back and attack her guards, they will overwhelm you. Now we can only escape, and try again another day."

"You should have let me kill her."

Loren did not answer, but she wondered if the Mystic was right. Yet Kal had been clear: justice was worthless if delivered in secret. Should Damaris die here, in the bowels of this mountain, who would ever even know? Especially if Loren and the rest of them did not escape to spread the tale. And if they killed her like common assassins, that would make them no better than the traitors they fought against who had tried to murder the High King.

But she had no time for such thoughts, not if she wanted to get them all out alive. They ran up the first stairway they saw, but it only took them up one floor, and they did not know which direction to turn.

"We do not know the way out," said Chet. "We will never get out of here before they catch us."

"Oh, stop your *whining*," said Niya.

"There is no other choice," said Loren. "We have to keep looking and hope for the best. One floor at a time."

They turned this way and that through the halls, trying to create a weaving, winding path so that they could not be followed easily. Loren, Chet, and Gem wore only cloth, and Niya was strong enough to run fast even with her chain shirt, so that they soon left the guards behind them. But they could hear the pursuit, their shouts and footsteps thundering in the halls.

At last Loren spotted another stairway. "There!" she cried, leading the way to it. But at the foot of the stairs they skidded to a halt. Above, they heard more shouts and the sound of running. Another group of guards, and this one making its way down towards them.

"We are trapped," whispered Loren.

"Then it is a fight after all," said Chet. He looked

to Niya. "I suppose we should be glad we have your sword."

"Wait," said Gem. He looked up at Loren with wide eyes. "There may be a way. The shaft."

She frowned at him. "It is shut, Gem. We cannot go up that way."

"Not up," he said. "Down."

Her mind raced. Down, down, into impenetrable darkness—but where they had heard the sound of running water. It might be a river deep enough to swim. It might be only a few fingers deep. Or the rope might not be directly over the water at all, and end ten paces above a rocky cavern floor, and they would kill themselves if they tried the jump. But they did not know that, and they *did* know what would happen if they stayed and fought the guards.

"We must try it," she said. "Come."

They ran on, and now they ducked their heads into each room as they went, searching for one that had a hatch. Chet found one in a few moments. Loren threw it open and looked up, just to be sure—but there was the metal grate, blocking the way in this shaft just as it had in the other.

"Very well," she said. "Down it is."

They slipped through the hatch as quickly as they could, with Niya going last. She pulled the hatch as far shut as she could, though she could not latch it from the inside. It would have to do. Loren led them all down the rope.

Fifteen floors they had descended before they found Damaris. Loren thought they passed at least fifteen more, but it was hard to keep count, for no light came through the hatches on the lower levels. Soon they were in pitch blackness, and when they looked up they could only barely glimpse the soft glow that had lit their way before.

"How will we even know when we reach the bottom?" called Gem. The sound of rushing water had grown loud enough now that he had to raise his voice to be heard.

"I imagine the rope will end," said Loren.

"That is not comforting," said Chet.

Loren chuckled—and then she cried out, for the wall had vanished under her feet. She had reached the bottom of the shaft, and when she put out her foot to take the next step down, it met only empty air. For a terrifying moment she swung there in the darkness, swaying back and forth on the rope as she tried to tighten her grip.

"Loren!" cried Chet, for he could not see her.

"I am all right!" she said. "The shaft has ended, but the rope has not."

"Can you see the floor?" said Niya.

I cannot see anything at all, thought Loren irritably. But she only said, "No."

Hand over hand she lowered herself once more, but now the way was harder without something to brace herself on. Her hands began to chafe on the rope, and she did not know how much longer she could keep hold. *As long as you must,* she told herself, tightening her grip again. This place must have a bottom. They would reach it eventually.

And then the rope ended.

Loren felt it with her feet first, where they were wrapped around the line. Suddenly they encountered the curving loop at the bottom of the rope, where it turned and ran back up the shaft to the crank that must be at the top. She went a little farther down and stuck out her feet, but she already knew she would not find the ground. The rushing water was loud, thundering below them, but too far for her to reach.

"We are at the bottom," she called up.

"Thank the sky," said Gem.

"I mean the bottom of the rope," said Loren. "The floor is still far below."

"Ah," said Gem. "That is somewhat less good news."

"What do we do?" said Chet.

"A moment," said Loren. "I am thinking." At least she was able to put a knee in the loop of the rope and take some of the weight off her arms. But that only made her realize that her friends had no such support, and their grips must be as tired as her own. Her mind raced, desperate for an answer.

They could risk the jump. Though she could not be sure, it sounded as though the water was below them. They could drop from the end of the rope, and hope that they would land in the river that would carry them out into the valley. But then again, if the river indeed emerged out into the open, would they not be able to see the light of the opening from here?

See.

She cursed the darkness. If she only had a torch, or moonslight, or—

Loren almost struck herself, she was so angry. *You stupid, stupid fool,* she thought.

The magestones. She had them in her cloak, the same place she always kept them. But she had not used them since Ammon, and had nearly forgotten about them.

"I cannot hold on to this rope forever, you know," said Gem. The boy tried to fill his voice with bravado, but Loren could sense the fear quivering beneath it. "Even one so strong as I am has his limits."

"One moment!" she said, fumbling with her cloak pocket. With hasty fingers she seized a magestone and broke off a piece, which she shoved in between her lips. Then she reached for the back of her belt and drew her dagger.

The cavern erupted in light, silver and pale, like the glow of the Elves. Now Loren could see as though she stood in the sun, or better, for every detail was enhanced, from the ridges in the rocky cavern to the cobwebs that collected in the corners.

She looked down and was glad she had not risked the jump. There was a river, yes, mayhap fifteen paces below them. But it twisted and turned through a fissure in the floor, and just beneath them was only rock, pocked with spikes of stone that jutted up from the ground towards them, like hungry teeth eager to devour.

"We cannot jump!" said Loren. "There is only stone below us."

"What?" said Chet. "How do you know?"

"My eyes are adjusting," she lied. "Are you not getting used to the darkness?"

"Then what do we do?" said Niya, her irritation plain.

Loren looked about. She could see other ropes hanging down from other holes in the ceiling—other shafts leading up to other wooden platforms, and all of them too far away to reach. But then she turned the other way, and saw that they were very near to the cavern wall, and there were shelves in the rock there. But it was at least five paces away—too far to jump, and certainly too far to reach.

"We must swing!" said Loren. "Swing the rope . . . this way." She reached up and tapped Gem's leg, on the side where the rock wall was. He did the same to Chet, who did the same to Niya.

"I see nothing that way," said Niya.

"Trust me," said Loren. "Draw back your legs, and . . . now!"

They did it, back and forth, back and forth. At first they were awkward and uncoordinated, but as they all sensed the rhythm of each other, they soon moved in unison. The rope only moved a pace at first, and then two. Then they got within reach of the shelf, but Loren missed her grasp. She tightened her grip on the dagger with one hand, and her hold on the rope with the other.

"This time!" she cried, and when she swung towards the shelf, she reached it at last. She threw herself onto the stone, and a lump in the rock struck her in the ribs, making her wince. But she seized the rope and pulled it tight, and just managed to keep from sliding off the edge again by wrapping her arm around a lump in the stone. The rope hung there, her three friends upon it, dangling over the rocky floor far below.

"Quickly!" she said through gritted teeth. "Climb down."

Gem descended like a spider, and she sighed with relief once his weight was off the line. Then came Chet, and by the time only Niya was left, it was easy. The Mystic reached the shelf at last, and Loren released the rope with a sigh. But above her she saw that the other three were fumbling blindly in the dark, their hands on the wall to hold themselves steady.

"We have to climb down from here," she said. "The wall is rough. There are handholds aplenty."

"How can you see?' said Chet. "It is black as tar."

"What matters is that I *can* see," said Loren. "I will go down first. When I tell you to, guide your foot to the edge, and I will give you your first handhold."

They did as she bid, and one by one they slid over the edge and began to climb down the stone wall. Loren put the dagger in her teeth, careful not to let it touch her lips, for it was frighteningly sharp. She was gratified to see that its magical properties remained even when she held it so.

With its help she took them all the entire long, dark, frightening way to the floor of the cavern, and when they had reached it they sighed with relief.

"If anything, I can see less than before," said Gem. "If this place is so dark, is there even a way out?"

"The water must emerge somewhere," said Loren. "It forms the stream in the valley outside Yewamba. Chet, put your hand on my shoulder, and the rest of you in a chain. I will take us to the water, and we will follow it out."

So they progressed to the water's edge. Loren could see that the river was nowhere near so deep as she had thought; she doubted it came up to her chest. But it was wide, and the way beside it was not always clear, so that it took them some time to follow it through the cavern.

When they reached the end of it, Loren hoped to find a curve in the rock, some sort of passage that would take them to the open air beyond. But to her dismay, the water ended at a wall, against which it frothed and bubbled.

"The water has ended," she said.

"What do you mean, it has ended?" said Niya.

"It dives under the cave wall here. If it emerges in the open air beyond, it goes underground for a ways beforehand."

"Then there is no way out?" said Chet.

"There is," said Loren. She turned to look at him, but then realized that was pointless, for he could not see her. "The river."

Niya snorted. "Underground? We do not know how far it is. We could drown."

"Yet there is no other way."

"Loren, I cannot swim," said Gem, and now all his bravado had fled him.

She cursed inwardly, for she had forgotten. "I can take you, Gem. You can hold my shoulders."

"He had better come with me," said Niya. "You are not as strong as I am."

Loren studied the Mystic for a moment, thankful now for the darkness. "I would rather bring him my-self," she said carefully. "Gem and I have done some-thing like this together before."

That was true enough—in the city of Wellmont, they had swum under a gate that blocked the river. But in truth, Loren was not sure that she trusted Niya with the boy's life. The Mystic had always scorned him, like-ly thinking him too young to be on such an important quest. If the way became blocked, and Niya faced the choice of saving the boy or saving her own skin, Loren did not think it would be a difficult decision.

Niya only shrugged. "If you insist."

"Loren, are you certain this is the best way?" said Chet.

"Of course not," she told him. "But it is the only way. Now come. Dawdling here will not make the swim easier."

She shucked off her boots and tied them to her belt. They would not help with her swimming, but once they emerged out the other side, she could not go barefoot all the way back to their camp. Quickly she helped the others do the same, for their fingers fumbled in the darkness, and soon they were ready.

"All right," said Loren. "Gem, take my shoulders. Follow the flow of the water. It comes out the other side in the end, so it knows where it is going. Good luck."

"Luck," said Chet, laughing suddenly. "How can we think ours is good, after all that has happened?"

Niya scowled in the direction of his voice, likely thinking no one could see her in the pitch-dark cavern. Then, without warning, the Mystic flung herself into the water. After letting Gem take a deep breath, Loren followed.

The water snatched her at once and dragged her into the tunnel beneath the rock. Immediately it slammed her into the wall, and she felt Gem's grip shift. Keeping one hand on her dagger hilt, she reached up with the other and clutched his arm. It was useless to try to swim, for the current was too strong here. She only twisted and turned, keeping her body between the boy and the rocks, and used her legs to brace against the impact. Chet and Niya would not be able to see a thing, and Loren only hoped they did not take too hard of a battering.

Her lungs grew weak, and then began to burn. The tunnel ahead showed no sign of ending. She took her hand from Gem's arm and tried to swim as best she could, desperate to speed their progress. If she was losing her breath, Gem must be near to drowning. Niya and Chet were nowhere to be seen. Had they become separated? Did the water run in different passages, ones she had missed as she went by?

A dim light appeared, different from the night vision of the dagger, illuminating the channel. The end of the tunnel at last. But though they could see the glow, they still could not see the exit, and spots had begun to dance in Loren's vision.

Around her neck, she felt Gem's grip slacken.

No, she thought. She seized his arm and kicked as hard as she could, striking for the light ahead. *Hold on. Hold on, you little brat.*

Sunlight erupted above them, almost blinding in its intensity. Loren shoved her dagger into its sheath and swam up, still clutching at Gem. Her head broke the surface with a great splash, and she sucked in a greedy lungful of air.

The shore was only a few paces away, and she kicked for it. Niya was there already, on hands and knees in the grass, gasping and heaving. Loren flung Gem up on the bank first and then dragged herself from the water. Her black cloak had become dead weight intent on trying to drag her into the river again, so she undid the clasp and threw it off. She fell on the shore as all her strength left her at once, and her chest heaved with her breathing.

But then she thought of Gem and rose once more. She crawled to the boy and flipped him onto his back, pounding on his chest. For one heart-stopping instant he lay still. Then at last he coughed up water. She hauled him up to sitting and bent him forwards, and he kept coughing until no more water came out.

Loren looked up towards the stream. *Chet. Where is Chet?*

Then he appeared, breaking the surface just as she had, a little upstream. He saw them and fought to swim to the shore, gasping. Loren sighed with relief. Chet had always been a good swimmer.

"Is he all right?" said Chet, once he had gained the land.

"Well enough, considering," said Loren, giving Gem's back a final pound.

"Leave off," said the boy, waving a limp arm in her direction. "I am fine."

Loren smiled down at him. But the smile died on her lips as a horn cut the air.

She had not had time to take in their surroundings, but now she looked up. They were at the foot of the stronghold, with its peaked prow jutting out into the air straight overhead. A few hundred paces away was the bottom of the long, winding ramp that led up to the main entrance. And down that ramp figures were running and shouting, their weapons drawn.

"They have spotted us," said Loren. She fought for her feet and snatched up her cloak. "Come. We must flee if we are to survive."

Quickly she removed her boots from around her waist and pulled them on. Niya struggled to don her own boots, her movements slow and sluggish.

"I would wager that now you wish we had killed the guards in the valley as we approached."

"I do not, but thank you," said Loren, frowning. "Now is not the time for gloating, but for running."

Run they did, following the stream. Soon the guards were behind them, giving chase along the opposite side of the river. But Loren and her friends were waterlogged and exhausted from the swim, so that they could not gain much ground, and soon their lungs burned anew.

"We are not gaining any ground," said Chet. "They will follow us straight back to Uzo and Annis."

"And—" Loren almost stopped in her tracks, and only resumed her flight when Chet snatched her arm and pulled her along. "Shiun. Where is Shiun?"

"She will look after herself," said Niya. "Likely she fled the fortress as soon as the alarm was raised, for who could think that we would escape?"

It was not a comforting thought that Shiun would leave them to their fate, but certainly they could not go back to see. If they somehow evaded the guards, they would return later. But she did not see how that would happen.

And then they ran over a hillock, and an arrow struck Loren in the chest.

She stumbled in her run and barely kept herself from falling on her face, sinking to her knees instead.

Dazed, she stared at the feathered shaft that protruded from her torso, on the left side and just under the collarbone. Her gaze drifted upwards.

Three guards stood there. Mayhap they were the ones Shiun had shown to Loren on the valley floor, two days ago when they had discovered Yewamba. Mayhap they were another three. But one of them had a bow, and she had loosed the shaft that now pierced Loren's body.

Was that the arrowhead she could feel, protruding from her back?

She tried to lift her left arm to see, but it did not move. She lifted her right arm instead, reaching behind her back. But a pain shot through her, and she dropped her hand.

Someone was screaming. Who was screaming? She looked up. Chet, Chet who held her shoulders, who was trying to place his body between her and the archer.

Why do that? she thought. *I have been shot already.* It struck her then that that was a foolish thought, and her mind was wandering.

Someone else was there. Shiun, her dark eyes wide and anxious as she beheld Loren's wound. And looking over Chet's shoulder, Loren could see two of the Yerrin guards had now been shot as well, and lay still on the ground. Shiun must have done it. The third guard lay on his back, hands raised feebly as Niya plunged her dagger into his chest, over, and over, and over.

Loren fell backwards and knew nothing more.

FORTY

Blinding pain was her only companion when she awoke, but that was better than the memory of a nightmare.

Loren tried to sit up. She failed, gasped, and lay still. Her chest was wrapped with bandages that covered a great pad of cloth. She tried to probe at it with her left hand, but as soon as her arm moved the pain redoubled. Hissing through her teeth, she waited for it to subside before using her right hand instead, though that limb was weak and shaking.

Touching the pad of cloth was not too bad, but

when she tried to lift it, dried blood peeled from her skin. She winced and left it alone, and then looked around.

Where were the others? She knew she was in her tent, but Chet was not with her, and she heard no movement outside.

"Is anyone there?" she croaked.

She heard movement on the grass, and then the tent flap flew open. Chet eagerly poked his head in, eyes shining as he beheld her. "You are awake," he said, his voice shaking.

"I am, and I am thirsty."

"Of course," he said. "One moment."

He vanished, only to return shortly with her water-skin. She could not sit up without his help, but once she did she drank deep, ignoring the way it burned in her throat. When she was done she patted his arm, and he moved the skin away.

"How long?" she said.

"It is the evening of the day after our mission."

Loren's eyes shot wide, and she tried to look out through the tent flap. "They have not found us?"

"We moved the camp," said Chet. "Shiun found this place, and we were on constant watch in case they drew near it. But then, sometime during the night, they simply gave up."

"Why?" said Loren. "Why would they?" She frowned, looking into her lap. Then a guess came to her, and she surged forwards, trying to leave the tent.

But with a grimace and a cry she fell back, and Chet only just caught her in time.

"Sky above, Loren, give yourself a moment at least. You took an arrow. That is no scratch."

Once more she looked at the bandages on her chest. "Who did this?" *Niya,* she guessed in her mind.

"Uzo," said Chet. "He has some little skill as a healer, it seems, though he told us often that he is no master at it. He did say the wound could have been much worse. The arrow struck only flesh, nothing vital."

"Nowhere near as bad as your wound upon the Seat, then?" said Loren.

Though he tried to restrain it, a guffaw burst out. "Darkness take you, Loren. We are not in contest to see who can suffer the greater injury."

Loren smiled at him and put her hand on his cheek. "Did everyone get out safely?"

"They did," he said. But then his face darkened, and his voice grew quiet. "All but Weath, of course."

"I am sorry," said Loren. Then she shook her head. *Darkness take me, my thoughts are wandering.* "But we have little time. I know why the Yerrins stopped searching for us. They mean to leave—"

"They mean to leave Yewamba," said Chet. "Annis guessed the same thing. She said it was a good thing Damaris did not know she was close by, or else she would never have left the stronghold. But now the family Yerrin feels too exposed, for their location is known, and mayhap word has already reached them that Kal marches west towards them. Whatever the reason, they are preparing to leave."

"Then this is our last chance to stop Damaris," said Loren. "We must—"

"She will ride out ahead of the rest," said Chet. "Annis guessed that, too. She thinks she knows the route Damaris will take, unless there is some road west of the mountains she can escape to. But Uzo and Shiun have gone to guard the main road, and if Damaris passes that way, they will see her. If they believe they can take her guards, they will. If not, they will mark her passing so that we may follow in due time."

Loren stared at him in wonder. "Annis did all this?"

"Annis and Niya," said Chet, smiling. "Niya commanded Uzo and Shiun to go. They should return in a few days. But all of the plans came from Annis."

"That girl has more wit than even I realized," said Loren, shaking her head. But then something he had said caught her attention, and she frowned at him. "You said Niya told Uzo and Shiun to go. She did not accompany them?"

"She is here," said Chet. "She took wounds herself, you will remember."

"I do," said Loren. "Only I wish Uzo and Shiun were not alone."

"They will not endanger themselves," said Chet. He sat back, leaning on his hands. "I for one am just glad we escaped in time, and that you are still alive."

"I am, too," said Loren, smiling at him. Despite

the pain from her wound, she felt as though a great weight had left her shoulders. "Indeed, my mind is easier than it has been in some time."

"Even though we lost Damaris?" said Chet, his brows rising.

She thought of her dream, and then of Hewal's corpse. "Even then," she said softly.

He shook his head. "Well, then my mind is eased as well. Only now I should go."

"Go?" said Loren. "Where?"

"To hunt," he said. "Our supplies run low, and Niya fears to visit that little town nearby, in case the Yerrins have placed agents there to watch for us. But I will send Annis in to sit with you, and help you if you should need anything."

Loren nodded. He kissed her forehead and left.

A while later she heard footsteps again and smiled as the tent flap opened. But it was not Annis. It was Niya. Her regular clothes were gone, replaced with dark brown trousers and a cream-colored tunic, the same as Loren's. It was the nondescript outfit most of them had worn on the journey to avoid attracting attention.

"Hello," said Loren softly.

"You look well enough," said Niya.

"I suppose I am," said Loren. "At least I am not dead."

"Though not for lack of trying."

Loren smiled. "How is your shoulder?"

Niya glanced at her own bandages. She wore fewer than Loren did. "It pains me less and less. I have been going for walks. They make it easier."

"I may do the same," said Loren.

It seemed as though Niya meant to say something else, or mayhap even to come inside the tent to continue speaking. But there came the snap of a twig, and she looked off to the side. She frowned at Loren. "You have another visitor. When you decide you are strong enough for walking, tell me. I shall bring you along."

She vanished from sight, only to be replaced by Annis. The girl crawled into the tent with her and took Loren's hand with a happy smile.

"It is good to see you awake."

"And it is good to see you at all," said Loren. "I heard that you have become quite the master strategist while I have been resting."

Annis' cheeks darkened. "I suppose I have been industrious in my planning."

"Thank you for seeing to things after I was injured," said Loren. "When I woke, I feared that we had lost everything. I should have known better."

"Stop it," said Annis, shaking her head. "You make it sound as though I have performed great deeds. I have only looked at maps and read a few signs."

"Kingdoms have been conquered, or more importantly, saved, by ones who sit and stare at maps," said Loren. "Our party would neither have come so far, nor come so close to achieving our aims were it not for you. I am glad you and Gem are with me."

At the boy's name, Annis' smile dampened considerably, though she tried to maintain it. But Loren saw, and frowned.

"What is it?"

"Nothing," said Annis. "Nothing you should trouble yourself over at any rate. You should be resting."

Loren raised her hands—the left one moved far more slowly than the right. "I am resting, and I cannot do anything else. Speak on. Did Gem do something wrong?"

Annis shook her head quickly. "No, not at all. Only . . . do you remember the night before you went to Yewamba, when I decided to tell him how I felt?"

"How can I forget?" said Loren, smirking. "I have rarely seen you with your blood up to that extent."

"Well, I did it," said Annis miserably. "And in return, he told me . . . that he felt affection for another."

Loren cocked her head, wondering at the girl's despair. "Another? Who . . . ?" Then a horrid thought struck her. "Oh, sky above. Do not say he means me."

Annis snorted—which Loren did not think was very complimentary—and shook her head. "No. It is Uzo."

Loren only stared for a moment. Then the meaning of it assembled in her mind. She closed her eyes and heaved a deep sigh. "I see. That . . . I am sorry, Annis."

"Why should you be?" said Annis, shrugging. "It

is not your fault, nor his. And is that not the most irritating thing? If he *did* pine after you, I could box his
ears for being a fool, when I have shown him plainly
how I felt. But now . . ."

"Yes," said Loren, thinking of Xain, and then of
Jordel. "I learned the same thing myself, just before we
left the Seat. Sometimes the deepest cut comes from
the one who did not intend it, and who had no other
choice in the first place."

FORTY-ONE

She rested that day, and went to sleep shortly after the sun went down. When she woke the next morning, her chest hardly hurt at all, at least not with any sharp pain. There was a gentle soreness that penetrated deep into her chest, and it swelled when she tried to move her arms. But Chet changed her bandages, which Uzo had shown him how to do, and she got a good look at her wound for the first time. It was much smaller than she had thought it would be, only a little larger than her fingernail, and the blood was already solid.

"The guards of Yerrin use narrow arrowheads," said Chet. "It lets them pierce chain, and sometimes plate, but it lessens the wound, and thank the sky for that."

With his help, she got dressed and left the tent. Outside, she found she could walk quite easily. She did not hurt anywhere but the shoulder, and as long as she did not move that too quickly, it was almost as though there was no injury at all.

"That is good," said Chet. "Uzo told us that the injury was not very serious, and that it was only the shock of it that made you fall senseless. Even so, you seem to be healing remarkably quickly."

It was true. She wondered about it, and then recalled what Xain had told her in the Academy's bell tower about the mystical properties of magestones. Was this another of them? In any case, she was glad of it.

As she sighed and stretched in the early morning light, Niya came out of her own tent. She smiled to see Loren up and about. "Good morn, Nightblade. How is your wound?"

"Better than yesterday," said Loren. "And I suppose that is all that can be expected."

"That is good to hear," said Niya. "Are you ready to try a walk? I found a path in the jungle yesterday that leads to a beautiful clearing. I think you would enjoy it."

Loren glanced at Chet, but he smiled and patted her hand. "I should go out hunting again," he said. "Go. It will be good for you."

"I will not be gone long," said Loren. Then she followed Niya, who struck out at once, heading south between the trees.

Soon Loren saw the trail that the Mystic had spoken of. It was an easy enough walk, and went up and down a series of hills that ran along the base of the mountains. Once or twice it crossed the stream, the same one that ran out of the mountain and came flowing all the way south. Loren remembered their escape from that place with a slight shiver.

Niya saw it and looked her over. "Is something wrong? Does it hurt?"

"No," said Loren. "I only remembered the cavern under Yewamba."

Niya nodded, and then fixed Loren with a crafty look. "And I remember you guiding us through it without pause. How did you see down there, anyway? Do not tell me you have good eyes—the place was pitch black."

Loren shrugged. She had not revealed her dagger to any of the Mystics, for she could not know who among them was trustworthy with its great secret. Even now she could feel it pressing against her ankle in her boot. "I cannot explain what I do not understand. I could see, and I do not know why you could not."

"Hm," said Niya, frowning at her. "Very well. Keep your secrets, Nightblade. But come along. We are near the place I wanted to show you."

The ground rose up now, up to the top of a ridge

that was like a first step leading up a grand staircase, all the way to the mountains high above. There on the top of the ridge was the clearing. When they reached it, Niya waved her arm expansively out towards the lands below, as though presenting a fine feast.

It took Loren's breath away. They were not so very high, but the land before them fell down and down, so that she could see for what seemed like endless leagues. Jungle stretched without breaking, except to the southeast where she could see the village of Sara-fu, smoke rising from its chimneys. But the rest was a verdant rug that went on forever, and the sun a golden coin glinting in a sky like the ocean.

"It is wonderful, Niya," said Loren. "I am glad you brought me here."

"Come, sit with me," said Niya. "Do you need help?"

Loren dropped and crossed her legs upon the ground. "No, thank you. It is as I said—the wound hardly troubles me if I do not jostle it."

"That is good," said Niya. She flashed a smile. "I will try not to jostle it, then."

Loren returned the smile, but she did not feel the same thrill course through her that she had during all the long journey across Feldemar. The memory of Niya's battle-rage, of the way she had cut down those people inside Yewamba, would not quit her mind. "You will not have an opportunity to."

"Oh, come now," said Niya. "At least be coy when

you rebuff me. After what we went through in Yewamba together, I deserve at least that much."

"It is Yewamba that is the problem," said Loren. "You went half-mad in there. You did not only attack guards, but unarmed merchants. It was as though no amount of blood could sate you."

Niya frowned. "We needed to escape, and we were bringing a prisoner with us. Any pursuer could have overtaken us easily. They were a threat, and I removed them."

"I . . . I understand that," said Loren. And inside she thought, *Do I honestly? Am I that different from the girl who left the Birchwood so long ago?* But the answer was the feeling of unease in her heart. "Yet I saw you, Niya. You enjoyed it."

The Mystic's nostrils flared, and she looked away. "Mayhap I did, but not in the way you think. I have always been angry. You must have seen that yourself. Long ago I learned to control that when I fought, to harness it into a sort of madness. It makes me strong. In the moment I may be a killer." She put a hand on Loren's knee. "But that does not mean I am always a killer. I can be gentle as well."

Loren wanted to pull her knee away, but she restrained herself. "Once, I wanted that. But I have told you that I am Chet's, and he is mine. More clearly than ever now, I know why. Chet and I have been by each other's side for most of our lives. We know each other. We understand each other. He feels the same way about killing as I do. You are a fine woman, Niya, but you and I will never have what Chet has."

"How many times must I tell you that I do not want what you and Chet have?" growled Niya. She leaned forwards, trying to kiss Loren.

"Stop!" said Loren. She shot to her feet, awkward without the use of her left arm, and her right fist clenched. "I have spoken plainly, and already you have skirted dangerously close to the wrong side of the law. Leave me be."

Slowly Niya rose to her feet. She looked down at Loren with a wry smile and shook her head.

"Oh, little Loren," she said quietly. "What a foolish, foolish little girl you have been."

Loren recoiled—and then her heart stopped. From Niya's eyes, a pale white light shone forth.

Her form shifted and rippled. First she shrank, so that she was of a height with Loren. Her dark hair grew by a few fingers and then turned so blonde that it was almost white. Her brown skin darkened further. Her lips grew fuller. And as the light faded from her eyes at last, they were a light hazel, a hazel that captivated Loren just as surely as it had the first time she saw it.

Her lips curled in a devilish grin.

"Hello, Loren," said Auntie. "I can only imagine how much you have missed me."

FORTY-TWO

Loren turned and fled for her life.

Her feet pounded down the path back towards camp, jostling her shoulder and making her wince as she plunged into the trees. She feared to look behind her, to slow even that much.

"Oh, Loren," called Auntie. "Why have you always been so coy?"

The voice sounded close, forcing Loren to turn against her will. But the weremage had vanished. Loren whirled, seeking her in the jungle, but saw nothing.

"Why—how long?" she called out. If she could get Auntie to talk, she might be able to tell the woman's location. "When did you take Niya's place?"

"You stupid, stupid girl." The voice came floating from her left, and Loren turned. Still she saw nothing. "It has always been me. From the very first time when you made your moon-eyes at me upon the Seat."

"That is a lie," said Loren at once. "You were kind. You were even . . . you acted as though you—"

"As though I *wanted* you?" Auntie laughed, long and cruel. "As I said. A stupid girl. So stupid, you very nearly betrayed the love of your life for a pair of strong arms."

She was trying to circle around, to come between Loren and the path back to camp. *"Chet!"* screamed Loren, breaking into a sprint and ignoring the pain in her chest. *"Chet!"*

The jungle was silent. For a moment she wondered if Auntie was still there, stalking her, or if the weremage had decided not to chase her, and instead to go back for the camp. She must reach it first. If Auntie hurt any of the others—

Auntie pounced from the trees, right in front of Loren, who tried to skid to a halt. But the weremage's hand darted out and seized her shoulder. Loren cried out with pain and fell to her knees. Auntie sneered down at her.

"The mighty Nightblade," she said. "How long I have waited to bring you low. But I could not have imagined how sweet it would be—almost as sweet as the taste of you upon my lips."

"Why?" gasped Loren, as Auntie continued to squeeze her wound through the bandage. "Why all of this?"

"Oh, it was so very hard not to kill you until now," said Auntie. Without removing her grip, she knelt, her face only a handbreadth from Loren's. "Even the delightful charms of your eyes, darkness take them, did not still my wrath, my desire to taste your blood upon my knife. But I knew I must be patient. I knew I must wait. For I knew in the end you would bring me to Damaris."

Her free hand pulled down her collar. Then Loren saw that she still had a ruined throat, the mass of scar tissue that spoke of a grievous wound. It had not changed with the rest of Auntie's body.

"She gave me this. She gave me this because of *you.* I lay in that sewer for days as I tried to stitch my own neck together, and still it is ruined. Because of *you.*" Her voice was little more than rasping breath now, sweet and pungent in Loren's nostrils. "That is why I needed you, needed you both, you see. But while I waited, while I followed you as you bumbled your way across Feldemar in search of her, I decided that you would be mine before the end."

Loren struck all at once, hoping to surprise her. Her right fist slammed into Auntie's neck, and the weremage coughed violently just before Loren crushed the woman's nose with her forehead. She fought to gain her feet, but Auntie recovered, sweeping her legs out from under her with a vicious kick. Loren crashed down upon her back, screaming as agony lanced her shoulder.

Auntie straddled her, drawing something from her pocket. She threw it in Loren's face—a fine powder, burnt orange. Loren gasped without thinking and felt it enter her lungs. Her body seized up, arms twitching, and then they ceased to move at all. She lay utterly limp, her limbs refusing to answer the call of her mind. Auntie grinned down at her.

"A poison," said Auntie. "It may kill you in time, if I use enough of it. For I will use a very great deal, Loren, a *very* great deal. But mostly, I will use it to hold you in place. Because I do not wish for you to go anywhere, *Nightblade*—not while I carve you up, a piece at a time."

She drew a knife from her boot and held it up. Loren tried to recoil, but she could not move.

It was the knife from her dream. Old, rusted, dirty. Far below the quality one would expect of a merchant—but just right for a madwoman who lurked in the sewers of Cabrus.

Loren could not even scream. Only her eyes obeyed her, and even that was sluggish.

"I want you awake for all of it. I want you to feel every bit of it—every cut. And I want you to remember all the while, Loren." She leaned down, her lips brushing against Loren's ear. "I want you to remember that you almost chose me. That you almost gave yourself to me, in every way, instead of the boy you claimed to love."

"Loren!"

Auntie whirled. The voice was Chet's, but it came from a distance, somewhere off through the trees. He called out again. He was closer now. He was coming this way.

No, no, sky above, no, thought Loren. *Run Chet, please, darkness take me, run. Why did I call out for you?*

Atop her, Auntie gave a growl—but then she froze. She turned and looked down at Loren, an evil glint in her eye.

"You told me that Chet knows you. That he *understands* you. You are wrong. Let me show you."

Light flowed from her eyes once more, and her body began to shift. Her blonde hair turned black and grew out, and brown skin turned to cream.

The transformation ended, and panic seized Loren's breath—for she stared into her own eyes. Auntie had taken on Loren's likeness; indeed, she looked identical, for they wore the same dark brown trousers, the same white shirt, though Auntie's was somewhat too large, for it had been sewn for Niya's larger frame.

"Come along, girl," said Auntie, and Loren shuddered inwardly to hear her own voice from that mouth. "I mean to give you quite a show."

The weremage rose and threw her arms beneath

Loren's, dragging her off to the side of the path. She rolled Loren beneath some bushes there, and ripped some branches from the trees, throwing them over her body. But then she knelt and moved the branches slightly so that Loren could look out.

"You can see me, can you not, girl?" whispered Auntie. "I would not want you to miss a thing."

Then she rose and turned, just as Loren heard Chet approach from down the path.

"Loren!" he exclaimed. "There you are. I heard you call my name, and I feared something was wrong."

Sky above, no, thought Loren. She railed at her body, screaming for her arms to move, but they would not comply.

"Wrong? What could be wrong?" said Auntie. She waited for Chet to come to her, so that she could be sure Loren would see them. Chet stepped up to her, and Auntie slid her arms up to lace her fingers behind his neck. She drew him close and gave him a long, passionate kiss. Loren wanted to close her eyes, but even that was beyond her power. "Nothing can be wrong when you are with me."

"I am flattered, though that has not proven to be the case in recent days," said Chet, giving her a wry smile.

Chet, look to the left, thought Loren. *Please, please. Look to the left. See me.*

His head jerked up, and a mad hope filled her that somehow he had heard her. But he looked the other direction. "Where is Niya?"

"After she showed me the clearing above, she went off on her own. She said she would make for the camp in a while. I am surprised you did not see her—but glad as well, for it means I have you alone." Slowly her hands slid down his chest, and then around his waist. He responded by wrapping his arms around her and leaning in for another kiss. "And while we are here, and alone . . ." Her hands slid around to his front, toying with the buckle of his belt.

Chet drew back, laughing with embarrassment. "I— Loren, what are you doing? We are in the open jungle."

"And why should that matter? No one is near to see us." Auntie smiled up at him and cocked an eyebrow. Her lips had a wry twist, and her eyes shone with promise.

That is not my smile, Chet, screamed Loren. *You know it. You know my eyes. Look at them!*

But he only glanced back over his shoulder, a silly grin stealing across his face. "What if Niya should return and look for you?"

"She will not," said Auntie. "I told you, she makes for camp." When he still seemed hesitant, she kissed him again and finished removing his belt while their lips were still locked.

They fell to the floor of the path, tearing at each other's clothes. Soon Auntie rolled Chet onto his back and sat atop him. Their low, hushed moans mingled with the sounds of the jungle, while Loren could do nothing but watch.

And then she blinked.

At first she did not notice, but then it happened again. She tried once more, consciously—and her eyelids responded.

Loren tried to move her hand. Her fingers twitched.

Could the poison be wearing off already? Auntie had made it sound as though she would be frozen for hours. Surely the weremage would not have left her here if the paralysis would wear off so soon.

Then she heard Xain's words again. *The remedies of the apothecary have little effect upon a wizard who eats magestones, and the same is true for poisons.*

The magestone she had eaten in Yewamba. It was still within her, burning the poison out of her blood.

She tried again, and this time her hand moved, jerking from her stomach and landing on the dirt beside her. She heaved again, and it edged towards the path a little more.

Chet and Auntie were growing more passionate with every moment, and the weremage sounded nearly frenzied at their tryst. She looked down at Chet, smiling fiendishly at him. "Do you love me, Chet?"

"Of course," he said, breathless.

"Do you *know* me?"

"I—what?" Distracted for a moment, he frowned up at her.

Slowly, painfully, Loren dragged her feet up towards her body, her knee bending up into the air. Her body jerked towards the path as she let the knee fall, but though the branches that covered her rustled, it was not loud enough to hear.

Without warning, Auntie slapped Chet's face. "Do you *know* me? Better than any other?"

"Loren, what in the darkness below—"

"Tell me!" cried Auntie. Neither of them had bothered to remove their tunics, and she seized the front of his now. "Tell me you know me, better than any other in all the nine kingdoms."

Chet shook his head and tried to push up on his elbows. "Enough, Loren. I do not know what you—"

Auntie slammed him back down on the ground. In an instant her old, rusted knife was in her hand. She pressed it against his throat.

No! thought Loren.

She saw Damaris holding the knife in her dream, saw it part Chet's skin, saw his blood splashing upon the ground.

"Chet," she croaked. She lifted one hand, shaking as it rose into the air, helpless. "Chet." But he could not hear her.

"Tell me," rasped Auntie.

Chet went white with fear. "Loren, what are you—"

Loren heaved herself out of the bushes, crashing down on the grass of the path. The sound drew Chet's attention at last, and he looked over at her. His face became a mask of confusion, and then terror as he looked up at Auntie.

"Chet," gasped Loren. "Run."

Auntie smiled at her, a vicious grin, and her eyes began to glow. She transformed back into herself again, keeping the knife pressed to Chet's throat. Chet recoiled with a cry, but he could not move from under her with the blade pressing against his skin.

"Well met, lover," said Auntie. "Are you not enjoying yourself? Am I not twice the bedfellow Loren is? She is little more than a girl, after all."

Chet panicked and tried to snatch her hand away, but Auntie seized his wrist and slammed it back into the ground. She did not move the blade from his neck, nor did she stop her writhing on top of him.

"Oh, but you are no longer so excited," said Auntie, pouting down at where they were joined. With a flash of magelight, she turned into Niya. "Do you prefer another? I noticed you eyeing me from time to time as we rode together. Or was that only jealousy? No, you desired someone else, did you not?"

Another flash of magelight, and now she was Weath.

"Yes, little Weath, your 'friend.' The one whose fragile little neck broke so easily, just before I pitched her from the walls of Yewamba."

"Stop," groaned Chet, turning his head as though he could sink into the ground away from her. "Please, stop it."

Loren tried to rise, tried to crawl towards them, but her legs were still sluggish. Only her arms would obey her commands.

Then she remembered her dagger. It was still in her boot. Shaking, she reached for it.

"Do not tell me you did not want her. You have had a greedy mind, little boy." Auntie's cruel smile dissolved into a grimace of hate. "And I will make you pay for your every untoward thought."

The dagger slid easily from its sheath. Loren hefted it, feeling the weight.

The handle is the heavier end, she thought, turning it to hold it by the blade. *Sky above, do not let me miss.*

She threw the dagger.

It sank into Auntie's arm. The weremage screamed in pain and reared back—and her blade came away from Chet's throat.

He rose up and snatched her wrist, and then struck her in the face before wrestling her to the ground. With his weight he pinned her, driving a knee into her chest and holding both her hands above her head. She screamed again, but it turned into a harsh laugh. He shook as he held her down, his hands grasping at her throat. Auntie turned to glare hatefully at Loren.

"You promised, you sniveling little liar. You promised you would not throw the knife at me."

"Be silent!" screamed Chet. "Be silent, you vile . . . you—" He shoved her hands away as she tried to fight him off, pressing her face into the dirt.

"Oh, is this all you wanted?" sneered Auntie. "To be in control? You should have said so. Have me then, if you wish."

"You—you took me, you took me without—" Chet's eyes were wild, his lips drawn back in a snarl. He seized the hilt of Loren's dagger and twisted it in Auntie's arm, drawing a fresh scream from her. "I will kill you."

"I believe you," said Auntie. "What are you waiting for?"

"Chet," groaned Loren. "Chet, wait."

His gaze turned to her. "Wait? You tell me to *wait?* You saw what she did, Loren. It is what the High King's harshest law commands."

Loren tried to rise to hands and knees, but her legs would still not obey her. "You are not a killer, Chet," she said. The words came thick and slow upon her tongue, for the poison had not entirely left her. "Remember what happened on the shores of Dorsea, how Xain—"

"How dare you?" cried Chet, his voice rising to a great shout. "That was a prisoner. He surrendered! How dare you call this the same?"

Incredibly, Auntie giggled. "The law is clear. And I have violated it so very badly."

"Be silent," growled Chet.

"Let the Mystics do it," said Loren. "They serve the King's law."

Chet looked at her for a moment. She thought she saw the fury fading from his eyes. But at last he shook his head, and she saw that the anger was not gone—it had only turned to ice, a terrible, bloodless rage.

"We are the King's law," he said. "This is not revenge, Loren. It is justice."

He was right. Of course he was right. Every child in Underrealm knew this edict. Loren would not have blinked at Auntie's sentence, not if anyone else were to carry it out. But to see Chet with the blade in his hand, death in his eyes . . .

"Very well," she said softly.

Loren turned her gaze from him to look at Auntie instead. The weremage looked back, her eyes twitching, her teeth showing in a smile, as though she had never been happier.

She was still smiling when Chet lowered the dagger and slit her throat, sending her blood gushing across the ground. A burbling laugh poured up through her lips, along with blood. Then, even as Loren watched, where he had slit it the flesh of her neck began to knit back together. But not the mass of scar tissue—that remained as it had been, even when Auntie was Niya. The fresh cut, though—it healed as she watched. It healed.

It healed until Chet plunged the dagger through her eye into her brain.

Auntie's body spasmed once, and then lay still.

And then after a moment, a final glow came from the weremage's remaining eye.

Slowly she transformed one last time. Weath's face shifted and melted away. But she did not become the seductive, loam-skinned beauty Loren had first met.

Instead her skin turned lily-white, her face a little older, mayhap the age of Loren's mother. The hair that replaced Weath's copper was not white-blonde, but frizzy and black.

A woman Loren had never seen before lay there dead. Chet rolled away from her, covering his face to hide the tears that spilled forth.

FORTY-THREE

When Loren could rise at last, she went to Chet's side and tried to hold him. But he recoiled from her touch, pushing her away and shaking his head. So she merely sat by his side, trying not to look at the stranger who lay dead before her.

In time Chet's tears subsided, and he rose to his feet. Loren stood too, if more slowly, and together they made their way back towards the camp. They did not bury the body. Loren could scarcely bear looking at it, and asking Chet to touch it was out of the question.

Annis and Gem saw at once that something was

wrong, but when they asked, Chet only shook his head and went into his tent. Loren told them nothing she did not have to—only that Niya had been Auntie all along, and that she had attacked them, and now was dead. From the moment he heard the weremage's name, Gem's face went pale, and his eyes wide.

"Dead?" he whispered. "Are you certain?"

"Yes," said Loren quietly.

His look grew distant, and he turned from her. In a moment he, too, vanished into his tent, leaving Annis and Loren standing there, staring at each other, not knowing what to do, or even where to begin.

That night, Loren ate a meager meal. Afterwards she went to the tent she shared with Chet.

Something compelled her to stop a pace away from it. She stared at the flap for a long while. And then she turned from it, and slept in the tent that had once been Niya's.

Uzo and Shiun returned the next day. Loren was hardly surprised when they told her that Damaris had ridden south with too many guards for them to engage. So little had gone well for their party this far in the mission, that this latest lack of success seemed almost expected.

In turn, she had to tell them the tale of what had happened with Auntie. They listened in shock, and when they learned that Niya had been the weremage all along, they shook their heads in disbelief. Then, looking at each other in silent agreement, they set off into the jungle towards the path that Loren had described.

When they returned from burying her, the dark look in their eyes spoke volumes of how shaken they were. They had not buried their companion and captain, a Mystic. They had seen an utter stranger, and only Loren's word told them that she had once been their sister-in-arms.

"We should ride south when we can," said Shiun, after they had eaten a silent meal together around a small fire. "I can follow Damaris easily enough now, but the trail may grow cold, and it certainly will once she reaches Dorsea."

Loren thought for a moment. "We will spend one more night here," she said at last. "One more night of rest, for the toll has been great. On all of us."

She looked across the camp. Chet still had not emerged from his tent.

The next morning dawned grey and cold, and a light rain began to fall. Loren went a little ways off from the camp and sat on a fallen tree, face turned upwards, letting the water wash away the sweat and the dirt and the horror of the last few days. She sensed that the rest of them feared to disturb her, just as she herself feared to disturb Chet. But eventually, Annis came out to her and waited, hands clasped in front of her, until Loren met her gaze.

"Shiun says we must go. The rain makes it ever more urgent that we begin the hunt, lest we lose Damaris' trail."

"Of course," said Loren quietly. "I will rouse Chet."

"He is awake, and readying himself to leave," said Annis.

Loren shot to her feet and pushed past Annis to run for the camp. She came to a halt where the horses were tied up. Chet stood there, securing his pack to the saddle. He looked at her without smiling and nodded.

"We are riding south," she said, not sure what else to tell him. "Damaris has gone—"

"Towards Dorsea. I know," he said. "Annis explained. Let us get on with it."

He turned away and resumed readying himself for the journey. Loren ducked her head, and after a moment walked past him to take down Niya's tent—*her* tent now, she supposed.

Soon they had mounted, and Shiun led them through the jungle towards the main road. Once there, they increased their pace to a steady trot, and made their plodding way south. The jungle stayed thick on both sides of them as they passed the town of Sarafu, and long after, so that for many hours they could see nothing but the trees on either side of them.

Then the trees fell away, and they came to a lip in the land, from which it spilled down a long, long way towards a great basin. The western rim was the Greatrock Mountains, and a wide river formed the eastern side. They themselves stood on the northern lip, and where it ended in the south, the jungle gave way to a sparsely wooded land of light brown dirt.

"That is the border of Dorsea," said Shiun. "Damaris rides south, no doubt hoping to evade us, as well as Kal's host, which still marches west."

"She will not succeed," said Loren quietly. "We will capture her. I swear it."

There was no longer any question of whether they should continue to pursue the merchant or return to Kal. She knew without asking that every one of them would not have turned back, not for all the gold in all the nine kingdoms.

Still they did not ride on, but only sat upon their horses, looking down at the lush land as the falling rain soaked it. The day was winding towards evening, and Loren knew they should be pressing on as quickly as they could. Damaris would not slow for anything, not until she believed herself to be safe. But still she hesitated. And after a time, she glanced at Chet.

"Go ahead," she murmured to the others. "We will be with you in a moment."

The party obeyed without comment, and soon she and Chet were alone on the road. But he did not look at her, not even when he broke his silence at last.

"I do not care if you understand why I did it or not," he said.

"Yet I do understand," she said quietly.

He snorted. "Do you? I was not so forgiving when you showed Xain leniency in Dorsea."

"It is as you said. That was different, and I was wrong to gainsay you when it came to Auntie."

Chet turned his face away from her. "You may say it, you know. You may tell me I am a hypocrite. I scorned you, though it was not even your hand that held the knife."

"It has been a long journey, but I am not ready to take that step," said Loren. "Yet I no longer look with disdain on those who do. I still think justice should come from the law, and from the King's servants who deal in it. But there is not always time. And you *did* serve the law, Chet. I know that."

She reached across the space between them and put a hand on his shoulder, but he shied away from her touch.

"I cannot," he whispered. "Please. I still see—I see her. I am sorry."

"You have nothing to apologize for," she told him, feeling tears brim in her eyes. She blinked them away. "Never. Not to me."

A moment longer she waited, until he turned his face forwards again and nodded. Then she spurred Midnight into a walk, and Chet followed just behind. The sun neared the horizon, heralding the approach of night, as she led him down the long road into the lowlands.

KEEP READING

The Nightblade Epic will continue. But it is not the only tale of Underrealm.

The Academy Journals series tells the story of the Academy for wizards upon the High King's Seat—and its new dean, Xain Forredar.

The first book *The Alchemist's Touch*. Get it here:

Underrealm.net/AJ1

AUTHOR'S NOTE

This book's ending is, in a lot of ways, much darker than the ending of *Darkfire,* which is the book that's generated the most angry reader emails up to this point.

So in lieu of acknowledgements, I feel the need to leave my first author's note in the Underrealm novels.

From the beginning, Underrealm was meant to be a place that was different from the worlds of most fantasy. A place where prejudice and inequality haven't been removed—they were never there in the first place.

(Well, except for income inequality, which is the only form of discrimination I've ever been able to wrap my head around. I mean, I can put myself in the headspace of a rich man and see how the thought process works: "I have more money and have the ability to do more things, therefore I am better than the people with less money." They're not *right,* but I *get it.* Whereas I simply do not, cannot, and likely will never understand the mindset of the man who thinks he's better than women because he's got more vulnerabilities below the waist, or the white person who thinks they're better because their ancestors were exposed to less direct sunlight.)

Anyway.

A world without racism meant there was no reason the oldest and most prestigious family in Underrealm—the Yerrins—couldn't be black. It meant that the colonizers who came and established their kingdom in Underrealm could be "Asian"—the quotes being used because, of course, Asia does not exist. It meant that while some kingdoms were more likely to produce people who looked a certain way, no one made assumptions or was surprised when a black person came from Hedgemond, a Middle-Eastern person from Feldemar, or anything else.

A world without sexism meant that women were not considered lesser when it came to property, inheritance, or succession. It meant that King and Queen had to be gender-neutral titles. To me, it also meant that birth control and abortion were freely available and state-subsidized. And from that, it followed naturally—in my mind, anyway—that prostitution would not only *not* be criminal, but it would be state-protected. (Some have assumed that this developed in the reverse sequence, and I can say definitively here that it did not.)

A world without LGBTQIA+ discrimination was very easy to create in some ways—in others it still challenges me. It was easy to write characters who were utterly unfazed when they discovered a friend was gay or bisexual. But was it a problem not to use the *words* gay and bisexual? Why did I want to avoid them, anyway?

(The answer is because I try to keep my language as "old-timey" as possible, to create a certain mood, and those words are incredibly recent in the lexicon.

No matter how I tried, they felt anachronistic. And in the end I determined that a society that never saw homosexuality and bisexuality as wrong would likely not have invented words to describe them, when "love" already existed.)

It was easy to write a trans character. It was even easy to determine how a trans person in Underrealm would transition. For the curious among you, there is an order of very high-powered alchemists who can turn a person's body from one biological sex to another. They're almost a sort of charity, so they perform the service for free, and they have temples in every kingdom.

But if that happened early in a character's life, how could I reveal to the reader that they *were* trans, without some convoluted info-dump about their early lives that would have felt shoved into the story?

(Some of you are already rolling your eyes at the dumb cis guy—and I apologize profusely, because of course now, years later, I have realized the easiest solution: *just write a trans main character, you idiot.* I'm sorry. I still have a long way to go. And I *am* going to do that, in the very very near future.)

And by the way, while I'm scribbling down this note, let me take the opportunity to be explicit about a few things—to use some words people in Underrealm would never use, and to spell out the gender identities of some people who haven't had reason to talk about it yet:

Loren is bisexual

Jordel was bisexual

Gem is gay

High King Enalyn is a trans woman and bisexual

Lilith and Theren, from the Academy Journals, are gay (like, super gay—you definitely didn't need me to tell you that one)

Perrin Arkus, from the Academy Journals, is a trans woman

Matami Drayden, from the Academy Journals, was gay

Adara, from the Academy Journals, is pansexual and polyamorous

At least that's what I've got right now. I'm still learning. I'm not entirely certain whether Loren is bisexual or pansexual, for example—and maybe she isn't, either. Identities shift and change over time. People learn more about themselves, they grow, they change.

A lot of these labels are new. Some were invented or twisted to make people feel worse. Some were invented to help people understand themselves a little bit better.

I'm spelling them out here only because I've decided that none of the *labels* belong in Underrealm—but the characters' identities still exist, just as they've always existed throughout human history.

If that's a bad decision on my part, I truly apologize, though I hope this at least makes it clear why I decided to do it.

And if I've missed any characters, I apologize again. But the ones listed above are the big ones—and the ones readers *absolutely don't get* unless something explicit happens in the story.

Seriously: I tried to establish Loren as bisexual right from *Nightblade*. I tried to describe her attraction to Auntie when they first met. But everyone read, instead, that Loren was terrified.

Was that my fault as a writer? Or did readers make assumptions based on the "default?" I don't know. A little bit of both, probably. And so in *Weremage* I decided to make things about as explicit as I could without having her cheat on Chet.

Which . . . brings us to the whole reason I wanted to write this note in the first place.

That scene. With Chet and Auntie.

A necessary part of ending gender discrimination is ending sexual violence. It's incredibly common. It ruins lives. And, at least in our world, it is skewed heavily against women—though it happens to men, too. (Anyone who says otherwise or tries to erase that is a really terrible person.)

Also, our society seems *wildly* uninterested in doing anything about it. Most victims aren't believed even if they do come forward with their story. Those who are believed often can't win court cases. It's a giant mess that makes me furious every time I think about it.

It made sense to me that a world like Underrealm would hold rape as the highest of crimes. Punishable by immediate execution. The High King's harshest law—as horrific to them as torturing toddlers to death would be to us, and therefore just as rare.

Not only was it an important worldbuilding point, but it helped me as a writer. It meant that I could avoid sexual violence in my books. That would make them much more accessible to those who are frequently turned off by the shocking amount of rape in genre fiction.

A Song of Ice and Fire (the *Game of Thrones* series) is a well-known culprit, but Martin is by no means the only author to do it. He might not even be the worst one. Other men do it with shocking regularity and an almost vindictive glee. Even women authors participate, though usually not so much or so ham-fistedly.

It's a contributing factor towards fantasy being seen as a male-dominated genre (which it's not, by the way). And I wanted no part of it.

But I knew from the very beginning of Loren's story, the very start of Underrealm, that I couldn't completely avoid sexual violence. I had to say one thing about it first.

And that is that most of the time, male fantasy authors can't write it for shit.

Rape is treated as a plot twist, a scintillating motivation for a male character (who it didn't happen to), or even "character development" on the part of the woman it *did* happen to.

(Because it almost always happens to women, doesn't it? Men are supposed to be more powerful than that—a hideous idea that's not even a full step short of victim-blaming.)

The first thing I knew was that my one instance of sexual violence would happen to a man. And I had a suspicion it should happen to the love interest of the main character, to truly flip the roles and hopefully make a few male readers uncomfortable. We need to be made uncomfortable more often.

And since it was the worst crime in Underrealm, it had to be done by someone who was irredeemably evil—abusive to the point of no return.

And that is when Auntie was born.

Yes, that is why the character was created in the first place. It's why she was the way she was in *Nightblade,* and in this book. From the very beginning, this was her purpose. A psychopath who cares for nothing but her own satisfaction, who takes joy from the suffering of others.

That's what a rapist is. Full stop. Otherwise they could never enjoy themselves in the face of the pain— or sometimes unconsciousness—of their victims.

And there's one more aspect of this I wanted to touch on: the aftermath.

Because even if it only happens once, sexual violence can last for the rest of the victim's life.

Most books never go into that. Most movies won't touch it with a ten-foot pole. It happens to the girl, her guy goes on a revenge tear, and in the end the credits roll over a world where all is happy again.

That is sexual violence as viewed by men who don't know, don't care to know, and would rather not confront the reality staring them in the face.

So there you have it. For some, this explanation will not be sufficient. It will not mitigate the fact that *that scene* was included at all.

If that's the case for you, I don't blame you. I won't apologize for writing it, but I am sorry for any negative effects it may have had.

And to wrap up, I will promise these two things:

- That's the only such scene I'll write in an Underrealm book
- The aftermath will be written with as much realism as I can muster

If that's not enough, I get it. But it's all I've got.

As always, thank you for reading. I'm writing the next book, *Yerrin,* and I gotta tell you: the world *does* get better.

Not that everything is happy-go-lucky puppies and rainbows. How could it be?

Yerrin will have dark moments. And it's the end of the second trilogy, so it'll have a killer ending.

But I promise we'll have at least some fun first.

Because that is another truth: no matter how dark things get during our worst moments, the world can be bright after.

So I'll see you in a brighter world.

Love,
Garrett

CONNECT ONLINE

FACEBOOK

Want to hang out with other fans of the Underrealm books? There's a Facebook group where you can do just that. Join the Nine Lands group on Facebook and share your favorite moments and fan theories from the books. I also post regular behind-the-scenes content, including information about the world you can't find anywhere else. Visit the link to be taken to the Facebook group:

Underrealm.net/nine-lands

YOUTUBE

Catch up with me daily (when I'm not directing a film or having a baby). You can watch my daily YouTube channel where I talk about art, science, life, my books, and the world.
But not cats.
Never cats.

GarrettBRobinson.com/yt

THE BOOKS OF UNDERREALM

THE NIGHTBLADE EPIC
NIGHTBLADE
MYSTIC
DARKFIRE
SHADEBORN
WEREMAGE
YERRIN

THE ACADEMY JOURNALS
THE ALCHEMIST'S TOUCH
THE MINDMAGE'S WRATH
THE FIREMAGE'S VENGEANCE

CHRONOLOGICAL ORDER
NIGHTBLADE
MYSTIC
DARKFIRE
SHADEBORN
THE ALCHEMIST'S TOUCH
WEREMAGE
THE MINDMAGE'S WRATH
THE FIREMAGE'S VENGEANCE
YERRIN

ABOUT THE AUTHOR

Garrett Robinson was born and raised in Los Angeles. The son of an author/painter father and a violinist/singer mother, no one was surprised when he grew up to be an artist.

After blooding himself in the independent film industry, he self-published his first book in 2012 and swiftly followed it with a stream of others, publishing more than two million words by 2014. Within months he topped numerous Amazon bestseller lists. Now he spends his time writing books and directing films.

A passionate fantasy author, his most popular books are the novels of Underrealm, including The Nightblade Epic and The Academy Journals series.

However, he has delved into many other genres. Some works are for adult audiences only, such as *Non Zombie* and *Hit Girls,* but he has also published popular books for younger readers, including The Realm Keepers series and *The Ninjabread Man*, co-authored with Z.C. Bolger.

Garrett lives in Oregon with his wife Meghan, his children Dawn, Luke, and Desmond, and his dog Chewbacca.

Garrett can be found on:

BLOG: garrettbrobinson.com/blog
EMAIL: garrett@garrettbrobinson.com
TWITTER: twitter.com/garrettauthor
FACEBOOK: facebook.com/garrettbrobinson

EPILOGUE

A LIGHT SNOW HAD ONLY JUST BEGUN TO FALL, AND IT dusted the Yerrin camp. Damaris' tent was fine, more than fine enough to keep her head warm and dry. But she had eschewed that shelter to drink in the frozen air. She took deep breaths, standing to the north of the camp, only vaguely aware of the guards who stood close to hand. Her gaze lingered on the Dorsean landscape they had been traversing for the last several days.

Do you pursue me, Nightblade? she thought. *That is good. Follow me. Follow me and never stop. Let me draw you to your doom.*

A shout came from behind her, and she whirled on the spot. Her guards drew closer and unsheathed their blades.

Damaris' heart skipped a beat as a figure emerged from the camp. His form was in silhouette, rimmed by the firelight, but she knew him—not only from his size, but from the way he moved, every little quirk of motion that had accompanied her on all the long roads of her life since they were both children. The guards fell away before him.

"Gregor," she sighed.

He fell to one knee at her feet, bowing his head. "My lady," he said. His voice was thick with emotion, and he hid his face from her, as well as the guards to either side.

Damaris glanced at them. "Leave us," she said. They obeyed at once, marching back towards the camp.

"Rise, my friend," she said, taking his shoulders and lifting him up. "Sky above, I have missed you more than I can say." She drew him into an embrace for a moment only, but it was enough that she could feel him shaking.

"I should never have left you," he said. "If anything had happened at Yewamba, I would have taken my own life the moment I had slain the vermin who had harmed you."

"Left me?" said Damaris wryly. She did not smile, but she let her eyes crinkle with amusement. "If you will recall, I ordered you to remain upon the Seat."

"And I failed you there, as well," he said. "I could not secure the support you require, and then a boy—"

She raised a hand, and he fell silent at once. "I know," she said smoothly. "I have heard all the tale of it already. And I do not blame you, Gregor. We are stretched thin, you and I, and we will not win every battle. All that matters is that we win more of them than we lose."

"We will, my lady," said Gregor, bowing his head once more. "I swear it."

"I believe you," said Damaris. "And the next confrontation swiftly approaches. Something happened at the Battle of Wellmont."

"A rumor only," said Gregor.

She fixed him with a look. "It is not a rumor."

His eyes did not widen, nor did his brows shift by so much as a hair. Yet from a pace away she could feel his whole body go rigid. "Then . . . are we to make our way east?"

"Not yet," said Damaris, sighing. "At least not while hounds nip at our heels. I am being followed."

"I have heard." Gregor's voice rumbled with fury. His fists, each almost as large as her head, coiled by his sides. "The girl."

"The Nightblade of the High King, you mean," said Damaris, letting her mockery emerge plain in her tone.

"I will take a party. We will come upon them in the night and destroy them."

"No, no, that will not do at all. Loren herself played no small role in the Battle of Wellmont, though she cannot possibly have learned what has occurred because of it. Yet we will ensure she comes to regret it."

Damaris' eyes narrowed as she remembered the storeroom in Yewamba, where Loren had dumped her like a sack of flour with her wrists bound together. And she remembered the boy, the boy Loren's age who had been there with her. Damaris had seen the look in Loren's eyes when she beheld him. It sent a lance of vicious joy through her, and her breath quickened.

"And when we are sure she is well-acquainted with the deepest pits of sorrow—then, Gregor, you may do what I should have ordered the moment we first laid eyes upon her. Then, you may kill her."